T0363311

INTRIGUE

Seek thrills. Solve crimes. Justice served.

Smoky Mountains Mystery
Lena Diaz

The Silent Setup
Katie Mettner

MILLS & BOON

DID YOU PURCHASE THIS BOOK WITHOUT A COVER?
If you did, you should be aware it is **stolen property** as it was reported
'unsold and destroyed' by a retailer.
Neither the author nor the publisher has received any payment
for this book.

SMOKY MOUNTAINS MYSTERY
© 2024 by Lena Diaz
Philippine Copyright 2024
Australian Copyright 2024
New Zealand Copyright 2024

First Published 2024
First Australian Paperback Edition 2024
ISBN 978 1 038 93523 6

THE SILENT SETUP
© 2024 by Katie Mettner
Philippine Copyright 2024
Australian Copyright 2024
New Zealand Copyright 2024

First Published 2024
First Australian Paperback Edition 2024
ISBN 978 1 038 93523 6

® and ™ (apart from those relating to FSC®) are trademarks of Harlequin Enterprises
(Australia) Pty Limited or its corporate affiliates. Trademarks indicated with® are
registered in Australia, New Zealand and in other countries.
Contact admin_legal@Harlequin.ca for details.

Except for use in any review, the reproduction or utilisation of this work in whole
or in part in any form by any electronic, mechanical or other means, now known
or hereafter invented, including xerography, photocopying and recording, or in any
information storage or retrieval system, is forbidden without the permission of the
publisher, Harlequin Mills & Boon.

This book is sold subject to the condition that it shall not, by way of trade or
otherwise, be lent, resold, hired out or otherwise circulated without the prior consent
of the publisher in any form or binding or cover other than that in which it is published
and without a similar condition including this condition being imposed on the
subsequent purchaser.

All rights reserved including the right of reproduction in whole or in part in any form.
This edition is published in arrangement with Harlequin Books S.A..

This is a work of fiction. Names, characters, places, and incidents are either the
product of the author's imagination or are used fictitiously, and any resemblance to
actual persons, living or dead, business establishments, events, or locales is entirely
coincidental.

MIX
Paper | Supporting
responsible forestry
FSC® C001695

Published by
Harlequin Mills & Boon
An imprint of Harlequin Enterprises (Australia) Pty Limited
(ABN 47 001 180 918), a subsidiary of HarperCollins
Publishers Australia Pty Limited
(ABN 36 009 913 517)
Level 19, 201 Elizabeth Street
SYDNEY NSW 2000 AUSTRALIA

Cover art used by arrangement with Harlequin Books S.A.. All rights reserved.

Printed and bound in Australia by McPherson's Printing Group

Smoky Mountains Mystery

Lena Diaz

MILLS & BOON

Lena Diaz was born in Kentucky and has also lived in California, Louisiana and Florida, where she now resides with her husband and two children. Before becoming a romantic suspense author, she was a computer programmer. A Romance Writers of America Golden Heart® Award finalist, she has also won the prestigious Daphne du Maurier Award for Excellence in Mystery/Suspense. To get the latest news about Lena, please visit her website, lenadiaz.com.

Visit the Author Profile page at
millsandboon.com.au.

CAST OF CHARACTERS

Lance Cabrera—A cold case investigator employed by a private firm called Unfinished Business. Lance's secret past comes back to haunt him, putting everyone he cares about in danger.

Keira Sloane—Frustrated at her small-town police department not giving her a chance to become a detective, she secretly takes on a case they let go cold. The case heats up when she tracks the evidence to Lance Cabrera.

Ileana Sanchez—Lance hasn't seen Ileana, his old girlfriend, in years. Suddenly she's back on the scene, causing tension and raising all kinds of questions about what really happened back when they were a couple.

Ian Murphy—He was Lance's boss years earlier, and his death changed the course of Lance's life, along with his old investigative team. Was Murphy behind those deaths, or simply a victim?

Rick Cameron—Once a good friend of Lance's, Rick is murdered in a cheap motel. When the clues point to Lance, Keira is determined to solve this cold case and find out whether Lance is a killer.

Levi Alexander—Levi was killed three months before Rick, and the only link that seems to tie these two deaths together is that they used to work with Lance.

Chapter One

Keira Sloane two-handed her service weapon, elbows bent, pistol pointing up toward the ceiling as she flattened her back against the wall outside the motel room. The dim lights from the dark parking lot one story below glinted off the rusty railing across from her. Chuck Breamer, one of two fellow officers with her, mirrored her stance on the other side of the door. In front of him, Gabe Wilson held his gun pointed down. He glanced at Chuck, then Keira. After receiving their nods, he rapped loudly on the door again before jerking back to avoid potential gunfire.

"Maple Falls Police. Last chance. Open the door." As with the first knock, there was no response.

Gabe held up three fingers, silently counting down. *Three, two, one.* He delivered a vicious kick to the door-knob. The frame splintered. The ruined door flew open and crashed against the wall, making the large window beside the door rattle.

All three ran inside, sweeping their guns back and forth.

The metallic smell of blood struck Keira immediately. A wounded or dead man lay on the bed closest to the window. She quickly checked behind the chair in the corner for any hidden suspects while her fellow officers checked under both beds.

"Main room clear," she announced.

Chuck jogged to the doorway on the back left. Gabe checked the one on the back right.

"Bathroom's clear," Chuck said.

"Closet clear," Gabe echoed. "No one else is here." He motioned toward an indentation in the cheap floral comforter covering the empty bed where it appeared that someone had sat at one time. "At least, not anymore."

Keira holstered her pistol and rushed to the side of the victim's bed, grimacing in sympathy at the extent of his injuries. Dressed only in navy blue boxers, the approximately thirty-year-old Black man was mottled with bruises and cuts on all of his extremities, with most of the damage to his chest.

Beneath him, the formerly white sheet was turning red. Blood dripped down, adding to a growing wet tangle of carpet. When she pressed her fingers against the side of his neck, to her surprise it was warm. There was a weak, thready pulse.

"He's alive. Get a bus out here."

Chuck radioed for an ambulance.

Keira grabbed the edge of the comforter and used it to apply pressure to what appeared to be bullet entrance wounds on his chest. Someone had beaten and tortured this man before shooting him. He'd lost so much blood it was a miracle that he was still alive, even more of a miracle if he made it to the hospital.

A hand grabbed her wrist, making her jump. She was shocked that it was the man on the bed. He stared up at her with pain-glazed dark brown eyes, his hand clutching hers. But whatever strength he had immediately drained away. His hand fell back to the mattress.

"Hold on," she told him. "Don't go into the light, buddy. Help's on the way."

His face turned ashen as his lips moved. But she couldn't make out what he said.

She leaned close. "Say it again," she encouraged him.

"L… Lance," the faint whisper sounded.

"Lance," she echoed. "Hang on, Lance. I'm Keira. I'm a cop. We're here to help you and—"

"Move." Chuck roughly pushed her out of the way.

"He's bleeding," she said. "His chest—"

"I've got it." His prior experience as an EMT kicked in as he maintained pressure on the victim's chest with one hand and checked his airway with the other.

Keira watched with a growing feeling of helplessness as Chuck assessed the victim. She wanted to help. But of the three of them, Chuck had the best chance of keeping him alive until the ambulance arrived.

She turned to check on Gabe and saw him reaching for the top drawer of the cheap particle-board dresser opposite the two beds.

"We need a warrant," she reminded him. "Exigent circumstances are over." Even though the motel manager was the one who'd called 911, he hadn't formally given them permission to search once they'd responded to the report of "shots fired."

Gabe shrugged and dropped his hand. "The lieutenant's on his way. Knowing him, he'll already have the warrant anyway."

She smiled at his statement. They both knew no one, not even their scarily efficient supervisor, Owen Jackson, could have gotten a warrant that fast.

Chuck straightened and stepped back from the bed. "He's gone. On top of being treated like a punching bag and sliced with a knife, he was shot at least three times. There's nothing anyone could have done to save this guy."

Keira blew out a shaky breath. Her wrist tingled as if the man were still holding it. He'd wanted her help. But she hadn't been able to do anything to change his fate. "Lance. His name is Lance."

Chuck frowned. "You know this guy?"

"No. He whispered it. Lance. Might have been Vance or Vince. But I think it was Lance."

"Did he say it was *his* name? Maybe it was the killer's name."

She winced. "I hope not. I called him Lance."

"We'll know soon enough, once we get a warrant to search for his wallet. Assuming it wasn't stolen." He started typing a text, no doubt updating their boss on the current status.

She glanced around the small room. Even the blood spatter on the wall behind the victim didn't mask the years of grime. But, aside from the twisted, bloody covers on the bed, everything else was neat and orderly. The dresser and nightstand drawers were closed. No belongings had been dumped onto the floor and rifled through. The second bed was made with the pillows and comforter in place.

"The room doesn't look tossed," she said. "His business suit's lying over there on that chair, as if he'd planned on wearing it tomorrow. It's rumpled, so the killer may have checked the pockets. But if this was a robbery, you'd think they'd take the suit. It's not cheap. Could fetch a few hundred at a consignment shop."

Gabe joined them. "I doubt a robber in this part of

town would recognize the value of a suit or want to bother with it. But they'd definitely have taken the fancy Mercedes out front that the manager said belongs to this guy. Why would a man who can afford a car like that stay in a nasty, cheap motel?"

Keira glanced at the man on the bed, wishing he could answer those questions, that he'd wake up in the morning and call his family, his friends. Tell them who'd attacked him and why. "Maybe he was hiding out from someone who'd never expect him to stay in a place like this." She shrugged. "That's one of many things we'll have to figure out."

Gabe gave her a doubtful look. "What makes you think Owen is finally going to let you play detective?"

She stiffened. "I can play whodunit as well as anyone else. I'm ready."

He held his hands up in a placating gesture. "No argument here. It's the LT you have to convince."

Chuck slid his cell phone back in his pocket. "We need to identify potential witnesses before they scatter like ants in a thunderstorm. Gabe, you take the rooms to the right. I'll go left. Names and addresses, verified with ID. We can't force them to hang around. But at least we can follow up with them once we have more manpower."

"Or woman power," Keira said. "I'll help."

Chuck frowned. "You're on guard duty. If the EMTs get here before we're back, try to keep them from destroying evidence. Once they verify our victim is DOA, get them out of our crime scene."

Gabe sent her an apologetic glance as he closed the door behind him and Chuck.

Chapter Two

Keira swore. How was she ever going to advance in the tiny town of Maple Falls, Tennessee, if her fellow officers kept coddling her and never gave her a chance? She knew exactly why they'd told her to wait here for the EMTs. In spite of them all being sworn law enforcement officers, her male counterparts couldn't set aside their Southern manners to treat a woman like one of the guys.

Even though she had a uniform on, they saw the woman first, the cop second. They didn't want her doing knock-and-talks and putting herself at risk in this part of town. Three years. She'd been working with them for three years, and she was still the lowest one on the food chain, the last to be given real opportunities to make a difference.

A quick glance at the shooting victim had guilt riding her hard. Here she was worrying about her career, her future. At least she *had* a future. This man, who was in his prime, had no future. His life had ended in violence and pain. What mattered right now was getting justice for him.

She edged closer to the bed, careful to avoid the bloodiest section of the carpet. He was a handsome man, with closely shaved black hair, his skin a medium brown color. The absence of a gold band on his ring finger meant he likely wasn't married. But he still might have a child, or children, perhaps an ex-wife or girlfriend. If he had siblings or parents still alive, people who loved him, they'd be devastated by his loss.

This was why she wanted to become a detective.

It was too depressing being bombarded on a daily basis by the awful things that human beings did to each other without some ray of hope or happiness. She craved the good parts of the job. She wanted to be the one to give a family the answers they desperately needed, the why and the who behind whatever had happened to their loved one. That would be the ultimate reward. Putting a name with the face of tonight's victim was the first step toward getting him, and his family, justice.

She glanced at the closed door. Would it really hurt to look for his wallet? Just to check his driver's license so she'd be sure about his name? If she was careful, if she wore gloves, she wouldn't destroy potential evidence or muck it up with her own DNA and fingerprints. She could already hear faint, distant sirens. The ambulance would be here soon, a few minutes out at most. If she was going to cross a line and not get caught, she had to do it now.

Always prepared, she had a pair of latex gloves in her pocket. She quickly pulled them on and went on the hunt for a wallet. It wasn't in the pockets of the suit jacket or in the dresser drawer. Instead, it was neatly sitting in the top drawer of the vanity in the bathroom, along with a ring of keys and his car's key fob.

Her heart seemed to squeeze in her chest when she flipped open the wallet and saw a photograph in a plastic sleeve. A little girl, probably no more than two, was in his arms, pressing a kiss against his cheek. He'd been a father after all. Or maybe an uncle or family friend. He was clearly loved and would be missed. She swallowed against the tightness in her throat and pulled his driver's license out. When she saw his name, her stomach sank. Rick. His name was Rick Cameron. The name he'd given her wasn't his.

Forgive me, Rick. I'm so sorry that I called you Lance, especially if he's the killer.

The victim's address was in Baton Rouge, Louisiana. She snapped a quick picture with her cell phone camera. Then she risked a precious few more seconds to check the rest of the wallet.

There were more pictures, a couple of credit cards and two one-hundred dollar bills. This definitely hadn't been a robbery. She started to set the wallet back in the drawer when a flash of white stopped her. Tucked into a credit card sleeve was a small piece of paper. She took it out and carefully unfolded it. There were two words written in a neat cursive script.

unfinished business

Voices sounded in the hallway outside the room. Keira quickly snapped a picture, then hurriedly refolded the note and put everything back the way she'd found it.

The squeak of the exterior door told her that someone had just entered the motel room.

"Keira? You in here?"

Chuck. Dang it. "In the bathroom. Give me a sec." She flushed the toilet and then flipped on the faucet as if she were washing her hands and hurriedly shoved her gloves into her pocket. When she stepped out, Chuck was standing with his hands on his hips while Gabe directed the EMTs toward the bed with the victim.

"You couldn't wait and use the bathroom in the motel office?" Chuck's voice was frigid.

Her face flushed warm as the EMTs glanced curiously at her. She knew the rules, knew not to disturb the scene. Heck, she'd warned Gabe not to open a drawer earlier. But she'd rather Chuck think she'd forgotten or had gotten sloppy than to tell him the truth—that she'd rummaged through the dead man's belongings knowing full well she shouldn't have.

"Sorry. It hit me all of a sudden." She gave him a pained smile as she strode toward him. "How did you two finish your knock-and-talks so fast?"

Gabe joined them near the dresser, giving the EMTs space to confirm the victim was beyond help. "Most of the rooms were empty, curtains open, beds made. We could tell there wasn't anyone inside refusing to come to the door. Lots of vacancies in this place." He wrinkled his nose as he glanced around. "Go figure, huh?"

"Not exactly the Ritz."

Gabe smiled.

Chuck didn't. He stared at her, his disapproval thick in the air, before turning to respond to a question from one of the EMTs.

Gabe gave her a sympathetic look before joining Chuck.

Keira blew out a frustrated breath. *Stupid.* She should have waited for the official investigation to find out the victim's name. No doubt she'd hurt her chances to be included on the case. If it had only been Gabe who'd caught her, he'd have kept it quiet. But by-the-book Chuck Breamer would no doubt tell their supervisor what she'd done at the first opportunity.

Sure enough, when the LT arrived, Chuck's summary

of everything the three of them had done included her trip to the bathroom. Their boss's words fell on her like a death knell as he barked his orders.

"Wilson, secure the crime scene until we can borrow a CSI tech from the DeKalb County Sheriff's Office to assist out here. Breamer, interview the motel manager. Get their surveillance video, assuming the cameras outside even work. Sloane—" his flinty gaze zeroed in on her "—let's see if you can manage to return to the station and write up your report without touching anything on the way out."

Gabe winced. Chuck didn't even look her way as he headed outside, presumably to speak to the manager.

Keira straightened her shoulders and took the walk of shame past her supervisor without comment.

BY THE TIME Keira finished her report, she wanted to kick herself for screwing up.

Gabe, upon his return to the station, had reluctantly admitted that Owen had said he'd planned on letting her help on the investigation—until he'd heard about what she'd done. Now she'd likely have to spend several more months trying to earn another chance.

Murders rarely happened in Maple Falls. So even if she was given a chance, it probably wouldn't be on a case this important. It would likely be on a stolen property investigation or a domestic violence situation that she could wrap up in less than a day. Her original plan in leaving Nashville PD to join a small police department because there'd be less competition definitely wasn't going the way she'd expected. She was beginning to think it was the worst mistake she'd ever made.

Gabe, her only true friend around here, kept sending

her looks of pity from across the squad room. Unable to take it anymore, she locked up her desk and left the station ten minutes early. If that was enough for Owen to write her up, so be it. At this point, she was too depressed to even care.

Later at home, in a calmer frame of mind, she reluctantly admitted that Owen wasn't petty enough to worry about ten minutes unless it was habitual. She was almost never late and rarely left early. But she had no doubt she'd still be written up for not following policy at a crime scene. And he was right to do it. She hadn't followed the rules. In fact, she'd broken them far worse than anyone knew.

She thumbed through the pictures on her cell phone that she'd taken in the motel bathroom. Technically, she should log them into evidence and then erase them from her personal device. The fact that she had no intention of doing either of those things could mean that her boss was right in thinking that she wasn't cut out to be a detective.

Forget that. She'd make a great detective. The only reason she occasionally broke the rules was because it was the only way to be let in on the action.

She studied Rick Cameron's driver's license photograph and the picture of his note. *Unfinished business* was cop slang for a cold case. But that didn't make sense in this context, especially since there wasn't anything in Rick Cameron's wallet to suggest he was a police officer working a case. Then again, if he was truly undercover, she wouldn't expect him to carry official police ID.

But that theory seemed weak. What kind of cold case would lead a detective from Louisiana to DeKalb County and the tiny Middle Tennessee town of Maple Falls? With a population just over two thousand, it wasn't exactly a sprawling metropolis where criminals fled to from big cities around the country to escape justice. Rick Cameron had to be passing through. To where? There was only one way to find out. She'd conduct her own investigation. And she'd do whatever it took to solve it, get justice for Rick and his loved ones, and prove herself.

When she presented her findings to the lieutenant, he'd be forced to recognize her as worthy enough to be allowed to work as a detective when warranted. Their ten-person police force didn't have any full-time detectives. Maple Falls was too small to justify that. And only a select few were allowed to act as detective when needed—like Chuck.

She grabbed her laptop computer from the end table and opened up an internet search.

THREE WEEKS LATER, Keira had little to show for her secret investigation into the motel murder. But neither did anyone else. As she sat at her desk in the squad room snooping through the latest printed copies she'd made from the official case files, her stomach sank at the lack of progress.

The name Lance had led nowhere. There weren't any local thugs on their radar with Lance as either their first or last name. A brief bio stated that the victim worked in the computer tech industry, remotely from home. He was a contract programmer currently in between contracts. That explained why an employer hadn't reported him missing.

He lived alone. No one in his neighborhood had ever noticed any family members visiting him, in spite of those pictures in his wallet. They hadn't noticed friends visiting either. Keira had no idea who the little girl was in the photo in Rick's wallet. All she could figure was that it was a friend's child and that she'd read far too much into it. After all, if he was close to that friend, or that little girl was part of his life, wouldn't someone in that circle have contacted the police by now, asking where he was? Baton Rouge law enforcement was supposed to let Maple Falls know if someone inquired about him. So far, that hadn't happened. With no friends, family or loved ones to advocate for him, no one was pushing the Maple Falls Police to keep digging and figure out who'd killed Rick Cameron.

None of the potential eyewitnesses at the motel had offered much of value either. The last person to make any notes in the case file was Chuck. And that had been four days ago. The case was already cold. Soon it would go into a deep freeze.

Gabe stopped by her desk and balanced a hip on the corner. "Two weeks off starting tomorrow, huh? Bet you're looking forward to it. Where you going?"

She shuffled the papers on her desk, mainly to hide her copies of reports from the Cameron case. "Probably what I do every vacation. Sit at home and watch TV, take naps. Lots of naps."

He clucked his tongue. "That's a waste, especially for a cute little brunette like you. Go do something fun. Pick up a guy. Trust me. For someone with your looks, it would be easy." At her eye roll, he laughed. "Okay, okay. Maybe you should pay a visit back home. Nashville, right? You must have some family or friends back there who'd love to see you."

Her only response was to stare at him. Although they were friends, she refused to discuss her family with him or anyone. The situation was…complicated. Going to see them during her two weeks off definitely wasn't on her itinerary.

When he gave up with his less than subtle interrogation, he wandered off to someone else's desk. Keira stuffed the papers she'd hidden into her purse and headed out. Her suitcase was already in her car. Let the so-called vacation begin.

Ten minutes later, she was at the town cemetery standing at the back corner where those without money or with no one to claim their bodies were buried. Pauper's graves. That felt so wrong for Rick Cameron.

His suit was expensive. The car he'd driven to the motel was a late-model Mercedes. He could afford a better burial. But he'd left no will, and his estate was tied up in the courts. For now, at least, he was here.

Keira placed the white silk roses she'd purchased earlier in the little vase beside the grave marker. It was a small slab of marble with only his name and dates. Normally a grave the city dug would only have a cheap metal marker with numbers on it. But Keira had scrabbled together enough money to buy the little marble headstone and vase. The man had used his last bit of strength to clutch her arm and whisper his dying word. How could she not give him a headstone after that?

Unfinished business. That note from his wallet was what had set her on her current path. It had cemented where she was going during her time off. After performing hundreds of internet searches on that phrase over the past few weeks, resulting in millions of useless hits, this morning she'd had better luck. She'd keyed in a ridiculously long string of additional search terms and the top result that popped up had her staring at the screen for a long time.

Unfinished Business, with both words capitalized, was the name of a private company in Gatlinburg, Tennessee, about four hours from Maple Falls. The purpose of the company? They investigated cold cases for law enforcement throughout the East Tennessee region. Since Maple Falls was in Middle Tennessee, they didn't officially support her county, which was why she'd never heard of them before. But here was the kicker. One of the investigators listed on their website had a name she'd rarely heard, until a few weeks ago.

Lance.

The odds were astronomical against UB's Lance Cabrera being the Lance that the victim had whispered with his final breath. Or even that UB was the same unfinished business listed on the note, especially since Rick hadn't capitalized either word. But the two things together seemed like a sign, a good omen that going there might help. Somehow.

Best scenario, UB and this Lance guy might actually know Rick Cameron and could lead to a resolution of the case. Worst scenario, they knew nothing about the victim. But as cold-case professionals they might give her some expert advice on how to proceed. Either way, it was a win.

She touched a hand to the cold marble. "Chances are a million to one against this being a real lead, Mr. Cameron. Or that this Lance guy I've found is *your* Lance. But it's all I have. Hopefully something will come out of this that will put your killer or killers in prison. I'm off to Gatlinburg to take care of your *unfinished business.*"

A crunching sound had her whirling around. No one was there. The cemetery was empty. Her silver Camry was about fifty yards away, the only vehicle in the parking lot. She scanned the tree line behind the chain-link fence. Nothing. It was probably just the light breeze blowing through the trees, making some branches click together. Or an animal rooting around in the woods, stepping on dried leaves that were everywhere, with it being the middle of autumn. But that didn't stop the unease that settled in her gut. After one last scan, she hurried toward her car, pistol out and at the ready.

Chapter Three

Lance Cabrera had always known his days were numbered. That the past would catch up to him sooner or later. But he'd really been hoping for later. Much later.

He kept his expression bland as the pretty young officer from Maple Falls told her story to him and his fellow cold-case investigators. She sat across the table from him in one of the glass-walled conference rooms of Unfinished Business, perched near the top of Prescott Mountain overlooking Gatlinburg, Tennessee, far below.

In the past, someone bringing UB a case who wasn't from the Tennessee Bureau of Investigation or an East Tennessee law enforcement agency wouldn't have gotten past the front door. But that rule had been eased after one of their own was abducted because they'd turned away the wrong person.

Now, when they could spare a few moments, they'd at least listen to people lobbying for their help outside of their contracted area. That help usually took the form of advice or referrals to other agencies. But their main goal was to determine whether the person was a potential threat.

This petite, brown-eyed, dark-haired wannabe detective—Keira Sloane—probably didn't concern the other UB investigators in the room. But in the twenty minutes that she'd been speaking and answering questions, he'd recognized the enormous threat she offered not only to him but to everyone in this room—including herself.

She tapped the pile of pictures she'd set on top of the table—crime scene photos she'd admittedly copied from the official case file. She was painfully honest, not even attempting to pretend that she wasn't supposed to be working on this case.

"There's one more thing," she said.

Her dark gaze locked with his. He could almost feel the nails pounding into his coffin as he waited for her next words.

"I told you the note in the victim's wallet said 'unfinished business,' which led me here. But he also *said* something to me right before he died."

Grayson Prescott, the genius businessman billionaire and former Army Ranger who'd created UB, leaned forward at the head of the long conference room table. "Don't keep us in suspense, Officer Sloane. What did Mr. Cameron tell you?"

"It was one word, a name. With his dying breath, he whispered, 'Lance.'"

Lance couldn't help wincing, thinking of Rick whispering his name as he lay dying in a motel room. At least he hadn't died alone. Lance would be forever grateful that Officer Sloane's kind face was the last one Rick saw, not the face of his killer.

"Hell of a coincidence," Ryland Beck, their lead investigator, said.

"It is," Lance agreed, careful to keep his grief from his voice, his expression. He had to play this carefully. A lot was on the line. "But I wouldn't call it compelling. There's no obvious connection between the note and what he said. The words *unfinished business* weren't capitalized like they would be if it was our company's name. It was likely just a reminder that this Cameron guy needed to take care of something."

"That's one theory," Sloane allowed. "Another is that he knew someone was after him, so he wrote that note in lowercase letters on purpose to throw them off if they found it."

"Why even have the note if he was worried that someone might find it?"

"I've asked myself that same question. The only thing that rings true to me is that he specifically hoped someone *would* find the note if something happened to him. To the killer, it meant nothing. But to law enforcement, well, we dig. We don't stop until we make sense of the evidence. That phrase is a clue, a breadcrumb left by a murdered man who whispered your name as a second breadcrumb. He anticipated that an investigator would follow that trail here. The question is, Why? And what does it have to do with you, Mr. Cabrera?"

He chuckled as if amused. "There's no way he could have known there'd be someone with him when he died and that he'd be able to give them a name."

"That occurred to me as well."

"And?"

She shrugged. "If I had everything figured out, I wouldn't be here asking for help."

"Fair enough. How certain are you that he said 'Lance'? Could it have been Vance? Vince? Something else? You said he bled out. I doubt his mind was firing on all cylinders. He probably wasn't even aware of what he said. It was random."

Her face reddened slightly, whether from embarrassment or anger, he wasn't sure. "He was lucid, his eyes clear as he looked at me. Could I have heard him wrong? Possibly. But I truly believe he said Lance."

"You truly believe?" he scoffed, trying to make light of her rather impressive conclusions that were likely spot on. "Let's assume you're correct. Why link that name to his murder? Maybe it was the name of a family member or friend, and he wanted them to know he was thinking about them at the end."

"My team explored those possibilities. He has no family that we've been able to discover. No friends that we know of. The name Lance had to hold some kind of significance for him to use his last breath to give me that information."

Lance's fists were clenched so hard beneath the table that his hands were going numb. He forced himself to relax his grip.

"If he truly said 'Lance,' and was lucid, how does that help you? It's not a common name. But it's not exactly rare either. It could be someone's first name or their last name. I'm sure if you run an internet search, you'll come up with thousands of hits in Tennessee alone. Did you? Run a search?"

Her eyes narrowed. She didn't appreciate him challenging her investigative skills and wasn't doing well at hiding her resentment. Good. Her defensiveness would help cast doubt on her conclusions.

She crossed her arms over her ample chest, making her appear even more defensive. "I searched our local law enforcement databases, as well as some national ones for known criminals with that name. Nothing of significance came up for our area. And you're correct that my internet searches yielded a large number of hits. But the name

Lance linked to a company called Unfinished Business? That combination only came up once and led me to you."

A ripple of unease seemed to eddy through the room. Lance sighed heavily and sat back. "I don't buy that for a second. You'd have gotten thousands of hits on that phrase, tens of thousands. There's no way you hunted all of those down and then determined only one hit was connected to the name Lance in any way. You're reaching. I totally get that. I've been there, many times. But jumping from point A to point Z without anything in between isn't how you find the *right* answers. Please tell me you have something else—facts, some actual evidence—for you to have come all this way and taken up our valuable time with your theories."

An elbow jabbed his ribs.

Frowning at Faith sitting to his left, he rubbed his side. "What was that for?"

"Manners," she said. "Remember those? Our team doesn't belittle people who come to us for assistance."

He glanced around the table. Pretty much everyone was looking at him with disapproval. He felt a flush creeping up his neck. Belittling someone, as Faith had put it, wasn't how he typically treated anyone, especially a woman. Apparently he was coming across as a bully and Sloane the sympathetic victim.

If the stakes weren't so high, he'd apologize profusely and shut up. And he'd do everything he could to make it up to Sloane for how he'd been acting. But the stakes *were* high, and this wasn't just about him. If he couldn't discredit Sloane's theories, both her and anyone in this room who might decide to assist her with the case was in jeopardy.

"All right, all right." He held up his hands in a placating gesture. "I might have been overzealous in playing the devil's advocate, looking for holes in your conclusions. It wasn't my intention to be offensive, to come across as a—"

"Jerk?" Faith offered.

Several of those around the table laughed.

Officer Sloane's brows rose, apparently unsure whether they were teasing or not.

Lance waited for the laughter to die down. Time for a more direct approach, to go for the jugular.

"I won't argue that particular conclusion," he allowed. "I've behaved badly. And although I don't excuse how I've acted, I hope everyone can at least understand it. After all, it's not every day that someone comes to my place of employment and essentially accuses me of being involved in a murder. That is why you're here, isn't it, Officer Sloane? Because you think that I may have killed Mr. Cameron?"

She arched a brow in challenge. "Did you?"

Grayson rapped his knuckles on the table. "Enough." His hard tone cracked through the room. "Accusing one of my investigators of murder won't be tolerated."

Her eyes widened. "I...ah... I didn't mean to... I mean, I did, but I didn't—"

"Wait," Lance said, ready to play his trump card. "Now that I understand Officer Sloane's...intentions, I can easily put her concerns at rest by offering up an important fact to go along with her misplaced theories."

She stiffened, her expression wary. "What *fact*?"

"My alibi of course."

She blinked in surprise.

He motioned to Faith and her husband beside her, fellow investigator Asher. "Where was I on the night that Mr. Cameron was killed?"

Faith frowned. "I don't—"

"At the beginning of this meeting, Officer Sloane said the victim was killed on September 22. In the early evening. Isn't that correct, Officer?"

"Around eight thirty, yes."

"Oh," Faith said. "Of course." She gave Sloane a pained smile. "Lance definitely couldn't have been involved." She motioned to Asher. "My husband and I had a housewarming party for UB's investigators that night. We were celebrating buying our first home together as a married couple. And before you ask, no, there isn't any possibility that Lance could have left without someone realizing he was gone. Although UB has administrative staff, an IT department and a forensics lab, the actual investigative team is small, less than a dozen of us. We're all close, more like family than friends. His absence would have been noticed."

Grayson gave Lance a subtle nod of approval and relaxed back in his chair. He'd been at the party too and no doubt was relieved that this could be put to rest so easily.

"Faith took an obscene amount of pictures," Lance teased, chuckling when she tried to elbow him again. "I'm sure I'm in more than a few of them. The metadata on the camera cards can prove the date and time each photo was taken. You mentioned that Maple Falls is in DeKalb County. Can't say I've ever been there. But I know my geography. That county is a good three and a half hours from here."

"Four, actually." Sloane sounded defeated, as if she were finally accepting that she was wrong. "More if you hit traffic."

Lance smiled apologetically. "I'm truly sorry to have been so hard on you. But I hope you can see now that the two clues you've put so much credence in have nothing to do with me or this company. They probably have nothing to do with your case at all."

She nodded, looking defeated.

Lance regretted being the one who'd made her feel that way. But he was enormously grateful that they'd all managed to dodge a bullet.

She offered a sheepish smile to Lance and Grayson. "I'm sorry that things went sideways. Diplomacy and tact have never been my strong points. And now I really am back at square one. I'll have to reexamine the entire case file and figure out another starting point, the true reason for that note and for why Rick Cameron whispered the name Lance. Honestly, I'm at a loss."

Lance stared at her in dismay. "You're not dropping the investigation? Letting the detectives in Maple Falls handle the case?"

"Detectives?" She shook her head. "We don't have any, not really. There's no lab, no IT department like you have here. Mr. Cameron's murder was investigated by a couple of our officers who are deemed qualified to be detectives when needed. In an emergency type of situation, our chief will ask the county sheriff for assistance. But he hates to do that and hasn't with this case aside from using their crime scene techs to gather forensic evidence. At this point, it's as cold as a case can get, even though it's less than a month old. That's why I'm working it on my own time. My vacation ends in less than two weeks. If I haven't solved the case by then, it might never be solved. To that end, if someone here has any tips or suggestions, I sure would appreciate it."

Grayson motioned around the table. "Everyone here, except me, used to be a detective in law enforcement. I recruited Ryland to help me recruit the others to work in the private sector when I started this company. These investigators represent decades of experience solving crimes. And you already know their current specialty is cold cases. I'm sure they can offer you some pointers."

The look of desperate eagerness on Sloane's face as the team began offering tips shot a feeling of dread through Lance. All of his arguments had been for nothing. This determined police officer wasn't going to stop digging after all. But at least Grayson and the team lead, Ryland, hadn't offered to pull any of the investigators off their current cases to officially work with her. That might be the only good thing to come out of today's meeting. Him playing his alibi card had taken away the need for them to work the case to prove his innocence. As long as it stayed that way, his friends were safe. But Sloane might not be, not if she'd done something to attract the killer's attention.

That's what Lance needed to know, what exactly she'd done so far, in detail. Maybe it wasn't too late for her. As long as the killer didn't consider her to be a threat, she was safe. But for him, everything had changed. The past had reared its ugly head again. He couldn't ignore it without risking anyone associated with him becoming collateral damage. Finding Rick's killer, and keeping the lid on their shared past, was paramount.

While Sloane furiously typed notes on her computer tablet, Lance took the opportunity to briefly study each of his friends.

Grayson Prescott—their leader, a military hero who'd come home to a murdered wife and a missing daughter. Instead of buckling beneath his grief and ensuing frustration over a case that went cold for years, he'd formed Unfinished Business. After UB solved Grayson's cold case, he'd dedicated the company to helping other families dealing with similar situations.

Next to Grayson was Willow, his current wife, a former Gatlinburg detective who'd helped him solve his first wife's murder and find his missing daughter alive and well.

Ryland Beck, their team lead.

Trent. His full name was Adam Trent. But no one ever called him Adam. He'd gone through hell and back to save a woman who'd been on the run for years against unknown enemies determined to kill her.

He smiled at Callum Wright, who'd spent his life hating his last name because of all the jokes about him being Mr. Right. Callum had once despised lawyers. Now he was married to one.

Asher and Faith Whitfield. When they'd ended up together, the only people who were surprised were Asher and Faith.

A few members of the team weren't here. Rowan Knight, their liaison with the TBI. Other fellow investigators, Brice Galloway and Ivy Shaw.

Lance cared deeply about each and every one of them.

When he happened to glance at the end of the table again, he was dismayed to see Grayson intently watching him. There were questions in Grayson's eyes. No doubt he'd noticed Lance studying his fellow investigators and wondered why. Hoping to turn Grayson's attention, Lance pretended interest in what Ryland was currently discussing with Sloane.

To Lance's relief, a few moments later, Grayson stood, signaling the end of the meeting. "Best of luck with your investigation, Officer. I wish we could have done more."

She began sliding her photographs and computer tablet into her leather satchel. "Everyone's been exceedingly generous with their time and advice. I really appreciate it."

The team slowly filed out of the glass-walled conference room and down the stairs to the war room below. It was a large open area with lofty two-story high ceilings so that anyone in the conference rooms could look down and potentially signal to other investigators to join them. Or anyone below could see who was upstairs, including Grayson's office beside the largest conference room.

Lance waited for the others to leave so he could time his exit with their guest's. He held the door open. "Officer Sloane—"

She paused in the opening. "Call me Keira, please. I think after practically coming to blows, we should be on a first-name basis, don't you?"

He laughed, genuinely amused. "Keira. If any of us come up with more ideas for your investigation, where can we reach you? Are you staying in Gatlinburg for a while?"

Her eyes widened. "I appreciate you asking. Although I admit to being—"

"Surprised?"

She nodded.

"My apologies again. I really didn't mean to come across so rudely. Your visit, what you said, caught me off guard." Understatement of the decade. "But that's no excuse for the way I treated you. Forgive me?"

The smile she gifted him with completely transformed her. Where before she'd been pretty, now she was…stunning. In another lifetime, maybe they could have been friends. Or more. In addition to being incredibly attractive, she had qualities he greatly admired: honesty, integrity and a quick mind. Normally he'd appreciate her stubbornness and refusal to give up on an investigation too. But right now those qualities were extremely inconvenient.

"You're forgiven." She handed him a business card. "I'm booked in a chalet for a couple of days, up Skyline Road. It's a small A-frame hanging off the side of the mountain with a driveway sloping so steeply down toward the cabin that I refuse to use it." She shivered for effect.

"I think I know the place. People make bets about whether a tourist will slide down that driveway one day and barrel through the house and off the mountain." At her horrified look, he grinned. "I'm teasing."

She blinked. "Oh, well, I'm still not using the driveway. I park on the street out front."

"Four-wheel drive, I hope. It's not cold enough to snow yet, but sometimes you need that extra power to get up these mountains."

"My Camry's got all-wheel drive. So far, it's been great at hugging the curves and holding the roads. I think I'll be okay."

"I'm sure you will." He slid the business card into an inside pocket of his suit jacket.

She started to leave, then stopped. "If anyone needs to call me, be sure to use the personal cell number on that card. Not my office number. Because, well—"

"You're not there. And your coworkers don't know you're playing detective." At the light flush on her face, he smiled again. "Your secret's safe with us. Have a good day, Officer Sloane."

She gave him a grateful smile. "Keira."

"Keira."

As she headed down the stairs, Lance paused at the top landing to watch her. The two-story windows of the war room looked out at the parking lot. True to her word, she got into a silver late-model Camry. He couldn't see the license plate to take down and potentially track her. But he didn't need to.

He knew exactly where she was going.

A few moments later, he reached his desk and grabbed his laptop computer.

"Hey, Lance." Asher motioned to him from his desk two aisles over. "Can you take a look at this?"

"Sorry, buddy. I've got something I need to take care of." He headed toward the exit.

"Catch me later, all right?" Asher called out.

"Will do." The lie was bitter on his tongue, especially when he turned in the doorway for one last look at his team and noticed Grayson and Ryland watching from Grayson's second-floor office. Lance nodded, then turned away, knowing he'd never see them again. Because, contrary to what he'd just told Asher, he was never coming back.

Chapter Four

Keira looked up from her computer tablet, surprised to hear a knock on the cabin's door. She'd gotten back from Unfinished Business a few minutes ago and had only just now settled in front of the coffee table to review her notes from the meeting.

Although she wasn't expecting trouble, someone stopping at this remote rental cabin deep in the mountains had her grabbing her service pistol from an end table. When she looked through the security peephole in the front door, no one was there. Even more surprising was that a black SUV with dark-tinted windows was turning down her steep driveway.

When the SUV's door opened, a familiar broad-shouldered figure stepped out. She blinked in surprise. As he pulled his shades off and slid them into one of the pockets of his charcoal-gray suit jacket, she shook her head. What in the world was Lance Cabrera doing here? And good grief, was he this handsome, and tall, when she'd seen him earlier? She'd been so pumped with adrenaline and nervous energy when she'd presented her information to the room full of investigators that she hadn't really paid attention to how ruggedly good-looking he was.

She set her pistol on a decorative table against the wall before opening the door.

"Mr. Cabrera," she said as he climbed the steps of the front porch. "What happened? Did I leave my favorite pen at UB and you rushed over to return it?"

His deep blue eyes crinkled at the corners with amusement. "I didn't notice any wayward writing instruments in the conference room when I left."

"Then I confess to being confused about why you'd show up here. I couldn't have made a good impression by essentially accusing you of murder. So I'm guessing you're not here to ask me out on a date."

He grinned. "If I thought you'd be amenable, and the stars aligned, it would be my honor to ask exactly that." His smile faded. "Unfortunately, this isn't a social call. We need to talk." He motioned toward the opening. "Mind if I come in?"

"Oh, of course." She moved to the side and pulled open the door the rest of the way. "You're probably cold, and here I am running my mouth. I can get you a hot chocolate or a…" She stared at him in surprise when he immediately shut the door behind him and flipped the dead bolt.

A prickle of unease ran down her spine. "Okay, that's weird. First, a knock on the door with no one there. Then you show up and lock the door as if the devil's on your heels." She laughed awkwardly. "Is there an axe murderer on the loose in the Smoky Mountains that I should be on guard against?"

His intense gaze zeroed in on her. "Someone knocked on your door? Then hid?"

"Yes, I suppose, I mean…it sounded like knocking. But it could have been a bird or an animal making noise outside. I was just checking the peephole when you drove up."

His pistol was suddenly out, pointed down by his side. "Are all your windows and doors locked?"

"I, ah, I guess so. I mean, I haven't opened any of them since I got here. But—"

"Lock the door behind me. Wait here. Don't go outside." He was out the door, turning left and running toward the side of the cabin before she could stop him.

She shut the door harder than necessary and locked it as he'd told her. But when she started toward the couch, she stopped. "The heck with this. I didn't drive four hours to be treated like a helpless little woman. I get enough of that at work." She grabbed her pistol and headed outside.

Since Lance had gone left, she went right, hoping that if there was someone out here, she and Lance would corner them. It seemed a bit ridiculous having her pistol out, looking for what likely amounted to some teenager playing a game of doorbell ditch. Although there weren't any other cabins immediately nearby, there were some farther down this road. Definitely within walking distance if some kids wanted to play a prank on a tourist. But if Lance was concerned enough to pull his gun, she was going to follow his lead, at least until she found out why he was so worried.

As she continued around the side of the house, she didn't encounter any juvenile delinquents or anyone else. She didn't hear anyone either, or really much of anything. Other than a light cool breeze blowing through the branches overhead, making her long for her jacket, the woods were eerily silent. No squirrels chattering. No birds chirping. No rustling in the undergrowth as a raccoon or other small creature searched for food. She hesitated. Had it ever been like this since her arrival? It seemed as if there was always something making noise. Why was it so quiet now?

On high alert, she raised her pistol out in front of her, sweeping it back and forth as she checked the bushes near the cabin's foundation. To her left, she studied the thick undergrowth of the woods, looking for something that didn't quite belong. Listening for a potential threat.

Stopping at the back corner of the cabin, she ducked down. Keeping her head low, she peered around the corner through the maze of timbers driven deep into the slope of the mountain, anchoring the house to bedrock. Nothing. No rebellious teenagers. No bad guy hanging off a stilt, aiming a gun at her. But Lance wasn't there either. Shouldn't he have reached the other corner a few seconds before her?

Her stomach sank. Maybe he'd run into some trouble. And she was his only backup. She whirled around and jogged toward the front of the house.

It nearly killed her to stop at the corner. But running full tilt into the open without looking first was a newbie maneuver. With only six years in law enforcement, she didn't come close to matching the experience of those at UB. But she sure as heck wasn't a rookie.

Crouching down low again to make herself less of a target, she peered around the edge of the cabin toward the raised front porch. Empty. So where had Lance—

Crunching leaves sounded behind her. She jerked around. A man dressed in black dove at her from the trees. Before she could even react, he slammed against her, crushing her against the log wall of the cabin. Her gun flew from her grip, skittering across the ground. She twisted and clawed at his arms around her waist, furiously trying to break free.

He cursed in her ear and jerked her up in the air.

She raked her nails across both of his arms, but couldn't reach any skin through his long-sleeved black shirt. Clawing at his hands didn't work either. They were covered with leather gloves. Grabbing one of his gloved fingers, she yanked back, hard. A loud pop was followed by his shout of rage and pain.

He threw her against the cabin wall as if she were a rag doll. She slammed hard against it, letting out a yelp of pain as she fell to her knees. Her ribs hurt with every gasping breath. Her ears rang from the impact. But she couldn't just curl up in the fetal position. She had to push through the pain, defend herself. Where was her gun? Where?

He stood a few feet away, chest heaving from exertion, his injured hand clutched to his chest. Dressed completely in black, with a cloth covering the lower part of his face, all that showed were his dark brown eyes, staring at her with the promise of retribution.

Using his uninjured hand, he drew a long jagged knife from beneath his shirt.

"What do you want?" she demanded, desperately looking around. There, her pistol. It was about three feet away, half buried in some dried leaves.

He rushed toward her, knife raised high.

She rolled to the side, barely avoiding the swipe of his deadly blade. Then she dove for the pistol. His guttural yell sounded behind her. She let out a panicked whimper as she grabbed her gun and flipped onto her back.

Lance was suddenly there, tackling the man with the knife. They both fell onto the ground, locked together in a deadly embrace.

Keira leaped to her feet, her protesting ribs making

her breath catch. Stumbling, she pushed through the pain, bringing her gun up. But she couldn't get a clear shot.

She didn't need one.

The fight was over as quickly as it had begun. The man with the knife grunted and collapsed onto the ground, his own blade protruding from his neck. Blood quickly saturated his collar as he made a sickening gurgling sound.

Lance jerked his head up, eyes widening in alarm. "Keira, hit the deck!"

She threw herself to the ground.

Bam! Bam! Bam!

She gasped in shock as another man dressed in black fell to the ground a few yards from where she'd been standing. A gun skipped across the dirt from his lifeless hands. Lance had saved her. But why did she even need saving?

"What the heck is going on, Lance? Why did these men follow you here?"

"They didn't follow *me*. They followed *you*." He grabbed her hand. "Come on. We have to get out of here." He tugged her toward his SUV.

"What do you mean they followed me? The only people I've met around here are you and the others at UB."

"We'll figure it out later." He motioned toward the passenger side as he aimed his key fob at the vehicle. "Get in."

Gunshots echoed through the trees. Bullets shattered the rear window, raining glass across the concrete like pennies pinging against a metal pan.

He jerked back and fired toward the trees on the incline across the street. More bullets slammed into the back of the SUV.

Keira returned fire, aiming where she'd seen the flash of muzzle fire in the trees.

"Get in the cabin," Lance yelled. "I'll cover you."

"We'll cover each other."

He frowned, but didn't argue. They both fired their pistols toward the trees as they raced up the steps and charged into the house. This time, she was the one who slammed the door shut and flipped the lock. Lance pulled her to the floor beneath the front windows a few feet from the entryway. He covered her body with his as bullets slammed into the front door.

Keira shoved at him, her lungs straining for air beneath his tight hold even as her sore ribs screamed in pain. "You know I'm a cop, right?" she forced out, then dragged in another painful breath. "I can defend myself. Get off me."

"And you know I'm a man, right? And a former cop myself? I'm not going to cower while a woman takes a bullet for me."

She shoved at him, cursing.

He laughed. "Maybe you should have been a sailor. Those are some salty words coming out of that pretty mouth."

"You think this is funny?" She coughed, then dragged in another painful breath. "People are trying to kill us."

"Not the first time. Won't be the last." He cocked his head, listening, his weight still crushing her ribs. "The shooting has stopped."

She shoved against him again. "Good. Maybe they gave up."

"Don't count on it. Lucky for us that solid door and the log walls stopped the bullets. They're obviously not using high-powered rifles. Must be using handguns."

"And knives."

He grimaced. "And knives. I'm guessing we have a couple of minutes while they regroup and plan their entry."

"Then you really need to get off me. Now, before I faint from lack of oxygen."

He looked down, a wry grin on his face. "Sorry about that." He rolled off her but stayed on the floor beside her. "Don't stand up until we're clear of the windows."

"No kidding." She drew her first deep breath and immediately regretted it, grimacing in pain.

"What's wrong?" He slid a hand across her abdomen, then up toward her chest as if searching for wounds. "Did he cut you? Were you hit?"

She grabbed his hand before things got embarrassing. "No cuts. No bullet wounds. The guy outside threw me against the side of the cabin." She shoved his hand away. "I don't think anything's broken. Just bruised." She drew some quick, shallow breaths, relieved that the pain was much more bearable that way. Rolling slightly to her side, she slid her cell phone out of her jeans pocket.

He frowned. "What are you doing?"

"Calling 911."

"I'd rather not involve the police."

She gave him an incredulous look. "Seriously? I *am* the police. We're *already* involved."

He grinned. "Well, there is that. I don't suppose we really have an alternative at this point. I didn't expect them to move on you so fast."

She paused with her phone in her hand. "Move on me? That's the second time you've essentially said that I'm the target. Maybe it's you they're after."

"Oh, they are. No question. But they didn't know where I was until you led them to Gatlinburg, to Unfinished Business."

"You're blaming all of this on me?"

"Of course not. I was just explaining—"

A thumping sound came from above. They both looked up.

"They're on the roof," he said. "They're probably leery of trying the front windows, guessing we'll shoot if they do. Please tell me this place doesn't have a skylight."

"Kitchen, back left corner." She tapped the phone's screen, dialing 911. But when she put the phone to her ear, there was only static. She checked the phone to see if it had been damaged. It was pristine, not a single scratch. And there were four bars. Excellent reception. So why wasn't the call going through?

Lance grabbed the phone and held it to his ear. "Cell service is jammed."

"Jammed? What the—who *are* these people? What do they want?"

"At the moment? Both of us dead. Or, more likely, you dead and me alive long enough to be tortured for information. Then they'll kill me."

She stared at him in horror. "What did you do? Sleep with a mafia boss's daughter?"

He let out a bark of laughter. "I wish. At least then all of this might have been worth it."

"You're joking at a time like this?"

"I'm multitasking, trying to come up with a plan that involves both of us staying alive, minus the torture part."

"What's the plan?"

"Did you miss the *trying to come up with one* part?"

She rolled her eyes. "We need to get out of here. Hide somewhere."

"On that we agree. It's the how that I haven't figured out. Cabin layout?"

"Kitchen on the left, this family room, bedroom and bathroom through that door on the far right."

"What about the door beside the bedroom door? Closet?"

"Basement. The rec room. But there's no exit. No windows or doors. Solid concrete walls. We'd be trapped if we went down there."

"Those concrete walls will offer protection, with only one entrance to guard—the stairs. That's more than we have on this level."

"I don't like it," she said.

A loud bang sounded from the kitchen, followed by the sound of shattering glass.

Lance tightened his grip on his pistol. "Time to make our stand, General Custer. Outside, where the bullets were flying earlier? Or the basement without windows?"

"I'll take my chances outside." She jumped up to open the front door.

He tackled her back to the floor just before a barrage of gunfire shattered the window where she'd been standing, raining glass down on top of them.

She swore, grabbing the edge of a blanket from the back of a nearby chair and tossing it on the floor over the glass. Then she scrambled across it toward the front door.

He quickly followed, blocking her way so she wouldn't try to open the door. "About that plan—"

"I know, I know. As much as I hate it, the basement's our only viable option."

"Smart lady. *Go.*" He pushed her ahead of him. They both crawled as fast as they could, knees bumping against the hard wood floors, staying low to avoid becoming a target through any of the windows.

They were almost to the basement door when shouts sounded behind them.

"Hurry," Lance yelled.

Keira jumped up and shoved the basement door open. The dark, constricted space below had her hesitating and drawing a painful, bracing breath to try to tamp down her fears. At Lance's questioning look, she straightened her shoulders, then forced herself to hurry down the stairs. At the bottom, she anxiously whirled around, expecting Lance to be right behind her. Instead, he stood silhouetted in the doorway above.

"Lock the door," he yelled, then slammed it shut. Something thumped against it.

She stood there, stunned. What the heck? She whipped out her pistol and raced back up the stairs. But when she pushed the door, it barely moved. She strained against it, only managing to open the door a few millimeters. That thump she'd heard. Lance must have shoved a chair or something else under the doorknob to keep her in the basement.

The fears from her past battered at her, narrowing her vision with darkness. She had to get out. She yelled some choice phrases at him and slammed her shoulder against the door. Her ribs protested the abuse, making her double over in pain. She drew small shaky breaths until she could straighten. Then she beat her fist against the wood, over and over, her whole body shaking. "Lance! Let me out!"

Gunshots sounded from the main room. Grunts. Shouts. More breaking glass. How many of those lunatics were out there? She shoved at the door over and over, fighting through the pain, desperate to get out to help Lance. And desperate to escape this dungeon before she curled into a fetal position like the terrified young girl she'd once been. Out. She had to get out!

A few agonizing minutes later, the sudden silence

shook her even more than the shouts and gunshots had. Was this the calm before the storm, like earlier when the birds had stopped chirping? What was going on?

The door yanked open.

She stumbled back, grabbing the railing to keep from falling as she swung her pistol toward the man looming there. He immediately raised his hands. Recognition slammed into her. She jerked her gun down.

"Mr. Prescott?"

"Officer Sloane." He dropped his hands, sounding slightly out of breath. There was a fresh cut on his jaw. His business suit was torn in several places. And his formerly white shirt was now dotted with blood. "At the risk of sounding cliché, the coast is clear."

Lance appeared beside him, looking far worse than his boss. Blood was smeared on his clothes, his neck, his hair. Bruises were already darkening along his jaw.

She rushed up the last few steps to the doorway. "Lance. Are you hurt? What—"

"We don't have much time," he said. "It's taken them twelve years to find me. Now that they have, they'll come at me with everything they've got. Anyone here when their reinforcements arrive is in danger." He held his hand out to Keira. "We're leaving. Now."

She shoved her pistol into the waistband of her pants and brushed past him into the main room. Her eyes widened when she saw the destruction and death around her. Several men dressed in black lay crumpled on the floor in various locations, clearly beyond help. Asher, Ryland, Faith and two other UB investigators stood near the stone fireplace at the back of the family room, looking as disheveled as their boss, several of them bleeding from various cuts.

"What happened?" she asked. "Have any of you been seriously hurt?"

Lance shoved a fresh magazine into his pistol as he peered out the back windows looking up at the mountains.

Grayson stopped beside Keira. "Thankfully, everyone's okay. Lance got the worst of it. He was fighting two men at once when we got here."

Lance turned from the windows. "I had it under control. You shouldn't have come."

"You're welcome." Grayson rolled his eyes.

Lance let out a deep breath and glanced at his teammates, offering a quick nod of thanks. As he stepped over to Keira and Grayson, he flipped back his suit jacket and shoved his pistol into the holster on his belt. "I don't mean to sound ungrateful. But I'd really hoped to not involve any of you in this. How did you know where I was? Or that Keira might be in trouble?"

Asher motioned to the destruction around them. "We all got to talking after you left. You were really defensive during the meeting, trying far too hard to discredit Officer Sloane's investigation. It was obvious there was something going on and that it involved both of you. Figuring out what cabin she'd rented only took a few calls. We'd planned on coming over to talk to her first, then we were going to your place. We didn't expect to get caught at the O.K. Corral."

Keira put her hands on her hips. "What's going on, Lance? You said these men have been after you for years but that they followed me. Did it occur to you that you could have warned me earlier in the safety of UB's conference room?"

His dark brooding gaze locked on hers. "Nothing you told me in the meeting made me think you'd attracted the attention of these guys. I came here to talk, to make absolutely sure you hadn't done anything to put yourself at risk. And then I was going to try to convince you to drop the case, to *keep* you out of danger. If I'd known they'd followed you, that they were in Gatlinburg, I sure as hell wouldn't have let you walk into an ambush. I'd have taken you with me when I left UB and protected you."

"Hold it," Faith said. "Do I have this right? Someone's been trying to find you and kill you for *years*. Rick Cameron is somehow involved. And you were worried that Keira may have led these enemies to you. Yet, instead of telling us about it and asking us to help, you risked your life, and hers, by trying to handle this alone?"

Lance winced. "It sounds way worse when you put it like that."

Asher stepped closer to him. "You had an odd look on your face in the war room when you told me you'd see me later. You were lying, weren't you? When you left UB, you were leaving for good, not planning on ever coming back. Tell me I'm wrong, Lance. Please, for God's sake, tell me I'm wrong."

Lance looked away.

Asher swore.

Keira pulled out her cell phone.

"Don't tell me you're trying to call the police again." Lance sounded alarmed.

"Assuming the cell signal isn't still jammed, dang straight I'm calling the police."

He grabbed her phone. *"No."*

Grayson motioned toward the others. Suddenly Keira and Lance were surrounded by the UB investigators, a wall of men and one woman—Faith—blocking them from leaving.

"The police are already on their way," Grayson told him. "And you're not going anywhere without telling your teammates, your friends, what exactly is going on."

Lance looked like he wanted to argue, but the sound of sirens coming up the mountain had him fisting his hands by his sides.

Grayson put his hand on Lance's shoulder. "I can practically see the wheels spinning in your mind, trying to weave some kind of story to make us leave you alone. You're trying to figure out how to keep all of us safe while you, and potentially Officer Sloane too, face something incredibly dangerous on your own. These obviously aren't your run-of-the-mill criminals out to settle a score. They appear to be highly organized, trained and well funded. You need our help, whether you want it or not."

Lance's jaw tightened. "I don't want any of you hurt." He glanced around at them, then let out a shaky breath. "Any more hurt than you already are."

Grayson dropped his hand from Lance's shoulder. "I don't want that either. Which is why you need to level with us, give us information so we know who we're fighting against. Then we'll fight them together." He looked at the others. "Am I right?"

"Damn straight," Faith said, her words echoed by the team.

Keira arched a brow at Lance and raised her voice to be heard over the approaching sirens. "I'm already in this. And I'm not letting you leave without me."

Grayson motioned toward the front windows, or what was left of them after being shattered by bullets. "Gatlinburg PD is going to pull up out front any minute now. Lance, give me your word that you're going to work with us, that you'll explain everything, and we'll come up with a plan together. No playing this solo."

He gave all of them a pained look, then nodded. "All right. I'll tell you everything. But not in front of the police."

"The police can help us," Grayson argued.

"Not with this. Trust me."

He stared at Lance a few moments, then nodded. "All right. I'll accept that, for now. But we've got to come up with a cover story. Fast."

"Sticking close to the truth works best," Keira said. "Less chance of our stories not matching. That should be easy since Lance is the only one in this room who knows what's going on and who is after him."

He gave her an odd look, as if he were going to correct something she'd said. Instead, he shrugged and remained silent.

"Sirens have stopped." Faith motioned toward the jagged openings where the front windows used to be. "I don't see the police, so they've likely parked down the street in case there are active gunmen. But they're probably running through the woods toward the cabin as we speak. Keira's right. We should stick to the truth where we can. We can honestly say that we all came here to see Keira and were surprised that Lance was here too and that these ninja guys were trying to kill them. But how do we explain Keira being here in Gatlinburg? Why we were coming to see her? Or you, Lance, coming to see her, without us bringing up Rick Cameron's case and whatever it has to do with your mysterious past?"

"That part's easy." Lance gave Keira a half smile and put his arm around her shoulders. "You and I are dating. My friends found out this morning when I told them at

UB. After I left, they came over to see you, to push for information about our relationship. I, of course, was already here, you being my girlfriend and all."

Her cheeks flushed and she pushed his arm off her shoulder. "Try to kiss me and I'll punch you."

His grin widened. "Noted."

Movement caught their attention out front. Police in flak jackets emerged from the cover of the trees, boots thumping as they raced up the porch stairs and aimed long guns through the openings.

Lance swore.

"Gatlinburg PD," one of them yelled. "Drop any weapons you have. Come out with your hands up."

Grayson straightened his suit jacket, frowning at the drops of blood and rips in the expensive fabric. "Everyone say as little as possible." He spoke low so those out front wouldn't hear him. "Stick to the story Lance just made up. Don't offer any extra information." He shook his head as if in disgust. "May God help us all. We're about to lie to the chief of police."

Chapter Five

In all her twenty-eight years, other than the awful things that had happened during her teen years, Keira couldn't think of a single day that was crazier, scarier, more frustrating, painful or confusing than today had been. And it wasn't close to being over. The sun was only just now beginning to set. But instead of being warm and cozy in her cabin as she'd planned when she first woke up, she was back at Unfinished Business.

One of the differences between this morning and now was that instead of being in a conference room, she was sitting in a chair in the middle of the so-called war room. Chairs had been arranged in a large circle. But few of them were occupied. The UB investigators were standing around in small groups talking, drinking and eating sandwiches their boss had ordered for their dinner.

The biggest difference from this morning was her reason for being here. She wasn't just looking into a cold case now. She was trying to find out why she'd been shot at, beaten, almost stabbed, locked in a dark basement and, perhaps worst of all, been forced to lie to fellow police officers. Rather than tell them she was here to investigate a murder, she'd told them she was Lance's girlfriend.

As if something like that could ever happen. She couldn't

imagine the stars ever aligning between them, not after their inauspicious start.

Making everything worse was that she'd been black-mailed at the cabin by Gatlinburg's police chief Russo to go to the hospital. She'd argued that she knew her ribs were only bruised, not broken. *After all, she'd had broken ribs before.* Of course, she hadn't shared that information with him. Still, it was only because Russo threatened to call her boss to order her to the hospital that she'd finally given in.

Now here she was, with bruised, not broken, ribs—as she'd predicted. And instead of being happy and grateful to have some tips and suggestions from a group of experienced investigators like she had been earlier, she was now desperate to find out how she could avoid the same fate as Rick Cameron.

She glanced around the room. Everyone who'd been at the cabin sported bandages or stitches on their various cuts and scrapes. Lance by far had the most injuries, with stitches on both forearms, his left calf and his scalp. Keira considered herself lucky that she'd only sustained a few minor abrasions. And that it only hurt when she breathed. Okay, maybe that wasn't something to exactly be thankful for. But considering how much worse it could have been, she wasn't complaining. Especially since none of her cuts had required stitches.

She hated needles.

And doctors.

And hospitals.

All they did was bring up bad memories.

Chief Russo had no way of knowing that. But it didn't keep him from being added to her list of people she'd rather avoid in the future. After all, it was only because of him that flashbacks of her childhood kept parading like a horror movie in her mind's eye. She didn't need that added stress on top of everything else, not today.

Impatient for everyone to join the circle so they could start the discussion, she looked past them through the two-story windows that overlooked the front parking lot.

Where the asphalt ended, the scary, twisty two-lane road up and down the mountain began. Just past that, the mountain rose steeply, its peak one of the tallest in the Smokies. From what she'd been told, the road ended at the very top of this particular mountain, at Grayson Prescott's estate. And since the mountain was called Prescott Mountain, she could only assume he owned the whole darn thing. How incredible was that?

Even if she ever had the money to afford it, she wouldn't want a mountain. Her multitude of fears from claustrophobia to heights and a ridiculously long list of other things would keep her from wanting to travel up and down a winding road every day. But, man oh man, could she appreciate the natural beauty around here.

Even in the fading sunlight, the scenery was so surreal that it made her want to stare out the windows and forget everything else around her. Tall, spindly oaks devoid of leaves marched up the steep slope beside thick, dark evergreens. Jagged rocks in varying shapes and sizes jutted out at odd angles, catching the light and forming a tapestry of colors that would make an artist weep. It was so much more picturesque than flat Maple Falls. But what struck her the most were the little puffs of white mist that gave the mountains their name—the Smokies.

When she'd first visited the Great Smoky Mountains National Park as a small child, she'd been terrified at the white puffs, convinced that the woods were on fire.

Thankfully, her mom knew otherwise and had reassured her. Those were the good times, when her family had been a real family. Before her father had turned to alcohol and painkillers to drown his guilt. Before everything had gone so horribly wrong.

"Never seen a mountain before?" Lance sat beside her. The teasing note in his voice was tempered by the lines of worry on his forehead.

"Not in a very long time."

His gaze sharpened, the lines of worry deepening. "That sounded ominous. What's wrong?"

"Other than someone wanting to kill me?"

"Don't."

"Don't what?"

"Lie to me. Don't pretend that you were thinking about the mess we're in. Something else was on your mind, something that put haunting shadows in your eyes. What is it? Something from your past? You seemed so lost, a million miles away." He gently took one of her hands in his and turned it over, revealing the ugly scars. "Is this part of it? The reason for the shadows?"

Her breath caught and she snatched her hand back, curling her fingers against her palms to cover the angry red welts. She forced a laugh. "Haunting shadows? Really? When did you become a poet?"

He didn't crack a smile. Instead, he simply waited, as if he expected her to confess her deepest, darkest secrets.

That was never going to happen.

"If by something in my past you mean being attacked by ninjas," she scoffed, "then you're right on target. Yes, my past...my *recent* past is bothering me. When do we get to hear the truth about what's going on? The truth about *your* past?"

He studied her, his expression turning sad. Or was it more that he was...disappointed?

Finally, he shrugged and motioned to the others. "As soon as everyone's settled—" his voice was raised so the team could hear him "—I'll start."

The little groups broke apart. The newest arrivals grabbed their laptops or computer tablets and hurried to take their seats. Faith and her husband, Asher, were already sitting across from Lance and Keira. Ryland, the team lead, was next to Faith. The other two men from the cabin sat close by. They had been reintroduced to Keira as Trent and Callum since she had forgotten their names from the earlier meeting.

The remaining members of the UB investigative team were here too, with the exception of their boss, Grayson, and his wife, Willow. They were both at the police station, where Grayson was trying to placate the chief. There'd been no way to hide what had happened from the media with so many gunshots and the destruction at the cabin. Not to mention the body bags being carried out to coroner's vans. The chief wasn't letting this go with a simple "home invasion" explanation.

Apparently he was a close friend of Grayson's, and he was also Willow's former boss. Their history together was the only reason the rest of them were allowed to leave the hospital after being treated without enduring lengthy police interviews. But they'd had to agree to go to the station later for more questioning if Grayson wasn't able to satisfy Russo with his answers.

Once everyone was seated and quiet descended upon the room, every eye turned to Lance. This man whom Keira viewed as the epitome of confidence and decisiveness now seemed uncertain, hesitant. After briefly glancing around the circle at his fellow investigators and Keira, he drew a deep breath and began to speak.

"Officer Sloane, I mean Keira, and all of my friends here at Unfinished Business, everything you think you know about me is a lie."

Chapter Six

Lance would rather face a roomful of gunmen with only a pistol and one magazine of ammo to defend himself than the people sitting around this circle. He cared deeply for them, and even felt a deep connection to Keira. After all, she'd been through hell because his past had followed her to Gatlinburg. His biggest regret was that he was responsible for putting both her and his work family in danger. Because of his actions, or inaction, he was about to lose the friendship of everyone in this room.

On the opposite side of the circle of chairs, Faith gave him an encouraging smile. "Come on, Lance. We know you. You can't fake the stuff that really matters, the kind of person you are. That comes out in actions, not words. So whatever it is that you've been hiding, don't be afraid to share. We're all friends here, family really." She smiled at Keira. "And future friends. We can't fix this unless we know what's going on."

He grimaced. "Some things aren't fixable."

Keira surprised him by briefly squeezing his hand. "We can at least try."

He smiled, but he already knew this meeting wasn't going to help. And he still wasn't committed to fully disclosing everything in spite of his promise to Grayson. It was too dangerous.

"As I said, everything you think you know about me is a lie, starting with my name. Lance Cabrera is the alias I took on twelve years ago. My birth name is Lance Mitchell." When the huge outcry he'd expected didn't happen, he hesitated, frowning. "I don't come from out west like I've led you all to believe. My hometown is in central Florida, a city called Gainesville. My résumé that I used to join Unfinished Business is a fabrication."

Ryland shook his head, his gaze locked on Lance. "No. It isn't. I recruited you. You were working as a detective in Nashville. I visited you there at your job. Spoke to your peers, your boss. He gave you a glowing recommendation, said you were the best detective he'd worked with in his forty-year career. Are you saying he made all that up? That he allowed a civilian to pretend to be a detective the day I was there?"

"Well, no, of course not. He told the truth as he saw it. I worked for Nashville PD for over eight years."

"As Lance Cabrera."

"Yes."

"Then if you're expecting shock or recriminations from us because you changed your name prior to that, you'll be disappointed. People change their names for all kinds of reasons. Heck, Faith changed her last name from Lancaster to Whitfield when she married Asher. We still consider her to be a friend, more or less."

Faith made a rude gesture.

Ryland grinned. "My point, Lance, is that we already know from what happened this morning and what little you've told us so far, that something bad in your past has caught up to you. If I felt that changing my name would help me get a much-needed fresh start, I wouldn't hesitate. What we need to know is who these people are and why they're after you." He motioned toward Keira. "And why they went after Officer Sloane. Stop worrying about how we'll feel and give us the facts. Tell us what we're up against. Then we'll all deal with the fallout. All right, brother?"

Lance was shocked at the nods of agreement from everyone in the room, including Keira. He hadn't expected that. He offered up one last warning. "I appreciate the support, more than you know. But if we continue, if I tell you everything, it puts all of you in danger. As it is, it will be difficult to put a slant on whatever stories the media is already spinning, to placate the bad guys. We need to make it convincing that UB being at the cabin truly has nothing to do with my past. Doing that should keep you all safe. Keira and I can leave and deal with this alone. My primary concern for her is to figure out how she got involved in this and find a way to get her out of it. The rest is on me to handle."

Ryland shook his head again. "No way. You aren't facing this alone. You've saved my life on numerous occasions, plus a few more of us. You were part of the team that helped save Asher on his last big case. We owe you for that."

"You've saved my life too," Lance argued. "You owe me nothing."

"Then consider this," Ryland said. "As far as I'm concerned, we're family. Family doesn't run when one of theirs is in trouble. Not this family anyway. Am I right guys?"

"And gals," Faith and Ivy chimed in, laughing because they'd both said the same thing.

Faith smiled. "We are family, Lance. And Keira is too, because her fate is apparently tied with yours, at least right now. None of us is running away from this, no matter how hard you try to convince us."

Everyone voiced their agreement.

Lance let out a shuddering breath, his throat tight. He'd never met a group of better people. And while he didn't want to involve them any more than they already were, it was clear they weren't going to give him that choice. All he could do now was prepare them.

He nodded his thanks, and when he'd composed himself enough to speak again, he began his story.

"To understand what's happening, I have to start where this began for me, my senior year in college. My on-again, off-again girlfriend, Ileana Sanchez, was off-again. Thankfully she was majoring in IT, computer programming, and I was following the criminology track. With radically different majors, the only times we crossed each other's paths was at sporting events or the restaurants on campus. I was just a few months shy of graduation.

"Most of my classmates were applying for jobs with police departments, hoping to move up the ladder from beat cop to detective eventually. I was determined to start out right away doing what I loved, solving mysteries, figuring out whodunit. I didn't want to spend years earning my stripes and paying my dues. My naive, overinflated ego had me applying for jobs with the big dogs—FBI, CIA, Homeland Security, you name it. If it was an agency with a glitzy reputation, I tried to get in."

Trent chuckled. "Ambition with a capital A. Those places prefer their candidates to have real-world experience in other careers or agencies before signing on with them. I imagine you got turned down flat."

"You'd be right," Lance said, "with one exception. A man I'd never met—Ian Murphy—working for an agency

I'd never heard of contacted me. He said he had been given my name from one of those other agencies. But who he got it from exactly, and how, was vague. He never quite explained that part."

"Red flags, buddy," Trent said.

"Where were you when I was naive and twenty-two, Trent?"

Trent laughed. "Just as young and naive as you, I'm guessing."

Lance smiled. "The sales pitch was incredible. The agency was brand-new, super secret and flush with money. They wanted young, energetic, smart people who would bridge the gap between the rules the law enforcement entities were forced to abide by versus what civilians could get away with. An example he gave me was that the FBI might not be able to secure a warrant they need in order to conduct some kind of surveillance because a judge doesn't agree that they have probable cause. But there's nothing stopping a civilian from performing his own surveillance and passing along any evidence he obtains. It provides the FBI with something tangible to convince a judge to give them a warrant. But it doesn't quite cross the line that would get the evidence thrown out. It's a legal loophole. Murphy was tasked with exploiting that loophole to help ensure the safety and security of the American people and our country. I was practically foaming at the mouth to sign up."

Keira nodded. "They appealed to your patriotism and the idealism a young man would have, not being jaded yet from the real world."

"They definitely knew which buttons to push. But, honestly, I was more excited about the prospect of getting to be a detective right out of the gate. The money he offered wasn't anything to sneeze at either. And once my ex-girlfriend got wind of the job offer I was considering, she was suddenly flirting with me again. I was too stupid to realize it was the money, not me, that she wanted."

Ryland shook his head in commiseration. "She must have been really hot."

Lance laughed. "She wasn't bad to look at, that's for sure. And I was still young enough and shallow enough that I liked having a beautiful woman on my arm, regardless of whether we got along well or not."

Keira rolled her eyes. "Was she blonde?"

"Ouch," Faith complained, pointing to her long blond hair.

"Sorry." Keira's face reddened.

"No, she wasn't blonde," Lance answered, smiling. "She had Spanish heritage and used that to her advantage. She'd never have dreamed of coloring her dark hair. It was her pride and joy." He shook his head. "Anyway, my point is, you can see the allure of the job offer on many levels, and I jumped at it.

"We took huge risks every day, putting our lives on the line with the bad guys we were after. And there was a risk that if we crossed a line too far, we might end up getting arrested. If that ever happened, we were sworn to secrecy. If we said it was part of our job, our employer would deny even knowing us. The agency's cover was that it was a private-eye service. And that's what they'd stick to, denying we even worked for them. We'd be completely on our own. Since I never expected to get caught, I wasn't worried. And since I made more money in one month than most police detectives make in a year, I had no intention of heeding the little warning bells that kept going off in the back of my mind. The money was a powerful incentive to someone fresh out of school. I paid off my student loans in the first six months of the job."

Asher whistled. "It took me a decade to pay mine off. I can see the appeal of working for this place. What was it called? Are they still in operation?"

"It was a nondescript front in a strip mall in a tiny central Florida town called Ocala. The official name is Ocala Private Investigations, or OPI. If there was an official government name for the agency, we never knew about it. Everything was on a need-to-know basis. Each of us knew a different piece of the overall puzzle. But no one knew it all, except our boss. As to your second question, OPI went out of business years ago."

Keira motioned for his attention. "Since you're focusing on this OPI, can you confirm they're the ones behind what happened this morning? That's where you're heading, isn't it?"

"Yes and no. OPI was the catalyst for everything that went wrong. But I don't have any proof that they're the ones behind what happened."

"What *did* happen?" Keira asked.

"After a handful of years working there, I was the team lead over eight other people—seven men, one woman. We were given a complicated mission that required the whole team. Each of us was supposed to develop dossiers on people whose names we were given. They weren't ordinary, everyday people with their lives plastered on social media. It was tough getting any information on them and took a lot of surveillance work. But we did it and gave the files to our boss. From there, he handed them off to his contact at the appropriate alphabet agency. Job done. Move on to the next assignment. Only, that's not exactly what happened."

He rested his forearms on his thighs and clasped his hands together, forming a fist as he thought back. "The very next day, I was surfing the internet and stumbled onto a routine story about some person getting mugged and killed that morning. The police were asking for any witnesses to come forward. When I saw the name of the victim, it sent ice-cold chills down my spine. It was one of the people whom I'd investigated. I'd given his file to my boss the night before."

Keira's eyes widened "Are you sure it was the same person? Maybe someone else had the same name?"

"I'd hoped that very thing. But it didn't take long to confirm it was the same person. I told my boss. He assured me it had to be a coincidence and to not worry about it. But it kept niggling at me. I couldn't let it go. I created some automated searches on the internet to alert me if more coincidences happened. A week later, I got a hit."

"Another person on the list was killed?" Keira asked.

Lance nodded, clasping his hands so tightly his knuckles ached. "Not just one." He glanced at his team. "All of them. There were nine people we'd investigated in that most recent assignment. In the span of one week, every single one of them was dead. Each alone didn't seem suspicious—random accidents, common health ailments like a heart attack, nothing particularly concerning. But together, it was a pattern. An incredibly disturbing pattern. One that I reported to Murphy. He glossed it over again, seemed uninterested. But I couldn't ignore it."

Asher leaned forward in his chair. "You dug into your other cases, didn't you? To see if anything like that had happened before."

Lance nodded grimly. "As you might guess, it had. Nothing recent. In fact, most of our cases were proven to be on the up and up. We found where cases we'd worked ended up going to trial and the guilty parties went to prison. The evidence we'd collected, things like recordings of people in bars or other public places spilling their secrets, most of it went to a good cause. Or so we told ourselves. We rarely did anything outrageous enough to truly cross any lines, at least, not any lines on the civilian side of things."

He shook his head and sat back, stretching his legs out in front of him. "But as we dug back over the years, we found a disturbing number of people that we'd investigated had turned up dead within days of us turning in our information. Needless to say, we were stunned. All of us had spent years thinking we were helping people and getting rich in the process. But in reality, we were being used to hurt people. It didn't take much of a leap to realize other information we'd passed along probably wasn't used for legit purposes either. We were devastated."

Trent shook his head. "Man. That sucks."

"That's putting it mildly," Lance said.

"What did you do?" Keira asked, caught up in the story. "Did you go to your boss again?"

"We did. The whole team so he couldn't blow it off this time. We'd gathered all of our data on the suspicious cases and presented it in a meeting with him one morning. He couldn't deny it in front of him in black and white. And, honestly, he didn't try to. He seemed as shocked and disgusted as we were. He told us to give him twenty-four hours to contact the right people and get the ball rolling on figuring out who was behind this abuse of power. The assumption was that one of his liaisons was a mole, a dirty agent. Three hours later, Ian Murphy was dead. He was killed in a drive-by shooting in a restaurant parking lot. The police theory was that it was a gang member who mistook him for someone else. The actual shooter was never caught."

Asher scoffed. "Sounds fishy, to say the least."

Keira nodded.

"I'll cut to the point," Lance said. "In the next few weeks, one of our teammates, Allen Stanford, was also killed. Single car accident. Ran his car into a tree. No witnesses. His blood alcohol level was twice the legal limit. But here's the catch. Allen didn't drink. Ever. Someone staged his murder to look like an accident, not realizing he'd sworn off alcohol for personal reasons. A few weeks later, another team member, Brett Foster, was framed for a crime he didn't commit. While he was in jail waiting for bail to be set, he was shanked by another prisoner. He didn't die. But it was close."

"Let me guess," Ryland said, "the prisoner who shanked him was later shanked himself."

"Close enough," Lance said. "He was found hanging in his cell. Apparently, he committed suicide even though he was slated to be released the following week."

Ryland swore. "This is crazy scary. Your team was falling like dominoes."

"It doesn't stop there either. Now we get to Rick Cameron."

"We already know what happened to him," Keira said. "He was beaten and shot in his motel room."

Lance nodded. "But there's more. Before that, when OPI was falling apart, he too was framed for a crime he didn't commit. That's when we all agreed we were on someone's hit list and needed to do something drastic if we were going to survive. We bailed Rick out of jail, picked up our other friend from the hospital where he was recovering from being stabbed, and disappeared. We took on new identities, which in this post-9/11 world was no easy feat. And we went our separate ways. Rick's birth name was Rick Parker. Cameron was his new identity."

"What about your families?" Keira asked. "And your girlfriend? Did you leave them behind?"

"We did. Breaking up with Ileana was the best part of it for me, for both of us really. We were never healthy for each other, fought more often than not. I'd broken up with her many times. But she was gone for a few weeks, sometimes longer, then she always came back and managed to convince me to try again. This time, after I explained that I'd quit my job and that my massive paycheck was no longer going to be coming in, she didn't argue. She left. And since I went underground, I haven't seen her since. Though even if I hadn't gone on the run, I doubt she'd have tried to rekindle our relationship. She loved the money far more than she'd ever cared about me." He shrugged. "And I obviously didn't care for her the way I should have, considering how long we'd been together. Rather than pine for her, I was relieved the drama was finally over."

"Good riddance," Keira murmured.

"A hundred percent," Lance said. "The part that was really difficult was leaving our families. We considered it our duty, like joining the Witness Security Program, WitSec. We were forced to let go of our past so that we could protect the ones we loved." He gave her a baleful look. "I haven't seen or spoken to my parents, sister or brother since."

Keira swallowed, her eyes looking suspiciously bright. "From your expression, you must have really loved them."

The wonder in her tone confused him. It was as if she

couldn't fathom actually loving your family. Didn't she have a family who loved her?

"What about your team?" Keira asked. "The OPI team. Have you kept in touch with them? Is that what happened to Rick? Someone traced an email or phone call from an OPI teammate back to him?"

He locked away the questions she'd raised in his mind about her family and focused on their current, dire situation. "I can't imagine Rick being that careless. The story I've given all of you is a pared down version of everything that went on. There were other close calls. We didn't know who to trust. Every time we tried to pursue this so-called mole, to find out who was behind everything, an attempt would be made on one of our lives. The only reason more of us weren't killed was because we were hypervigilant, fully aware that someone very powerful with a lot to lose was after us. Believe me, if we could have outed them and put a stop to what they were doing, we would have. But we didn't have the resources, the ability. Going underground was our only choice. We all agreed we wouldn't call, email or contact each other in any way. That's how it's been ever since."

Faith frowned at him. "Rick was far closer to Gatlinburg when he was murdered than to his home in Louisiana. It's only logical that he found out you were in danger and was trying to reach you when he was killed. He must have given them your name and location. That's why the bad guys went after you, after Keira."

Lance was shaking his head before she finished. "We never shared our aliases or locations. We each kept our first name, but not our last. And we all moved away from Florida, not telling each other where we'd gone. Even if Rick was tortured for current information on his OPI team, he couldn't have told them what he doesn't know."

Keira stared at him, her eyes narrowed. "There's more to it. There has to be. You said they followed me to Gatlinburg, then to you. But I came here because Rick left that note and mentioned your name. He must have been in Maple Falls because he'd figured out where you were, thus the note. And he was on his way here to see you, maybe to warn you that the past was catching up."

Lance shrugged. "I believe you're partially right. Rick must have figured out where I was and felt he needed to come warn me. But he didn't want to put me in danger by trying to contact me in any way that could be traced."

"But he must have done something for them to know where you were."

"They didn't know where I was until they followed you to Gatlinburg, then to UB. Otherwise, when they'd killed Rick weeks ago, they'd have come straight here. Something else happened in Maple Falls, something you uncovered or did without even realizing it. That's why they followed you here. Was there any time when you told someone else about the words 'unfinished business' and my name? Maybe someone was watching you and the others involved in the investigation and saw, read or heard something substantive about the case."

"No way. We didn't know anything to tell. And I'm the only one who connected you to the note. The only one I told about that was Rick." She gave him a half smile. "I visited his grave on my way out of town, told him that I was trying to…" Her eyes widened. "Oh no."

"Go ahead," Lance urged her. "What are you remembering?"

She clutched her hands against her middle as if she

were feeling sick. "I spoke out loud to him, mentioned that I was going to find his killer and get him justice. I said I'd take care of his unfinished business and see if this Lance guy was his Lance guy."

"Were you alone?"

"I thought I was. But literally right after I said that out loud, I heard something in the woods. I thought it was an animal rooting around in the dried leaves. But I was spooked enough to take out my pistol until I was in my car."

"That's it," he said. "Must be. Someone was watching you and heard enough to think you knew where I was."

She put her hand on his forearm. "I'm so sorry. I had no idea."

He gently took her hand in his. "Of course you didn't. I'm grateful you figured out where I was. At least now I know someone is actively hunting my team again." When he would have let go, she held on for another moment.

"I really am sorry I put you in danger, Lance."

He gently squeezed her hand. "You did me a favor. Now that I know they're here, I can do what I need to do to protect myself. And you. We have to figure out how to extricate you from all this so you can return to Maple Falls without living in fear that they'll go after you."

This time, it was Keira who let go, pulling her hand back to clasp it tightly with the other, her face pale.

Lance was about to try to reassure her when Ryland spoke.

"The key to this seems to be in figuring out how Rick knew where you were. Any ideas on that?"

"I have a few, one in particular. It goes back to three months ago, when yet another one of my old teammates from OPI was murdered."

"Oh no," Keira said. "I'm so sorry."

He nodded his thanks.

"How did you find that out?" Ryland said, continuing to press for information.

"As you might imagine, being a team lead yourself, I've always felt responsible for my old team. I couldn't figure out the identity of whoever killed our boss and has tried to pick off each of us. So the least I could do was try to look out for them, in some way, without endangering them."

The pained look in Ryland's eyes confirmed that he well understood the feeling of responsibility and the guilt whenever any of them ran into trouble.

"One of the ways I've tried to do that is to set up automated searches of the internet. Every story that goes through the major news outlets, like Associated Press, gets fed into my searches. The first names of my team go through an algorithm I set up, something we used at OPI actually. It compares known details about my team with the news stories and uses a decision tree to determine whether to alert me via email. One of the most accurate parts of the decision tree that produces alerts is when pictures are involved. The algorithm uses facial recognition software. Three months ago, one of the searches found a picture of one of my old team members, Levi, with a reported last name of Alexander. Not his original birth name of course, but it was definitely him. He'd been killed in a mugging in New York. Most people aren't killed during muggings, so it wasn't typical. But there wasn't anything obvious to link it to our time at OPI either. But since then, I've been more aware and careful, keeping a lookout for signs that I'm being watched, followed."

"Man, that's a lot of baggage and stress to live with for so long," Asher said.

Lance shrugged, not feeling particularly worthy of any commiseration. Not when two of his teammates had been murdered in the past few months and he'd been unable to prevent their deaths.

"It's smart to keep tabs on your team as best you can," Ryland said. "But if you can use that kind of technology, especially the facial recognition searches, so can your enemies."

"Which is one of the reasons we've all agreed to steer clear of the media in any way so our photos aren't plastered on the internet. It's why I typically avoid photo ops on our cases, if you haven't noticed."

Faith nodded. "We've noticed. We figured you were one of those people who was camera shy."

He arched a brow. "*Shy* isn't in my vocabulary."

She laughed. "Okay, okay. We assumed you had your reasons. But now that you've explained it, that makes sense. You can't possibly avoid cameras all the time though. Airports alone will have you on their video systems from the moment you drive onto their property."

"It's a risk, for sure. Luckily, that post-9/11 security I mentioned earlier is top-notch on airport online systems, if not their physical security. I've flown many times and haven't found any photos of me from the security scans leaked to the internet. My algorithm searches for stories about me too, just in case something pops up, so I can try to take it down. So far, I haven't been targeted. Until today of course. But I also haven't done anything to stir up trouble. None of us has. So maybe that's the bigger reason why we haven't been found."

"Until three months ago," Keira said.

He winced. "Until three months ago. I've wondered if maybe Rick has done the same thing as me over the years.

He could have been running his own searches and saw that story about Levi. If he decided to go to New York to look into what happened, he could have been spotted, assuming the mole had seen the story and went there to see if any old OPI team members showed up. Rick could have been on the run since then, maybe after a close call. And he started digging, trying to find me, as the old team lead, so we could figure out what to do. And how to warn our other teammates. But they found him before he got to me."

Lance looked around, making sure that everyone was paying attention. "All of you who were at the cabin today saw the manpower the mole sent after Keira and me. There were a couple of guys outside, a few more who got into the cabin—"

"Eight total," Asher said.

Lance winced. "All heavily armed, trained and wearing identical outfits to conceal their features from any potential witnesses. From what I heard of the police talking to each other as they checked everything out, none of the bodies had ID. Ryland, I assume that you've been communicating with Grayson off and on today. Heard anything about any of the bad guys being identified?"

He shook his head. "Nothing at all. None of their fingerprints have come up as a match in any databases so far. AFIS will take a while. The FBI database checks always take longer than our local ones. Gatlinburg PD will check DNA too. But that'll take a while unless Grayson can convince them to use our lab, which isn't snowed under with queued up requests. But from everything you've said, I don't expect any matches on any criminal DNA databases, certainly not CODIS. No way would this mole hire someone with past arrests or convictions that would mean their DNA has been logged. He's got too much at stake for that."

"Agreed," Lance said. "This guy, or gal, running this operation has access to significant resources. And I don't have any clue as to his or her identity. That was the problem twelve years ago, and it's still the problem today."

The atmosphere in the room had gone somber and tense. Everyone appeared to be trying to absorb everything that Lance had said. It was finally sinking in that this was far more serious, and deadly, than anything they'd ever faced.

He rested his forearms on his knees again. "My OPI boss and three members of my old team have been murdered. It's possible more of them have been killed and I don't know about it. Assuming that hasn't happened, I have five teammates left. And I need to find every one of them to warn them. All of us from OPI need to change our aliases again, start over, again. On top of that, I need to figure out how to get Keira off the mole's radar so this doesn't destroy her life and force her to go underground too."

Lance gave her a weak smile. "I'm so sorry about all of this. But I swear to you that I'll do everything in my power to keep you safe, and get your life back."

She gave him a weak smile but was clearly upset.

"What's your plan?" Ryland asked. "It sounds as if you've made some decisions."

"My first priority is to get Keira somewhere safe where she can lay low. After that, I'll work on finding my team and warning them. Then I'm going to figure out once and for all who this mole is. I'm going to end this."

"No." Keira's brows were drawn down in a frown. "For one thing, you can't do this by yourself. It's impossible. And I'm not hiding out while you face this alone."

"Keira, with all due respect for your experience and

abilities as a police officer, you're not ready for this sort of thing. And more importantly, this isn't your fight."

"It became my fight the moment those maniacs tried to kill me. I want to bring them down as much as you. I made a promise to a dying man who entrusted your safety into my hands by telling me your name. That's sacred. I'm not running. I'm sticking with you. And I won't be a liability. I'll be your wingman or woman or whatever. Besides—" she gave him a saucy look "—you're not dumping your new girlfriend that easily."

Faith burst out laughing.

Lance frowned at her before turning back to Keira. "This isn't a laughing matter."

"I'm not the one laughing."

"Sorry," Faith called out. "I'll stop." She chuckled again, then grinned.

Asher smiled at his wife, then winked at Keira. "I agree that Lance shouldn't dump you so soon in your relationship." He arched a brow at Lance. "And you're not dumping your work family either. We're in this with you."

"Agreed," Faith added.

"When one of us is in trouble, we all are," Ryland said.

The others joined in, voicing their agreement. Every one of them.

"The time for debate is over," Ryland warned. "From now on, this case, your case, is the only one that Unfinished Business is working. And we're damn well going to solve it."

Lance hadn't been this frustrated, or touched, in a long time. Part of him wanted to shout at them to stop being so selfless, to just let him walk out the door. But the other part was so moved by their determination to help him that he was having difficulty forming words.

Keira seemed to sense his turmoil when she yet again took his hand in hers. "All for one and one for all. Is that the Unfinished Business motto?"

He cleared his throat, threading his fingers with hers. "Apparently so. Though I imagine the Three Musketeers might disagree."

Ryland stood. "We need to clear our schedules, make plans, hand out assignments. Lance, you'll have to go far more in-depth about OPI than the overview you just gave us. We need information on the cases you worked, dates, the names of anyone and everyone you had contact with while you worked there, no matter how unimportant it might seem. Let's get some coffee going and get comfortable. We'll likely be here most of the night. And many more after that."

Lance held up a hand to stop everyone. "One more thing, not that we need any added stress at this point. We don't think any other gunmen were still alive after this morning's attack, but we should all consider that someone may have remained in the woods watching. They could be watching all of us now, maybe even outside of this building. Everyone needs to be hypervigilant about your safety, and your loved ones' safety, until this is over."

Chapter Seven

Keira yawned in the back seat of UB investigator Adam Trent's truck, keeping her gaze averted from the steep drops down the side of the mountain road as they bumped along in the dark. Lance was in the passenger seat in front of her, talking to Trent. The night had been much longer than any of them had expected. Sunrise was only minutes away. And none of them had gotten any sleep yet.

Turned out, Grayson and Willow's influence with Police Chief Russo hadn't gone as they'd hoped. Eight dead bodies was just too much to explain away without a proper investigation. Russo had insisted on interviewing everyone again who'd been at the cabin and wouldn't back down. The only concession he made was to conduct the interviews at Unfinished Business because of Grayson's insistence on wanting to keep his team out of the media spotlight.

The interviews had gone well, considering. The roughest part for Keira was trying to pretend that she and Lance were a couple. Not knowing exactly what he was saying about her in his interview, she'd vaguely glossed over their relationship details and kept her answers brief. They must have both satisfied the detectives, because they were told they could go.

After a seemingly endless trip along winding narrow

roads they finally turned onto a relatively straight and flat one. The sun's first rays revealed that they were in a valley. The Smokies formed a misty white backdrop to a sparkling pond with a fountain in the middle. White three-rail wooden fences lined the road, only falling away when the truck turned once more and approached an ultramodern take on a traditional farmhouse.

Two stories of black siding were trimmed in crisp white. Charcoal-gray stone framed the bottom of the home. And a slate chimney rose up the left end. Instead of a wraparound porch, there was a stone-wrapped portico in front, held up by thick cedar posts. A three-car garage flanked the large house on the right side.

This was Lance's home, the horse ranch he'd told her about when he'd arranged for them to get a ride with Trent. They certainly couldn't return to her rental cabin. And both of their vehicles had been shot up and were still being held as part of the ongoing crime scene investigation.

Lance had assured her and Trent that it would be safe to go to his home for a short time. The property deed wasn't registered under his name. It was listed under a tangle of shell companies that would take someone a long time to unravel. Still, they didn't plan on staying. He was retrieving his OPI files for Trent to take back to UB. And he had another vehicle in the garage for him and Keira to use.

Packing a suitcase was another item he'd said was on his to-do list, along with arranging for the care of his handful of horses while he and Keira left town. For her part, she already had her suitcase. That was yet another concession made by Chief Russo. He'd had a police woman pack her things at the rental cabin and take it to Unfinished Business for her.

"Do you prefer to wait in the truck?"

She blinked and realized that Lance was standing beside the truck, holding her door open.

"Oh, sorry. Was just…admiring your house. It's beautiful."

He smiled. "It's home. Wish we had more time and I could give you the grand tour. You're welcome to explore inside on your own while I get what I need."

"I just might." She hopped out of the truck, and the three of them headed inside.

Just like the outside, the interior of the house was a study in masculinity, blacks and browns with lots of dark stone accents. The ceilings were unusually high on the first level for a two-story home. She wouldn't have even realized there was a second level if she hadn't known from the outside. This open, expansive house was something she could breathe in. Her discomfort with tight spaces wouldn't be a problem here at all.

Lance motioned toward a massive cedar-and-granite island on the left side of the room. "Help yourself to something to eat if you're hungry. Otherwise, we can grab breakfast on our way out of town."

She would have thanked him, but he and Trent had already turned away and were heading toward a door on the far right side of the room, presumably to Lance's office. She heard their deep voices in conversation as they disappeared inside. With all the stress of the long day and night behind her, she was more inclined to want to sleep than eat. But if she lay down on one of the two groupings of black leather couches, she'd probably never get back up. They looked far too comfortable for her weary body. Instead, she meandered around, learning about Lance from the way this bachelor had chosen to furnish and decorate his home.

Dark colors were definitely his thing. There were no pinks or pastels, no feminine touches anywhere, except perhaps for a few pillows and blankets thrown over a chair and one of the couches. But she imagined those were more for comfort and warmth than to soften up the place.

He was a reader, something they both had in common. She practically drooled over the chunky floor-to-ceiling bookshelves she could see through an archway by the kitchen area. A ladder attached to a brass rail declared it to be his home library. And as she got closer, she could see there was nothing techie to interfere with the ambience. There were only books here, comfortable reading chairs and a gas fireplace on one end. She would have preferred the coziness of a wood-burning fireplace. But she could see the advantage of gas in this particular room. There wouldn't be any concern about smoke or soot damaging the books.

Part of her wanted to check the rest of this gorgeous house out, give herself that grand tour. But the reader in her couldn't pull herself away from this room. She scanned the bookshelves, delighted and in awe of his collection. There was one whole section of classics, many leather bound. Several appeared to be first editions. But she didn't want to risk damaging them by touching them, so she couldn't be sure.

Other shelves held all kinds of nonfiction, with a heavy emphasis on autobiographies and biographies of people all throughout history. Those were the most worn books, reflecting his love of knowledge rather than a desire to lose himself in a good story. Her preference was fiction, tales of every kind, from thrillers to fantasy, and her personal favorite, historical romance. Unfortunately, she didn't find any romance on his shelves. But there was a thick fantasy novel she'd love to sink her literary teeth into. Perhaps it wouldn't be too much to ask to borrow it.

The pleasing timbre of male voices again had her turning around, clasping the novel to her chest. Trent and Lance stood at the end of the foyer talking. Two large boxes were on the floor beside them, presumably the promised OPI files.

She headed over, relieved to see Lance smile at her holding the book, nodding as if to let her know he approved of her choice. She waited beside him as Trent summarized the plans they'd made earlier, as if to double-check that they were all on the same page.

"Asher and Faith are tasked with finding former OPI team member Melissa Temple. Ivy and I will search for Sam McIntosh. Callum and Brice are in charge of locating Jack Scanlon. You and Keira will look for Brett Foster. That leaves…" He thumbed through some texts on his phone.

"Mick Thompson," Lance told him.

"Right. Thompson. As soon as one of the teams I just mentioned frees up, they'll look for him. Grayson, Willow, Ryland and our TBI liaison, Rowan, will provide support from UB for all of us. They'll also run interference with Chief Russo. And they'll get started right away on these OPI files to help us locate your former teammates and to take a fresh look at what happened. Hopefully they'll find a thread to pull, something that will lead us to the mole sooner than later. Sound good?"

"Sounds real good. Thanks, Trent."

Trent responded by clasping Lance on the shoulder and nodding at Keira. "Both of you, please, keep in contact. If anything concerning pops up, let us know. We'll do the same."

Keira smiled her agreement.

Lance motioned toward the boxes. "Let me help you with those."

They each carried a box out to Trent's truck. When Trent was driving away, Lance rejoined Keira in the main room. He motioned toward the book in her hand. "One of my favorite epic fantasies. You read Rebecca Yarros?"

"Not yet. I've heard great things about this book and have been wanting to try it. Do you mind?"

"Of course not. Although I don't know how much reading time we'll get in the next few days, or however long this takes. If nothing else, you can take it back to Maple Falls once we've secured your safety and ability to return." He gave her an apologetic look. "I really am sorry you've been caught up in all this."

On impulse, she set the book on an end table and took one of his hands in both of hers. The warmth of his skin sent a shiver of delight up her spine and had her face flushing hot, especially when his eyes widened in surprise. But he didn't pull away, and she didn't let go.

"I don't think I've ever heard a man apologize as much as you have to everyone over the past—what?—twenty-four hours? I wish you'd stop. None of this is your fault. Seems to me that you've spent the past decade, even longer, fighting just to stay alive while keeping track of your team to try to keep them safe too. You didn't choose this path. But you darn well have the integrity to see it through and protect others, including me. That's not something to apologize for or feel bad about. It's admirable, honorable. Can we stop with the apologies?"

Ever so slowly, he lifted his other hand toward her face as if to give her time to stop him.

She didn't.

He feathered his fingers lightly across her cheek, then through her hair, gently pushing it back before dropping his hand. "You're something else, you know that?"

She drew a shaky breath, more affected by that light touch than she could have imagined. "Is being 'something else' good or bad?"

His lips curved in a sexy smile that had her hot and cold all over. Mostly hot.

"Definitely good," he said. "Maybe after this is all… resolved, I should take my chances about asking you out."

"Maybe you should."

He grinned. "Don't think for a second I'll forget you said that."

She would have made another sassy retort, but her brain cells seemed to have drowned in the rush of hormones flooding her system.

"Keira?" His deep tone was laced with humor.

"Um, yes?"

"I need to check on the horses before we leave."

"Right. Okay."

He glanced down at his other hand tightly clutched in hers.

"Oh!" She immediately let go, her face flushing hot. "Sorry."

He leaned down and pressed the lightest, barest kiss against her cheek, then winked. "I'm not. Wait here and I'll just step out back—"

"No. I'm going with you."

At his raised brows, her face flushed again. "I'd rather go with you to back you up if something happens." She tapped the holster concealed beneath her jacket, where she had her pistol. "Cop. Remember?"

"I remember. I used to be one too, you know."

"For eight years. In Nashville. Heck of a coincidence."

"Coincidence?"

"Nashville. My hometown."

"Right. Where your...complicated family lives, I assume?"

She stiffened. "Out back you said? That door off the kitchen?"

His smile widened. "Your excellent detecting skills are showing again." He held out his hand. "Come on. I'll show you my horses."

"That pickup line needs work," she teased, ignoring his hand as she headed toward the back door.

He chuckled and followed behind. Once outside, however, his amusement evaporated. Instead, he was fully alert, scanning the property and the outbuilding they were heading toward.

Feeling silly for flirting with him when both their lives were potentially in danger, she went on high alert too, in full police mode. She kept her right hand down near the holster she'd donned from her suitcase earlier and scanned for any hint of trouble.

When they reached the building, she expected him to pull out a key to unlock the doors to the stables. Instead, there was an electronic keypad beside it. But he didn't press the buttons. He pressed his hand against a black square beneath it. The doors clicked and a barely audible motor hummed, making the doors slide open.

Inside was no less modern and masculine than his house had been. Black metal rafters supported the roof instead of wooden beams. Pristine stone floors that gently sloped to rectangular drains on either side of the aisle no doubt made cleaning much easier than the dirt floors she'd expected. Sturdy cedar formed the stalls on either side.

"There are only four horses here right now," he said as she followed him down the aisle. "But it can hold up to eight. I figure one day, if I'm lucky enough to turn old and gray and still have this place, I'll fill the other stalls with little fillies and colts for my children and grandchildren."

"That sounds wonderful," she breathed, picturing it in her mind.

He stopped and looked at her over his shoulder. "You like horses?"

She laughed. "Honestly, I don't know. I've never seen one up close. Our family couldn't afford things like that when I was growing up."

He slowly nodded. "I forget sometimes just how blessed I am. We always had horses. Now I suppose I'm carrying on the family tradition. I just wish my dad could see this place."

She looked up at him, the sadness in his voice making her throat tight. "Maybe when this is over, when we stop the person behind what happened at OPI, you can see him again."

His jaw tightened, but he didn't say anything.

She stopped at the next stall, shaking her head in wonder at the beautiful animal poking its graceful head over the top of the stall door. "I can't imagine any father not approving of this. The house, the land, this place and, oh my goodness, these beautiful babies. They're amazing." She laughed when the reddish-brown horse closest to her snuffled at her shirt.

When she reached up to touch its muzzle, Lance grabbed her hand.

"Careful," he said. "She's looking for something to eat. I'd rather you kept your fingers."

Keira blinked and took a quick step back.

"I didn't mean to scare you. She's not mean. But she might bite on accident if you stick your fingers out like that. Here." He opened a metal bin in the wall behind her and pulled out a carrot. "Do it like this. Flatten your palm."

He broke the carrot in half and put one piece on his palm and held it up toward the horse. She snuffled his hand, grasping the carrot and pulling it into her mouth.

"Want to try?" He handed Keira the other half of the carrot.

"Definitely." She did what he'd shown her, laughing when the horse's velvety lips tickled her hand and took the carrot. "Oh my goodness. She's so sweet. And so very beautiful."

His dark eyes captured hers as he responded. "She most definitely is."

The wink that followed told her he definitely wasn't talking about the horse. She tried to respond and again couldn't seem to find her voice.

He took mercy on her, taking her hand in his. "Come on. We need to hurry. I don't think anyone will figure out about this place. But I'd rather not risk it. I need to get something from this last stall over here, the empty one on the left."

When they reached the stall, he let her hand go and crossed to the far wall.

"You mentioned the horses were hungry. Should I feed them?" she asked.

"If we had time, I'd love to show you how to do exactly that. They need oats, fresh hay, water. The carrots are treats, not a meal. I called a friend from my home office earlier to take care of that. He'll be here soon to get them." He reached above his head toward a piece of cedar trim.

"Get them? He's taking the horses away?"

Lance half turned, all serious again without a hint of his earlier lightheartedness. "If the wrong people figure out this is my place, I don't expect it to be standing when I return. The horses will be at my neighbor's stable, someone I trust." He turned back to the wall.

The idea that someone would destroy his beautiful home and this stable brought tears to her eyes. But whatever she might have been about to say was forgotten when the back stall wall slid open to reveal a narrow hidden room.

He headed inside, and by the time she followed, lights had flipped on, and he was pressing on another panel. It too slid open, but instead of another room, it revealed a metal safe built into the wall. There was a small desk and chair beside it, but nothing else. He crouched in front of the safe.

"Lance? What is this place? What are we doing here?"

"Saving my team. Hopefully."

"Saving your...which one? OPI? Or UB?"

He glanced back at her. "Both." He quickly pressed a sequence of buttons. The door on the safe popped open. A small leather duffel bag sat on the bottom shelf. Above it was a dark brown accordion folder about three inches thick.

"Lance, please. What are you...?" Again she stopped, this time in shock. He'd pulled out the duffel bag and opened it on top of the desk. Even from a few feet away, she could easily see what was inside.

Money.

A *lot* of money, bills of various denominations banded together.

"My goodness. That has to be thousands of dollars."

"It's enough."

"Enough for what?"

"To ensure our safety." After double-checking the contents, he zipped it closed and set it onto the floor. "We can't use credit cards, ATMs, anything traceable. We'll pay for everything we need in cash. I've also got IDs in the bag under various aliases, extra pistols and magazines of ammunition."

"I've heard of people having go bags to grab in an emergency, but normally they have clothes and toiletry items in them."

"I always figured I could buy those things wherever I ended up, if I didn't have a chance to pack a suitcase of clothes before I left. ID, cash, weapons—those are harder to get when traveling."

"Makes sense, I suppose. I've never felt the need for a go bag. Until now. I wish I'd packed extra ammunition before coming here."

"You've got a nine-mil right?"

She nodded, patting her jacket, hiding the bulge of her holster. "A Glock seventeen."

"My primary weapon is a Sig Sauer P320, nine millimeter. We can share ammunition. I'll pack extra."

"Thanks. I'll pay you back if we end up needing that ammo."

"Let's hope we don't." He sat at the desk. It barely surprised her this time when he slid more panels back and suddenly had a computer monitor in front of him with a keyboard on top of the desk.

She stepped to his side, glancing down at the bag of money, IDs and weaponry. "Lance. It's fine for you to use your money for your own protection. But I don't want you using it for mine. It had to have taken you years to save all that. We can make one stop at a local bank, and I can pull out my savings."

He'd been typing on the keyboard but stopped and looked at her. "It didn't take any time at all. I had terrible judgment when I first started out in joining OPI. But the one thing it did was give me more money than I could ever spend. And Grayson Prescott, my current boss? He's a billionaire, Keira. He pays us enough that we'll never have to worry about financial security. So don't worry about using that cash. There's plenty more."

She swallowed, then nodded. "Thank you. For helping to protect me. You're exceedingly generous with your money, your time. I just hope it doesn't end up costing you your life." She motioned to the room around them, the safe, the computer. "For you to have gone to all this trouble, the people we're up against must be far more dangerous than I'd even suspected."

"They're dangerous, yes. But only because they hide in the shadows. The mole, even with all the resources at his disposal, is still just a person, Keira. He's not superhuman, no more powerful than anyone else. All we have to do is bring him out of those shadows and into the light. We're going to survive this. Together. Trust me. And trust yourself. I've seen your courage. You ran out of the cabin when you could have stayed inside and been safe. But you didn't. You ran outside thinking I needed help."

She rolled her eyes. "Fat lot of good I did. You didn't need help. I did. I almost got you killed."

Again her hand somehow found its way into his. He threaded their fingers together, his large, strong hand engulfing hers, but gentle. So gentle her heart seemed to shift in her chest.

"You ran toward possible danger, Keira. For me. You

didn't know what or who might be out there. You still went outside. You're a good cop and a good person. And stronger than you know. Rely on your training. Trust yourself."

She offered him a tremulous smile. "Whatever happens, don't forget to ask me out on that date, okay?"

He pulled her hand to his mouth and kissed the back of it, just like the heroes in those historical romance novels she loved to read.

"I won't forget," he whispered against her hand, his warm breath making her shiver. He gently squeezed, then let go. "Just one more thing before we leave."

She pressed her hands together, covering the warm spot where his mouth had been. But the warm feelings flooding through her began to cool and freeze as she saw what he was doing. And began to understand.

The first call he placed through the computer was to someone the computer screen listed as Melissa. As soon as a voice answered, the computer voice spoke. "It was the best of times, it was the worst of times."

The call ended.

Lance pressed a few buttons and a second call went out. To Sam.

The computer announced the same phrase. "It was the best of times, it was the worst of times."

Another call. This one to Mick. The next was to Jack. Then, finally, Brett.

After Lance made the computer disappear and closed the wall over the safe, he straightened and stood directly in front of her.

She didn't meet his gaze.

His hand gently but firmly pressed her chin up until she was looking at him, his gaze locked with hers. "Ask me," he said. "Say it."

She stared at him for a long moment. Finally she said, "I'm surprised you chose Charles Dickens as your safe phrase to warn your old team."

He stared at her for an equally long moment. "What would you have chosen?"

She clenched her fists at her sides. "Nothing at all. Because I wouldn't have lied to my current team. I wouldn't send the UB investigators on a useless mission to try to find the OPI team members when you've known all along where they are. You knew Rick was in Maple Falls too, didn't you? Before you answer, think very carefully. Because I'm mad as hell. Don't lie to me. Did you or did you not know that Rick Cameron was in Maple Falls coming here to see you?"

The skin along his jaw whitened. "Do you honestly think that if I knew my friend was in trouble that I wouldn't have gone to help him? That I'd just let him die?"

She leaned toward him. "Isn't that what you're doing right now? Or at least risking the lives of your current friends when there's no reason to risk them at all? You can simply pick up the phone and call Trent, call the others and tell them there's no need to look for anyone. What kind of game are you playing?"

He swore, then scrubbed his face with his hands. "This isn't a game. You think I'm risking my UB friends' lives by sending them on a wild-goose chase? Just the opposite. The information in those files that I gave Trent is ancient history. It won't lead them to danger. It will keep them away while I take care of this damned mole once and for all."

She stared at him, blinking in surprise. "What the...? Everything you told them was a lie?"

He arched a brow. "Actually, my very first statement

was the truth, that everything they know about me is a lie. I just continued the charade. Not because I'm some sadistic jerk but because I care about them. They're married, have girlfriends, families. Grayson has a little girl from his first wife who was murdered. He only recently found her after she'd been missing for years. I don't want to be the reason she loses her father after only just meeting him.

"Today, with everyone confronting me, I was trapped. Trapped by my own team trying to force me to involve them in my own mistakes. Well, that's not going to happen. When I left UB this morning, heck, yesterday morning now, to go see you, I wasn't going to return. Ever. If things don't go the way I hope they do, that will still be my plan."

"Wow. I can't believe this. Did you not hear anything they said? It makes sense for them to help you. To help us. What makes you think that you can fight this mole on your own when you haven't been able to figure out who he is in over a decade?"

His jaw worked again. "Do you honestly think I haven't been searching for the mole ever since I left OPI? He forced me to give up my own family, forced all of us to do that, to keep them safe. I'm close, Keira. I've got all kinds of information, evidence, showing this mole's movements over the years. His electronic trail. And I've eliminated dozens of people through my investigation."

He let out a deep breath. "There are only a handful of people left who could be the mole, people who were in a position of power back when we were at OPI. People who hid behind the scenes and who I've discovered and focused on. I'm ready to end this, once and for all. I just need to find that one crumb, that one more piece of the puzzle that makes the whole picture come into focus. Then I can bring him to justice. I can end this."

She stared at him, stunned. "You think you're close to solving it?"

"I know I am. The death of Levi was a huge clue. Something he did put the mole on his trail. But I didn't take it as a clue or realize the significance until you came here and told me that Rick had been murdered. Their deaths, so close together, can't be a coincidence. All I have to do is find the link between them. That will be the key to narrowing my list of suspects down to one."

"That's a lot of speculation and uncertainty to be betting our lives on being able to take this mole down without help from Unfinished Business. Are you forgetting what happened at my cabin? We were almost killed."

"Don't you think I know that? It's all I can think about, how close you came to being killed."

She stared at him in surprise, then cleared her throat. "Okay. Then it's clear that I should have a say in this too. My fate is tied up in the results of this new search, finding this guy and stopping him. Because of that, I get input into what we do. And I want UB working with us. I don't think we can win this without them."

He stared at her a long moment, then swore beneath his breath. "I'm not going to change your mind on this, am I?"

"No."

"Good to know. If you're scared and don't have confidence that we can handle this on our own, then you shouldn't come with me."

"I shouldn't…wait. No. That's not what I meant."

A thumping noise sounded from somewhere inside the stables. "Lance? I'm here, like you asked. Where are you?"

Keira frowned and looked over her shoulder.

"In here," Lance called out. "Last stall on the left."

There was a sudden yank at her waist, and then something cold snapped around her left wrist. She whirled around, shocked to see Lance tossing her pistol onto the desk. He must have grabbed it from her holster. And there was a silver circle of metal shining around her wrist.

"Handcuffs? What the...?" Lance tugged her forward and snapped the other cuff around a metal ring on the wall that she hadn't noticed earlier. "What are you doing? Take these off."

A tall, imposing-looking man in his mid to late forties peered in through the opening, seemingly unsurprised to find the secret room. But his eyebrows rose when he saw Keira with her arm cuffed to the wall. "Hey, Lance. If you two are in the middle of something kinky, I can come back later."

"Shut up, Duncan."

Duncan laughed.

Keira rattled the cuffs. "This isn't funny. Lance, take these off."

"Duncan, can you give us a minute?"

"I can give you a whole lot of minutes while I load the horses. I'll come back after." He disappeared back into the stables.

Keira yanked on the cuffs again.

Lance swore and grabbed her arm. "Stop. You're going to hurt yourself."

"*You're* hurting me. You did this. You're responsible. Take them off now and I won't press charges."

He sighed heavily and let her go. "I'm sorry about this. I really am. I'll have Duncan take those off as soon as I'm gone. Have him take you to Unfinished Business. You can tell everyone the truth. It won't matter once I leave. They won't know where I'm going."

He turned away.

"Wait," she called out, panic making her voice shake.

"What now?"

"Please. Please let me go with you. I can help. I'll watch your back."

"No." He started to turn away again.

"Lance!"

His answering sigh could have knocked over one of the cypress timbers on the other side of the door. "One more question," he said, "then I'm out of here."

She licked her dry lips. "Why are you doing this? Why are you cutting me out of the investigation? It's not just about UB, keeping them out of it. There has to be more to it. You don't actually believe what you said earlier, about me being smart or courageous or that I could be an asset in your search. You think what, that I'd be a hindrance?"

His gaze locked on hers, and he was suddenly standing right in front of her. "I never lied about my belief in your abilities, Keira." He slowly shook his head as he stared down at her. "You're just as smart and courageous as I said, probably more. And you would definitely be an asset in any investigation."

"Then why? Why don't you want me to go with you?"

He flattened the palms of his hands on the wall on either side of her, his body so close they were almost touching. "I was going to. But when you were so adamant about not wanting to do this without my UB team, it made me rethink why I'd involve you when the whole reason I'm not involving them is to protect them. God knows I don't want anything bad to happen to you either. So why risk it? As impossible as it sounds, you're the best thing that's happened to me in a long time. We barely know each other, but I know this. I *want* to know you, learn everything about you. I want to take you out on a date, two dates, a dozen. But most of all, I want—I need for you to be safe."

Her whole body seemed to catch fire with his words. "Lance, are…are you saying you want to be my boyfriend?"

He choked on his laughter, coughed, then grinned. "Yeah. I guess that's what I'm saying."

"Prove it. Kiss me."

The sound of horses' hooves clopping through the stables had him stepping back. "I have to—"

"Lance. *Kiss* me."

His eyes darkened to a stormy blue. His gaze dipped to her mouth.

She closed the short distance between them, her breasts crushed against his chest as she angled her lips up toward his. "Lance?"

"I'm going to hell for this."

"Worth it."

He groaned deep in his throat. Then she was in his arms, and his mouth was doing all kinds of incredible things to hers. Good grief, this man could kiss. She wanted to wrap herself around him and hold on and never let go, give him back as good as he was giving her. And at first, she allowed herself to respond, to enjoy. After all, a piece of heaven was being dangled in front of her. And she was too weak not to take it. But as amazing as being in his arms felt, the awkwardness of her left arm being cuffed to the wall was enough to help her keep her wits about her and remember why she'd initiated this embrace in the first place.

She suddenly twisted against him and yanked his pistol out of his holster.

His eyes flew open as she pressed the gun's muzzle against his flat belly.

Ever so slowly, he pulled back and looked down between them at his gun, and her finger on the trigger.

"You've got two choices, Lance."

He slowly raised his head and waited.

"You can unlock these handcuffs and promise that you'll take me with you to find the mole."

His jaw worked, anger darkening his eyes even more. "Or?"

She shoved the gun against him. "Or you can bet your life that you know me well enough, after only a day, to be sure that a trained police officer isn't going to shoot a man who kidnapped her and chained her to a wall."

Their standoff went on for nearly a minute. Finally, Lance pulled the handcuff keys out of his pocket.

Chapter Eight

"You wouldn't really have shot me, would you?"

Keira sat beside Lance in the dark blue SUV he'd had in his garage, once again bumping down mountain roads. But this time, thankfully, they were heading out of Gatlinburg. Soon they'd be on wider, safer roads without the constant drop-offs beside them.

"I guess we'll never know for sure," she said.

He frowned and glanced at her, then focused on the road in front of them. "Regardless, you earned the right to be a part of this hunt for the mole. But once this is done, we're done. Before we ever got a chance to get started."

His words caused an ache in her chest that was hard to hide. But she did her best to pretend they didn't bother her. "You really know how to hold a grudge."

"A grudge? You had your finger on the trigger, not the gun frame. The trigger."

"I had to. Otherwise you'd have made some kind of move, tried to grab the gun away from me."

He glanced at her again. "Fair enough. Still, your finger could have accidentally jerked or squeezed just enough on that trigger to kill me even without meaning to. That's not something I'll forget."

"I guess that first date is no longer on the table then."

"We both know the answer to that."

She smiled, but inside she was raw, hurt, tired and so angry she wanted to hit something. To shatter some glass. Bust a chair into little pieces like they did in those action movies. All she'd wanted when she came here was to get justice for a murdered man. And now her entire world had been yanked out from under her. This...thing, this bond or whatever the two of them felt for each other, shouldn't even matter with everything else that was going on. But, dang it, it did. And every time he looked at her in derision or anger or said something like he'd just said, it was another dagger to her heart.

It would be comical if it wasn't so painful. In spite of all those romance novels she enjoyed, she didn't believe in instant love. But she did believe in instant connections, in feeling powerfully drawn to someone even before knowing them all that well. After all, she'd felt that with Lance. She *still* felt that way in spite of her heart being battered and bruised. And the hopeless romantic in her would probably always wonder *What if?* when it came to Lance Cabrera.

LANCE'S GRIP RELAXED on the steering wheel at the sound of Keira's deep, even breathing. She'd fallen asleep against the passenger door, looking as miserable as he felt.

How had everything gone so wrong?

All he'd wanted was to protect the people in his life who'd had no part of his bad decisions at OPI. They were innocent, both his friends at UB and Keira. It wasn't right to drag any of them into the danger that he'd brought to their door. Instead, he'd likely alienated his UB family, once they found out he'd tricked them. And he'd certainly ended any chance he'd had with Keira.

Was he angry with her? Hell yes. But that anger was already beginning to fade, and regret was digging its talons into him. Could he have taken his pistol away from her without getting shot? Maybe. Probably. But he hadn't tried because of one element to the situation that she hadn't thought through.

Duncan.

He was one of the few people Lance trusted completely outside of Unfinished Business. He wasn't just a guy Lance hired when he needed someone to look after his animals. He was a close friend. If Keira had shot Lance, Duncan would have shot her. And that wasn't something Lance could risk. So he'd gone along with her threat, letting her believe it was only because he was concerned for himself, when he was more concerned for her. And rather than go back on his word to let her accompany him on the search for the mole, he'd stood by his promise.

Lying to her again and not letting her come with him wasn't something he could stomach. But he still would have, in a heartbeat, if he thought she'd be safer that way. However, having seen firsthand how obsessed she was with finding the mole, he'd finally realized that nothing was going to keep her from pursuing this. It made more sense to keep her with him so he could look after her than to constantly wonder when and where she'd show up. He couldn't bear being the cause of her getting hurt, or worse. So the lesser of two evils seemed to be to keep his word and treat her as his partner in this hunt.

As for this crazy obsession he had for her, well, he'd just have to get over it. There was no way she'd ever forgive him for what he'd done. And he wasn't sure he could forgive her either. She could so easily have killed him. All because he'd cared enough to try to protect her. That whole stupid incident had destroyed their trust in each other. Without trust, a relationship was impossible.

He silently swore. He hadn't been this mixed up in the head since Ileana. She'd twisted him inside and out, leaving him, coming back, over and over until he didn't know what he felt anymore. With her out of his life once and for all, he'd finally been on an even keel again. And now here he was letting another woman tilt his world. Not in a good way either.

Maybe the disaster at the stable was fate's way of waking him up, of keeping him from potentially making another mistake. But he hated that it had taken well over a decade for him to finally meet someone he could immediately see himself with long-term. And then for all of that to come crashing down.

Sleep deprivation. That's what all of this had to be. He wasn't normally this quick to anger, this confused. He'd matured since his days of being so easily manipulated by his ex. Now he approached life with logic, not his hormones. All he needed was a good night's sleep. He'd been up for well over twenty-four hours now. Heck, it was edging closer to thirty.

Lucky for both of them, the next exit had a decent hotel with a vacancy—a two-bedroom suite with two king-size beds. And the cash bribe he gave the night clerk was enough to get her to look past the fact that he didn't have a credit card to secure the room. His false ID and a wad of cash was all she'd needed in order to hand over the room key.

A bleary-eyed, exhausted Keira mumbled good-night without meeting his gaze, then clicked her bedroom door shut with him still standing in front of it.

His shoulders slumped in defeat. He so wished that he

could have a complete redo of the past day and a half. But life didn't come with a rewind button. And as he'd told his team earlier, some things couldn't be fixed.

Chapter Nine

When Keira stepped out of the hotel bedroom, freshly showered, in clean clothes and wearing enough makeup to hide the dark circles under her eyes, she stopped in surprise. The kitchenette had a pot of coffee made with a mug and packets of sweeteners beside it. Next to that was a box of delicious-looking breakfast pastries in varying types from apple to cinnamon to cream cheese and a handful of others. And just in case that wasn't what she fancied, there was a large bowl of sliced fruit and a loaf of bread sitting beside the toaster. But Lance was nowhere to be found.

His bedroom door was open, the bed visible through the doorway neatly made. The folder he'd had in his safe yesterday was open on the coffee table in front of the couch. Papers and pictures were spread out as if he'd been studying them earlier this morning. But the suite itself was sadly empty.

A slight movement to her left had her turning. Through a slit in the curtains she could see a man in a dark leather jacket standing at the balcony railing, a cup of coffee in his hands as he looked out at the Smoky Mountains. Lance.

The guilt that had her tossing and turning last night rode her hard. It was an uncomfortable feeling, one she wasn't used to.

She fixed herself a cup of coffee. One packet of sugar, none of that fake sweetener for her. And some creamer she'd been unsurprised to find in the refrigerator. After all, he'd thought of everything else she might want or need.

After returning to the bedroom to put on her long jacket against the chilly fall air, she grabbed her mug of coffee and headed outside. When she stepped onto the balcony, Lance smiled. But it was a shadow of his usual ones.

"Morning," he said.

"Morning. I come unarmed."

He lifted the edge of his jacket to show his pistol holstered to the belt of his jeans. "Can't say the same."

She wanted to joke about that, to say something to cut the tension. But nothing clever came to mind, so she didn't try.

They stood silently beside each other for several minutes, sipping their respective cups of coffee and staring out at the beautiful vista in front of them. This time of year, the Smokies were dressed in fading golds and oranges. Not the full-on brilliant colors that would have attracted leaf peepers a month earlier. But still colorful enough to steal her breath.

In spite of all those winding, narrow, terrifying roads without guardrails all over these mountains, she couldn't deny how amazing and awe-inspiring it would be to see this kind of scenery out her windows every day. But she'd prefer to see it from a valley looking up at the mountains rather than actually driving through them.

As she watched, thin white clouds moved over the peaks, dressing them in mist and dipping down into the higher elevations. A few minutes later, the mist rose, revealing the peaks again. But shadows from other clouds passed across the sun, emphasizing the deep variations of color dancing up and down the slopes.

"It really is beautiful here," she murmured, mostly to herself.

He set his coffee mug on the railing. "I've lived in this area for over three years and have never tired of the scenery. It's ever-changing. One minute, you can see for miles. The next, the mist settles in and you can barely see anything. In the summer, it's every shade of green you can imagine. Once the last of these autumn leaves drop, it will be gray and barren-looking to the casual observer. But if you pay close attention, you'll see things you couldn't see before. Bald spots and clearings between groves of trees. Evergreens interspersed between the spindly, naked birch and oak."

When he went silent, she prodded, "And in the spring? What's it like then?"

He smiled, as if at something only he could see. "Everything comes to life. Wildflowers dot the ranges. Trees leaf out, fill out, new branches climbing toward the bright blue sky. Baby rabbits, squirrels and chipmunks can be spotted hiding in the bushes, climbing trees, chattering at you when you encroach on their domain. At sunset the deer come out, mothers watching over their spotted fawns. Bucks scratching their antlers on the trees. Black bears are all around these parts. Mostly they stay hidden, but that time of year they wake up hungry from hibernation and eat everything they can. You'll spot some in the mountains or in town trying to score an easy meal from a careless tourist who tosses out their food without realizing it will attract wildlife."

She was mesmerized by the emotion in his voice, the wonder in his expression.

"You really do love it here, don't you?"

His smile faded as he faced her, resting his hip against the railing. "How could I not?"

"Well, for one thing, there are those narrow death-defying curvy roads up and down the mountains. I don't see how anyone could love those."

His mouth quirked up at one corner. "Believe it or not, you get used to them, barely think about it once it's part of your daily routine."

"I suppose. But it's hard to imagine. If I lived here, I'd rather stay in a low-lying area with some gently rolling hills. The mountains could form a gorgeous backdrop, in the distance."

"Sounds like my ranch."

She blinked. "Exactly like your ranch. It's beautiful."

They were both quiet for a minute, then…

"I'm sorry—" he said.

"I'm sorry—" she said at the same time.

They both laughed.

She stepped closer and put her hand on his, which was resting on top of the railing. "I mean it, Lance. I'm so very sorry for yesterday. I was shocked, angry, when you put those handcuffs on me. Even more angry that you were going to leave to pursue this investigation without me when my fate is involved as much as yours. But that's no excuse for what I did. I never should have put my finger on that trigger. You're right, one shake of my hand and I could have shot you." She swallowed against her tight throat. "I could have killed you. I'm so, so sorry."

He looked down at her hand on his, then slowly turned it so that they were holding hands. "I appreciate that. I'm sorry too, more than you can imagine. We both made mistakes. But it was my poor decision that started it all. Truce?"

She tightened her grip. "Truce."

He studied her, seeming uncertain. But then, as if he couldn't help himself, he gently pulled her toward him. He cradled her against his chest, his arms around her, hugging her close. When a brisk breeze made her shiver, he opened his coat and wrapped it around both of them, forming a warm cocoon.

Like a weary traveler finally coming home, her body relaxed against his. It felt unbelievably right being in his arms. And, man oh man, did he smell good, a mixture of coffee, soap, leather and the clean outdoors. The hard planes of his sculpted body fit against her curves as if he'd been made for her. It seemed silly even thinking that way, as if she were writing one of those romance novels. But it was true. She could have stood there forever, held by him. And dang if she didn't want to. But the world intruded all too soon. His cell phone buzzed in his coat pocket.

He murmured an apology as he extricated himself and stepped back to check his phone. When he saw the number, he grimaced and took the call.

"Hey, Trent."

She watched in surprise as he held the phone slightly away from his ear. Even from a few feet away, she could hear Trent's raised voice. He definitely wasn't happy.

Lance pressed the phone back to his ear. "I know, I know. I shouldn't have—" He winced again, then shook his head at Keira, his mouth quirking in that half grin she was beginning to become so familiar with.

"That's not going to happen." He sighed heavily as he listened to Trent's response. He stepped to the end of the balcony, leaning back against it, speaking on occasion but not really saying much.

When the call ended, he held the phone in his hand rather than slide it into his jacket pocket. "That was fun."

"What happened?" she asked. "He sounded angry."

"Yeah, well, he wasn't happy when Duncan told him I'd contacted my old team already and he and the others didn't need to try to find them."

She drew in a surprised breath. "You had Duncan tell them the truth?"

"Someone I know made me feel guilty." He winked. "At least now everything's in the open. He wants us to come back so we can work on this together since there's no reason to go searching for my old team now."

"Is that what we're doing? Going back?"

"We? No. But if you've changed your mind and don't want to go with me, I can have Duncan pick you up here and take you to UB."

"We haven't spoken about your plan. I'm guessing you're heading to New York City to look into Levi's death." She winced. "Long drive but I guess there's no other option or you wouldn't be able to bring your duffel full of weapons with you. From there, you'll try to find out whether Rick was there and whether it cost him his life too. At some point you'll head to Maple Falls to see the scene of the crime firsthand, the motel where Rick was murdered. Am I right?"

"I guess my answer depends on whether you've changed your mind about wanting to go with me. And yes, we'd be driving. Shouldn't be too rough with two drivers to switch off."

"We're in this together. Nothing's changing my mind. And I'm fine helping with the driving."

He smiled. "All right then. Heading to Maple Falls isn't in the equation. It's likely too dangerous."

"You think the mole's people are still there, watching for one of us to show up?"

"It's what I'd do. Besides, you're a walking, talking treasure trove of information about that investigation. And your copy of the case file has the crime scene photographs. We can review those together. But the first order of business is to look into Levi's death, as you said. It makes sense with everything that's happened that his murder was the catalyst to stir things up again. I want to try to figure out why he was killed and what put a target on his back. But he wasn't killed in New York City. He was killed in a small town in upstate New York called Newtown. When I mentioned New York in the UB meeting, I purposely implied that it was NYC to keep my team away from the actual location where Levi was killed."

She gave him a doubtful look. "If you found Levi's mugging story on the internet, so can your UB friends."

"I'm sure they will. But it will take time. It was a small article in an obscure paper. It's not going to come up high on any internet search engines. By the time they figure out the location, I'll have finished my investigation there and moved on to the next step."

"The next step?"

His jaw tightened. "I'm going to end this."

A feeling of dread snaked up her spine. "What, exactly, does that mean?"

Rather than answer, he checked his watch. "Trent's had all of three minutes to trace my phone. Even jumping through hoops with the phone carrier, I imagine he can bribe or threaten someone into helping him rather quickly. We probably have another five minutes, at best, before he has our location. It should take the team a good forty-five minutes to reach this hotel. But I wouldn't put it past them to call in help from Chief Russo and send a police car over here to cut that response time. We'll have to pack our breakfast to go." He winked, then picked up his phone and hurtled it deep into the woods beyond the balcony.

Keira stared at the trees where his phone had disappeared. "I sure hope that was a burner phone."

"Unfortunately, no. It was my personal phone. From here on out, we use burners so that my well-intentioned UB friends can't trace us. I do have another smartphone under my alias. It's never been used. No one will have any history of it to find us, so it's safe for internet searches or whatever else we may need. There are cheap burner phones in my go bag too. Untraceable, only good for phone calls. I'm happy to share." He held out his hand. "I will of course reimburse you for your loss."

She stared at him. "Please tell me you're kidding."

"Afraid not."

She swore and handed him her phone, cringing as he sent it hurtling into the trees.

Chapter Ten

Keira sat on the foot of the second of two queen-size beds in her and Lance's second-floor room in the only bed-and-breakfast in Newtown, New York. Lance stood a short distance away peering out the window down at Main Street.

"What do you see out there?"

He dropped the frilly curtain back into place. "Questions without answers. We walked the whole length of that street and back in, what, ten minutes? Fifteen? Newtown is even smaller than I thought it would be. There's absolutely nothing here to attract someone like Levi."

"He wasn't a nature lover? Hiker? Antique store aficionado?"

He scoffed. "Not even close. He hated living in Ocala, Florida, during our OPI days. He complained that there were more horses per capita than people." He smiled. "He might have been right. He was only there because the financial company his father worked for had transferred the family there when Levi was still in high school. He craved excitement, neon lights, plays, opera—the finer things in life. He was only biding his time in horse country until he felt he had enough money to quit and move somewhere like, well, New York City."

"Which is a good four hours from here," she said. "If he's a city-slicker type, why settle in Newtown?"

"That's what we need to find out."

"We should make a list of our to-do items," she said. "Divide and conquer. We can meet at the little café on the corner in a couple of hours and share what we've found."

He immediately shook his head no. "As small as this place is, I don't see any reason for us to split up. Without knowing whether the mole has people in town, watching for anyone asking about Levi's death, I'd rather not risk us each being on our own."

She shook her head in frustration. "You don't trust me to take care of myself. Still."

"Of course I do. I just don't see the need for it."

"The quicker we look into things here, the quicker we can move on to something else. Splitting up is the best way to do that."

He cocked his head. "Is it just me?"

"Just you…what?"

"That makes you defensive every time I suggest we do things a certain way."

"I'm not defensive. I'm just… I don't want to be coddled, that's all."

"Is it coddling to want to work together as partners, backing each other up rather than working separately?"

"Splitting up makes more sense," she insisted.

"No. It doesn't. It's far more dangerous, and you know it. So why are you getting your hackles up?"

She stiffened. "My *hackles*?"

"Poor choice of words. Come on, Keira. What is it? What am I doing wrong here?"

She blew out a deep breath, then shoved her hair back from her face. "Nothing."

He waited a moment. When she didn't say anything else, he asked, "Nothing meaning what exactly?"

"It's not you, okay? It's…men in general. The guys I work with in Maple Falls. The ones who ordered me around at my Nashville job. My father who…who…smothered me. Who wouldn't let me out of his sight. The man who… who…" She shook her head, squeezing her eyes shut. "It's not you. I'm sorry. It's just… I don't like being told what to do. Or protected. I don't… I don't—"

He sat beside her and pulled her onto his lap and into his arms. She stiffened, ready to push him away.

"Keira," he whispered against the top of her head. "Please, let me hold you. I'm asking. Not telling. I'm not coddling or protecting or telling you what to do. I'm here for you. You're in control. Please, let me be here for you. You're the one in control. It's okay."

You're the one in control.

And just like that, the floodgates opened. Instead of pushing his arms away, she held on tight, sobbing against his chest.

"It's okay," he whispered, his arms tightening around her. "It's okay. Let it out. You're in control."

His intuitive words had her sobbing harder, holding on to him so tightly it probably hurt. But she couldn't seem to let go or stop crying.

He rocked her back and forth, whispering over and over against the top of her head. "It's okay. It's okay. You're in control."

When she finally stopped crying and straightened, she gasped in embarrassment at his shirt. "I'm so sorry. Your shirt is soaked."

He smiled. "You can soak it any time you need to. I have other shirts."

She should have immediately gotten off his lap. But somehow, she couldn't seem to make herself even want to.

Instead, she stared into his eyes, just inches away. "How did you know that's what I needed to hear? I didn't even know I needed it."

Ever so gently, he feathered her hair back from her face. "Every time I make a decision for both of us, you push back. I thought maybe it was just me, that you didn't want to feel as if I was trying to force you into anything. But then, what you said…before you started crying… I realized it's not just me. It's something that happened to you, isn't it?"

She squeezed her eyes shut a moment, then let out a shaky breath. "Yes."

He waited. When she didn't say anything else, he asked, "Do you want to talk about it?"

For the first time in a very long time…no. For the first time *ever*, the idea of sharing what had happened instead of being forced to felt…right. As if she could somehow lighten the burden on her soul by sharing that burden with him. But when she opened her mouth to tell him, the words wouldn't come. She shook her head. "I…can't."

He gently kissed her forehead. "If you ever want to tell me, I'm here."

"Thank you," she whispered. "And… I really am sorry. For everything. You're right that I get prickly when someone tells me what to do. But I've been doing the same thing to you. I've been forcing you to let me come with you. That's not right either. I'm sorry, Lance. Truly."

He cocked his head. "You think you've been forcing me?"

"Well, yes. Like back in the stables, when I…" She squeezed her eyes shut for a moment. "When I made you promise, at gunpoint, to take me with you. That was wrong on so many levels."

"Kind of like me handcuffing you in the first place?"

She laughed. "Well, that was somewhat outrageous. I guess we both messed up."

"To a point."

She frowned. "What do you mean?"

He gently set her on her feet beside the bed and pulled out his pistol.

"Um, Lance? What are you doing?"

"Letting you know that you don't have to apologize." He dropped the magazine out of the pistol onto the bed, then ratcheted out the bullet in the chamber. Then he stood in front of her and handed the gun to her, pointing it at his belly just as she'd done back in the stables.

She swallowed and lowered the pistol. "Why are you doing this?"

"Trust me. It's not loaded, so it's safe. Hold the gun exactly as you did at my ranch."

When she hesitated, he said, "Please."

Hating what she was doing, and feeling worse than ever for having pointed it at him before, she held it in her right hand. Mimicking the way her left hand had been hand-cuffed to the wall, she raised her left arm.

"Now what?"

"Put your finger on the trigger."

"Lance, I don't..."

"Please."

She sighed heavily and did what he'd asked. "Okay, now—"

He moved with blinding speed. One moment the gun was in her hand. The next it was in his but aimed at the floor.

She blinked in shock, then looked up at him. "Oh my gosh. I never really had a chance, did I? At the stables."

He reloaded the pistol and holstered it at his waist. "I'd like to think not and that I could have taken it away just as easily. But there's always a possibility I couldn't have. Regardless, I think it's safe to say that you don't need to feel guilty for forcing me into anything I didn't want to do."

She nodded, humbled by his skills and reminded again that her few years in law enforcement didn't come close to his experience. "You need to teach me that trick sometime."

"After we bring the bad guy down, absolutely. Anytime. Maybe I'll show you how to ride a horse too, if you're game."

She smiled. "It's a date."

He grinned. "I knew I'd get you to say yes at some point."

"Overconfident," she chided.

"Highly motivated." He looked her up and down, then let out a slow sexy whistle.

She burst out laughing.

He laughed too, then crossed to the closet and pulled out a fresh shirt. She was about to tease him but whatever she was going to say flew out of her mind when he shrugged out of his wet shirt. His golden tanned skin rippled over his back muscles as he reached into the closet. His jeans hugged his narrow hips and cupped his perfectly proportioned backside. When he turned around, she had to bite back the low moan of desire that caught her by surprise. There wasn't an ounce of flab on his golden muscular abdomen. His chest and biceps would have made an artist weep at the chance to paint him. Heck, they made her want to weep with the urge to reach out and touch.

As he buttoned up and began tucking his shirt into his jeans, it did nothing to cover up the picture of him now firmly branded in her mind. How was she supposed to work with him now after having seen what was hiding underneath his clothes? Her gaze dipped to his jeans and her belly tightened.

He took some small photographs from his OPI folder and slid them into his shirt pocket. She took advantage of his inattention to hurry into the adjoining bathroom to compose herself.

"Let me fix my makeup and I'll be right out," she said as she closed the door.

"Take your time. Want me to wait downstairs?"

She blinked in horror at the dark tracks of mascara on her face from all her crying. "If you don't mind, that would be great."

"The key's on top of the dresser. I'll chat up the inn-keeper for any information I can get about Levi and Rick."

"Good idea."

At the sound of the door closing, she let out a pent-up breath. His reminder about his teammates had her want-ing to kick herself. She'd been on an emotional roller coaster, thinking about her past. That must have been why she'd gotten in such a dither over Lance's drool-worthy body. She shook her head. Yes, he was gorgeous. But that wasn't important right now. She had to focus on what really mattered.

Staying alive.

Chapter Eleven

Lance stood across the street from the police station thinking through possible scenarios of how he and Keira could get a copy of the case file and coroner's report on Levi's death.

Keira put her hands on her hips. "I can't imagine they'd tell me no after I explain that I'm in law enforcement. I've got my badge. I don't have to mention Rick's case. We can tell part of the truth—that Levi was a friend of yours and we'd like to find out more about what happened to him."

"The chief probably would let us look through the file. But we have to weigh the advantages versus the disadvantages. Although the innkeeper this morning didn't recognize Levi's picture when I showed it to him, he did recognize Rick's. So we've verified our theory that Rick was in town shortly after Levi's death notice was placed in the paper. We've already asked nearly every store owner on Main Street about Levi and Rick. The more we do that, the more we risk attracting the wrong kind of attention."

"You're not worried the mole will find out we're here, are you? We're registered at the B-and-B under your alias. Paying cash everywhere we go. Are you thinking the local police are in league with the mole and would tell him we're here in Newtown? That seems far-fetched."

"It does. But it also seems far-fetched that the mole would discover and murder two of my teammates a few months apart over a decade after we went on the run. Something has happened to stir things up. Without knowing what that was, we have to do everything we can to not broadcast our location. I'd rather find him before he finds us.

"To answer your question, though," he continued, "I have no reason to suspect the local police are involved in any of this. However, if you show your badge to the police chief, he's likely to want to call your boss to talk it out with him before providing access to the files. We already know the bad guys were in Maple Falls, that they followed you to Gatlinburg. They could still have the Maple Falls Police Station under surveillance. Maybe they've even got a wiretap to see if you check in with your boss. A call from here to your boss could be exactly what the mole needs to find us."

She shook her head. "Either you're ridiculously paranoid about this mole's reach and capabilities, or you're right and I need to get paranoid."

He smiled. "Maybe a little of both. We do have another option to get the files. It would be illegal. And risky."

She held her hands up. "We're not breaking into the police station or hacking into their computer system. I draw the line there."

"You wouldn't have to go with me. I could take care of it late at night when they have a skeleton staff. In and out."

"Are you serious?"

He sighed and scrubbed his jaw. "I'm serious that it's an option. I haven't made any decisions yet."

"You can't honestly believe that risking getting caught

and going to jail is better than me going the legal route and simply asking for a copy of the file."

He arched a brow. "I wouldn't get caught."

She rolled her eyes. "Someone needs to help you with this confidence problem of yours."

He laughed and checked the time on his phone. "I vote we grab an early dinner at the café and think all of this through."

"On that we can agree. Maybe that's why you're coming up with crazy ideas. We skipped lunch and your brain is running on empty."

He grinned. "Maybe that's it."

A few minutes later, they were sitting across from each other in a large booth at the back of the Corner Café. With it being between the traditional lunch and dinner hours, there weren't that many customers. And Lance had purposely asked to sit in that booth so he could have his back to the wall and keep an eye out for anyone coming close enough to overhear anything he and Keira talked about.

No sooner had their food arrived than the little bell over the entrance announced someone was coming in. Lance looked up, then swore.

Keira glanced at him in question, but before she could turn around, Trent and Asher were sliding into the booth beside them.

"What the hell are you doing here, Trent?" Lance demanded as Trent grabbed a french fry off his plate and set a file folder on the table. "And scoot over, Asher. You're crowding Keira."

Asher smiled at Keira and moved over. "Nice to see you again."

She slid closer to the wall, giving him more room. "Um, nice to see you too."

"No," Lance said. "It's not. What are you two doing here?"

Trent's shoulder brushed against him. Lance reluctantly moved over and shoved his plate with a cheeseburger and fries out of the way.

"Aren't you going to ask how we found you?" Trent asked.

"I'm sure it wasn't difficult. All you had to do was trace Levi to this town and then you called the only hotel here, gave them our descriptions, and the innkeeper ratted us out."

Asher laughed. "He totally did."

Lance shook his head. "I thought after I had Duncan give you the information I'd been accumulating about the mole and the people on my short list, you'd focus on that. Why interfere with Keira and me looking into my team member's deaths?"

Trent motioned toward Keira. "Knowing that the mole tracked Keira from Maple Falls to Gatlinburg suggests that he may still be watching for Keira and you. Which means you couldn't formally ask the police chief here in Newtown to give you the information that you need about Levi's death without risking having your names entered online and possibly triggering a notification to the mole." He tapped the folder. "So Asher and I got it for you."

Lance stared at him, afraid to hope. He flipped open the folder. Sure enough, the first few pages were the police reports about the mugging. After that were the hospital ER reports. And underneath that, even more notes on the investigation.

Trent motioned toward the folder. "That last group of pages is the coroner's report."

Lance started to pull that section out, then decided

against it. Levi was his friend. He wasn't mentally prepared to view autopsy photos and records of his injuries just yet. He'd wait and review them later at the B-and-B. He closed the folder. "I'm not sure what to say."

"You don't have to say anything." Trent clasped his shoulder. "We told you that you and Keira aren't in this alone. Whatever help you want or need from us, just let us know. We respect your decision to work this angle by yourselves. We'll continue looking into the higher-ups in the agencies you pointed out in your research. When you're ready to regroup and share information, let us know."

Trent slid out of the booth and stood.

Asher did the same but paused to place another folder on top of the first. "We're working in shifts at Unfinished Business so that we've got someone moving your investigation forward at all hours. That's the summary of what we've pulled together already. Of the five men you believe could be the head bad guy, we've eliminated two of them."

Lance looked up in surprise. "You're sure?"

"Positive. At the time various events you pointed out back at OPI transpired, those two wouldn't have had the opportunity, or the power, to pull them off. The others would. We're focusing on those remaining three now."

Asher nodded at Keira, who smiled back. She turned the full wattage of her smile on Lance, who was still reeling from everything that had just happened. When he was finally able to break free from her beautiful smile, he realized his friends were almost to the door of the café. He slid out of the booth and strode after them.

"Trent, Asher." They stopped at the door. Lance held out his hand. "Thank you. I mean it. I've been an ass. And it's taken me too dang long to realize it. I'll keep you both posted on any progress that Keira and I make. Please thank the team for us."

Trent clasped his shoulder again. "We're only a phone call away, buddy." He stepped outside.

Asher shook Lance's hand, but his earlier amusement seemed to evaporate as he held on tight.

"You and I went through hell together when Faith was almost killed a few months ago. You were there for both of us. We're both here for you now. Don't forget that. And whatever you do, don't let your thirst for justice, or revenge, get you or Keira killed."

With that, he stepped out the door.

Lance watched as Trent and Asher crossed the street to Trent's car, more affected by Asher's words than he would have expected.

Don't let your thirst for justice, or revenge, get you or Keira killed.

"Lance? Everything okay?"

He turned at the sound of Keira's voice. *No. Nothing is okay.* He forced a smile and joined her at the table. "We can discuss the investigation later. Let's eat before our dinner gets cold."

"Late lunch, not dinner. Depending on how late we're up working, I may still require additional sustenance."

"I consider myself warned that I may have to raid the B-and-B kitchen at midnight."

"Count on it." She laughed and they sat down to their respective burgers and fries.

At the end of their meal, Lance picked up the folders to leave.

"Wait," she said. "At every place we've been today, we showed Levi and Rick's photographs. Might as well do that here too." She held out her hand. "I'll ask the staff. You can wait here."

He nodded his thanks and handed her the pictures from his shirt pocket.

A few minutes later, she returned and gave him back the photos. "No memories of Rick having been here. But Levi definitely ate here often. He was somewhat of a regular. One of the waitresses remembers him meeting a woman here maybe once a week."

"A woman. As in a friend?"

"More than friends, according to the waitress who remembers them best. Before you ask, no, she never heard their names. And since they paid in cash, there aren't any credit card receipts to look through. I asked her if she could describe the woman with Levi, and she said she was very pretty, with long dark hair and light brown skin. She was tall too, about the same height as Levi."

His stomach dropped, as if he'd just jumped off a cliff. "She's just shy of six feet tall then. A couple of inches shorter than me."

Keira's brow wrinkled with concern. "Lance? You don't sound right. What's going on now?"

"I need to ask the waitress something. Which one is she?"

"Alice, the same waitress who took our orders. The young blonde woman on the right by the drink machine."

He pulled out the smart burner phone that had internet capabilities and pulled up a picture. When he reached the waitress and tried to show her the picture, she kept smiling and blinking her obviously false eyelashes. It took several attempts to get the information he needed. And several more minutes to extricate himself from her groping hands without providing his phone number that she'd asked for.

Keira wasn't at their table anymore. Instead, she was standing by the door, watching through the glass as she clutched the folders against her chest.

"Thanks for getting the folders." Lance stopped beside her. "Ready?"

"That depends. Did you get what you wanted from that Dolly Parton wannabe?"

He blinked. "Our waitress? Alice?"

"Oh. Was that her name? I forgot." She pushed the door open and stepped outside.

He caught up to her and stopped her with a gentle hand on her shoulder. "Keira? Did I do something to upset you?"

She let out a deep breath, her cheeks flushing a light pink. "No. No, you didn't. I'm being...just forget it. Sorry. I'm not myself." She drew a steadying breath and he began to wonder if she could actually be jealous. Of groping Alice. The very idea was ludicrous. And interesting too if Keira was upset that Alice had been so clingy. Very interesting.

"Was Alice able to provide more information about Levi? Or his apparent girlfriend?"

He scrubbed his jaw, forcing himself to focus on the case. Not his attraction to the beautiful woman working the case with him.

"I showed her a picture from many years ago that my old roommate in college posted on our fraternity's website. It was a frat party. The picture was of me and some of my buddies with some women we were dating at the time. In spite of the years that have passed, Alice recognized one of the women in the photo as being the one she'd seen at the café. It was Ileana Sanchez."

Her eyes widened. "Your ex?"

He nodded, his throat tight. He still couldn't believe she'd turned up in the middle of this investigation.

"Yikes. How incredibly awkward for her to have dated your friend all these years later."

He slowly shook his head. "Ileana and Levi never would have dated. Levi Alexander was gay."

Chapter Twelve

Keira sat on her bed, thumbing through one of the stacks of papers that Trent and Asher had given them. On the other bed, Lance was doing the same.

She motioned toward the notes she'd been taking on a legal pad. "I've been thinking about Ileana and Levi acting lovey-dovey in the café. With him being gay, I can't figure out any reason for them to do that."

"The only one who can explain is Ileana."

"I'm guessing you have no clue where she lives these days, other than close to this place, in theory, if she was coming here on weekly visits."

"She wasn't part of OPI in any capacity. I had no reason to keep up with her after we all went underground. That might be something Trent and Asher can look into for us."

"You're going to take them up on their offer to help?"

He looked up from the page he was reading. "I've finally given in. I'm waving the white flag. I surrender to my team's good intentions in spite of my own intentions to keep them out of this."

She gave him a suspicious look. "And none of this sudden willingness for them to help has anything to do with you wanting to avoid your ex?"

He grinned. "It's a definite side benefit."

She laughed. "Want me to give Trent the good news?"

"If you don't mind. Take a burner phone. We'll only use it for contacting Trent. Make sure he knows that and not to pass the number around and only to call if or when absolutely necessary. We'll toss that phone in a couple of days."

As she got the burner from his duffel bag, she asked, "You don't really think the people looking for us would set up a massive trace for all of the UB investigators' phones do you?"

"No. I don't. But I'm still not willing to risk it." He told her Trent's number and she punched it in.

After she made the call, she went back to the reports on top of her comforter. The room went silent while they both read through the information they'd divvied up between the two of them. It was probably an hour later when she stiffly slid off the tall bed and stretched her aching back.

"I'm too young to feel this sore."

"We've been at this for hours. Take a break. Go downstairs and get that snack you talked about earlier."

"I remember you agreeing to pilfer from the kitchen when I'm ready for a snack. But you can relax. I'm not hungry yet. And I'm not ready for a break, not a long one at least. I just need to stretch and walk it off until I'm ready to bend over those papers again." She motioned toward his bed. "Find anything interesting yet? Any leads for us to follow?"

"Not much. Mainly I'm looking through the data that made UB conclude they could mark two people off my suspect list."

She stretched up toward the ceiling, then leaned over and touched her toes, her long hair falling over her face and sweeping the floor. When she straightened, and stretched toward the ceiling again, she asked, "Do you not agree with their conclusions?"

When he didn't respond, she lowered her arms and looked at him.

He was staring at her, his eyes darker than usual, tension in every line of his body.

"Lance? Is something wrong?"

He looked away, his jaw working. A moment later, he let out a long, deep breath. "Maybe we shouldn't have agreed to sleep in the same room."

She waited, but when he didn't say anything else, she asked, "Why not? There was only one room available. If we didn't stay here, we'd have had to drive an hour out of town to the next hotel."

She stretched again, trying to relieve the pressure in her shoulders.

"Keira?"

"Um?" She touched her toes again, reveling in how much better her back was starting to feel.

"That hotel might be safer."

She turned to face him, hands on her hips. "Safer? You think our location has been compromised?"

"It's not our enemies that are at issue. It's me. If you stretch one more time, pulling that T-shirt tight across those luscious breasts of yours or tightening your pants across that curvy little ass, I may have to handcuff myself so I'll keep my hands off you."

She blinked, then swallowed, understanding now why he was so tense, his eyes so dark. His hunger for her was palpable, his hands fisting in the comforter as his gaze slowly traveled over her face, her breasts, down, down, down. His Adam's apple bobbed in his throat. When a small bead of sweat rolled down the side of his face, she licked her suddenly dry lips.

Lance groaned and started gathering up the papers on

his bed. "You can stay here tonight. No need for both of us to leave. I'll grab a change of clothes and get a hotel room down the highway. In the morning I'll meet you downstairs and—"

She climbed up onto the bed and tugged the papers out of his hands. His gaze flew to hers.

"Keira, what are you—"

She tossed the stack of papers onto the floor and straddled his lap.

His eyes widened. "I wasn't kidding, Keira." His deep voice was raspy, sending shivers of desire straight to her belly. "You're playing with fire." He grabbed her by the waist as if to lift her off him.

She grabbed his wrists. "I'm a big girl, Lance. I know what I want. The question is, what do you want?"

His nostrils flared. "What I *don't* want is for you to have any regrets. We're both under stress, tired. We've been through a lot together in a really short time." His hands shook as he gently set her to his side and scooted back.

Her face flamed with embarrassment. "Okay, guess I totally misread the situation. No harm. No foul." She gathered herself to slide off the bed.

He stopped her and pulled her back across his lap, sitting sideways instead of straddling him. Even so, the evidence of his desire for her pressed thick and hard against her bottom. He stared down at her, and slowly, so very slowly, ran his thumb across her lower lip. She shuddered and closed her eyes. He rested his forehead against hers, his warm breath fanning across her face, making her shiver with longing.

"Keira, my desire for you isn't something I can hide."

"I'll say," she teased, slightly shifting on his lap.

He sucked in a sharp breath, then laughed. "You're killing me here."

"You're killing me. Mixed signals much?"

He groaned, then slid his hands around her and twisted to the side, setting her on the bed between his outstretched legs instead of on his lap. Then he gently pulled her back against his chest and loosely looped his arms around her waist.

"When this is over," he whispered next to her ear, "when I know you're safe, you're going back to your life in Maple Falls."

She stiffened and started to push away.

"Let me finish." His arms tightened around her. "Please."

She huffed out a breath, then leaned back against him. "What? Just say it."

"Don't be angry." He feathered his hands across her arms, massaging her taut muscles. "You're a breath of fresh air, Keira. You're smart, courageous, gorgeous, funny and honest. But this, us, it happened so fast, under extraordinary circumstances. Our emotions are running high. At any other time, I'd gladly accept the precious gift you just offered me. I'd be honored. But you're special. This...thing between us is special. It should be treasured, not rushed. We need to be sure it's as real as it feels right now. Making love is a line that, once crossed, changes everything. If we act without taking our time to get to know each other, we may later find that what feels real right now causes regrets later. Do you understand? Does that make sense?"

She pushed out of his arms and turned on her knees to face him. "You're saying you don't want me to wish we hadn't made love weeks down the road."

"Yes."

"There is no planet on which that could possibly happen."

He laughed. "Well, I appreciate that. And I wish I could be as sure as you that you'll still feel that way weeks from now. But I'd rather risk you being upset with me than to do anything that can't be undone later. I want us both thinking clearly and to be sure before we take a step like this."

She shook her head. "Wow. I didn't think guys like you existed in the real world."

He frowned. "What do you mean?"

"Just that... I didn't know there were...any gentlemen left out there. Men who value a woman for her mind, her personality, more than they want to jump her bones."

He choked on a laugh. "I'm not the saint you're painting me to be. The line I'm drawing in the sand is shaky at best. And the only reason I'm drawing it, to be clear, is because I care about you. I don't want you for just one night. I want it all."

She stared at him, afraid to ask what "want it all" meant. To her, it meant white picket fences and churches and babies. It meant forever. The thought of forever with him, with anyone, was the bucket of ice water she'd needed. It cleared her mind like nothing else would have. Because it scared her. He was right. They needed to take a step back, a huge step back. And explore a relationship at normal speed, not warp speed.

As impossible as it seemed, he might be right that in a week, two, more, when things were back to normal— whatever normal was—they might not feel the way they did right now. And, holy moly, neither of them had any protection. What had she been thinking? The repercussions of that could link them forever, even if they decided forever wasn't in their cards.

She slid off the bed and straightened her shirt. "Well. I'm glad one of us had the strength to stop things before they got out of hand."

He gave her a doubtful look. "Are we okay? Can we still work together as a team and this not cause problems between us?"

"Absolutely. Of course. We're both professionals." She cleared her throat. "I've decided to get a snack after all. I'm going to raid the kitchen. Want anything?"

He arched a brow. "I thought it was my job to ransack the kitchen."

"Yes, well. I'm not sure what I'll want until I take a look. If I see something really yummy down there, I'll bring you some. Deal?"

"Deal."

She slid her feet into her slippers and practically ran out the door.

LANCE STARED AT the closed door for a long moment. His heart was racing so fast he was surprised he wasn't having a heart attack. And his erection was so hard it was painful. Keira had no clue how difficult it had been for him to turn down her invitation. And while the reasons he'd given her for waiting to take that step were true, he hadn't told her everything.

Like that he didn't want to risk jumping into a relationship this quickly because he'd been burned so badly by Ileana.

He knew Keira wouldn't appreciate being compared to his ex. And he wouldn't blame her. But he'd fallen fast and hard before. And that had ended in disaster. He'd waited too many years for someone as special as Keira to come along to rush into things and possibly make another mistake. He was a different person now, a man instead of a boy. Mature instead of ruled by his hormones.

Or at least, he'd thought that, until he'd very nearly pounced on Keira when she'd straddled his lap.

Realizing he was so close to losing his control had scared him. It had him thinking about Ileana and the mistakes he'd made. Keira deserved better. She deserved a man who respected and loved her, not a man ruled by physical desire who didn't know his own mind. The two of them needed time. And they didn't have that luxury right now. They had a killer to catch and stop before he hurt or killed someone else, most especially Keira.

Ever so slowly, he slid off the bed and stood. He winced and adjusted himself, then headed into the bathroom for a long cold shower.

MORE THAN AN hour passed before Keira mustered the courage to return to the room that she and Lance were sharing. She hesitated in the hallway, her hand on the doorknob. She hadn't ended up getting anything to eat. Instead, she'd sat in the front room that the innkeeper called a library even though there weren't any books in it. She hadn't needed anything to read anyway. Her jumbled thoughts were enough to keep her occupied.

What had happened, and almost happened, between her and Lance had her confused and restless. But mostly, it had her frustrated that she'd allowed her wants and desires for him to get tangled up in what they were trying to do—find and stop a killer. All the times that the lieutenant back home had chided her for not staying focused or for being impulsive, she'd chalked up to him not taking her seriously because she was a woman. But just a few days into investigating this so-called mole, she'd let personal things cloud and distract her from the case.

Maybe the LT was right, and she wasn't ready to be a detective just yet. Surprisingly, that thought didn't make her angry. Instead, it had her thinking hard about those dues she'd wanted to avoid paying as she zipped up the ladder to get a coveted detective spot. Maybe she really did need more experience first. She needed to hone her skills and truly be ready before taking that next step.

As soon as she'd come to that conclusion, her mind cleared. A sense of relief swept through her, and much of the tension and pressure she'd been under for so long lifted. She wasn't sure what that meant for her future in law enforcement. Did she want to keep going along as she had been? Or was there something else out there she was more suited for?

Whatever the eventual answers to those questions might be, for now she was eager to get back on the current case and help Lance in any way that she could. Then, well, she'd see where things went, both professionally and personally. She just hoped she could handle the embarrassment of facing him again after practically jumping his bones earlier.

Straightening her shoulders, she drew a bracing breath and opened the door to their room. When she saw Lance standing by the bed looking at some pictures on top of the comforter, she hesitated again. He hadn't even looked up when she'd opened the door. He was dressed in some soft-looking plaid pajama pants and a dark-colored T-shirt. His short dark hair was damp and curling at the ends, indicating that he'd recently had a shower. But it was the angry look on his face that had her concerned.

She closed the door. The loud click had him looking

up. He gave her a brief nod, then looked down again as if still lost in thought.

When she reached the bed and saw what he was looking at, she winced. Although she'd been to a few autopsies, they'd always been a struggle for her to endure. These photos of Levi Alexander were no different. No wonder Lance was upset. Seeing his teammate and friend laid out on a metal table brought the loss home on a completely different level. It made it painfully real.

Thankfully, the black-and-white outline of a human body on the opposite page that indicated the wounds didn't show many. He'd been stabbed twice. In the abdomen. The other cuts and bruises were relatively minor, no other true stab wounds. And the cause of death was listed as exsanguination. He'd bled out.

She motioned toward the report. "Hopefully the speed and shock of the attack meant he didn't feel much pain."

He was frowning, staring down at the report. "It says he had stage four prostate cancer, which had spread to his liver and brain."

"That's awful," she said. "I'm so sorry about your friend. This all has to be such a shock. I can't imagine your pain, seeing Levi this way. He's a pale shadow of the vibrant man in that other picture you have of him. Maybe the cancer helps explain why he looks so different."

He gave her a strange look, then selected the photograph she was talking about and set it beside the autopsy photo. "You mean this one?"

"Well, yes. That's the picture we used all day when asking if anyone had met him."

He took another picture from the stack and set it beside the first. "What do you see when you look at this photo?"

"Happier, healthier times, I guess. In this one, Levi is

smiling. His face is fuller and his skin color looks much better."

His jaw worked. "That second photo isn't Levi. It's another teammate of ours, Sam McIntosh. And this—" he pointed to the autopsy photo "—isn't Levi. It's Sam." He looked up from the pictures, his eyes dark with anger. "Now I know why Levi was flirting with Ileana. It wasn't Levi at the café. It was Sam."

She drew a sharp breath and looked at the pictures again. Now, knowing they were two different men, she could see the small differences. But someone who didn't know either of them would likely do what she and others had done, including the waitress. They'd confused the two and thought they were one and the same.

"For Sam's body to have had Levi's ID on it, Levi had to have been involved and switched their identification," Lance continued. "I believe that Levi took advantage of how much he and Sam looked alike to fake his own death. Then, when Rick read about Levi's death, he must have come here and spoken to the police. When they showed him a picture from the autopsy report, Rick would have known it was Sam. Levi was either watching for any OPI teammates to show up, or he was hanging around town for some other reason. Either way, he knew that Rick knew the truth. So he kept tabs on him, made plans, then likely lured him to that motel in Maple Falls and tortured him, looking for information on the rest of the team. Then he killed him." His jaw worked again. "My old teammate and friend Levi Alexander is the mole."

Chapter Thirteen

Since Trent and Asher had told Lance that the team was working the case 24-7, and it was already late, Lance decided to call the main line to Unfinished Business rather than wake anyone. When the line finally clicked, a woman's voice came on.

"Unfinished Business, Ivy Shaw speaking."

"Hey, Ivy. How'd you get stuck with the night shift?"

"Lance! It's great to hear from you. How are things going? Is there an emergency? I can send someone to you and—"

"No, no. Sorry. Didn't mean to worry you. No emergency, thankfully. Trent told me you all were taking turns keeping the investigation going. Is anyone else there with you?"

"Callum will be back in a few minutes. He headed down the mountain to grab us some food."

"Let me guess. Pepperoni pizza and beer."

She laughed. "You know Callum well. For me, he's grabbing a salad. And breadsticks of course, with marinara sauce for dipping. A woman can't live on salad alone."

"You're currently trying to track down the OPI mole, right?" he asked.

"Yep. Making good progress too. We're down to two of the men on your list—Eli Pratt and Chris Landrew. Both are higher-ups in Homeland Security and held positions of power even back when you worked at OPI. It's looking promising that one of them at least had the potential to be involved, with the authority and opportunity to order or do the things you pointed out in your research."

"Homeland Security." Lance looked at Keira standing by his bed, watching him intently as he spoke to Ivy. "HS fits. They'd have the power, as you said. But more than that, back in the agency's early days, they'd have the reach and vaguely defined guidelines that were the rule more than the exception. I can see them having interests in many of the cases we worked that I later found out went south—for all the wrong reasons. Have you gotten any idea of the motive behind the breach? Money, revenge or power all work in this situation, I'd imagine."

"My vote is on money," she said. "It would be pathetically easy, as you said, during the inception of HS, to hide expenditures, mislabel and channel money to other items or people. But that's speculation at this point. As to deciding whether Pratt or Landrew is our mole, it's a toss-up right now. Maybe they worked together. We'll figure it out. Shouldn't take much longer. The information you amassed over the years was incredibly detailed. You'd have eventually figured it all out on your own. But I'm glad you trusted us to help you wrap it up more quickly. Is that why you called? For a status update?"

"Actually, I called to update you and the others. Keira and I have been digging into the deaths of my teammates, Levi Alexander and Rick Cameron. We've found out that there was mistaken identity that seems to have been intentional. Levi Alexander isn't the one in New York who was killed. It was another teammate, Sam McIntosh. He and Levi look a lot alike. We used to tease them that they could be brothers. I believe that Levi capitalized on that resemblance to kill Sam and take over his identity. Although, as to why he'd do that, I really don't know yet."

"Oh no. I'm so sorry, Lance. That's a heavy thing to deal with, grieving for one friend only to find out he's double-crossed your team and you have yet another teammate dead. Wow."

"It's been a surprise, for sure. Although it's nothing I ever considered before, having both a mole inside and outside of OPI helps fit a lot of the pieces together that I had trouble with while investigating everything that happened. Our missions came from multiple alphabet agencies and were vetted through our boss, Ian Murphy. What never made sense was that the murders of people we investigated were happening regardless of whether the mission was for the CIA, the FBI, Homeland Security or other agencies. I was trying to find someone with enough power that they could tap into the other agencies, maybe in conference calls with the higher-ups. If Levi was a mole inside OPI, he'd have the information on all the cases regardless of which agency it was for. He could then give that info to the agency mole, such as Homeland Security."

He shook his head, disgusted with himself. "I should have seen that years ago. But I trusted my team. I was blind to any of them being involved."

"Don't beat yourself up over it," Ivy said. "It's hard to be objective about friends, especially when they're your team that you rely on to watch your back and help you in dangerous situations. That objectivity problem is why we've been doing a deep dive into the backgrounds on each of your teammates. We'll switch gears now that we know Sam is gone and Levi is still around. With him stealing Sam's identity, he's definitely moving to the top of our priority list. I'll pass along anything we find out."

"Thanks, Ivy. Thank everyone for me. Keira was right to push me from the beginning to trust my UB family to help with this. Just be alert. Stay safe, all right?"

"You bet. Callum's pulling up in the parking lot out front. Want to talk to him about this?"

"I'll leave you to relay it," he said.

"No problem. Are you and Keira staying where you are or heading somewhere else to continue hiding out until we know it's safe for you to return to Gatlinburg?"

He held Keira's gaze as he answered Ivy. "I'll discuss it with Keira and we'll decide together. We'll keep you posted."

Keira smiled, no doubt appreciating that he was consulting with her now, rather than telling her what they were doing as he'd done at first. She sat on the foot of the bed, waiting for him to update her about the call.

"Lance," Ivy said, "you and Keira be really careful. I don't want to have to help train a newbie around here."

"Well, thanks for the concern."

Ivy laughed. "You know we love you. Later."

Lance ended the call and tossed the burner onto the bed. After he updated Keira on what Ivy had told him, she shook her head.

"It's beyond disappointing to think that someone high up in Homeland Security would use their power to have people killed to further their own greed or other objectives," she said. "My fear is that someone like that could no doubt spin a story to cover their tracks, even now. The guys who came after us were probably hired mercenaries without any traceable links to him. If he finds out that you've discovered Levi is his contact, he'll do everything he can to take us out. We're in a perilous situation, more now than before. I don't think we should stay here in Newtown any longer. We've been asking lots of questions. And Trent and Asher, even though the police and autopsy information they provided is helpful, it could also have put us on someone's radar."

He smiled. "On that we agree."

She arched a brow. "Which part?"

"All of it."

"Oh. Good. So, we're leaving?"

"As soon as possible." He pulled each of their suitcases out of the closet and set them on their respective beds.

Keira grabbed her clothes from the top dresser drawer. "Sounds like UB is well on its way with the investigation into Homeland Security. Are they trying to figure out where Levi might be too?"

He set his duffel bag of money, IDs and weaponry into his suitcase. Then he tucked his socks and underwear beside it. "Ivy said he's now at the top of their priority list."

When he turned around, she was watching him, concern evident in her expression. "You don't sound very confident. You don't think they'll find him?"

He shrugged. "I know they can and they will. Eventually. I just think I might have a better chance of finding him than them, now that I know specifically who to look for. UB can chase after HS. Our boss and our company have the type of connections to make the inquiries that I wasn't able to make when I worked this on my own. What I want to focus on is Levi. Something is off there. If he's the OPI mole, why would he trade identity with Sam and make it look as if he's the one who died? The only answer that makes sense to me is that he's on the run, hiding."

She checked the drawers, apparently making sure that she hadn't missed anything, her back to him. "You think he's fallen out with the HS mole?"

"That would explain why he's on the run." Lance took the few shirts and jeans he'd brought and quickly folded them. He and Keira had assumed they'd be here several days or he wouldn't have unpacked at all. "The mole probably knows everything about Levi, including where he lives. But Sam's identity ends here, in Newtown. As long as Levi doesn't go back to his own home or places he normally frequents, he has a chance at getting away."

"Right," she said. "As Sam, he's fresh, brand-new. It's a dead end for the mole to look for him as Sam anywhere other than in Newtown." She shut the dresser drawers and turned to face him. "But if HS doesn't know where to look for him, how will we know where to look for him? And something else is bugging me about all of this too. Why would your ex, Ileana, show up around here with Sam? Do you think she could be involved with what happened at OPI?"

"All good questions, Detective Sloane. Questions for which we need to get the answers."

She smiled at his use of the detective title. "Guess we'd better get busy, then, and find those answers."

When they were in his SUV, Keira fastened her seat belt and took a cautious look around, as if watching for a slew of mercenaries to come running at them. Her right hand was poised near where her gun was holstered beneath her jacket.

He hated that she had to be worried about her safety. She still felt guilty about coming to Gatlinburg and leading his enemy there. But none of this was her fault. It was his, for making the decision to run and hide all those years ago. If he could have a redo, he'd have dedicated himself to finding the mole, or moles, in the beginning. Then Sam and Rick wouldn't have been murdered. And Keira wouldn't be caught up in all of this, with her life in danger. Meanwhile, an incredibly selfish part of him was thankful that things had gone the way they had. Otherwise, he might never have met her.

"Since we don't know yet where to search for Levi," she said, "I'm thinking we should head to Tennessee, maybe the western region so we're close enough to UB for assistance if we need it but far enough away from Gatlinburg and Maple Falls that our enemies won't stumble across us."

He started the SUV. "Ever been to Kentucky?"

She blinked. "Kentucky? No. What's in Kentucky?"

"In the southwestern corner, there's a tiny one-light farm town called Wingo, population a little over five hundred."

"That's a really small town. I'm guessing they don't even have a motel. Why would we hide out there?" Her eyes widened. "Wait, I'll bet Levi grew up there. You think he might have returned to his roots? Wouldn't that be dangerous if the HS mole knows all about him?"

"It would be. Agreed. But Levi's roots are in the bright lights of LA. He wouldn't dream of living in a rural area like Wingo. He'd be worried he'd get horse or cow manure on his wing tips."

"Oh." She sounded disappointed.

"Sam, now, he's a different story," Lance continued. "He was born and raised in Wingo on a large farm. His parents grew corn, tobacco, soybeans. But it was their small stable of thoroughbreds that they raised for the sheer love of horses that he was so proud of. He took me there on vacation many times to go riding and show me the hundred-acre property that he loved."

"Wait, so you're thinking Levi—pretending he's Sam now—would go to that farm?"

"If he's desperate, it could be a first stop until he gathers his resources and figures out his next move."

"No, it would be foolish," she insisted. "Anyone could look up Sam's birth records and trace him to Wingo. The HS mole would think of that and check it out."

"I disagree. It goes against all logic and common sense to go to Wingo, which is why the HS mole wouldn't bother. He wouldn't think Levi was that foolish. Instead, he'll focus on trying to find Levi through other means. The more I think about it, the more I think Levi would hide out there."

"I'm not sure I agree," she said. "But if we do decide to go there, at least for a quick look, what about Sam's parents? Do they still live on the farm?"

"They passed away years ago. But Sam kept the property. I checked on it a while back as part of looking into finding the mole and doing what I could to ensure the team was still safe. Sam didn't live there, of course. He'd gone underground, new identity and all that like the rest of us. But he kept the land under a web of shell corporation names. He was too sentimental to give it up. It's rental property now, a farm that a management company leases out. With no one knowing Sam is actually dead, that likely hasn't changed. If Levi did decide to go there, he would have told the management company to clear out any renters so he could stay there. With enough cash, I imagine it would have been easy to make that happen." He glanced at her, his hands on the steering wheel. "It's all conjecture. But since we need to get out of Newtown—"

"Why not head to Wingo?" She smiled. "Let's do it. Let's go find Levi."

Chapter Fourteen

The drive from Newtown to Wingo took almost twelve hours. Keira was grateful that Lance had agreed with her that driving straight through without any sleep wasn't safe. They'd stopped at a hotel just before dawn, separate rooms this time. Keira fell asleep the moment her head hit her pillow. Lance had told her he'd pretty much done the same, except for a call first to Trent to update him on their plans.

With the sun beginning to sink on the horizon, they'd finally arrived at their destination—Wingo, Kentucky. When Lance told her that Wingo was small, she'd pictured a quaint Southern town with a square anchored by a historical-looking city hall sporting a clock tower on top. Surrounding the square would be little mom-and-pop restaurants, old-fashioned dime stores and antique shops. Instead, the "town" part of Wingo consisted of one street that was probably no more than a city block long.

At the top of the hill at the beginning of the street was a funeral home. The bottom of the hill boasted a handful of abandoned boarded-up stores, rusty railroad tracks and what appeared to be a clothing factory that might have been in use during the last world war. At the top of the other side of the hill was a church.

That was it.

Wingo, the town, had apparently died long ago. Wingo, the surrounding community, wasn't much to look at either. Or, at least, at first glance it wasn't. As Lance drove slowly down potholed gravel streets out to the paved rural two-lane highway, Keira was astonished at how friendly and outgoing the people were that they passed. And how *not* stressed everyone seemed to be.

No doubt, they all struggled like anyone else to go to work each day or work their farms, pay their bills, buy groceries. But they came home every night to a place where neighbors sat on front porches and called out to each other. Children tossed footballs beneath hundred-year-old oak trees in enormous unfenced backyards. Everyone they passed waved and smiled at them, as if they were lifelong friends. And the farms, they were nothing like she'd pictured in her mind either.

These weren't corporate-run monstrosities with miles of corn waving in the fading twilight. These were family farms, with thriving gardens up by the homes to provide fresh vegetables and spices. Chickens ran free across the yards, no doubt providing delicious eggs to their owners. And fences were used to keep the chickens and other animals safe from predators, not to keep the neighbors away.

She drew a deep breath of cool, fresh air through the open window, watching the quaint little homes as they drove past. And green plants that Lance had told her were soybeans, dotting the hills in neat rows.

"It's so beautiful here," she said. "Peaceful. No one honking horns or jostling past each other in a rush to go someplace else. I could get used to this."

He chuckled. "You say that now. But you may change your mind when you realize the only shopping around here is that mom-and-pop grocery store we stopped at a few miles down the road. Real shopping is a good forty-five minutes away. If you have a medical emergency, God help you. The closest hospital is even farther away. And I'm sure you noticed the lack of movie theaters and fancy corner coffee shops around here. They don't even have a bowling alley."

"Bowling? You don't have the potbelly to convince me you like to bowl."

"Ouch. I have a lot of friends who would resent that remark. No potbelly required. It's fun, especially if there's a pool hall attached."

"Ah, there we have it. The real reason you'd go to a bowling alley—so you can play some pool and down some beers."

He grinned, not denying her assumption.

"Enough with trying to ruin my fairy-tale impression of this charming town," she told him. "Okay, maybe you're right, and I couldn't live here full-time. But to unplug, disconnect and relax for a few weeks? Absolutely. It's really not much different than you living on your ranch, right? It's pretty far out of town. Isolated."

"The nearest Wally World is only fifteen minutes from my place."

"Ah. Walmart. The epitome of civilization. Twenty self-checkout lines and not a cashier in sight."

"Exactly."

She shook her head, smiling. "How much farther to the short-term rental you got us?"

"Another mile, maybe less. But Sam's place is down that next turn on the left. We could do a quick drive-by to see if anyone's home. It'll be dark soon. This is our only chance to get a look before morning light."

She straightened in her seat. "Let's do it."

"Windows up. The dark tint should help disguise who we are if Levi's there and sees us in the SUV."

They closed their windows. When Lance turned down the driveway to Sam's farm, instead of the gravel she'd expected it was paved and wider than the rural highway they'd just left. Maybe that was to make it easier on the horses when they had to be moved in or out of the property. She knew next to nothing about horses but didn't imagine a bumpy road would be good for them while keeping their balance in horse trailers.

With the sun setting, Lance turned off the headlights to avoid anyone seeing them from the house as it came into view. He stopped, and they both took in the lay of the land. Like everything else out here in the true country, Keira thought it was absolutely beautiful. The road continued for a good quarter mile across rich green fields to the one-story white farmhouse with a black shingle roof.

A porch with white railings and four brown rocking chairs ran the entire front of the home. White three-rail fences, like those at Lance's place, lined the long driveway and split the fields into smaller sections.

"Those are the stables over there to the back left side of the house," Lance said. "I remember some large wooden outbuildings directly behind the house for storing tractors and other equipment, including the horse trailer. I imagine they're all still there."

"Why would they need tractors? The fields are all grass, not soybeans, or whatever else they grow around here."

"A riding mower would take weeks to cut these fields. You can do it on a tractor in a few hours."

Her face warmed. "Mowing the grass. Right. City slicker here. Guilty."

He squeezed her hand. "You're coming around though. Before long, you'll want your own chickens and a little garden to raise tomatoes."

She wrinkled her nose. "No chickens. And I prefer spinach to tomatoes, thank you."

He shook his head. "We'll have to work on that. No self-respecting horse rancher prefers spinach over tomatoes."

"Maybe you can train me in the ways of ranchers."

His mouth curved in a slow, sexy grin. "I can teach you a lot of things."

"Promises, promises." She winked, her face warming at her audacity to do so.

He laughed, and she looked out the windshield toward the house, her face flushing hotter. She'd never been one to flirt or tease like she did with him. Something about Lance brought her out of her shell and made everything fun. Here they were, essentially on the run for their lives, and he could make her forget the danger and actually laugh. That was a rare gift. But also dangerous. They both needed to focus right now. Playing could happen later. If she was lucky.

Her fingers dug into her palms. She *really* hoped playing happened at some point between them. She craved Lance like a drunk craved his next drink. And she wanted to find out what it was like to move past that one amazing kiss they'd shared. She had a feeling that being with him would be spectacular.

"I don't see any lights on in the house," he said. "No sign of a car or truck either, although he might have parked around back."

They both watched the place for several more minutes, but even though it was getting almost too dark to see, no lights came on.

"We'll conduct some surveillance tomorrow," he said. "Let's get out of here before I can't see the road without headlights."

He backed the truck up until they reached a wide enough spot beside the driveway to allow him to turn around. Then he flipped the headlights on and sped to the main road.

A few minutes later, he pulled into another driveway, this one short and filled with gravel. It ended in front of a small white house with a front porch only large enough to accommodate two small cane-backed chairs, one on each side of the door. It wasn't all that different from the other little cottages they'd passed. But it was just similar enough to another cottage in her memories that it sent a chill up her spine.

A few minutes later, they were inside, their suitcases sitting in their respective bedrooms. They'd have to share the only bathroom, but it was a Jack and Jill. They each had their own sink and toilet. The only shared amenity was the shower.

Just like the other cottage.

She waited inside the eat-in kitchen as Lance carried in the few bags of groceries that they'd grabbed at the mom-and-pop grocery mart just outside of town. Normally, Keira would have helped. But the queasiness and panic that had been building ever since they'd pulled up outside finally won. She pressed a hand over her mouth and ran for the bathroom.

Her misery as she threw up her lunch was compounded by embarrassment when Lance was suddenly kneeling beside her, gently pulling back her hair. She would have pushed him away, but her stomach wouldn't stop heaving.

A cool damp cloth pressed against her forehead, her cheeks, her neck. It felt so good that her embarrassment was forgotten. He held the cloth against her forehead, whispering sympathetic words. When her stomach finally settled, he started to wipe her mouth. Her face flaming hot again, she grabbed the cloth from him and took care of it herself.

He stood and helped her up. Without looking at him, she flushed the toilet and moved to the sink to wash her hands. When he again made no move to leave, she finally drew a bracing breath and glanced at him in the mirror. "I need some privacy now. Please."

"Of course. Call out if you need me."

When he closed the door behind him, she almost called out for him to come back. The intimacy of him seeing her in such a vulnerable and awful way was embarrassing. But being shut in the bathroom alone in this house was so much worse.

Desperately longing for some toothpaste and a toothbrush, she gargled warm water over and over until her mouth felt clean again. Then she was out the door, running through the house.

"Keira. What's wrong?" Lance called out somewhere behind her.

"Can't. Breathe. Air. I need air." She didn't even slow down. She threw the front door open and ran onto the porch, her shoes catching on the threshold. Pitching forward, she threw her arms up to try to catch herself. Lance managed to grab her around the waist and jerk her back, saving her from tumbling face-first down the stairs.

He turned her and clasped her tightly against him. "My God. Keira. You almost...my God." His hands shook as he held her, rubbing her back and resting his cheek against the top of her head.

His kindness, his strength, his obvious concern, had

her fighting back tears. Again. But she absolutely refused to cry all over him as she had at the bed-and-breakfast. Mortified on so many levels, she pushed out of his arms.

"What is it?" he asked. "Are you sick? Do we need to—"

"Drive forty-five minutes to a doctor?" She forced a wobbly smile, still fighting the urge to curl into a ball and cry like the young girl she'd once been before she'd been forced to grow up far too fast so very long ago. "I'm not sick. I'm..." She squeezed her eyes shut, drew a deep breath, then another. Feeling more in control, she opened her eyes. "I'll explain later, but...can we...can we please go somewhere else? To stay? I can't... I can't go back in there. I'm so sorry. I know it must have cost a lot to get this place on short notice. And you might not get your deposit back and—"

"Shh. It's okay." His smile was so sweet, so compassionate, it had her heart squeezing in her chest. "I'm blessed that I don't have to worry about money. And I should have consulted you about the rental to make sure you were okay with it before I reserved it anyway."

"What? No. I knew you were calling to reserve something for us. If I wanted to provide input, I would have. I just...it never dawned on me that the place we got would remind me...would look like..." She shook her head and wrapped her arms around her middle. "Just please take us to a different house, one that's nothing like this one. Okay?"

He pressed the sweetest kiss against her lips. "If my marching orders are to get us a place nothing like this one, then that's what I'll do. No worries. Come on." He took her hand in his and led her to the truck, helping her inside and buckling her seat belt as if she were a precious gift, not the burden she knew she'd become.

"Give me a couple of minutes to call the rental agency again and grab our suitcases and groceries. I'll be right back."

She gave him a shaky smile and nodded her thanks. After he shut the passenger door, she immediately pressed the lock, not even caring that he must have heard it and thought she'd lost her mind. He jogged up the porch steps, and a moment later the porch lights came on. But they weren't bright enough to reach much beyond the porch itself.

As she waited, she huddled against the seat, her hand on her holster. She'd forgotten how dark it could be out in the middle of nowhere, without streetlights or the so-called light pollution of a city close by. And she'd forgotten just how oppressive that darkness could be.

When she realized she was sliding down in her seat, huddled like a child, she swore and forced herself to sit straight. She wasn't that miserable young girl anymore. And there was no reason to be afraid of an empty house. There were far scarier things to be afraid of right now, like Levi Alexander and whoever he might be working for to try to kill Lance and her.

Funny how so many years had gone by and it was still her past that had the power to frighten her far more than her present. Facing gunmen as an adult, using her police training and excellent marksmanship to protect herself and potentially Lance, was something she was prepared for. She could control her reactions, and how she approached the situation. It was the nightmares of her childhood that she still didn't know how to control.

A few minutes later, Lance jogged down the steps with

their two suitcases. He stowed them in the back of the SUV. One more trip into the house and he had the grocery bags. The porch light clicked off, and he hurriedly set the bags in the rear seats.

"Everything's set," he assured her, with an encouraging smile. "The next place is a bit farther, about five miles down the highway. We'll be there in a few minutes."

She watched in relief as the eerie cottage faded into the darkness. When the new rental house came into view, the tension in her shoulders began to ease. But the guilt inside her flared to life. This was definitely not a cottage. One of the more prosperous families in the area must own this one. Or a city slicker had it built as their summer vacation home. It was as modern as the other house was historical. Two stories of glass and steel were softened by gray ledge stone and cedar posts holding up the overhang above the double front door. Landscape lighting chased away the darkness.

Lance cut the engine and gave her an inquiring look. "Better?"

She unfastened her seat belt and impulsively kissed his cheek. "Much."

He grinned. "I can find a bigger house if it will get me a kiss on the lips."

Without missing a beat, she raised on her knees and pressed her lips to his. He groaned and picked her up, lifting her over the middle console and onto his lap as if she weighed nothing. Their first kiss had been full of heat and wonder. This one was scorching. She answered his every touch with her own, their bodies deliciously in sync with each other. He slid a hand around her back and one in her hair and deepened the kiss.

The honk of the horn as her back pressed it had both of them jerking apart. They burst out laughing.

"Talk about a mood killer," he teased. He popped open the door, lifting her in his arms and hopping down from the SUV. When she was standing in front of him, he leaned down and gave her another quick kiss. "The lock code for the front door is 4371. Let's check it out and make sure you're okay with everything before I bring our things inside."

"No. It's fine. Really. You did great. It's nothing like the other place. I'll grab the groceries if you don't mind getting the suitcases."

"All right, but if you change your mind about the house, I can—"

"It's perfect. Let's hurry. It's cold out here."

"Personally, I'm burning up." He winked.

Her face flamed as it did so often around him, and he laughed in response.

The house was everything the outside promised it to be. Clean, bright, open and modern. There was absolutely nothing to make her feel claustrophobic or remind her of her past. But since those dark images had already been resurrected, they were fighting to consume her. She doubted she'd get much sleep at all tonight.

While Lance put their suitcases in two of the bedrooms upstairs, she put away their groceries. There were snacks, peanut butter and jelly, crackers, bread, soup, beer, bottled water. And coffee of course, along with powdered creamer and sugar. Things that didn't need refrigeration. Neither of them planned on being in town long. A few days at most, less if they found Levi right away.

When she finished and turned around, Lance was a few yards away leaning against the massive dark quartz island.

"Are you hungry? I can make us some soup and sandwiches."

"I'm starving, actually. I'll heat the soup and—"

"I'll make the ribbon sandwiches."

"Ribbon sandwiches? Fancy name for a PB&J. Did you learn that in home economics class at school?"

"Actually, Mamaw, my grandmother on my father's side, showed me. You'd be amazed at my culinary skills. I can boil water too."

She laughed, and soon they'd both wolfed down their small hastily thrown together meal. Once the kitchen was clean again, they dried their hands on a kitchen towel.

"Seems rude to eat and run," she said. "But I'm practically asleep on my feet. Which bedroom is mine?"

"Top of the stairs, first room on the right."

"Thanks. For everything." She started past him, but he tugged her hand, pulling her back toward him. She looked up in question.

"Do you want to talk about it?" His voice was gentle, soothing, his expression one of concern.

She'd managed to avoid a discussion about why she'd panicked at the cottage. Dinner had consisted of small talk and plans for tomorrow's surveillance. But it was only fair to explain. She opened her mouth to do exactly that, but the shadows swirled in her mind, stealing the words.

"Just know that I'm here if you ever need to talk." He kissed the top of her head. "I'm not quite ready to call it a night. I'm going to log in to UB to check on their progress with the investigation, maybe catch a football game rerun. Sleep well." He headed into the main room with its U-shaped arrangement of black leather couches facing an enormous television on the far wall.

She flipped off the lights in the kitchen, leaving the

dimmed canned lights in the main room as the only lights on downstairs. "Lance?"

He'd just picked up the laptop that he must have set on the coffee table after taking their luggage upstairs. He arched a brow in question.

"Thank you. For everything."

He smiled. "Anytime, Keira. Anytime at all."

Chapter Fifteen

A slight movement had Lance opening his eyes and sitting up, surprised to find that he'd dozed off in the family room. He was even more surprised to see Keira sitting beside him, facing him with her legs crossed in her lap. Her hair was mussed, giving her a sexy just-got-out-of-bed appearance. But the pink pajama tank top and shorts with cartoon cats all over them had him grinning.

"Nice pj's."

She didn't even crack a smile. It was then that he realized how pale she looked.

He glanced up the stairs, his hand automatically going to the gun still holstered on his hip. "Did you hear something? See someone through the windows?"

"What? No. No, I haven't heard or seen anyone. No one real anyway. Or, at least, not anymore." She threaded her fingers through her hair, mussing it even more. "Sorry. I know I'm not making sense. I just, well, I couldn't sleep. Or when I did, the nightmares came again." She drew a shaky breath. "I can't remember the last time that happened. Years, I suppose."

"I'm a little lost here."

She sighed heavily, her hands nervously clenching and unclenching each other. "I owe you an explanation about earlier. The cottage."

He shook his head. "No, Keira. You don't. Everyone has demons they deal with, something from their past or some kind of phobia. That's for you to tell or not. Completely up to you."

"Okay, well. I need to tell you. I don't want you thinking I'm losing my mind. I want you to understand."

"All right. Take your time. Whatever you need."

She twisted her hands together, then turned, sitting close beside him, her right thigh snuggled up against his left one, warming him through his jeans. He swallowed, his entire body heating as she tentatively clasped his hand with hers and rested their joined hands on her thigh. She obviously had no idea how much he wanted her, how the simple feel of her pressed against him had blood flowing to all the wrong parts. Hating himself for even thinking about sex when she was obviously struggling to gather her thoughts and tell him something important, he used his free hand to pull a light blanket off the back of the couch.

Lifting their joined hands, he settled the blanket over both their laps and then set their hands back on top.

"Thank you," she murmured, no doubt thinking he was just worried about her being cold.

He tried to relax against the back of the couch, a bead of sweat running down his temple. But at least she couldn't see his painful erection straining against the front of his jeans with the blanket covering him.

When she still didn't say anything, he was about to remind her that she didn't have to and they could just sit quietly until she was ready to go to bed again. But her soft, hesitant voice broke the silence first.

"I was fifteen," she whispered.

And just like that, those three little words killed the desire flooding through his veins. Instead, he was now filled with dread, hoping, praying that she wasn't going to say what he feared she would say—that someone had hurt her when she was little more than a child.

Please, don't let it be that.

She rested her head against him. He automatically pulled his hand free from hers and settled his arm around her shoulders, drawing her close. She didn't pull back. Instead, she nestled into the crook of his arm. He wanted nothing more than to protect her, to keep her safe. But he knew that whatever she was about to tell him wasn't something he could save her from. It had already happened.

"I'd stayed a few minutes late with my algebra teacher, getting help with a homework problem. Missed the bus. Home was only a couple of miles away. At the time I was on the cross-country team, so I didn't bother calling my parents for a ride. I changed into my running shoes and took off jogging down the road. I can't tell you how many times my dad warned me not to run with earphones in both ears. He said it was dangerous, that I couldn't hear if a car was getting too close, that I should always keep one ear uncovered. Of course, I ignored his advice. Music was jamming. I never heard the van."

His stomach tightened. "Did it hit you?"

"I wish that's all that had happened. No. The driver parked on the side of the road, then came up from behind and grabbed me. I kicked and scratched for all of about fifteen seconds. He shoved a needle in my neck and everything went black. When I woke up, I was tied up in the back bedroom of a little cottage like the one we went to earlier tonight."

He swore softly and rubbed his hand up and down her arm.

"I won't... I won't go into the particulars. I did that in

court, and it was like being violated all over again. I never want to relive it like I did those three days on the witness stand."

"You don't need to," he whispered against the top of her head. "You don't have to."

She nodded against his chest. "I know. But I wanted you to understand. He held me captive for fifty-six days. Tied up most of the time. Kept in a darkened, tiny room. Only let out to shower when I stank too much for him to be able to stand me."

"Good grief," he said. "He was a monster."

"Yes. He was. And it was only through luck that I was eventually rescued. He was pulled over in town for a traffic violation when he was picking up supplies. An observant policeman remembered a witness's description of the van and a girl jogging on the side of the road the day I went missing. They'd driven by, not thinking anything of it until they saw the missing-person posters a few days later. If they hadn't reported it, and the policeman hadn't been suspicious, and my abductor hadn't been dumb enough to have kept my purse in his van, I wouldn't have made it."

She slid her arms around him, holding tight. "I wasn't the first girl he'd taken. But I was the last. And the only one who survived."

His hands shook as he lifted her onto his lap and held her like the precious gift that she was. Barely contained fury roared through his veins. The need to feel the monster's bones crunching beneath his fists was palpable. "What happened to him?"

"He was convicted and sentenced to life, without the possibility of parole. But he never served a day in an actual prison. He took the coward's way out, hung himself in the county jail."

"Good. I don't like the idea of you both sharing the same planet together."

She pulled back and smiled up at him. "Here I am thinking about the most horrific period of my life, and you have the power to make me want to laugh. You're an amazing man, Lance Cabrera."

He softly kissed her but couldn't dredge up a smile of his own. "You're an amazing woman. To have gone through what you did and have gone on to be a functioning, contributing member of society is an achievement of its own. To become a police officer, to face the evil others do day in and day out after experiencing the worst of the worst, is awe-inspiring." He pulled her close again. If she didn't need a hug right now, he sure as heck did. He wished he could take away all the hurt. But all he could do was be there for her. For now, hopefully it was enough.

"That's why you didn't want to go into the basement at the cabin," he said, his cheek pressed against the top of her head. "I imagine you're not a fan of dark, tight spaces."

"And being trapped. No windows or doors."

He winced and pulled back. "I was being stubborn, thinking I knew what was better for you than you knew yourself. I never should have locked you in that basement."

She smiled again, the color slowly coming back into her cheeks and the light returning to her brown eyes. "Apology accepted. You're a strong man used to being the protector. I get that. And I appreciate it. But as you said, I'm a cop. I've been trained and I can shoot pretty darn well, top of my class for marksmanship at the academy. We need to trust each other. As a team, we're much more capable than on our own."

He shook his head in wonder. "I've been on two significant teams over the years, and you're teaching me more about teamwork than I've learned in all that time."

"Slow learner, I guess."

He laughed. "Maybe so. I know I'm pushing my luck in asking any personal questions after what you just shared. But I'm curious about something else."

"I can't imagine anything more personal than what I've already shared. Go ahead."

"Your family. You're estranged from them, right? Is that because of what happened to you? Or something else?"

Her smile dimmed but didn't go away completely. "The ordeal as I've come to think of it happened in Memphis. Everyone in town knew about it. I couldn't escape the cruel comments of other kids at school or the looks and whispers whenever I went anywhere else. My parents tried to protect me by uprooting the family and moving us to Nashville. My younger brother and sister blamed me for them losing their Memphis friends. My parents were overprotective and practically smothered me. Dad turned to alcohol, trying to drown his guilt for not having been able to protect me when I was abducted. I was miserable. We fought constantly and I rebelled, got into trouble. When I turned eighteen, my mother gave me an ultimatum. Straighten up or move out. I was gone that same day, never went back."

"That has to be hard, not having the support of your family anymore."

"No harder than you being forced to give up yours."

"We're both orphans, in a way. Maybe one day we'll both be able to move forward, overcome our pasts and reunite with our loved ones."

"Maybe," she said, sounding doubtful. "Or maybe we move forward by creating a new family. Or, ah, families."

Her face flushed a delightful pink, letting him know he hadn't misunderstood what was probably a Freudian slip. The thought of the two of them starting a family, together, having a real future as a couple, should have scared him. His last serious relationship, Ileana, had been so awful it had soured him on the idea of ever getting married or having children. And yet, that kind of future with Keira didn't sound like a life sentence. Instead, it sounded more like winning a lottery.

She carefully stood, suddenly seeming shy as she adjusted her pajama shorts and then crossed her arms over her chest. "Seems like I'm always thanking you. But I really do appreciate everything you've done, how protective, strong and kind you've always been to me. And for listening. It helped. Talking to a therapist, a stranger, never seemed to work. But telling you just a little about what happened feels…like a weight dragging me down has been lightened considerably."

"I'll always be here for you, Keira. I mean that. Always."

Her eyes widened. Had he frightened her? Or was she surprised—in a good way? Before he could try to reassure her, she called out a hurried good-night and rushed up the stairs.

Chapter Sixteen

Keira was feeling raw and off-kilter the next morning. Her emotions were far too close to the surface, and it was difficult to concentrate. She was frightened of the situation that she and Lance were in, worried about some as yet unknown enemy wanting to kill them. Concern for Lance, in particular, weighed heavily on her. He'd become so important in such a short amount of time that she was more worried about his safety than her own. Part of that was because she felt that she was in over her head, both personally and professionally.

Her law enforcement experience was nothing compared to Lance's. She was good with a gun. And she'd always had a knack for setting witnesses at ease when talking to them as part of her beat-cop duties. But her detective skills were nowhere near what she'd once falsely believed them to be. The tips and suggestions that the UB investigators had given her seemed obvious—after they pointed them out. And Lance's suggestions did as well. But their ideas had never been her ideas. They'd never even occurred to her.

The longer she worked this case, the more she was beginning to accept that maybe being a detective, or even a cop, wasn't the right fit for her. And she was finally starting to understand why. After giving Lance a watered-down version of the trauma she'd endured as a young teenager, it had dawned on her, a real light-bulb moment, that maybe the whole idea of being a cop was just her response to that trauma. Being in control and making her own decisions were crucial to her feeling calm, to staving off the panic that was never far from the surface. Maybe working in law enforcement was just her way of maintaining that sense of control. It helped her feel stronger, less vulnerable. But did it make her happy? Fulfilled? Maybe she'd been wanting the detective title as just another way to try to search for whatever would fill the empty void inside her.

It was something to think about.

As to her personal dilemma that circled around Lance and her feelings for him, they obviously were attracted to each other. But in spite of the teasing and flirting they did so often, one or both of them always seemed to find an excuse or a reason to stop before they crossed a physical line they couldn't uncross. Was it because they really weren't meant for each other? Or was it simply because each of them was unsure of what their own future might look like once this current crisis with Levi and the other mole was over?

It was all so confusing. And it made it hard to focus and do a good job backing up Lance when her thoughts were such a jumble. But at least after pouring her heart out to him last night, she'd been able to get some much-needed sleep. For the first time since the attack at her Gatlinburg cabin, she felt rested and ready to face whatever obstacles were in their way. She just had to lock up the distracting thoughts about her career and Lance, and focus on their mutual goal of stopping the mole, or moles, and reclaiming their lives. The sooner they could do that, the sooner she could make some decisions about her future.

In spite of her worries that things might be awkward between them when she finally came downstairs freshly showered and ready for the day, things weren't awkward at all. After a quick, light breakfast and easy conversation, they headed out to Sam's farm to spy on it and see whether there were any signs that Levi was there.

They parked at the back of the property this time, using a road that Lance knew about from his many times visiting with Sam. From the way the tree branches and bushes encroached on the road, it was obvious that the most recent occupants of the farm didn't use the back entrance. So it was easy to drive up fairly close to the outbuildings in the woods behind the house and not worry about being seen. From there, it was a long boring day of watching and waiting for signs of life from the house, with just a couple of breaks to head out for something to eat and much-needed bathroom trips. Once back at the rental that evening, they'd used their respective laptops to look for clues about the fiasco that OPI had become.

The only thing of note that happened both days was that a man arrived at the stables in the mornings to feed the horses and turn them out into a pasture. Around the dinner hour, he showed up again and bedded the horses down in the stables for the night. But he never approached the house or any other outbuildings. And there were never any signs of life from the house itself.

The surveillance lasted two days. Both were essentially carbon copies of each other. No lights came on in the house. The blinds on the windows stayed closed. No one drove up the driveway toward it and no one came outside.

At the end of the second day, Keira and Lance sat down

at the kitchen table to eat dinner. Keira had slow-cooked a Crock-Pot of roast with potatoes and carrots, thanks to a trip to the little market for more supplies the day before. They'd both realized that living on peanut butter and jelly sandwiches wasn't going to cut it, even for a short stay.

Lance set his napkin on his plate and leaned back in his chair. "Either I was starving, or you're one fine cook, Ms. Sloane."

"Probably a little of both. I can steer my way around a kitchen when I want to. And we're both tired of junk food." She reached for his empty plate to rinse and wash, but he stopped her.

"I'll clean the kitchen," he said. "It's the least I can do after you cooked this delicious meal. But let's get our daily call to Trent out of the way first. I'm hopeful he's found something. We're coming up with zero on our end."

"Works for me." She moved their plates out of the way and sat beside him.

Lance got Trent on the phone and put it on speaker mode while they gave him their updates—which was basically that they'd made no progress.

Lance added, "I also tried tracing both Sam and Levi's phones that I had programmed into my computer. But regardless of which phone Levi was using when I sent the warning to my team to go underground, he's not using it now. It's either turned off or has been destroyed."

"We tried the same thing here," Trent said. "Even went through the phone carriers for their official records, courtesy of a subpoena secured by Chief Russo. Your team is well trained to ditch phones and switch to burners, is all I can say. We came up empty. This Levi character has gone completely off the radar. He hasn't returned anywhere that we've been able to trace him to in his past.

And from what you've said, he hasn't gone to Sam's one hold-out property from his early life either. As much as I hate to say it, we're at a dead end on finding him unless something happens to expose his location. Are you going to perform surveillance tomorrow or switch gears?"

Lance motioned toward Keira. "What do you think?"

She shrugged. "Without another lead to chase on Levi, I'm inclined to give it one more day."

"One more day it is then," he agreed. "After that, we'll need to find a new location to keep ourselves off the radar. Even though we're using alias internet accounts, cash and burner phones, we're still leaving an electronic trail. That makes me nervous. I'd rather head out sooner than later. But I agree with Keira that one more day feels right. I really thought Levi would show up here. And I don't have any more ideas on where to look for him at the moment. Any updates on the Homeland Security link?"

"Good and bad news on that front. The good news is that we finished our investigation into both of the HS guys we'd zeroed in on. The bad news is that neither of them are the mole. We're going to have to look at everything again, see if we missed something. One thing that has come out of this is that we did deep dives into the cases you'd researched where people were killed, the ones you and your team provided intel about. Although it's not obvious at first, when you peel back the layers, you'll find that many of the people who were killed had alleged links to organized crime. If that's the common thread, then a mole in the Justice Department makes far more sense than someone in Homeland Security. He could be in the FBI or even the US Marshals, turning over locations of witnesses to a mob boss to take them out. Making this entirely about money for the moles. They get rich, the mob protects its own people, who would have gone to prison if the witnesses had been around to testify."

"FBI," Lance said. "I looked at them but found nothing."

"Like I said, we had to go deep. We've used Chief Russo's influence, our TBI liaison and his connections to the Florida Department of Law Enforcement, as well as our boss's considerable influence on governors and other politicians. It's only through their hard work that we've gotten the subpoenas we needed, in record time I might add. And because of that we got access to information you and I would never have gotten otherwise. You wouldn't have found that link on your own. Trust me."

"I still hate that I didn't. I'll look at my FBI interactions in my OPI files again and see if I can pull any threads."

"Sounds good."

Lance motioned to Keira. "Anything you want to add? Suggestions on how to move forward?"

She cleared her throat, nervous about bringing this particular item up.

Lance smiled. "Whatever you've found, don't worry about sharing it. You might have figured out a clue that will put all the pieces together."

"Doubtful, but okay. I do have one thing I wanted to mention. And the only reason I'm bringing it up is because of Trent mentioning the Justice Department. That could mean any link to the FBI is important for the case, so—" she drew a deep breath "—something I was looking into last night, or rather someone, is, um, your ex-girlfriend, Ileana Sanchez. Or her married name now, Ileana Vale." At Lance's doubtful look, she rushed to explain. "I figured you might have had difficulty being objective about her, so I wanted to take a look just to make sure she's not the one who spied on the OPI missions. You haven't mentioned her when talking about who might have been double-crossing your team, so I—"

He held up his hand to stop her. "It's okay, Keira. You don't have to explain why you researched her. It makes sense to cover all our bases. The reason I haven't brought her up is because she didn't have any access to OPI case files. I didn't share my ID or password at any time. And I never discussed our cases with her."

"I would expect nothing less," she assured him. "But it's not you I was thinking could have had their access to OPI's computer system compromised, not on purpose anyway. She was with you for several years. She would have attended social functions with your team and their significant others, right? She knew them? Was friends with them?"

He was silent for a moment, then slowly nodded. "Yes. She was friends with them. But everyone knew the rules. No discussing our cases with anyone not on our team."

Trent chimed in on the phone. "Rules are made to be broken, Lance. You admitted you've kept up with your team as best you could in spite of agreeing that everyone would go their separate ways and not ever try to contact each other again. Maybe someone on your team stretched the rules too. Especially in the early days, before you realized someone was taking the information and using it to target people for execution."

Lance scrubbed his jaw. "Even if you're right, and she somehow managed to get someone on my team to talk about their cases, she wouldn't have had the power or connections to do anything with the information."

Keira cleared her throat again. "She got married shortly

after OPI broke up. The man she married is Hudson Vale. He currently runs the FBI field office in New York City."

Trent whistled. "If Vale is our guy, the mole, that just might be the connection we're looking for."

"I've never heard of Hudson Vale," Lance said, still sounding unconvinced. "Did you look into him too?"

She nodded. "He was an assistant in the same office as the FBI managers you looked into early on. While he wasn't at the top, he did have access, at least location-wise, to the offices of the big fish. If he's dirty, if he has relationships with those in organized crime, he might be someone we should look at more closely. Maybe Trent and the UB team can dig in and see if it pans out."

"Lance?" Trent asked. "If you feel strongly about this, I won't look into it."

He frowned. "Of course you should look into it. Keira did an excellent job discovering a potential link to someone in the FBI who could be passing information along. But I'm still not convinced that Ileana would have the access to even get the information. There's only so much my team would have shared, even over a few pints of beer at a team gathering."

Keira twisted her hands together on top of the table.

Lance arched his brows. "There's more?"

"Just one more thing I wanted to mention that goes along with what you just said. Back at UB headquarters, when you were telling all of us about how you got started with OPI, you mentioned that you were following the criminology track in college. You also said that Ileana was majoring in information technology, computer programming specifically. I just wondered how good she was and whether she may have been swayed to put her skills into, well, hacking. If so, she could have hacked into your

OPI computer system. Did you two, um, live together at some point? Where she'd have access to your computer when you were gone or sleeping?"

His jaw worked, and the skin along it turned white as if he were clenching his teeth. Finally, he nodded. "We shared an apartment my senior year. And once I bought a house, she moved in and out depending on how our relationship was going at the time. I have no idea if she's skilled enough to have hacked into OPI's system. But she definitely would have had plenty of opportunities."

Trent filled in the awkward silence that had fallen over the meeting. "We'll jump on this and look into what Keira found. Should have at least an initial status update for tomorrow's call. Anything else?"

Lance looked at Keira. She shook her head. "No. That's it. Thanks, Trent." He ended the call and shoved the phone into his pocket. But instead of getting up, he remained seated, staring off into space.

Keira wasn't sure what to do. She could sense his anger, the tension in his body. It pained her that she'd done that, upset him. No doubt he was remembering his old girlfriend, both the good and bad times. Maybe the best thing to do was just let him be. Give him some space.

She stood and quietly took their plates to the sink. After quickly rinsing them, she loaded them in the dishwasher. She'd clean the rest later, once he left the kitchen. When she turned around, she jumped in surprise to see him standing directly in front of her. His face seemed drawn, his eyes a darker blue than usual. And his brows were drawn down in a frown.

She cleared her throat. "I'm sorry if I overstepped. I was trying to cover everything, make sure we hadn't missed a clue. But I probably should have asked you first—"

He ever so gently pulled her against his chest and rested his cheek on the top of her head. She was so surprised that she didn't even hug him back. She just stood frozen, not sure what to think.

"No, Keira," he murmured, stroking her back. "You didn't need to ask me first or apologize. You did exactly what I should have done and I'm glad that you did." He let her go and stepped back. "Any feelings I once had for Ileana died years ago. I'm not upset that you dredged her memory up. I'm upset that you felt you had to because I hadn't done my own due diligence. Not enough, anyway. I should have…"

He shook his head. "My point is that my ego wouldn't consider that I'd made any mistakes, or that my team had, to allow her—or anyone else—access to our files through any of us. I always assumed someone we did work for in the agencies, or their boss, would have used their meetings with my boss to obtain knowledge about the cases we were working. Making assumptions appears to be my downfall. None of the people I thought could be the mole have panned out. And now you've offered an entirely new avenue to explore as to how the information may have been leaked."

He finally smiled. "If you ever need a recommendation to help you with advancement to detective, I'll be happy to provide you one. You're proving to be a better detective than me."

She almost choked, then coughed. "Uh, no. I'm not. But I appreciate the compliment and offer."

He cocked his head. "There seems to be some hesitation there."

"I just, well, honestly I've been thinking that law enforcement may not be the right fit for me. The more I think about it, the more right it feels not to return to my old job. It was a way for me to heal, to feel I was in control after having that stolen from me so long ago. But I don't get the satisfaction at my job that I always expected."

"You have the skill set, Keira. Don't let anyone tell you otherwise. Maybe Maple Falls just isn't the right place to exercise it. Whatever you do, I hope you don't make a quick decision. Think long and hard before giving up a career that might end up providing far more satisfaction—in the right place, working for the right boss—than you might expect."

"I appreciate the advice."

"Or you're secretly thinking it's none of my business."

Her face warmed.

He laughed. "Now that all of that is out of the way, let's get to work."

"Right. Dishes." She started to turn and he tugged her hand, keeping her where she was.

"I already told you that I'm doing the dishes, cleaning up the kitchen. But that can wait. The work I was talking about is finding Levi. Even if Ileana is the true leak at OPI, I'm not convinced that Levi isn't involved too, or responsible for Sam's murder."

"Because he stole Sam's identity."

"Exactly. Watching the farm for two days hasn't gotten us any new leads. Rather than spend another day doing the same, I'm suggesting that we do some nighttime surveillance. Maybe he's somewhere else during the day and coming back at night. We haven't seen evidence of any vehicles coming in or out, other than the man taking care of the horses. But what if he's doing what we've been doing, coming in the back way? And only coming at night? It's something to check out. We can park somewhere outside of the property and walk in through the woods this time. And see if he shows up."

She glanced at the darkness beyond the kitchen window.

His warm hand urged her face back toward him. "If you don't feel comfortable outside at night, I can do this on my own. I totally get why you're afraid of the dark."

She shivered. "It's not the dark that worries me. It's the people who hide there. Plus it's extra cold tonight. Have you seen the weather reports? It might even snow in the early morning hours."

"Like I said. I'm fine doing it by myself—"

She lightly punched his arm.

"What was that for?" He mockingly rubbed his arm as if she'd hit him really hard.

She rolled her eyes. "You're not going by yourself. I'm your backup. We'll dress in layers and bring blankets. But if my feet start to lose feeling from the cold, we're leaving."

"Deal. Wheels up in ten minutes."

She laughed and they both headed for the stairs.

THE MOON WAS bright enough that they could see fairly well outside. That helped make up for the lack of lights on Sam's property. But two hours of being there, sitting on the cold ground in the woods behind the house, had Keira shivering. Lance swore and shifted around behind her, stretching his long legs out on either side of her thighs to form a warm cocoon around her. He pulled her back against his chest and wrapped both of them in the blankets they'd brought.

His warm breath fanned her cheek as he leaned down next to her ear. "Better?"

Oh boy, was it. The heat of his body warmed her all over, turning her hormones into a flood of lava in her veins. All she had to do was ease back, unzip her jeans, turn around and they could—

"Keira? If you're still too cold, we can leave."

"What? Oh, no. I'm…much better now. Thanks."

He bent down again, giving her a doubtful look. "If you shiver again we've leaving."

"I won't. I'm warm now." *Scorching.*

He watched her for a moment, as if waiting for another shiver. When she didn't, he straightened and wrapped his arms around her waist.

They sat that way so long she really was getting toasty. In spite of the pleasure in being held so intimately by him, she was about to ask him to move back a little before she started to sweat. But then a sound interrupted the night. It was a mechanical sound, a familiar sound but one that they hadn't heard since beginning their surveillance.

She turned and looked at him. "The condenser unit just kicked on."

He nodded, hurriedly pulling the blankets off both of them. "Someone turned on the heat. Let's see who's home."

A few minutes later, they were at the back door, one on each side, pistols drawn. Keira couldn't help comparing it to the same type of situation when she and her fellow deputies were outside Rick's motel room in Maple Falls. She desperately hoped they weren't about to discover the same kind of horrific scene.

Lance silently counted down, holding up his hand. *Three. Two. One.* He stepped back and delivered a vicious kick to the doorknob. The frame split and the door crashed open. They ran inside, pistols sweeping out in front of them. A dark-haired pale man was standing in front of a couch in the main room. Moonlight coming through the ruined back door illuminated the terrified look on his face as he stared at them in shock.

Lance aimed his gun at the man's head. "Make one move, Levi, and I'll kill you just like you killed Sam."

Chapter Seventeen

Levi didn't move, not even to raise his hands as Lance pointed the gun at him. Keira wasn't even sure if he was breathing.

"Light switch?" she asked.

Levi didn't say anything. He simply stared at Lance.

"Behind me," Lance said. "To the left. Unless the place has been renovated since I was here last."

The switch was right where he'd said. She flipped it on, and overhead pot lights lit up the main room and small eat-in kitchen area off to her left.

"Cover me," Lance said, holstering his gun.

"You got it." She aimed her pistol in Levi's direction, careful not to get Lance in her sights as he pulled the other man to his feet and searched him.

Lance took a pistol from Levi's front pocket and a knife from a sheath on his ankle. After putting them in his own jacket pockets, he ordered, "Sit down."

Levi slowly sat, his gaze flitting from Lance to Keira and back again. "If this is about Sam, I swear to the good Lord above, I didn't kill him."

"Right," Lance said, his voice angry, clipped. "You just happened to be in Newtown at the same time as him, saw him get killed, then switched IDs."

Levi's eyes widened. "That's exactly what happened! Except that I didn't just happen to be there. We were friends. I was visiting. We were walking down a side street, and a car with dark-tinted windows pulled up. The passenger window rolled down and—*bam bam*—Sam fell. I ran behind a building. As soon as the shooter drove off, I rushed to Sam. But there was nothing I could do. He was… he was gone." Levi's eyes glistened with unshed tears.

"I didn't have a clue who'd shot him or why," Levi continued, "so I switched IDs in case they were going to come after me too. Sam lives, or lived, in Newtown. So there was nowhere else to look for him. But I lived in Rochester. There were plenty of places connected to me if someone was trying to find me. I hadn't exactly been living off the grid. So I figured if I pretended to be Sam, they wouldn't know where to find me as long as I didn't go anywhere I'd normally go. I had to act as if I really was dead."

"They. Who is 'they'?"

"I don't know. I assume it's whoever was after us from our OPI days. I'd honestly thought we'd left all that behind. But since I didn't know anyone else who'd want to kill Sam, I assumed our past—OPI—had caught up to us. And without knowing how they found Sam, I didn't know if they'd know how to find me. That's why I went on the run, came here to hide out until the heat died down and I could figure out my next steps."

Lance watched him intently, as if weighing his words for signs of deceit. Keira didn't know Levi or what reactions were typical for him. But every word he'd said bore a ring of truth to her. She didn't think he had anything to do with his friend's murder, which meant he likely wasn't involved in the attempted murders of her and Lance in Gatlinburg.

"What about Rick?" Lance asked. "Did you kill him too?"

Levi shot up from the couch.

Lance pulled his gun out of his holster so fast it was a blur. "Sit. Down."

The tears that had been threatening rolled down Levi's cheeks as he sat. "Rick's dead? What happened?"

"You tell me."

"I don't know. I swear."

Levi was sweating and looking down as if ashamed. He was hiding something. But Keira still couldn't picture him having killed Rick. He seemed too devastated.

As if reading her mind, Lance said, "You're hiding something, Levi. If you want to survive the night, tell the truth. All of it."

Levi swore, anger darkening his eyes. "Enough, Lance. Okay? If you don't believe me and you want to kill me, just do it. I'm tired of being accused of killing my friends."

"What are you hiding?" Lance showed no reaction to Levi's anger and cut him no slack.

Levi swore again. "Rick was religious about staying underground, using aliases, burner phones. He was more careful over the years than Sam and I have been. But he showed up in Newtown after the news reported that I'd been killed in a mugging. And before you ask, yes, I hung around a few weeks after the shooting, and that's why I know Rick was in town asking questions. I was watching for that car again, the shooter. If he'd shown up I'd have taken him out. But he didn't. And Rick left soon after checking around town. I never saw him after that and I don't think he ever saw me. I don't know where he went. And I certainly didn't know he was dead. What happened?"

Lance stood in silence.

Keira took mercy on the frustrated-looking man on the couch. "He was shot. Much like Sam was."

He squeezed his eyes shut, in obvious pain. When he opened them again, his eyes were bloodshot. "Did he suffer?"

Lance slowly holstered his gun, signaling to Keira that he'd finally accepted Sam's story.

"I was there," she told Levi, "with Rick when he died. He went...peacefully." The lie was heavy on her conscience, but she didn't want to hurt this man any more than they already had.

Lance gave her a subtle nod, letting her know he appreciated her compassion.

He sat beside Levi and put his hand on his shoulder. "I'm sorry, man. When I found out that Sam was the one who'd been killed and his ID was switched with yours, I thought you must have been the mole inside OPI."

Levi frowned. "Mole *inside* OPI? I always thought one of the higher-ups in the alphabet agencies we worked with was the one who went after us. You think it was an inside job?"

"It's a long story. But Officer Sloane and I—"

"Keira," she corrected, smiling at Levi.

Levi nodded but didn't return her smile. He seemed shell-shocked by the knowledge that yet another friend of his had been murdered. She certainly couldn't blame him.

"Keira and I," Lance said, "along with some people I work with, have been looking into why our past has come back to haunt us all again."

"Us? Did someone go after you too?"

Lance nodded. "After Keira and me. She worked Rick's case. As I said, long story. But we believe someone in the

FBI, and someone either in OPI or close to someone in OPI, worked together to pass information to some organized crime bosses. My team is probably a few days from getting the evidence together to prove it."

"This is absurd. I mean, good that you think you're close to solving this puzzle after all these years. But crazy, and scary as hell, that someone in OPI is working against us. And coming after us again." He raked his hands through his shaggy hair, which badly needed a cut. "First Murphy, then Allen, Sam, Rick. Mick too, of course."

"Mick? He's dead?"

Levi nodded. "Just a few days ago, from what I heard. Cancer. Sam had cancer too. He wouldn't have lasted much longer, a couple of months at most. That's part of why he wanted to enjoy life, quit hiding. And it's why he reached out to Ileana. He was tired and wanted to spend the rest of his days with friends. He wanted to return to Wingo too, back to his horses." He shook his head. "Now he never will." He looked up at Lance. "You didn't know about Mick? Seems like you know everything else."

Lance shook his head, no doubt hearing the bitterness in Levi's voice but choosing to let it go. "I didn't know. There aren't that many of us left. Most of the team is gone."

Levi smiled for the first time. "Guess that makes it easier to figure out who in OPI was spying on us. But for the life of me, I can't imagine any of them—Brett, Melissa, Jack—leaking information to someone to murder people." Levi cast a bleary look at Lance. "I certainly didn't spy on us and pass along information."

Lance pulled the confiscated gun and knife out of his jacket pocket and held them out to Levi. "I know you didn't. And I'm sorry I put you through hell tonight. I needed to be sure."

Levi stared at him a long moment, then nodded and took his weapons. After he sheathed the knife and slid the pistol into his pants pocket, he asked, "You said you expected to have proof soon about who's behind this. Who's your money on at OPI? Brett, Melissa or Jack?"

"Actually, Keira has a theory about that, a solid one. We've been toying with the idea that it might be—"

Headlights flashed onto the front window blinds.

Lance leaned over the couch and peered between some slats in the blinds. "A car's coming up the driveway, fast."

"Only one?" Keira asked.

He nodded. "Just one." He watched while the lights flashed away from the blinds.

A few moments later, the sound of an engine indicated that the car must have pulled up right in front of the house. Then the engine cut off, leaving nothing but eerie silence.

Chapter Eighteen

A loud knock sounded on the front door of the farmhouse. Lance motioned for everyone to be quiet. He knew exactly who it was. What he didn't know yet was whether they were the mole or just another unpleasantry from his past coming back to haunt him.

He mouthed the words *Stay here* to Keira. Then, aiming his pistol toward the floor, he jogged to the ruined back door and slipped out into the night. He carefully circled the left side of the house to the front corner, using it to shield him from their visitor's view until he assessed the situation.

Headlights no longer shone from down the long driveway. The stillness of the night wasn't broken by the sound of idling engines from hidden vehicles. Moonlight didn't reveal any dark figures skulking through the pastures. The only sound at all was repeated knocking, pounding really, on the front door. And the sound of a voice Lance had hoped never to hear again in his lifetime.

"Levi, you're in there, right? Come on. It's me, Ileana. Open up. I need to talk to you."

Lance used her distraction to run behind the car, a dark-colored Mercedes. He peered through the back windows, then the front, although it was difficult to see much because they were tinted. No movement caught his attention. And no one shot at him. So the car was likely empty. Unless someone was hiding in the trunk, she'd come alone. Or there were more people hiding in the woods somewhere, unseen and unheard.

"Levi, please. Open the door!" Ileana pounded on it again.

Hoping he was right, that she truly had come alone, Lance crept up behind her. Going with his instincts, that she was the one who'd betrayed them all, he pressed the muzzle of his gun against the back of her head.

She froze, her hand in the air, ready to knock again.

"What do you want, Ileana?" he demanded.

She stiffened, then slowly turned around, eyes wide as she backed up a step. "Lance?" She looked past him, then left and right, as if expecting others to be with him. "What are you doing here?" She frowned. "And for goodness sakes, put the gun down. I'm not a burglar or robber or whatever you're thinking."

"You have no idea what I'm thinking. What do you want?"

She frowned at the gun he had aimed at her midsection now. "Can I at least lower my hands?"

"No."

She swore, calling him several unsavory names. It certainly wasn't the first time he'd heard them from her.

"I'm not going to ask you again," he warned.

"Oh for the love of... I'm here to see Levi. Is he here or not?"

The door behind her opened. Levi stood on the threshold. "I'm here," he said.

She whirled around. "Oh my goodness. You're okay? I

was so worried. I thought he'd killed you too." She smiled and held out her arms as if to hug him.

He held up a hand to stop her. "Wait."

Her arms slowly lowered. "What's going on? Why are you both treating me as if I'm a stranger?"

"Keira," Lance called out.

"Right behind you."

He glanced over his shoulder, surprised to see her emerge from a crouch behind the car, her pistol down toward the ground. "You followed me?"

"I'm your backup. One day you're going to learn to stop telling me to wait while you run into danger. It's never going to work."

"It appears that I'm a slow learner."

"You certainly are." She winked.

He chuckled. "I was going to ask if you would pat Ileana down."

"Pat me down?" Ileana practically shrieked the words. "What the heck does that mean? Who are you anyway? Lancelot's future ex-girlfriend?" She smirked.

"Officer Keira Sloane," she said, as she moved past him. "I need to check you for any weapons."

"What? No way. Don't you touch me, you little—"

Keira grabbed Ileana's arms and whipped her around, then thoroughly searched her. All the while, Ileana called her even more colorful names than she'd tossed at Lance. Keira straightened and held out her hand. "Give me your purse."

Ileana clutched it against her chest. "No. This is ridiculous. I'm leaving." She stalked toward her car. But as soon as she passed Keira, Keira snatched Ileana's purse.

"I assume your keys are in here," she said. "I'll return

this inside." She jogged up the steps and brushed past Levi, heading inside.

Ileana sputtered in outrage. "You have no right to treat me this way. You all have some explaining to do."

Lance holstered his pistol and motioned toward the house.

She huffed and marched back to Levi. "Are you really going to let them treat me this way?"

Levi looked at Lance, his expression unreadable. "Lance has his reasons. I'm sure he'll explain them to us." He put his hand on the back of her jacket and ushered her inside with him.

After one last look around, Lance headed in as well and bolted the door behind him.

"She has a gun in her purse." Keira tossed it onto the kitchen island.

"Yeah, well," Ileana said. "I'm a woman, traveling alone. Of course I have a gun, for protection. You're one to talk, whoever you are. Everyone here has a gun except Levi."

Levi didn't bother to correct her on her assumption that he was unarmed. "You have a black eye."

"Well thank you for stating the obvious," she said.

He stepped closer, clearly concerned. "How did you get that?"

She arched a perfectly plucked eyebrow. "My husband's fist. It's not the first time either."

Levi pulled Ileana to the couch and sat beside her. "You never told me or Sam that he ever hit you."

"It's not exactly something to brag about."

"Do you need some ice for that?" Lance asked, doing the right thing when he really wanted to throw some handcuffs on Ileana and interrogate her.

"Finally found your manners, Lancelot?"

He gritted his teeth. "Don't call me that."

"Whatever. No, I don't need any ice. Like I said, my... difficulties with my husband aren't new. And they're no one else's concern. That's not why I'm here."

"Why *are* you here?" Lance asked. "And how did you know that Levi would be here?"

The sound of running water had them looking toward the kitchen area. Keira had just wet a paper towel under the faucet and was wringing it out. She pumped a few drops of soap onto it, then took it to Ileana.

"What do you want?" Ileana frowned up at her.

"Proof." Keira rubbed the paper towel across Ileana's black eye.

Ileana cried out and shoved her hand away. "What the heck? Are you a sadist or something? Why did you do that?" She gently patted at her eye. "That really hurt, you little witch. And you've got soap all over it."

"I've been called worse." Keira held up the paper towel for Lance's inspection. "No makeup. She's not faking her injury."

Lance grinned. "Smart."

Keira smiled back and threw away the paper towel.

Levi faced Ileana on the couch, his expression one of concern as she continued to wipe at her eye. "Some... stuff is going on here. I'm sorry you got caught up in it. Now isn't a good time for a visit—"

"It's three in the morning," Lance announced. "She's not here on a social call. Why, exactly, are you here, Ileana? And how did you know that Levi was here?"

Levi frowned at the suspicion in Lance's tone but didn't interfere.

Ileana seemed disappointed that he'd let Lance speak that way to her. But she also seemed to realize that refusing to explain wasn't getting her anywhere. "I'd hoped that Levi was here. But I wasn't sure. I'd already looked everywhere else I could for him. And I called a million times without an answer. Either his phone is off or broken. This farm is Sam's family's place. I was hoping against hope to find Levi here."

She put her hand on his thigh. "I'm so relieved that you're okay. Hudson snooped in my phone and discovered I was having an affair with Sam. He shot Sam. And he bragged about it to me." She dabbed at both eyes this time, which were shiny and bright as if she were holding back tears. "When he saw in the news that you were killed in a mugging, he was furious. He said he must have gotten the wrong guy. He's been on the warpath ever since, trying to find you. He thinks you're Sam, with you two looking so much alike and all. If he finds you, he's going to kill you too."

"You came here to warn me?"

"Of course. What other reason would there be? Hudson is finally out of town on a business trip. This is the first time I've been able to get away in months." She motioned toward her black eye. "Of course he gave me this as a parting gift before he left, a warning not to go anywhere."

Levi patted her shoulder. "You should have told me about him." He winced. "Or told Sam. We'd have helped you. He might be a big shot at the FBI, but he's still going to get what's coming to him. We'll get justice for Sam, and for you. I know you really cared about Sam."

She sniffed. "Of course I did. Not telling both of you about what Hudson was doing was me trying to protect you. I wanted to take care of it on my own. But he found out anyway. And I couldn't... I couldn't protect Sam." She sniffed again.

"Is that true, Levi?" Lance asked. "Ileana and Sam were having an affair?"

Ileana rolled her eyes. "Of course it's true. Why would I lie?"

"Levi?" Lance repeated.

Ileana stewed in anger but didn't say anything.

Levi nodded. "Like I said earlier, neither of us was staying low under the radar. He saw something in the society pages in the *New York Times* about her one day. He'd always...always liked her. But of course, when you two were together, he never would have dared to act on his feelings."

"I know. Sam was a good guy."

Levi smiled sadly. "He was. Anyway, he was lonely, you know? He just wanted to see an old friend, a familiar face, again. She agreed to come visit in Newtown and, well, things progressed from there."

"Ileana," Lance asked, "how did you know it was Sam who was killed and not Levi? As you said, the news reported Levi as the victim of the mugging."

She shook her head in exasperation. "My husband was bragging that he'd killed my lover. Then he saw in the news that Levi was killed instead and was furious. I needed to know the truth, whether it was Sam or Levi who'd been killed. And I wanted to warn whichever one was still alive to hide from Hudson. What do you think I'd have done? Nothing? Just sit on my hands while my husband killed another one of my friends? What kind of person do you think I am, Lance?"

When Lance didn't answer, her face reddened. "Good grief. We had our bad times, plenty of them. But we had good times too. I don't understand why you're interrogating me like this. I had to go to the police in Newtown and look at that awful autopsy photo to confirm it was Levi. And then, of course I knew it wasn't."

"Did you tell the police that?" Levi asked.

"No, no, dear. I don't understand why you let people think that you were dead instead of Sam, but I assumed you had a good reason. Part of me wondered whether you knew Hudson had killed Sam and you switched places to try to keep Hudson from going after you too. After all, the three of us visited quite often in Newtown when Sam and I were an item. Hudson probably realized that when he snooped through my phone."

She sniffed again, although Lance didn't notice any actual tears.

"Once we get you somewhere safe, we need to switch that headstone in the cemetery," she said. "It's not right that your name is on Sam's grave. He deserves better than that."

Levi patted her shoulder. "He does. I agree."

Ileana motioned toward her black eye. "This thing hurts like the devil. Get me some ice. But first I have to pee, and clean the rest of the soap off my face. You're not going to try to stop me from using the bathroom are you?"

Levi held his hands up apologetically. "Course not. It's the last door on the—"

"I know where it is. Been here before." She glared at Lance. "Years ago, with my ex." She marched down the hallway and into the bathroom, slamming the door behind her.

Keira let out a long breath. "She's something."

Levi's chin raised. "She's a good person. She's obviously been through trauma with her husband and losing Sam. And it didn't exactly help that we held her at gunpoint when she got here."

Lance and Keira exchanged a long glance. He sighed and scrubbed his jaw. "Right before she arrived, Keira and I were going to explain that we believe Ileana may have used her computer programming expertise to hack into our OPI databases. With her marrying the head of an FBI field office later on, it lends more credence to that theory."

Levi shook his head. "No way. Whoever got that information is responsible, either directly or indirectly, for people being killed. Ileana would never want any of us hurt. That's why she's here. To protect me."

"Would you bet your life on that?" Keira asked.

Levi frowned at her. "As a matter of fact, I would."

"You saw her Mercedes out front," Lance said. "It's black with dark-tinted windows. Could that have been the car used by the shooter who killed Sam?"

His face reddened. "Of course it could have. Because her husband, Hudson, was driving it."

Lance and Keira exchanged another glance.

"What?" Levi demanded. "What aren't you telling me?"

Keira gave him a sympathetic look. "Lance and I were performing surveillance earlier, to see if you were here. Since Hudson Vale's name recently came up in our investigation, Lance tapped some resources and contacts that his company has with the FBI. Hudson was out of the country when Sam was shot."

"Levi," Lance said, "when Sam was shot, is there any possibility that a woman could have been driving the car?"

Levi's face turned pale. "I don't...maybe." He glanced down the hall.

"Ileana's been in that bathroom a long time," Lance said. "Keira, did you see a cell phone in her purse?"

"Ah, shoot. In her pocket. I noticed it when I searched her for weapons and didn't think anything about it."

They both drew their guns and took off down the hallway.

Lance busted in the door without even knocking. He swore when he saw the empty room, and the open window above the toilet.

Keira sucked in a sharp breath. "The mirror."

Written in toothpaste were three words.

You're all dead.

They whirled around and ran out of the bathroom.

Levi's eyes widened in shock when he saw them. "She's gone?"

"Out the window," Lance said. "We need to—"

"I'll stop her." Levi ran for the front door.

"Wait," Lance yelled, rushing toward him.

Levi threw the door open. The crack of rifle fire filled the house. Levi's body jerked as the bullets struck his body. He was dead before he even hit the floor.

"No!" Lance yelled. "Damn it. Not you too." He started toward his friend.

Keira jumped in front of him and shoved at his chest. "He's gone. There's nothing you can do for him. We need to get out of here." She tugged his arm, trying to pull him toward the back door.

He stood frozen, unmoving. Blood pooled beneath Levi's body. The door gaped open, revealing the moonlit front yard. And the sound of an engine starting up.

Ileana.

He started toward the door again.

Keira slammed her body against him, knocking him to the side a few feet, but he managed to keep his balance. "Stop it. She's getting away."

She slammed the flat of her palms against his chest,

blocking his way. "Wait. Listen to me. What if Ileana wasn't the one who shot Levi? You saw what she wrote on that mirror. Do you really think she would try to take on all three of us without help? She's not alone in this. Her hired hands must have just arrived and hid out front. Heck, she probably gave herself that black eye to get Levi's sympathy. Rather than her being a victim of domestic violence, I'd bet money her FBI husband is in on this with her. His men are likely out front right now. We have to—"

Another round of gunfire shattered the night. Bullets strafed through the open front door. Lance and Keira dove behind the kitchen island, low to the ground. As soon as there was a pause, they both jumped up and ran out the back door.

Chapter Nineteen

The rumble of more engines had Keira and Lance turning when they reached the woods, looking back toward the house. Three SUVs with gunmen hanging out the windows were barreling down the long road into the farm.

"Good grief," Keira said. "How many of them are there? We need help. A lot of help."

Lance shoved his phone in his pocket. "I just tried to call Trent. They're jamming the signal. We need to get out of their jammer's range."

They took off running again, crashing through the woods, leaping over the pallet of blankets they'd left from their earlier surveillance. They'd almost reached Lance's SUV when a flash of moonlight on metal had both of them stopping and ducking behind a tree. More vehicles were roaring up the back road.

"It was an ambush all along." Lance swore. "I'll bet all Ileana wanted to do was confirm how many people were in the house before she signaled her husband to bring in his mercenaries. Come on, this way." They took off running through the woods, leaving the back road and the house behind.

"What exactly attracted you to that woman in the first place?" Keira asked as she struggled to keep up with his long strides while scanning the trees for signs of gunmen.

He grinned. "I was young and stupid, and she had a figure."

"Men."

The sound of shouting off to their left had them jumping behind some thick pine trees.

Keira held her pistol in both hands, her lungs screaming for air as she tried to drag in quiet, short breaths to avoid anyone hearing her. Behind another tree, Lance mirrored her position, his chest heaving as he too tried not to make any noise. Very slowly, he leaned around his tree, then jerked back. He held up two fingers and motioned to his right. Then he held up two more and motioned to the left. She nodded to let him know she understood.

Could she and Lance take four guys out without being shot themselves? Possibly. Probably. She was good with a gun. And Lance, well, he was good at everything, as proven by his performance at the cabin. But eliminating four enemies when there were dozens out searching for them would only give away their location.

The sound of voices gradually faded amid shouts of a man somewhere behind them ordering someone to get some flashlights.

Lance leaned around the tree again, then straightened. He gave her a thumbs-up, then a rolling motion with his hand for her to follow him. The two of them took off in a jog toward the right end of the property in relation to the back of the house.

She was soon considering begging for mercy, desperately needing to stop and catch her breath. He was obviously in great shape, and their fast jog through the woods didn't seem to bother him at all. But she had a stitch in her side, her ribs were still bruised and she was gasping for air. There would definitely be more Pilates in her future, if she survived tonight.

Thankfully, Lance raised a hand and signaled her to stop so she didn't have to embarrass herself by asking for a reprieve. But when she saw why he'd stopped, she vigorously began shaking her head.

No, she mouthed, afraid to talk out loud in case any gunmen were close by.

He pointed at the building that housed the horses and nodded yes.

No, she mouthed again, shaking her head so hard her hair flew around her face.

Lance pointed in the direction of the house, mimicking a gun with his thumb and forefinger and firing over and over, reminding her they were severely outnumbered and had no choice.

And, dang it, he was right. They didn't. No matter how good a shot either of them were, they couldn't win against such overwhelming odds if they were discovered.

She glared her displeasure at him.

Sorry, he silently mouthed, then motioned for her to follow him again.

I can do this. I can do this. She silently repeated the phrase over and over in her mind as she followed him into the stables.

Taking everything one step at a time helped. She was the lookout at the door while he did whatever he needed to do inside. It gave her a task to focus on instead of wondering how in the world she was going to manage riding a horse when the closest she'd ever been to one before was at Lance's stables in Gatlinburg. Feeding a horse a carrot without getting your fingers bitten off was one thing.

Clinging to its back without falling was something entirely different.

Sending up a quick prayer, she pulled her burner phone out. *Please let there be a signal.* She pressed the numbers 911 and listened. Nothing but static. Dang it.

The sound of hooves shuffling against the hay-covered floors had her turning around. She immediately backed up, bumping into the doorframe as four impossibly tall horses surrounded her.

Lance appeared between them and grabbed her hand. "Come on," he whispered.

"Wait. Which one is mine? They don't even have anything to hold on to."

He grinned and whispered, "Saddles and reins?"

"Whatever," she whispered back. "I'll take my chances with the gunmen." She backed away from the horses milling around and started for the door.

Lance tugged on her hand. "Come on. We're not riding these horses. Those are the decoys."

A moment later she was standing in front of a huge black horse with a saddle and reins, as he'd stated. But there was no way she was getting on it. "It's huge. Way bigger than the others."

"That's why I picked him. He can handle both of us."

"Wait. Both of us?"

"You didn't expect me to ask you to gallop all by yourself when you've never sat on a horse before, did you?"

"Well, yes. I guess I did. Wait. Gallop? That's the really fast gear, right?"

He chuckled and put his foot in the metal thing hanging from the saddle. Then he vaulted up onto the horse. She stared at him, at his hand as he reached down for her.

"Sorry, I can't. I just can't." She hurried toward the other horses that were docilely standing just inside the door.

The sound of hooves clicking and stomping against the floor had her whirling around. Lance leaned down with both arms and snatched her around the waist. He swung her up behind him without even slowing down. Keira let out a squeak of fear as she landed on the horse's bottom behind the saddle and it gave a light kick.

"Hang on," Lance called out.

She wrapped her arms around his waist, locking her hands together against him.

"Hang on," he repeated.

She let out another squeak as the horse leaped forward. The other horses, the ones he'd called decoys, bolted out through the doors and raced toward the house. Lance jerked the reins of the horse they were on, and it dug in its heels, rounding the building and then taking off in a run deeper into the woods.

Keira knew she should have had her gun out and watched for anyone after them. But even if she somehow managed to hang on with one hand to free her gun, she'd never be able to aim it while bouncing on the back of this beast. She'd likely end up shooting herself, the horse or, worse, Lance. She suddenly realized that every spaghetti Western she'd ever seen was a passel of lies. No hero could manage this jolting, bumpy roller-coaster ride and manage to aim a gun at any bad guys. It just wasn't possible.

Bam, bam, bam.

Her eyes flew open, her ears ringing. Lance was holstering his pistol, having just shot it. She looked off to their left and saw two bodies lying on the ground, their guns dropped beside them.

Holy moly.

She blinked in shock and immediately revised her negative view of those spaghetti Westerns. Or, rather, she revised her view of Lance. He'd already been amazing. Now he was a hero in a whole other way. Her earlier fears dimmed and she straightened a bit, still hanging on for dear life. But no longer convinced they were definitely going to die.

Maybe they had a chance after all.

Bam. A gunshot sounded close by.

Lance suddenly arched against her. The horse whinnied as Lance jerked the reins. Then they were falling onto the ground. Her breath left her in a rush as she rolled underneath a scratchy bush, headlong into a mound of pine needles. Gasping like a fish out of water, she desperately tried to make her lungs work again. Her ears were as useless as her lungs. All she could hear was a low buzzing sound.

The horse bolted past her, its hooves flashing in the moonlight through the branches of the shrubs surrounding her as it galloped away from the house, minus her and Lance.

Where was he? He had to be near her, somewhere.

Her lungs finally expanded in a rush of cold air. She coughed and gasped, everything hurting as she got up on her hands and knees. What had happened? Gunfire. She'd heard a shot. Only one this time. And it wasn't Lance who was shooting. Oh God, please, no. Lance couldn't have been shot, could he?

The answer to that was brutally clear when some men shouted about ten yards away, motioning toward something on the ground. A man, a tall broad-shouldered man with a dark jacket and short dark hair. Lance.

A sob rose in her throat. She pressed a hand to her mouth to keep from crying out. Four men. There were four of them, poking at Lance as if he were roadkill. He suddenly moaned and swiped at one of the men's hands. Keira had never seen something so wonderful in her life. He was alive. Lance had either been shot or knocked out from the fall off the startled horse. But he was alive. Which meant there was still hope. It also meant that it was up to her to save him. She didn't know if she could shoot four men quickly enough to avoid being shot herself. But she was sure going to try.

She clawed for her pistol as two of the men grabbed Lance's arms and legs, hoisting him up between them. Her mind reeled in horror when she realized her gun was gone. It must have fallen when she was thrown from the horse.

Three more men, each holding rifles, joined the original four. They seemed to be arguing about something. Then they split up, some heading toward the house, others going in the direction that she and Lance had been riding. And another...coming straight toward her.

She bit her lip against the urge to cry out in pain as she scrambled around in the leaves, searching for her pistol. Everything hurt. She didn't think any bones were broken, just badly bruised, like her ribs that were really hurting again. But that was the least of her worries. If the man didn't stop or turn away, she was about to be discovered. And then Lance would have no one to save him.

The gun was nowhere to be found. And the man was getting far too close, scanning the woods near her. He didn't seem to know she was there. But he'd see her soon if she didn't do something. She continued to flail in the leaves, trying to find her pistol. Something sharp seemed to slice into her hand. She sucked in a breath, then pulled it up out of the leaves. It was just a stick, but it was thick and sharp on one end where it must have twisted and broken from the shrubs as she'd fallen. It was also slick with blood from where it had cut her hand. Stealing herself against the pain, she grabbed it and swung it up and out just as the man peered over the bushes.

It jammed deep into his throat. His eyes widened in shock, his hands clawing at his bleeding neck. Then he slowly crumpled to the ground.

Keira stared at his lifeless body, shocked that she was the one who'd done that. She'd never once shot anyone in the line of duty. And here she'd just stabbed one to death. With a branch. Hysterical laughter started to bubble up in her throat. She swore and forced herself to draw deep even breaths.

Think, Keira. Think.

How could she save Lance against dozens of armed gunmen with only a tree branch as a weapon? The answer was painfully clear. She couldn't. She had to get help. But how? There were men all through these woods. How could she escape all of them and make it back in time to help Lance before it was too late?

If it wasn't too late already.

She reached in her pocket for her cell phone, relieved when her hand tightened around it. Maybe she was far enough away that the cell signal was no longer blocked and she could call Trent or 911 or both. She pressed Trent's number and Send, then listened. The same buzzing sound she'd heard before sounded again. The signal was blocked. She'd heard somewhere that text messages went through better than calls when signal strength wasn't strong. She tapped in a quick message to Trent and pressed Send. Then she sent the same message to Asher. But both texts popped up on the screen with red exclamation points beside them.

Text failed to send.

She groaned and shoved the phone back in her pocket. Despair like she'd never felt before flooded through her. If she could trade her life for Lance's, she would willingly do so. But she was under no pretenses that the men after them would take that trade. They'd kill both her and Lance.

Lord, please. Help me figure out what to do. Give me a sign.

A whinny sounded behind her. She slowly turned around. The horse that she and Lance had been riding stood only a few yards away, calmly munching on some brown grass beneath a tree.

Keira swore and looked up at the sky. "You couldn't have given me a different sign? Like maybe a truck?"

As if in response, lightning cracked across the night sky. And it started to rain.

"Okay, okay. I won't look a gift horse in the mouth. Ha ha." She pushed herself to her feet and slowly advanced on the scary beast staring at her as if she were a bug it wanted to squash.

Chapter Twenty

Lance glared at the no fewer than ten men crammed into the small farmhouse's main room, milling around as the worst aggressor stood in front of him. No doubt him being tied to a dining room chair made Ileana think she was safe. She certainly thought so, the way she kept smirking at him and pacing back and forth. But she wasn't that confident, or she wouldn't be staying out of reach of his feet.

One step in the wrong direction and he'd sweep her legs out from under her. He'd follow that up by slamming on top of her, chair and all. He had every movement planned. But it was his last resort. Because the one thing he knew for a certainty was that if he attacked Ileana, every man in the room would riddle him with bullets.

Since there didn't appear to be a way out of here with his life anyway, the only thing really holding him back was Keira. When the bullet had grazed his head, knocking him silly, everything had gone fuzzy. He'd managed to climb out of the fog when he was being hauled out of the woods. But he had no idea what had happened to Keira. For her sake, he was trying to hold his temper. Stall. Do whatever he had to do to stay alive. Because if there was even one chance in a thousand that he could do something to help her, to save her, he would.

No matter how much torture he had to endure.

Ileana glanced at her phone again, her still-beautiful face drawn with impatience.

"What's wrong, Ileana?" he goaded. "Not allowed to make any decisions without hubby's permission?"

She scoffed. "Hubby? Are you kidding me? That weak, useless excuse for a man?"

"Ah. So you feel the same affection for him that you once felt for me."

"Shut up."

"If he's so weak, why are you taking orders from him? Why did you feed him information about OPI? Why do you let him beat you?"

She let out an angry screech and motioned to the man closest to Lance. He slammed his fist against Lance's jaw, whipping his head to the side.

Lance held back a groan. And smiled. The man raised his fist again.

"Stop," Ileana ordered. "I need him conscious and able to talk. Break his jaw, and he won't be able to answer my questions."

"I thought I already answered your questions," Lance said. "There are more?"

She stopped in front of him, her hands fisted at her sides. "You haven't answered anything! Where's the rest of your team? Where's Brett? Melissa? Where's Jack? Tell me and I'll let you go."

"Where's Keira? Tell me and I'll let you live."

Her phone buzzed in her pocket. She glared at him before checking the screen. Then she smiled. It was that smile that had him going cold inside.

"Bring another chair over here," she called out. "We're about to have company."

It took every ounce of control that Lance had not to shout in rage when two men stepped through the back door opening, dragging Keira between them. A chair was brought over close to Lance. And Keira was quickly tied into it, just like he was. Her head hung limply. Lance watched in terror for her chest to rise. Finally, it did. Thank God. She was alive.

Ileana was suddenly there with a glass of water. She tossed it in Keira's face.

Keira jerked in her chair, blinking at the water dribbling down her cheeks. She blinked again, then looked around as if only just then realizing where she was. She groaned, and Lance could have sworn he heard her curse beneath her breath.

"Hey, beautiful," he whispered.

Her eyes widened. Tears sprang into them and she smiled, drawing his attention to her cracked and bleeding lip. "My hero," she whispered back. "Glad to see you still breathing."

"I'm hardly a hero. But ditto on the breathing thing."

"Well, isn't this sickeningly sweet," Ileana said. "Two little lovebirds right before they die."

Keira completely ignored Ileana, keeping her gaze on Lance. "I rode that beast to get help. Unfortunately when I got to the road, I didn't quite clear the fence."

He stared at her in shock. "You rode the horse? By yourself?"

"I'm pretty sure it felt sorry for me. Well, until it saw the fence. Then it decided to get rid of me and veer the other way. The horse went left, I went straight. Before I could get my feet under me, some of Ileana's jerks grabbed me. So much for my attempt to save you."

"Enough!" Ileana yelled. "I'm about to vomit. Let's

get down to business. Our dearly departed Sam was nice enough to get cancer and decide he wanted to reunite with old friends before he died. That's what finally got the ball rolling again on the stupid OPI train and opened the door for me to find and eliminate the rest of you. I failed my uncle when things fell apart with that company. I finally have a chance to redeem myself now. All I need to do is find the last three team members. If you tell me nicely, I'll have both of you killed quickly. Continue to defy me and you'll suffer a slow, agonizing death. Your choice."

Keira finally turned and gave Ileana her full attention. "Don't you have to call your husband for permission to do any of this first?"

Ileana slapped her so fast Lance didn't get a chance to whip his legs out to stop her.

Keira ran her tongue over her freshly bleeding mouth, then smiled.

Lance was proud of her courage. But he wanted to shake her for angering Ileana further. He spoke again to distract Ileana from hurting Keira again.

"I don't know where they are," he said. "Who's this uncle you mentioned? Is he yours and your husband's mob contact? The one you both sold information to for years, causing innocent people to die?"

"Stop dragging Hudson into this. He's as moral and ethical as they come. And he never hit me by the way. This black eye was my doing, to get sympathy from Levi. Hudson would never hit a woman, even if she deserved it." She rolled her eyes, obviously not thinking of that as a compliment. "He never knew I was the one getting information. And the people who died were far from innocent. They were traitors, snitches, the worst of the worst. They deserved exactly what they got."

Lance made no attempt to hide his disgust. "How I ever thought you were a decent human being all those years ago is a mystery I'll likely never solve."

She screeched her rage again. But this time, she didn't stop to direct someone else. She hauled back to slap Lance just as she'd done to Keira. But this time he was ready for it. He whipped her legs out from under her and crashed down on top of her, twisting so the arm of the chair slammed against her throat. He was almost immediately yanked back up, still tied to the chair. But the damage was done. Ileana's face was already turning blue as she made gagging sounds and clawed at her crushed windpipe.

Her men all seemed to be in a state of panic, converging on her and dragging her into the dining room. They placed her on the table and started shouting orders at each other, trying to figure out how to help her.

Lance had been twisting and pulling at the ropes behind his back ever since he'd been captured. With the fall to the floor and him and his chair being hastily set back up, the ropes had loosened enough that he was able to yank his hands free.

Keira stared at him, her eyes wide with concern as he made short work of the rest of the ropes and knelt down behind her to work on hers.

"Go, go," she whispered. "Get out of here before they realize you're free."

"I'm not leaving you." He yanked and tugged at her ropes, swearing at how tight they were.

"I mean it, Lance. Please. I can't handle seeing you die. I'd rather die myself knowing you were going to be okay. Go."

He tugged at her ropes, finally loosening them. "I love

you too," he whispered, grinning as he yanked her up to standing.

"Hey, hey, stop!" one of the men yelled. He drew his gun.

Lance jumped in front of Keira, shielding her with his body.

"Wait," another man yelled at the first, shoving his hand up toward the ceiling just as the gun went off. "We can't kill them until she's done with them."

"Look at her," the shooter argued. "She's purple. She's not telling us anything."

Lance and Keira were already running for the front door, not waiting around as the argument continued behind them.

He threw the door open and they both ran outside. Lights flashed across their faces, making it impossible to see past them. The sound of dozens of guns being ratcheted and loaded had him glancing at Keira in frustration. "I'm so sorry."

She smiled. "Me too. I wanted to see how this thing between us ended. And I really wanted to find out what comes after the kissing part." She winked.

He grinned. Then they both raised their hands.

The sounds of men jogging toward them had Lance stepping in front of Keira again. She swore and tried to stand beside him. Just when they expected to be shot, the men passed them and ran inside the house.

Gunshots boomed. Glass shattered. Shouts and screams sounded.

"Get them out of here," a voice that Lance didn't recognize called out.

"We've got them."

That voice, he did recognize. He blinked against the harsh lights, then grinned when Trent and Asher ran up to them. Trent grabbed Lance's arm. Asher grabbed Keira.

They all raced off to the side of the house, away from the gunfire that was already slowing.

Kneeling down behind the engine block of one of the cars that had pulled up, the four of them waited until someone called for a cease-fire.

"All clear," someone from inside shouted.

People started running in and out of the house, taking control of the scene. Lance hugged Keira close to his side as they straightened. When yellow crime scene tape came out and someone began using it to cordon off the area, Lance and Keira looked at Trent and Asher in question.

"What's happening?" Lance asked. "Who are these people? How did you find us? What are—"

"Enough, enough." Trent grinned. "Ask Keira here. She's the one responsible for us getting here in the nick of time."

She blinked. "I am? What do you mean?"

"The text messages. We were already in the area because we'd hooked up with Hudson Vale to find Ileana and—"

"Wait," Lance said. "Ileana's husband? Isn't he the FBI mole?"

Asher shook his head, joining the conversation. "No. Ileana was the only mole. No one in the FBI was involved. She hacked OPI's computers and fed the info directly to a mob boss."

"Let me guess," Lance said. "Her uncle."

"Later you'll have to tell me how you knew that. Her relationship to him was buried under a web of changed names and forged birth certificates."

"It wasn't any brilliant investigative skills on my part," Lance said. "She told me a few minutes ago."

"Can we get back to these text messages you mentioned?" Keira said. "They blocked our cell phones. Nothing I sent could have gone through."

"They did," he said. "You must have gotten the phone out of the cell signal jammer range at some point, because the texts told us exactly where you were and what was going on. We—us and the FBI guys—were trying to figure out where exactly this farm was located. But until those texts came in, we were flying blind." He patted Keira on the shoulder. "You did it. You saved the day."

"No, I didn't. You all did." She smiled up at Lance. "And you did. You gave us both the time we needed to survive. You're my hero, truly."

He smiled and pressed a tender kiss against her forehead. "That's debatable. I'm just glad it all worked out. Or has it? Trent, Asher, you said you brought Vale here. Does that mean what I hope it means?"

They nodded. Trent said, "We have all the evidence we need to put Ileana away. And her uncle. Hudson Vale, the FBI, they had nothing to do with anything that happened. He was livid when he found out what Ileana had done. Due to a conflict of interest, of course, there's another FBI guy running this scene. But Hudson is here too. He wanted to be there when she was arrested."

"I don't think that's going to happen," Lance said.

"No? Why not?"

"I'm pretty sure she's dead."

They stared at him in surprise.

"I'm not proud of it," Lance said.

Keira tightened her arm around his waist. "There were at least a dozen armed men inside—"

"Ten," Lance corrected.

"Dozens more outside," Asher added.

"Right," Keira said. "In spite of all that, Lance did everything he could to protect me. And he did. Ileana would have killed us both. And even with all those thugs around us, and him tied to a chair, he managed to take her down. He truly saved both of us." She smiled. "But you two get credit too. You did arrive, as you said, in the nick of time."

They laughed, then sobered as a body bag was carried out the door, escorted in part by a very pale, defeated-looking man. Lance recognized him as Hudson Vale because of the research he'd done. From Keira's gasp beside him, he knew she did too. The man was moral and ethical, just as Ileana had accused. And in spite of what she'd done, which would no doubt end his career with the FBI, he'd ensured that justice was served.

An EMT ran up to Keira and Lance. "I was told you were both hurt. Do you need a stretcher?"

Keira looked up at Lance. "Your head is bleeding."

"It's mostly stopped now. You're black and blue. And your lip is bleeding."

"It's mostly stopped now."

They both laughed.

"We're fine," they told the EMT, laughing again when they said the same thing at the same time.

He gave them an odd look, then headed off in search of someone else to help.

"Hey, Lance. Catch."

He turned, and Trent tossed him something. A key fob. Lance looked at him in question.

"The only white SUV out here." He pointed. "Go on. You two have been through enough tonight. Head back to wherever you've been staying. Asher and I will catch a ride with someone else and we can talk tomorrow."

Keira frowned. "There aren't any hotels around here.

You can come to the house Lance rented. It's big enough for all of us."

Trent grinned. "I don't think Lance would agree with you. Like I said, we'll catch up tomorrow."

"Really late tomorrow," Lance called out.

Trent laughed as Lance grabbed Keira's hand and practically dragged her to the SUV. When they reached it, he turned her around so he could look in her eyes. He cupped her face with his hands and stared down at her in wonder. "I know it seems crazy to say this, so soon. But I've never been more sure of anything in my life. Keira, I—"

"—love you," they both said at the same time.

"Wow," she breathed.

"Wow," he echoed.

They kissed, and when they broke apart, tears were streaming down her cheeks.

"Keira? What's wrong?"

"They're happy tears. I suppose this means you'll be asking me for a date now."

He shook his head. "No. I've decided against that."

Her smiled faded. "What? I don't—"

"I was thinking of asking you something else instead. Marry me?"

She stared at him, her mouth falling open in shock.

The confidence he'd felt moments before took a dive. "Or, if it's too soon—"

She burst out laughing. "Too soon? We've never even been on a date."

"Right. Too soon. I've been worried this whole time about going too fast, about you possibly regretting this later. I want you to be sure, even though I know that I am. I'll wait as long as you want. We can take it slow and—"

"Yes!" She smiled. "The answer is yes!"

He stared at her, his mouth going dry. "Can you repeat that? I'm not sure that I heard you correctly. My ears are ringing."

"Which part? The yes that I'll marry you? Or the part where I tell you I am madly, deeply, forever in love with you? There will be no regrets, Lance. We can have a long engagement, if you need that to feel secure about me, about us. But I've never been so sure about anything. I love you. With everything that I am."

He groaned and kissed her again. This one was scorching hot. He pressed her against the SUV, fitting their bodies together. He kissed her the way he'd wanted to from the moment he'd seen how bravely she'd faced the gunmen at the cabin. She was an amazing woman in so many ways. Whether she wanted to return to Maple Falls and continue to be a cop or move to Gatlinburg with him and choose another career, they'd work it out. The only thing that mattered was being with her and living the rest of their lives together.

Whistles and catcalls had them breaking apart.

"Get a room," Asher called out.

Keira laughed. Lance rushed her around to the passenger side of the SUV and hurriedly fastened her seat belt. Then he was in the driver's seat racing them back toward their rental house.

When they arrived, he tenderly picked her up and carried her up the steps to the front door. Pausing in the opening, he held her in his arms and looked down at the most precious person he'd ever met. "I know we aren't married yet. And this isn't our home. But I still want to carry you over the threshold."

"That's so sweet. Since we're skipping a few steps, I'm

thinking we could skip another one. Let's start the honeymoon right now. That is, if you want to."

He cleared his suddenly raw throat, staring down at the beautiful woman in his arms. "How did I ever get so lucky to find you?"

"Hmm, I'm not sure. But you're definitely going to *get* lucky. If you hurry."

He eagerly ran inside carrying her, both of them laughing the whole time.

* * * * *

The Silent Setup
Katie Mettner

MILLS & BOON

Katie Mettner wears the title of "the only person to lose her leg after falling down the bunny hill" and loves decorating her prosthetic leg to fit the season. She lives in Northern Wisconsin with her own happily-ever-after and wishes for a dog now that her children are grown. Katie has an addiction to coffee and X and a lessening aversion to Pinterest—now that she's quit trying to make the things she pins.

Books by Katie Mettner

Harlequin Intrigue

Secure One

Going Rogue in Red Rye County
The Perfect Witness
The Red River Slayer
The Silent Setup

Visit the Author Profile page at millsandboon.com.au.

MILLS&BOON

For Tom

CAST OF CHARACTERS

Eric Newman—Has he outgrown Secure One, or has Secure One outgrown him? Eric doesn't know, but he's tired of playing third fiddle.

Sadie Cook—She's on the run with a baby who isn't hers and accused of a murder she didn't commit. She needs help but doesn't know who to trust.

Houston Cook—This adorable baby boy is a pawn in a dangerous game. Who wants him and why?

Kadie Cook—This single mother has gone missing. Will she live to see her baby again?

Victor Loraine—His family is on the wrong side of the law, and he's guilty until proven innocent.

Selina Colvert—The responsibility of caring for traumatized women has taken a toll on Secure One's medic. She's ready to be an operative, but first, she needs the chance to prove herself.

Efren Brenna—As the newest member of the Secure One team, he's fit in well with everyone but Selina. She refuses to acknowledge his skills, but he will prove he can cut the mustard.

Chapter One

The radio crackled to life, and Eric Newman reached for it. His army team brother, Mack Holbock, climbed from the car ahead of him. "We've got him covered from the front," their team leader, Cal Newfellow, said over the radio. "What do you see from your vantage point?"

Eric brought the radio to his lips. "We're in position. Gunner ready to engage." Motion caught his attention, and he noticed the back door of the diplomat's car crack open. A little foot came out, and his breath caught. "The back door of the car is openin—"

He never finished the sentence. An explosion rocked the air, and he was blasted backward in his seat. His head smacked the side of the Humvee from the percussion wave, and his gunner fell into the back seat. Just as the acrid scent of war reached his nostrils, Eric slammed down the accelerator and whipped around the raging fireball of the diplomat's car. He had to get to the rest of his team. There was no way anyone inside the car had survived the explosion. He could only pray his team wasn't dead alongside them.

"Do you see the team?" Eric shouted to his gunner, but he got no response. He skidded to a stop when he saw the bodies. His three brothers had fallen alongside

each other but were all moving. Crawling. Clawing their way toward him.

Roman Jacobs was first to open the door, helping Mack and Cal into the Humvee, all three bleeding and covered in soot. Eric hit the accelerator and tore away from the carnage before Roman had closed the door. There was no need to render aid to the family in the car. They'd been vaporized the moment the bomb had gone off. They could do nothing for them, and it was time to get out of Dodge before someone decided they were a target too.

Eric pulled alongside the helicopter in a matter of minutes, slammed the Humvee into Park and jumped out, nearly falling when his world spun in one direction before it flipped to the other. Doggedly determined, he helped Roman carry an injured Mack to the chopper, both of his legs a bloodied mess from flying debris. Roman's lips were moving, but all Eric heard was the buzzing in his ears. He was used to that after an explosion. It had happened more times than he could count, but it was frustrating when he couldn't communicate with his team. Cal, Roman and Eric piled into the chopper as it lifted off the ground, the sandy hellscape growing distant with every spin of the helo blade. Eric worked with Cal to stabilize Mack on a gurney so they could take stock of his injuries.

Cal tried to wrap Mack's legs with gauze but kept dropping it. It was what Eric noticed when he went to pick it up that had him shouting for Roman. "His hand!" he yelled at the man who had grown up with Cal as his foster brother. "I've got Mack. Help Cal!"

Roman nodded and said something, but Eric couldn't

make out the words. He was dizzy and fell twice while trying to get Mack's legs covered to protect the wounds. He would not be the reason his buddy became a double amputee. Mack gave him a thumbs-up, his lips moving, but Eric couldn't determine what he said. He turned to face Roman when there was a tap on his shoulder. Roman had wrapped Cal's hand in a beehive fashion to hold it all together, but Eric had seen the truth. He no longer had five fingers on that hand. Roman was saying something, but the only thing Eric heard was silence.

"Can't hear you!"

Roman handed him earphones, and Eric threw them on, forcing himself to concentrate on listening below the ringing in his ears. That was when the truth hit him—under the ringing in his ears was nothing but radio silence.

A TAP ON his shoulder made him turn, arm up, ready to block a blow. He was face-to-face with Efren, who took a step back. "You okay, man?"

Eric dropped his arm and sighed. "Sorry—I got distracted by something."

"Hey, I know that kind of distraction," Efren said, shaking his head. "Sometimes you can't avoid it."

Efren had lost his left leg during the war. He knew how easy it was to get trapped in those flashbacks, which was one reason he fit in so well at Secure One—the team understood being in a war zone, foreign or domestic. No one judged you for slipping into the past when the conditions were right. Thankfully, the team was always there to bring you back to the present.

Eric pointed straight ahead. "The car reminded me

of the one that blew up the day everyone at Secure One got hurt."

The mission had gone perfectly wrong. Their team might have reached their destination, but the horrors that had transpired after were burned in Eric's memory forever. Every night for the last fourteen years, he watched the replay of a little foot coming out of the door and then it falling to the ground, unbound by its body. He watched the horror show of Mack walking a few feet away from the car before he was tossed forward in slow motion and fell to the ground. He was alive, but the debris had hit his lower legs and severed the nerves beyond repair. He wore braces on both legs to stay upright now, but he was lucky to be walking at all. Cal, their team leader and owner of Secure One, had nearly lost his right hand. They'd salvaged a few fingers, but the hand was grotesquely disfigured. Cal wore a unique prosthesis to compensate for the fingers he'd lost that day, and it shocked Eric every time Cal pulled out a gun and pulled the trigger with precision.

Eric had gotten the silent injury, literally and figuratively. By the time they'd gotten to the hospital, the ringing had started to subside, which had made how silent the world was even more evident. The doctors had told him that percussion injuries like his often resolved within a few days to a few weeks and to wait for his hearing to return slowly. After four months, they'd admitted that maybe there was a problem and ran some tests. They'd discovered he'd had severe sensorineural hearing loss, which meant his hearing would never return. While he wore top-of-the-line hearing aids, at the end of the day, when he took them out and set them on the bedside table, his world was silent again. It had been fourteen years, and he still wasn't used to it.

"Do you think we have a situation?"

Eric's gaze drifted back to the car parked in front of a darkened storage unit. "Time will tell."

"Should we call Cal?" Efren whispered from behind.

"Whatever for?" he asked defensively. "I'm team leader while he's in DC, and I've worked here as long as Cal and Roman. I can handle this."

Efren held up his hands in defense. "You're right. I'm sorry. I'm so used to Cal standing over my shoulder that I don't know what to do when he's not. I'm surprised he even went to DC with everyone."

"It took some convincing," Eric admitted, his gaze trained on the car in front of them as it sat idling by an empty unit at the back of the storage buildings.

Convincing was an understatement. Eric had to threaten to leave Secure One for Cal to listen to his complaints. For years, Eric had diligently worked to level up Secure One in the security industry, but the team never seemed to notice. If it hadn't been for him installing the latest technology and integrating their clients' information into the computers, it wouldn't have mattered that Mina was a world-class coder and hacker for the FBI. If he hadn't found the adaptive outerwear and clothing for uniforms to help Mack, Efren and Mina change quickly while on the job, the team wouldn't have been prepared when things went sideways. Ultimately, Eric was in the background, ensuring Secure One ran smoothly and efficiently. His ego didn't require recognition for that. He'd been a member of an elite team of army police when he'd served, and there was no place for ego there. All he wanted was to be on a level playing field with Cal, Mack and Roman—just as they had been when they'd served together.

Last spring, Secure One had been involved in a case that had gained national attention. Mack and his fiancée, Charlotte, had been responsible for finding and arresting the Red River Slayer, a serial killer terrorizing the nation. Charlotte was receiving a medal for bravery in DC, and Cal wanted to attend the event, so he'd asked Eric to lead the team in his absence. He had been stunned by the request since Roman wasn't going to DC with them, and Roman had always been Cal's right-hand man. Eric had jumped at the chance—but not to prove to Cal that he was capable. He'd proved that in the field time and time again in much more dangerous situations than surveilling a storage unit.

Eric wanted—no, he needed to prove that he could still be an effective leader who others respected. If he didn't, all the years he'd spent being a silent leader had been wasted—at least in his eyes. The rest of the team would say otherwise, but they were all coming from a place of leading the team in front of the public, which was an opportunity Eric had yet to have. He wouldn't waste this chance to show his boss his leadership skills were sharper than ever.

"I readily admit that I don't understand all the dynamics between you, Cal, Roman and Mack. That said, I'd trust you to have my back any day on the battlefield. You and Selina are the two most underappreciated members of this team," Efren said.

"I can't fault your observation skills, that's for sure.

I'm surprised you noticed Selina's contributions, considering her prickly attitude toward you."

"Probably why I noticed," he said, chuckling as he shook his head. "That said, it would be hard to miss. She's putting on Band-Aids when she should be out in the field. Don't get me wrong—she's great at what she does, but I think she's underutilized for her talents."

"I get the feeling you aren't the only one who feels that way," Eric said with a nod. "Selina may need to have a day of reckoning with Cal too. As for you, I don't know what you did, but you sure rubbed her the wrong way. Usually she's the sweetest, most easygoing person at Secure One."

"I wish I knew too. Selina has been prickly since the moment they introduced me to her. If you want my opinion, I think she's hurt and angry that Cal hired me when it should have been her."

"That's possible, but we needed help at the time, and Cal couldn't worry about whose toes he stepped on or who got their feelings hurt. We were hunting a serial killer."

"I can agree and disagree on this one," Efren said. "Yes, you needed help, but an EMT or nurse is easier to find than someone like me."

"Fair." Eric was forced to agree with his logic, especially since they'd only procured him because he was a friend of Mina's. "All I'm saying is I don't think that crossed anyone's mind. Mina knew you and said you'd come in fast." He sighed and shook his head. "I guess I'm just as guilty as Cal for not suggesting he bring Selina in and hire a new nurse. I hope Selina sticks around long enough to have it out with Cal. She deserves her day in court."

"I hope she does too, and hey, if it takes the heat off my back, you won't hear me complaining," Efren said, tongue in cheek.

The dome light came on inside the car, and Eric crouched low—Efren sat since his above-knee prosthesis didn't allow him to crouch. "Get this on video, and make sure to get the make and model of the car and the plate," he whispered, motioning for Efren to use the app on their tablet. It wouldn't be fantastic quality, but it would give them something to go on.

Two men climbed from the car, and Eric leaned in for a closer look. He had no doubt a crime had been committed or was about to be committed, and he wanted to see it go down in real time just in case he could still help the victim. Fettering's was a self-storage for the rich and famous, but it was the middle of the night, and the rich and famous didn't casually drop by their storage unit in the cold rain to pick something up. Efren and Eric were there to find holes in the client's security and close them before bad things happened. He knew they'd just found a hole and a bad thing was about to happen.

He motioned for Efren to pull on his night-vision goggles before he did the same. The lighting was nonexistent, which was another issue for Fettering to address, but the goggles would keep them from missing anything. He kept his gaze trained on the two guys opening the storage unit door while he pondered if what Efren had said was true. If it was, then he did owe Selina an apology. He knew what it was like to be constantly overlooked as an asset to the team, even when you were working your tail off every day. He'd chat with her and let her know that feeling hurt for being overlooked was okay. Then he'd encourage her to talk to Cal and demand the respect she deserved.

"What are they carrying?" Efren whispered as the guys grabbed something from the car and carried it into the storage unit.

"Whatever it is, it's heavy," he answered. The men shifted, and he caught a glimpse of the item. "It's a trunk." The two guys lowered it to the unit's floor and then stood. They turned to face each other for a moment before they pulled the door back down and locked it. "I don't feel good about it," Eric said as the car pulled out the back exit.

What he didn't tell Efren was that he could read their lips. Whoever the Winged Templar was, that was who these guys worked for. Their expressions had told him they also feared him. Eric ran a hand along the back of his neck to see if the hair was standing up. His in-grained military intuition told him what those guys had just dropped inside the unit wasn't seasonal clothing.

"My gut is clenched as well," Efren agreed.

"First of all, two guys don't go out at midnight to drop off something at a storage unit unless they want to be certain no one is around."

"True," Efren said, moving his goggles to the top of his head to check his tablet screen. "What's second of all?"

"Second of all, because of the first of all we're going to search that unit."

"Sure, it's unusual for two guys to drop something off late at night, but I don't know if it's break-in worthy."

Eric slid his goggles to the top of his head. "The property management has a right to search any unit that displays suspicious activity. It's in the lease they signed."

"And didn't read."

"Bingo," Eric said before he pointed at the tablet. "Are they gone?"

"Sure are. They drove out of the gate and headed down the road. I still don't understand why Fettering, who has more money than Heinz has pickles, put a storage business on his property. The clientele can be rather sketchy, and it's a lot of coming and going at all hours of the day and night," Efren pointed out.

"All true, but believe it or not, there are a lot of rich people in Minnesota who need a place to store their off-season toys and goodies. Dirk Fettering is one of those rich people. He built these units to cater to his kind of people. Classy, not sketchy."

"Well, that felt sketchy," Efren mumbled, motioning at the storage unit.

"Exactly," Eric agreed, taking his bolt cutters from his belt. "And that's why we're going to take a look."

Efren hoisted himself to standing and grabbed the tablet. "What does your gut say?"

"I give it fifty-fifty odds that it's either money or a body."

"A body doesn't make sense. Eventually it would start to smell."

"Then let's hope it's money," Eric said, pushing himself away from the building. He knew full well it wasn't money. He was almost certain it was a body. The men had struggled under the weight of it, and you didn't dump money in a storage locker and drive away. Why they'd dump a body here, he couldn't say, but this was his chance to prove himself to Cal, and he wasn't going to sleep on the job.

"This is the perfect example of why that back entrance and exit is a problem. The lack of security back here is disturbing," he said over his shoulder.

"They have to swipe their card to get in, right?" Efren asked.

"They have to swipe a card. It doesn't have to be theirs. It's easy to dupe a card with no one the wiser." There was a guard at the front entrance to check people in, but not the back one. It had been their first suggestion when they'd taken the job, but Fettering had refused to consider closing the back entrance and exit from 8:00 p.m. until 7:00 a.m. He'd said as long as the person had a card, they had every right to be there. Eric knew that wasn't the case, and after their initial walkthrough tonight, he'd put it back on the list as number one. What had just happened had proved his point.

The two men reached the storage unit, and Eric glanced around the space. "We need better lighting and cameras back here too. We just lucked out that we were back here when they pulled up."

"Agreed," Efren said. "Fettering built a state-of-the-art storage facility for big-name clients and then slacked on security measures. It feels a little suspicious to me."

"You'd be surprised how often that happens," he said. "They get so caught up in the idea of what they're offering people that they forget about the logistics of how to protect it. Got gloves?"

They each tugged black leather gloves from their waistbands and pulled them on. Eric inspected the lock and chuckled at the simple padlock you could buy at the local hardware store. As if that would stop anyone who wanted to get inside. Sometimes people were far too trusting of other humans. He cut the metal band quickly and rolled the door up. Efren flashed his light into the cavernous space, and Eric wasn't surprised to see the unit was empty other than the giant trunk.

"Something feels off. Why do they have this giant storage unit for one trunk?" Efren asked.

Eric shook his head as he stood with one hand planted on his hip. "I would guess that whatever is in that trunk is the answer. This was likely a drop, and someone else will come to pick it up."

"And if it's not a drop?"

"Then it's a body, and the climate control will buy them a few extra days before it starts to smell."

"Are we going to open it, or are we going to call the cops?"

"Oh, we're going to open it," Eric said, "and depending on what we find, we'll call the cops."

He knelt, inspecting the locks on the trunk. They were surprisingly easy to get open with his lock-pick set. Once the three locks were popped, they lifted the lid. A smell hit him that he knew all too well. Copper.

"Well," Efren said as he stared at the dead body inside the trunk, "you called it. Last time I checked, a man's head doesn't belong in the middle of his chest."

"Nope," Eric agreed. "Sure doesn't. It looks like a call to the Bemidji PD is in order."

Efren flicked off the flashlight. "This is gruesome."

"Yes, removing someone's head and sitting it on their chest to fit them in the trunk is a bit gruesome, but the manner of death also indicates—"

"A mob hit," Efren answered, and Eric tipped his head in acknowledgment.

"That or a gang killing. Either way, this guy is not a Secure One problem. He's a police problem." Eric pulled out his phone to call the police, but internally he was cussing out the universe. The first time Cal trusted him with a solo job and he found a body. Not that he had any control over that other than how things went now.

"Maybe we should wait and see if someone comes along to pick up the trunk," Efren suggested.

"We don't know for sure that anyone is. Now that I know it's a body, I'm legally obligated to report it. We'll leave it to the PD to sort out. A dead guy in a trunk is above our paygrade."

"Fair point. If nothing else, a dead guy in a trunk is also incentive for Fettering to tighten security."

"We can only hope." Eric's tone was dry and nonbelieving as he connected his hearing aids to his phone via Bluetooth.

After reporting the body to the police, they settled in to wait for a squad. Eric would update Cal as soon as he turned this over, and then he'd sit down with Dirk and find out exactly what kind of business he was running out here. Eric had every intention of proving he could do the job, even if it was the last thing he did.

Chapter Two

Sadie Cook pulled the curtain on a front window back slowly. She liked working the night shift because it was quiet and it was easy to finish her tasks, but tonight was anything but quiet. The rumor was they'd found someone dead by the storage units. She wouldn't be the least bit surprised if the rumor was a fact. It was only a matter of time before someone figured out that the lighting was nonexistent in the back of the units, and with an exit built right in, it was bound to happen. Maybe now Mr. Fettering would stop telling them, the housekeeping staff, that it was perfectly safe to park back there. Safe or not, she didn't have a choice but to stay and work for him as a housekeeper. The pay and the hours were what she needed to survive, but a dead body gave her pause. The last thing she wanted was to end up a dead body simply because she worked for Dirk.

The flashing lights made her anxious, so she let the curtain fall and turned away from the window. She wanted to head home, but no one was allowed in or out until the police had taken everyone's statements. She deduced that trying to sneak out would be an excellent way to end up in the interrogation room of the Bemidji Police Department. With a resigned sigh, she grabbed her phone. Since she had no idea when she could leave, she'd better make a call. She plastered herself along the wall farthest from the door before she dialed, just in case someone happened to walk past while she was talking.

"Hello?"

Sadie let out a pent-up breath with relief. "Julia? It's Sadie."

"What's up, girl?" her friend of five years asked.

"I've been held up at work. Can you keep him a little longer?"

"Of course. He's sleeping anyway, so there's no need to wake him. Everything okay?"

"I don't know," Sadie admitted, a shiver of undefined fear running down her spine. "The Bemidji PD showed up after the security guys were here. Rumors are floating around that they found a body, but I can't confirm. I also can't leave until I talk to the cops."

"That sounds ominous, Sades. Time to pull the rip cord?"

"I don't think I'd get off this property without being stopped by someone, nor do I want to end up in the clinker for leaving the scene of a crime. I'll be first in line so I can get home though."

"I meant in general," her friend said in the kind of voice that told Sadie exactly what Julia thought about Dirk Fettering.

"You know I can't quit this job yet, Jules. Once we find Kadie, then I'm out. I promise."

"Okay—be safe. No need to worry about our little guy. He's fine here. Take your time, and while the cops are there, ask them if they have any new leads on Kadie's whereabouts."

Sadie grimaced at the thought as she told her friend

goodbye. After stowing her phone back in her pocket, she picked up her cleaning supplies and left the bedroom. Julia was right. She would have to face the same detectives who kept telling her that her sister hadn't disappeared but had left of her own free will. Sadie knew that wasn't true. Her sister loved her baby boy more than life itself and would never willingly leave him. Something had happened to her, but the police refused to listen, much less look at the evidence.

In fairness to them, there had been a note that said single motherhood was too much for her and she was leaving town, but it wasn't real. Sadie knew her sister's handwriting, and what was on that paper wasn't it. If Kadie had written it, she'd done it under duress so Sadie would recognize the stilted writing as something other than her usual beautiful flowing penmanship. She'd even shown the police other samples of Kadie's handwriting, but they still refused to help her.

In the meantime, Sadie was trying to take care of Kadie's eight-month-old baby boy, Houston. Thank heavens Julia could keep him while she worked because there was no way he was going into the foster care system, even temporarily. It was her job to keep him safe until Kadie returned. Since Kadie had never named a father, Houston had no one but Sadie to protect him.

"Sadie Cook?"

She jumped and spun, her cleaning kit tumbling to the floor as she stumbled backward. Strong, warm hands grasped her arms and kept her from falling at the last second. The man who had called her name, and kept her upright, was the epitome of *tall, dark and handsome*. His skin was perfectly tan, he had black hair in a crew cut that said *military turned civilian* and coffee-brown eyes that were pinned directly on her lips. Her skin heated from his touch, and whispers of a sensation she hadn't felt in too long spiraled through her.

"I didn't mean to scare you. Are you okay?"

"Fi-fine," she stammered. "Sorry—I was lost in thought when you called my name."

"Are you Sadie Cook?"

"That depends on who's asking." She noticed his nose had a misshapen bump near the top, telling her without telling her that he'd broken it once or twice in the past. The bump added character to his already intriguing eyes. Both were overshadowed by his lips though. Full, plump and pink, they'd make any woman yearn for a kiss. The way he stared at her lips made her wonder if that was what he was thinking about right now. How would she feel if this man planted them on hers out of the blue? *Not even upset* was the answer.

Stop, she scolded herself. *You have a baby to take care of now. You don't have time for kisses from hot guys.*

After her internal chastising was over, she stiffened her spine and raised her chin as a slow smile lifted his lips. It was the kind of smile meant to be sly, but on this guy, it just screamed *bedroom sexy*. The worst part? He knew she was lusting after his lips.

"My name is Eric Newman. I'm part of the Secure One security team."

Well, she wasn't expecting that. She'd had the security guys pegged as much older and far less of a male specimen than the one before her.

"I noticed a bit of commotion."

"You could say that," Eric said with a chuckle. "I'm

helping the police question the staff. Since I witnessed the incident, I know you had nothing to do with it, so don't worry about that. I do have to ask the staff if they saw or heard anything unusual over the last few days."

Unusual? Like her sister disappearing into thin air? She resisted the urge to give this man more than he'd bargained for in answer to his question.

"I don't know what you mean by *unusual*."

Casually, he let go of her arms and placed his hands on his hips. "The same vehicle coming and going. People on the property you had never seen before. That kind of thing."

Sadie thought about it for a moment but finally shook her head. "That's the problem, Eric. There are always people coming and going in the house, but I don't know all of Mr. Fettering's friends. You'll have to ask him."

"I believe the Bemidji PD is doing that now." The tone of his voice was patient, but she could tell he was on edge.

"Something bad happened, right?" she asked. "Probably by the back exit." She gauged his reaction and noticed his eyes dilate for a moment. Her words had hit the way she'd hoped.

"What do you know about the back exit?" His tone told her this was no longer a friendly question-and-answer session. Now he wanted information.

"That's the exit Mr. Fettering makes us use, but I hate it. The lack of lights back there makes it unsafe as soon as the sun goes down, and I always told my friend if anyone wanted to commit a crime, that was the place to do it." A shiver racked her body, telling the man in front of her just how much she believed that statement to be true. "I knew it was only a matter of time, but Dirk didn't want to hear it."

"You're observant," Eric said. "Have you seen any suspicious activity back there before?"

"No," Sadie said, taking a step back. He was one of those men who pulled you into his atmosphere and held you there. It was disturbing and wonderful simultaneously, but Sadie knew she had to get out before she wanted to stay. "Can I go now?"

"You can. I'll check you off as having been questioned. You'll need an escort to your car."

Sadie nervously swallowed before she answered, "That's okay. I'll be fine, but thanks." She turned away to gather her supplies when he tugged on her apron.

"No, I mean you'll have an escort. No one is allowed in the storage area without a security guard. The back exit is closed, so everyone has to show identification and exit through the front. Are you working tomorrow?" Her nod was short. "When you arrive, someone at the entrance will direct you to the new parking area. I'll take you to your car now if you're ready."

Sadie frowned. They must have found a body. It was the only thing that made sense if they were being this cautious and demanding at the same time. Kadie's face skittered through her mind's eye, and she fought the urge to ask him if they had found a woman's body. The way he looked at her, she wondered if he suspected she was hiding something. She had to stay off this guy's radar if she wanted to find her sister and bring her home. "I just need to grab my coat."

He turned and motioned for her to go ahead, and that was when she noticed the device behind his ear with a thin wire attached to a translucent earpiece. It wasn't a security piece. It was a hearing aid. A second glance told her he wore one on the other side too. The memory of how he'd stared at her lips brought heat to her cheeks when she realized he'd simply been reading her lips and not thinking about kissing her.

Embarrassed, she grabbed her coat and keys from the closet and followed him out the door. After some fancy security talk and flashing her identification, they made it to her car without incident.

"Head to the front of the units and exit there. Another guard will be there to check your identification," Eric said, holding the door open for her while she climbed in.

"Wow, you mean the help gets to leave through the front door tonight?" she asked, her words laced with sarcasm so he knew she was kidding.

His sly smile told her he was amused. "Don't get used to it. I'm sure by morning you'll be parking at the pavilion and ridesharing on the back of a mule if Fettering has anything to say about it."

He shut the door on her laughter and waved her off as she headed for the front of the storage unit. She comforted herself with the knowledge that she may have to work tomorrow, but at least she wouldn't have to see Eric or his kissable lips ever again.

ERIC WATCHED SADIE drive off in a red Saturn that was probably as old as she was but showed no signs of rust from the Minnesota winters. The memory of her warm skin beneath his skittered heat through his body, sounding his internal alarm. Their short encounter had been enough to tell him she was a flame he'd better stay far away from to avoid getting burned. If this were a different time and place, he wouldn't have let her drive away without getting her number, but he had no time for this now or ever. He had a job to do, which didn't include wishing he could kiss those lips he'd read to the letter.

He'd had to read her lips, so he was grateful that she had the perfect set. His hearing aids were good, but background noise was impossible to control in some situations, no matter how good your aids were. He'd learned quickly to read lips if he wanted to concentrate on the conversation. It was easier than asking *What?* all the time. Sometimes it was the only way he could follow a conversation or even have a conversation if he wasn't wearing his aids. People took communication for granted until it became difficult. He'd been just as guilty of that sin until the moment it had happened to him. His experiences in the sandbox had taught him to take nothing for granted.

He couldn't stop thinking about Sadie though. Not just her girl-next-door looks or how tiny she'd been under his hands, but how he'd noticed a flicker in her eyes when he'd told her who he was. She'd been skittish, and his years of working security told him one thing—she was hiding something. If he had time to spare, he might look into her and her background, but he didn't, and by the looks of this place, he wouldn't have time for a while.

The trill of his tablet stiffened his shoulders. He'd been expecting the call, but that didn't mean he was prepared for it. He stepped into the empty guard booth at the entrance and answered the video call.

"Secure two, Echo," he said to the black screen, waiting for his boss to answer.

"Secure one, Charlie," Cal said, and then his face flashed on the screen. "Eric, what the hell is going on there?"

"Cal," he said, noting his boss's mood. "I wasn't expecting to speak with you until morning. It's late in DC."

"Or early, depending on how you look at it, but I got your message and wanted an update."

"Bemidji PD is here, and they've taken over the investigation."

"Of a body dropped in a storage unit? You and Efren witnessed it?"

"We did," he confirmed, his attention pulled away for a moment by the ME van as it rolled slowly toward the exit. "We were walking the property looking for security breaches. The suspects didn't know we were there when they pulled up. They unloaded a trunk that was a little too suspicious to be clothing or home goods. That was confirmed when we opened the trunk and found a dude with his head sitting on his chest."

"Mob hit?"

"Or gang. Either way, it was odd to dump him there and leave. Unless it was a matter of convenience for these guys." The name he'd seen on the guy's lips ran through his head and he said, "I was watching them with our night-vision goggles, and one of the guys said the name Winged Templar. Have you ever run across that name before?"

"Winged Templar?" Cal was silent for a moment and lifted his eyes toward his hairline while he thought about it. "No, but it sounds like a code name to me. If this is a mob hit, that could be the name of the hitman."

"Exactly what I was thinking," Eric agreed. "I suppose I should tell the cops about it?"

"Probably. At some point. Keep it under your hat for now. In case it has something to do with Dirk's place rather than the dead guy."

"Heard and understood," Eric agreed. "We always

knew that the back exit was a problem, and tonight proves it. Maybe now we can convince Fettering to fix it. He's not happy being the center of an investigation."

"That's your job now," Cal said. "But if it matters, I agree. He needs to close off that back entrance onto the property and add more lights. People should only be allowed to enter and exit through the front gate that's staffed."

"With cameras that record and hold the data for thirty days."

"Agreed. What is your plan moving forward?"

He asked the question in a way that told Eric to read between the lines. It was a test, and he'd better have the correct answer if he wanted to remain in control of the situation.

"Tomorrow I'll talk to Fettering regarding the security issues we discovered and how to fix them. After we go over all of the weak points of his property, Efren and I will head back to Secure One and let Fettering think about it for a few days. Once you're back, we can implement the most important changes, like lighting and cameras. That will make our lives easier back at headquarters as well. Right now, he only allows one camera at the guard booth that saves the data for twenty-four hours. That doesn't help us much."

"You know how hard I fought him on that. He hired us to be his security team and then tied our hands at every turn."

"True, but I've seen no less than five high-profile people in and out of the units over the twelve hours we've been on the ground. He promised discretion, and that's what he gives them."

"Maybe, but the time for all of that has passed. Now

it's time to let us do our job properly. Besides, *discretion* is our middle name."

"As well it should be, but getting Fettering to believe that will be a much tougher sell. Anyway, don't worry about us here. We've got this."

"I have no doubt that's true, Eric. We planned to be home in three days, but if you need us sooner, just say the word."

"We'll be fine. Roman and Mina are keeping things humming in the control room, and there isn't much to handle here outside the scope of our business. The cops will deal with the body, and Efren and I already gave our statements. Just enjoy your trip, and know that I'll reach out if something comes up that I need approval on."

"We'll be back in seventy-two hours. I'm counting on you to have everything ready to go for when Fettering decides to let us add additional cameras and security measures. I want to move on it the minute he gives us the go-ahead, so he doesn't have time to change his mind."

"Ten-four. Echo out," Eric said before ending the video call.

Eric let his shoulders relax and started a mental list of the equipment they'd need to do the job right this time. Unfortunately for him, his mind was focused on Sadie Cook and nothing else. She intrigued him, which was a rare occurrence when it came to women. He'd never been one to worry about what a woman was thinking when he was looking for a good time, but Sadie was different. He'd only spoken with her for a few short minutes, but that was all he needed to know she was the whole package. That was when he reminded himself that made her a woman he would never have.

Chapter Three

Why did I go this way? Sadie was kicking herself for taking that exit without checking if there was a way back onto the highway. The long, dark, winding road she'd been on for the last twenty minutes did accomplish one thing—it told her the SUV in her rearview mirror was following her. It had been behind her on the highway, and she'd convinced herself it was headed in the same direction until she'd taken the exit and they'd followed. She was exhausted after back-to-back shifts. She only had a few hours of sleep after getting home late the night before and heading back there this morning to do the work she didn't get done last night after the body was found. Sadie would do whatever she had to do to protect Houston though.

Now she was utterly alone on a dark road in middle-of-nowhere Minnesota, with a baby in the back seat. To add insult to injury, it had started raining about an hour ago, leaving the pavement covered in wet leaves and making it almost impossible to see. She couldn't stop or even think about pulling over until she was somewhere safe and she'd lost the SUV behind her. Houston was who she had to protect right now, so she'd take it slow and easy but wouldn't pull over. Pulling over was certain death, she had no doubt. If only she knew why. She hadn't done anything but work hard to keep Kadie and Houston in her life. Now someone wanted to end hers.

Sadie grasped the wheel tightly and accelerated, her gaze jumping to the rearview mirror. The other car was keeping pace. "Now what, baby?" she asked the sweetheart in the back. She'd planned to pull over and give him a bottle, but she hadn't bothered to stop when she'd noticed the black SUV follow her down the exit. She'd fished the bottle out of his bag and propped it against the edge of his car seat. The clock was ticking down to when he needed to be changed and fed again. She couldn't do that on the side of the road, so she had to find somewhere safe sooner rather than later.

Her gaze focused on the horizon, and she searched for the lights of a city. There were none. All that stretched out before her was desolate darkness without an end in sight. She should have turned around and returned to the highway, but she'd been afraid the SUV would overtake her if she'd tried that. With dread, her gaze dropped to the gas gauge. It was down to a quarter of a tank. The last road sign she'd seen had said the next town was fifty miles. She had to have gone at least thirty by now. If she could keep the SUV behind her, she'd make it to a well-lit and populated area before she pulled over. It wouldn't save her, but it might buy her time. She cursed the fact that she'd had to leave her phone at home and hadn't bothered to stop and pick up a burner phone immediately. Without one, she couldn't even call up Google Maps.

With it, they might find you.

Not that she knew who *they* were. Sadie had been minding her own business at work when she'd been called to the office and handed an envelope. The secretary couldn't tell her who had delivered it, but her name had been on the front. Sadie had thanked her and tucked it into her apron until she'd had time to read it on her break. Inside the envelope had been three letters cut from a magazine and glued to a notecard. It had said *RUN*. After what had happened the night before, Sadie had heeded the warning. She'd grabbed Houston and done just that.

With no idea where she was going, Sadie had made the short-term plan to get to Minneapolis and blend into the city for a few days until she could figure out what was happening. Did this have something to do with Kadie being missing or something to do with the body they'd found last night at Fettering's place? Or was this someone playing a game because they had Kadie and wanted Sadie vulnerable so they could get Houston too?

The truth stuck in her chest, and her hands tightened on the wheel a hair more. Suddenly, she wished she'd listened to Julia when she'd begged her not to go off alone with Houston. She'd said the note could have been a practical joke, which was possible, but Sadie knew better. The person who'd sent her that note knew something she didn't and wanted to warn her. In hindsight, it could have been sent to isolate her. If that was their goal, they'd succeeded.

Her mind drifted to that pair of lips she saw every time she closed her eyes. Was it Eric who had warned her? He ran security for Fettering's complex. He could have insider information. If he wanted to warn her without compromising the investigation, an anonymous note was the only way. That was a bit farfetched, but nothing was off the table when you worked for a celebrity.

Sadie had learned that truth several times over the last few years. Dirk had made his fair share of enemies.

Some would even consider him cutthroat. Maybe he was in his business, but not in his personal life. Fettering was essentially a forty-year-old college frat boy who thought he knew everything but also wanted to be everyone's friend. Sadie had served at and cleaned up enough of his parties to know who he was when the cameras weren't on him. Working at his private parties put her on a different plane of household importance than others. Not that she wanted even an ounce of that hierarchy, but she had been eager and energetic when hired. That was her way of saying she'd been naive to the ways of some peoples' worlds.

Headlights filled her car, and a glance behind her showed the SUV coming up fast on her. Maybe they wanted to pass. Crazy to do it on a curve, but she slowed, hoping they'd go around her and leave her in peace. The car swung into the left lane, and she eased off the gas more, relief filling her chest. They were following her, but not for nefarious reasons.

"We might make it after all, Houston," she whispered, holding tight to the wheel as the car came up on her left on the curve. "We'll find somewhere to stay and ditch this car," she promised, wishing the SUV would get past her before someone came at them from the other direction. She eased down on the brake as the SUV accelerated, giving them space to clear the lane.

Sadie sighed with relief when they swung over until she realized they wouldn't clear her. She slammed on the brakes, but it was too late. She heard the crunch of metal as her head whipped to the side. The car spun, and she screamed, the sound bouncing around as they twirled at a dizzying speed toward the edge of the road. Sadie desperately grabbed the wheel again and twisted it to the left. It didn't respond. Houston cried, glass shattered and then there was nothing but the rhythmic swish of the windshield wipers.

ERIC RUBBED HIS eyes with one hand while he gulped coffee from his mug with the other. He'd been back at Secure One for less than four hours and was already covering a shift in the control room. Mina wasn't feeling well, and Roman didn't want to leave her alone. Eric had told him not to worry about it, but now, two hours later, he regretted his decision. At least he and Efren were in the same boat. Neither of them had gotten much sleep after dealing with Fettering last night, and the trip back to Secure One only added to their fatigue.

"When is Cal coming back?" Efren asked.

The person who answered surprised the hell out of him. "Tomorrow late afternoon or evening," Selina said as she entered the control room. "He wants to get home sooner, considering the situation at Fetterings'. He'll file a flight plan once he knows for sure."

"Hey, Selina," both guys said in unison.

She had a pot of coffee in one hand and a tray of sandwiches in the other. "I thought you might be hungry," she explained as her gaze drifted across the monitors in front of Efren. "Everything status quo?"

"Quiet, just how we like it," Efren said, snagging a sandwich. He held it up. "Thanks."

"Don't get used to it, Brenna. I'm not a waitress."

"I wouldn't, and I'm aware," Efren said when he swallowed.

"Maybe you could cut Efren a little slack, Selina," Eric said, grabbing a sandwich. "If you've got a beef, it's not with him. It's with Cal."

Selina spun on her heel and gave him a look that would wither weaker men. "I didn't ask for your opinion, Eric. Nor his, for that matter. I was going to offer to take a shift so you guys could sleep, but I think I just changed my mind."

She stalked out in a way that left no room for argument.

Efren whistled and shook his head. "I don't even know what to say."

"Neither do I," Eric admitted, turning back to the screen. "That's not the Selina I've known for the last seven years. I wish she'd stop taking her angst out on you. It's not right."

The phone rang, so Efren picked it up, answering with mostly *yes*, *no*, and *are you sure?* When he hung up, Eric eyed him. "Who was that?"

"Bemidji PD. They have a warrant out for a suspect. That was a courtesy call to let us know they hope to have her in custody soon."

"Her?" he asked, and Efren shrugged.

"That's what they said. Apparently she works for Fettering."

Eric sat up straighter and leaned toward him. "What's her name?"

Efren glanced down at his pad and then back to Eric. "Sadie Cook? I have no idea who that is."

Eric's heart pounded, and his mind spun a mile a minute. What on earth? There was no way Sadie Cook had anything to do with that body drop.

"Efren, I interviewed Sadie. She's this tiny little thing who was terrified of me! There is absolutely zero chance she has anything to do with that murder. I'd stake my career on it. We were there when the two guys dumped the body." For a moment, he remembered that look of fear in her sweet blue eyes. Was it fear that she'd been discovered? No matter how hard he tried, Eric couldn't get there with it. It didn't make any sense whatsoever. There was no way she would order a hit and then have them drop the body at her place of employment. She drove a car almost as old as she was, which was a good indication that she didn't have a lot of cash to throw in on a murder-for-hire plot. Something was going on with Sadie Cook, but it had nothing to do with the murder last night.

"According to the PD, the dead guy was Howie Loraine." Eric leaned back against the chair with a groan, and Efren paused. "What?"

"A Loraine? They were involved in a multistate counterfeiting scheme about eight years ago. Last I heard, Dad was doing life, the stepmom was dead, and Randall Junior and Howie were running the legal business. Everyone suspected Randall Junior was also running a not-so-legal business, but no one could prove it. Howie was the youngest son and, shall we say, the most free-spirited. It still doesn't make sense that they suspect Sadie."

Efren held up his finger. "Except that they pulled in one of the guys from our video. His version goes that Sadie is the one who hired him."

"This makes less sense now than it did last night," Eric growled, turning to face the computer screens again. "Why would Sadie order a hit on Howie Loraine? Does she even know him?"

"According to the chief, the dude refused to answer that question."

"Well, of course he did! You know damn well someone sent him in there to say that. It's too clean and neatly drawn. The only way that guy got caught was if he wanted to—"

A blur caught his attention on the screen. Before he fully registered what he saw, he was on his feet and grabbing Efren's shirtsleeve on the way to the door. "Let's go!"

"What grid was that?" Efren asked as they ran out the door, weapons at the ready.

"Lake side, northern edge!" Eric yelled back as they ran toward what he thought was a car driving onto the property.

"Should we call Roman for backup?" Efren asked as he pulled up next to him.

"No, let's see what's going on first. I don't want to pull other guys from their grids until I know if this is a threat. If it is an attack, we can't leave those areas vulnerable for them to infiltrate."

They both knew all too well about people trying to infiltrate Secure One. The last few years had been one attempt after another. Roman's FBI partner and now wife, Mina, had been hunted by a madwoman and ended up at Secure One for protection. The Madame had then infiltrated Secure One and snatched Mina from under their noses. Cal had sworn that would be the last time Secure One was vulnerable to an outside force. They'd learned about the vulnerabilities of their property the hard way but put those experiences to good use. Secure One now had one of the most protected perimeters in the country. That said, they couldn't stop someone with an axe to grind from trying. He was in control of this base now, and this was his chance to prove himself to Cal. Eric couldn't risk taking the wrong action too soon. Once he assessed the situation, he'd make the call.

They closed in on the grid section that wasn't surveilled other than in the control room. It was outside Secure One property and owned by the county, which tied their hands. "It looked like a car driving into the ditch, but it's raining, so it was hard to tell," Eric said as they ran. What he didn't say was that he thought he recognized the car. "That bank is steep. The only way down it is to roll. I'm worried someone's hurt."

They reached the fence, and he grabbed his walkie. He'd set off the all-hands-on-deck alarm before he'd left, so he hoped Selina was in the control room by now. "Lights on, fence off," he requested.

Relief flooded him momentarily when the spotlights came on and the gate clicked open. Selina still had his back. His relief was short-lived when they ran through the gate and found the car. It rested on its side with a tendril of white smoke whispering its way through the bent hood. His fears were realized—he knew the car. An older-model red Saturn that, unlike last night, was now crumbled stem to stern as one wheel spun lazily in the air.

Eric paused for a moment. "Is that crying?"

"Sounds like a baby to me," Efren agreed.

They sprinted forward, reassured that this was an accident, not a planned attack.

"Help!" a woman screamed as their boots crunched through the leaves. "Help! I can't get out!"

"We're coming! Don't move!" Efren called out as they rounded the back of the car.

"Houston! You have to get Houston out of the car!"

"Sadie, it's Eric from Secure One. You're okay. Just let us assess the baby."

Glancing at each other, the men peered through the back windows. Sure enough, there was a strapped-down car seat holding a crying infant.

"Are you hurt, Sadie?" Eric called to her.

She pointed at her right leg. "My leg is stuck! Don't worry about me! You have to get the baby out!"

Efren grabbed Eric's shirt. "The same Sadie the cops are looking for?"

"It appears so," he said. "We need to get her out of the car before we worry about her legal situation."

With a nod, Efren called out to Sadie, "Just take a deep breath. We're going to help you. How old is your son?"

"Almost eight months, but Houston is my nephew."

"Call Selina. We might need her," Efren said before he ducked low again.

Eric hit his walkie and requested Selina's help at the grid. A medical professional would be helpful if they needed an ambulance, and if they couldn't get Sadie's leg free, they'd need to call the fire department. His gaze drifted to the smoke billowing from the engine, and he hit the walkie again, requesting fire extinguishers.

If his luck held, they'd be able to free Sadie and get her inside the confines of Secure One. If he could talk to her about what had happened last night before too many people realized she was here, he might be able to run interference for her. Why he cared so much about what happened to her, he didn't know, and he wouldn't—couldn't—take the time to figure that out right now. They had a job to do, starting with rescuing a baby and his aunt. Eric forced his gaze away from the baby's chubby legs as they pumped against the seat. Another baby wasn't going to die on his watch. He had enough to atone for. He didn't need to add more to his already full dance card.

The truth settled low in his gut. Sadie had been running. He didn't know if that made her guilty or scared until his gaze flicked to hers for a millisecond. Scared. Terrified, actually, and they had to help her. She believed their lives were in danger. There was no other reason she would be out driving in the rain with a baby.

Efren was walking around the car and pointed to the wheel well on the passenger side. "I think our best bet is to lower it back to four wheels and then try to get them out through the door that isn't smashed." He put his hand on top of the door facing up. "Opinions?"

"That's our only choice. Let's do it now before the engine decides to go up."

The car was a lightweight sedan made of more plastic than metal. The two of them easily lowered it back into position, and once the wheels touched the grass, they tried the back door. Locked.

"Can you hit the Unlock button?" Eric called out to Sadie. She said something he couldn't hear. The rain and the wailing infant had rendered his aids useless.

"She said it's not working," Efren said right next to his ear. Eric hated that the guys knew how much he relied on them to fill him in.

"Give me your shirt," he demanded, and Efren stripped off his sweatshirt and handed it over. Eric wrapped it around his arm and ran to the other side of the car. "Protect your head," he yelled to her. She turned away, and Eric smashed his elbow into the cracked driver's-side window. It fell inward, and he cleared away the extra glass to stick his head inside. "We're going to get you out. Others are on their way to help."

"The baby first!" she cried.

"I'm going to hand him out to my friend. His name is Efren Brenna. You're on Secure One property, which was a handy place to crash."

"I didn't crash. Someone followed me and then ran

me off the road!" Sadie's eyes were wild, and her chest heaved from adrenaline.

Someone had run them off the road? Son of a... "We're going to help you—just take long, slow deep breaths so you don't hyperventilate." Eric kept talking to her while he cleared glass off the seat and then turned to Efren. "I'm going to climb in and unlock the door that isn't smashed. We need to take the baby out that way."

"Got it," Efren said, lopping to the other side of the car to wait for him.

Eric carefully slid into the car, pulling his legs into the tight space. At six-four, he wasn't made for cars this size. "Everyone is going to be just fine. I've got a nurse on the way to check on the baby, so hang in there."

He finally got the door unlocked, and Efren pulled it open immediately. "How do I unlatch the car seat? I want to leave him in it until I'm sure he isn't injured." The baby had cried himself out and just whimpered as they worked to free him. He didn't look injured at first glance, but Selina Colvert, their on-site nurse, would be the one to determine that for certain.

"Pull the handle forward, and there's a red button on the back."

Efren followed directions and had the baby out in no time. When Eric knelt in the front passenger seat, he realized freeing his aunt—and wanted murder suspect—would be a lot more complicated.

Chapter Four

Air hissed between Sadie's teeth when Selina touched the wound with antiseptic. Selina glanced up and frowned. "I'm sorry. I know it sucks, but I'm almost done."

Sadie worked up a smile and waved her hand in the air. "No apologies. I appreciate you fixing me up so I don't have to go to the hospital. I don't know who's after me, but I can't risk taking Houston back out on the roads right now."

"You're absolutely certain that someone ran you off the road?" Eric asked as he walked around the med bay with Houston, jiggling and patting the baby as though his life depended on it. Despite the seriousness of their situation, she couldn't help but smile. He was terrified of hurting him—that was easy to see. Then again, she might be afraid of the same at six-four and over two hundred pounds. Eric's arms swallowed up Houston, and Sadie struggled not to love the whole image. Houston's father had been a no-show, so the baby had never had a man in his life. She wondered what it must be like for him to be held in the strong arms of a man who cared, even for a little while. Was Houston afraid, or could he sense that everyone here had protected him?

"I'm positive," she said. "I took the exit to look for a place to feed and change Houston but noticed a dark SUV follow me down the exit ramp. I was already paranoid, so I kept driving rather than stop at the gas station. They stayed behind me, which could have been innocent."

"Until it wasn't," Eric said just as Houston started to cry again.

Selina didn't say anything, but she grimaced, which worried Sadie. They knew something she didn't, but everyone refused to answer her questions.

Sadie knew things didn't look good for her. She was on the run with a baby that wasn't hers, his mother was missing and she'd been run off the road. She couldn't help but feel like the ante had just been upped and that her sister was in more danger than ever before. She had to find Kadie soon, or she worried her sister could be gone forever.

"This needs a few stitches." Selina broke into her thoughts, and Sadie snapped to attention. The plastic under the dashboard had crushed into a V during the accident and trapped her inside the car. They'd gotten her out, but not before a jagged piece had sliced her lower leg open. "I'm afraid it won't heal if I don't close it up."

"Do what you have to do," she said, gritting her teeth and waiting for the burn of the needle. Everyone at Secure One seemed to trust Selina Colvert with their life, so she was grateful she didn't have to leave the security Secure One offered right now. Selina set about her work, and Sadie was pleasantly surprised that she felt nothing but the sharp prick of the needle to numb it.

"All done," Selina said, applying a bandage to the wound before removing her gloves. "It only needed five stitches, but you're going to feel it in the morning," she explained, cleaning up her tray. "I'll give you antibiotics to ensure it doesn't get infected. It's safe to shower since I put the waterproof cover over it. We'll have to take them out in about a week."

"Thanks, Selina. I appreciate the help. Is there some-where I can go to warm a bottle for Houston? He's going to start screaming if I don't."

"Sure, Eric can take you down to the kitchen. There's no high chair, I'm afraid."

"No problem," Sadie promised, standing and fixing her pants. "I can feed him in his car seat."

"Eric, can you take Sadie to the kitchen?" Selina asked as he continued to walk around the room with Hous-ton, but he didn't respond. Selina held up her finger and walked over to them, tapping Eric on the shoulder. He turned, and she signed something to him, to which he nodded and walked over, handing Sadie the baby.

"Hi, Houston," she cooed to the little boy. She watched as Eric fiddled with his ears and gave them a rueful smile.

"Sorry—I turned my ears off when he cried and didn't hear you. Selina said you need to go to the kitchen?"

"Yes, please," Sadie said, standing and setting Hous-ton on her hip while she tried out her leg. It was sore, but she could walk with no problem. "He'll need a bottle and food before I do anything else."

Eric exchanged a glance with Selina, who nodded, and then he ushered her out of the room and down a long hallway. "Sorry about back there," he said, walking be-side her while carrying the car seat.

"Don't apologize," she said with a shake of her head.

"Sometimes I wish I could shut my ears off when he's crying. I never thought of it when I asked you to take him. I should be the one apologizing."

"I didn't mind. He's a good boy, just scared and confused." The shrug he gave at the end of the sentence told her that Eric had liked his babysitting job more than he wanted to let on.

"Once he eats, he'll be off to dreamland, which is good. I need to figure out what's going on."

"I can probably help with that." She glanced at him, but his face was a mask of neutrality. "Let's get him fed first, and then we'll talk."

He flipped the light on, and they walked into a large commercial kitchen big enough to feed a small army. Then again, this place looked like it housed a small army, so it was probably needed. Sadie busied herself getting Houston's food made and heating his bottle, but the whole time, her mind was racing to figure out who wanted her dead and why.

Once Houston had been fed and changed, Eric brought Sadie and the baby to the meeting room. He'd said he wanted to tell her what was happening but hadn't divulged anything so far. After the long day, she was starting to fade, but Houston wouldn't settle down like she had expected him to after dinner.

"Give me the baby. You need to rest that leg." He held his arms out for the little guy who practically threw himself into them.

Sadie collapsed into the nearest chair while he tucked Houston into his arm and grabbed the half-finished bottle, popping it into his mouth. Houston sucked at it hungrily, which offered blessed silence to the room.

"You look like you've done that a few times," she said, her keen eye ensuring he was doing everything correctly.

"I had six younger brothers and sisters, so I was feeding babies by the time I was seven."

"Wow," she said with a shake of her head. "I can't imagine having that many siblings. It must have been chaos."

"There were days I'm sure my mother drank once we were in bed." His smile was rueful, so she knew he was joking, and she cracked a smile herself.

"I would be surprised if she didn't too. It was only Kadie and me in our family. Kadie is older by barely a year, and Mom called us her Irish twins. That's why our names rhyme. Mom wanted us to be as close as real twins so we always stuck together in life. I have to find her."

Eric tipped his head in confusion. "Wait, find her? Is she missing?"

Sadie nodded and swallowed hard around the panic clawing at her throat. Pushing back the tears was much more challenging, but she managed to say the words that terrified her. "Kadie's been missing for almost ten days now. I told the police, but they don't believe me."

"They think she ran away?"

"Yes, but she didn't! I swear to you she didn't!"

He rested his hand on her shoulder to calm her. "I'm listening, Sadie. You're positive she didn't get overwhelmed taking care of Houston?"

"I have no doubt in my mind. Kadie is an excellent mother, and she has a strong support system. There was never a time that she couldn't tell me she needed a break, and I would take over care of Houston. Something happened to her, I'm telling you!"

Eric squeezed her shoulder to calm her, but it wasn't working. She was barely holding it together. Then again, maybe he was why she was still holding it together. By rights, she should've been in a bed nursing her leg wound.

"I'm listening," he promised. "Walk me through it."

She held her arms out for Houston, and he gently laid the babe in her arms. Houston immediately rubbed his face against her shirt while she stroked his head. Sadie loved him like a son; she'd do anything for him, including risking everything to find his mother.

"Kadie and I live together. I'm the younger sister but also the one with the most common sense. Kadie was always the fanciful child and the free and easy adult. At least until she had Houston," she added quickly, so he didn't think Kadie didn't take care of the baby. "When she found out she was pregnant, I convinced her to move into my apartment so I could help her with the baby and she could save money. We worked opposite shifts, so while I worked, she had Houston, and while she worked, I took care of him."

"Where does she work?" Eric asked. "At Fettering's?"

"No, she's a dental hygienist." She gave him a crooked grin. "I know, a strangely responsible career for someone as free and easy as Kadie, but it worked for her. She finished school first since she was the oldest, and then I was supposed to go."

"Supposed to?"

Sadie was embarrassed, so she kept her gaze glued to Houston rather than the eyes of the man who was too nice to her in her time of need. She couldn't stand to see pity or disgust in his eyes. "Life kept getting in the way and I kept putting it off. Then Houston came along. He was more important. I'm only twenty-nine. I have plenty of time to go back to school."

He lifted her hand and squeezed it. "You're a good aunt to that little boy. He's lucky to have you."

"That's why I worked nights," she said, finally glancing up at him. There wasn't pity or disgust in his eyes, just an earnestness to help.

"Why did you work the day shift today then?"

"Since Kadie disappeared, I've had to work my schedule around my friend Julia's since she watches Houston for me."

"Which means you worked back-to-back shifts."

"He's worth it."

"We do what we have to do, right?" She nodded rather than answer and kept her face turned to Houston's. Soon, he was tipping her chin up to face him. "I need to read your lips while we're talking, okay?"

"So-sorry," she stuttered, forgetting herself for a moment. "I'm tired and sore."

"Scared and hungry too?" he asked, and she nodded. "I'll get you some food once Houston is asleep. In the meantime, tell me what happened the day Kadie disappeared."

"It was like any other day," she said with a shrug. "I came home from work and took over Houston's care while she went to work. It was about an hour after she left when her work called to find out if she was coming in. She had never missed a day of work, and they were worried. Since I knew she'd left an hour earlier, I was frantic, thinking she'd been in a car accident or something dreadful like that. I drove her route to work, but she was nowhere to be found."

"Her car is missing too?" he asked, and she nodded. "You know that's a pretty good sign that she did run, right?"

"The note would also lead a person to think that," she added, chewing on her lip. His brow went up, and she sighed. "I found the note in my room later that morning."

"A note that said she was overwhelmed and leaving town?"

"Yes, but here's the weird part. It wasn't there when I changed my clothes after I got home from work, but it was there when I returned from searching for Kadie." His brow went up higher. "That freaked me out because someone was in our apartment. I immediately loaded up Houston and went to stay with my friend Julia. Here's the other thing. Kadie didn't write the note. It's not even close to her handwriting."

"Maybe she was in a hurry?" he asked, and she shook her head, setting her jaw.

"Listen to me," she hissed as she leaned toward him. "I know my sister and her handwriting. If she wrote that note, she purposely wrote it so I would know she was being forced. I showed the police. I even showed them samples of her real handwriting, but they aren't listening!"

He held his hand out, and she took a deep breath before she upset the baby. "I believe you, Sadie. You know your sister better than anyone, so if you say this is completely out of character for her, we work the case until we find her. Mina Jacobs, one of our operatives, could analyze the note's handwriting." He paused and grimaced. "I bet you don't have it with you."

"I do," she said with a nod. "It's in my luggage. I took everything I thought I might need to find her."

"Good. Efren brought everything in from your car, so we'll get Mina on that once Houston is settled."

"We need to call a wrecker for the car, right? I'm afraid it's done for after that crash."

Eric smiled. "Oh, that car has carried its last passengers. We've moved it to one of our equipment sheds for now. You don't need to worry about it until you're feeling better."

Houston let out a wail, and she rubbed his soft head to soothe him. "I'm worried about him," she said as he continued to fuss. "He was jostled in the accident. What if we're missing something, and that's why he's so fussy? Maybe he did get hurt in the crash."

"I'm sure he's got bumps and bruises the same as you do."

"I know I could use some Tylenol." Her tone was joking, but he could tell she was serious.

Eric turned, grabbed a black phone off the wall and then punched a button. "Hey, Selina," he said when she answered. "Could you come to the meeting room with some Tylenol or Advil? Sadie is hurting." He hung up the phone and swung back to her. "Selina is on her way."

"You didn't have to do that," she said in frustration. "I think I have some in my purse."

"Selina was on her way down anyway. She wants to check on you and Houston. Do you have any pain reliever for him?"

"In his diaper bag," she said, chewing on her lip. "I should give him some, but I don't want to mask any problems we don't know he has yet."

Eric was about to speak when Selina entered like a whirlwind. She handed Sadie a small cup with pills and knelt to check the bandage over her wound. Once she was satisfied, she stood up and glanced between them.

"How is everyone?"

"Houston is fussy, but hopefully he'll fall asleep now that he's had a bottle," Sadie said, swallowing the pills with the water she'd grabbed from the kitchen.

"I think he needs some Tylenol too," Eric gently said. "Sadie is worried about masking any injuries we don't know he has, which is a legitimate concern. What do you think?"

"I think if we don't, we'll have an unhappy boy on our hands all night." She turned to Sadie. "How about I take him to the med bay, give him the Tylenol and observe him for the evening? He can sleep on the gurney with side rails or in his car seat, whichever you think is better."

Sadie rubbed her palm on her thigh a few times before she answered. "I'm okay with that. I don't want him to suffer all night, but I'm worried about him."

"Completely understandable," Selina promised, kneeling next to her. "You love him and feel guilty about the crash, right?" Sadie nodded with half a shrug at the end. "Remember that someone ran you off the road. We don't know why, but this wasn't your fault. You had him buckled in correctly, and because of that, he wasn't severely injured. I'm sure he has some sore muscles like you, but he'll bounce back by tomorrow. I also have a heated blanket system to offer him some relief from those sore muscles if he sleeps on the gurney. I'll be right there by him, so you don't have to worry about him falling."

"Okay," she said with a grateful smile. "Houston needs

to sleep, and if you can offer him some comfort while keeping an eye on him, I would be forever grateful."

"I'm more than happy to," Selina promised, patting her knee before she stood and gathered Houston's diaper bag. "Would a bath be okay? It would allow me to look him over head to toe for large bruises or bumps without scaring him."

"He loves his bath time," Sadie said, pushing herself up. "I'll help you."

Selina held her hand out and motioned at the chair. "You have things to discuss with the team. I'll get Houston settled for the night while you do that. Then, when you're ready to sleep, you're more than welcome to join him in the med bay."

Sadie chewed on her lip for a moment before she spoke, her gaze glued to her nephew in her arms. "Call me with any problems?"

"Without question," Selina promised.

With a kiss to Houston's head and a whispered I love you, Sadie handed him over to Selina.

After they left, Sadie leaned back against the chair with a sigh. "Selina is an angel."

"Truer words were never spoken," he agreed. "When you meet the rest of the team, you'll see we all specialize in certain areas of the security business. That's how we work cohesively as a team."

"Everyone I've met so far has been wonderful, you included. Thanks for all your help, Eric. We'll get out of your hair as soon as I can figure out how to get a car that runs."

"I don't think so, Sadie," he said, sitting across from her. "Why were you running in the first place?"

Her shoulders were hunched, and she stared at the floor rather than make eye contact, remembering at the last minute to look up so he could read her lips. "I was at work, and my boss gave me a note someone had left for me."

"What did it say?"

"Run."

"That's it? Just *run*? So you did?"

Her nod was punctual. "My sister is missing, and they found a body the night before at my workplace. I don't need a college degree to know something is off. I grabbed Houston and left town."

"Where were you going?"

"I don't know!" she exclaimed, jamming her hands into her hair. "I don't know, okay? I just got in the car and drove."

"It's okay," he promised, awkwardly patting her shoulder. "Just take a deep breath." She did, and he patted her shoulder again. "Good. You picked up Houston and took the back roads to avoid the highways?"

She glanced up at him in question for a moment before she shook her head. "No, I was on the main highway headed to Minneapolis. I planned to get lost in the city for a few days until I figured out what to do. It was getting late, and Houston needed a bottle and food, so I took an exit, thinking I would stop at the gas station and take care of him. That's when things changed."

"That's when the SUV started following you?"

"Yes, but I wasn't sure if they were actually following me, so I drove past the gas station thinking maybe that's why they took the exit. If they stopped at the station, I'd turn around and go back."

"But they didn't."

"Nope," she said, shaking her head. "They stayed behind me, so I kept driving. After an hour, I thought they'd decided to pass me, so I slowed down in hopes they'd go around me and I could finish the twenty miles to the next town in peace."

"That's when they attacked?"

"Yep," she said with a sigh. "They swung the back of their SUV into my car, and you saw the result."

"If it makes you feel any better, slowing down probably saved your life."

"I'm glad I did something right tonight." She added a wink and a smile, so he offered her a smile back.

"You did many things right, including taking that note at face value. Are you aware there's an arrest warrant out for you?"

"What?" The gasped question was loud in the quiet room. "An arrest warrant? Why on earth would they put out an arrest warrant for me?"

"For ordering the murder of Howie Loraine."

Sadie gasped, her mouth open, but no words came out. She blinked twice and then crumbled into Eric's arms.

Chapter Five

Sadie blinked several times until she realized the man holding her was not a figment of her imagination.

"Welcome back," he said, helping her to sit up.

She accepted the water he offered and sipped it, her body zinging with the electricity of being touched by a man for the first time in too long. Sadie smoothed her hand down her neck and cleared her throat. "I don't know what happened. The last thing I remember is you saying there's a warrant out for my arrest, which is obviously a joke."

"I wish that were the case, but it's not. The cops picked up one of the men who dropped the body in the storage unit. He told the police that Sadie Cook hired them to put Howie Loraine in the grave."

Her head swam again, but she took a deep breath and let it back out. "There must be another Sadie Cook because I don't know who Howie Loraine is, Eric. You have to believe me!"

He put his finger to her lips to hush her. "I do believe you. We did some digging into your records and can see that you live paycheck to paycheck and have minimal savings."

"I help my sister care for Houston and pay all the rent." Her tone was defensive, and he took her hand.

"And that makes you a wonderful aunt and sister. I wasn't judging you. I was pointing out that there is no way you paid anyone to commit a crime. Do you know the Loraines?"

"Again, I don't have a clue who Howie Loraine is," she said, rubbing her temple with the hand he wasn't holding. She liked how his hand encapsulated hers. It made her feel safe as her entire world fell apart.

"The eldest Loraine, Howie's father, Randall, was arrested and jailed for a counterfeiting scheme he ran about eight years ago."

"I moved to Bemidji from Minneapolis five years ago, so that was before my time here. This Howie was his son?"

"Yes, his youngest of three. Let's just say Howie liked to play it fast and loose. Chances are whoever killed him was someone he owed something to."

"If that's the case, why frame me?" she asked. "They don't even know me."

"At least not on the surface—"

"I don't know them!" she exclaimed, jumping up and planting her hands on her hips.

Eric stood, making her feel diminutive as he gazed down at her. "I believe you," he said again, taking her hand. "What I'm trying to say is we can't say that your sister didn't know them."

Sadie tipped her head in confusion. Kadie? Her head started to shake before she even spoke. "No. Kadie tells me everything. I know everyone she knows and who she dates."

"Good. Then we need to start with Houston's father."

"Okay, so that's one thing she didn't tell me," Sadie admitted with a grimace.

"You don't know who the baby's father is?"

"No, but I assure you, it's not someone with the last name Loraine. She never dated anyone by that name. Full disclosure?" she asked, and he nodded. "I'm not proud to say this, but Kadie told me she isn't sure who Houston's father is. She had a one-night stand and never got the guy's name. About three months later, she found out she was pregnant."

"This is not an untold story," he said, probably to make her feel better. It didn't work. "That happens a lot. I'm saying that until we know why they accused you, we need to protect you and Houston."

"I don't know how we would find out why they accused me if I don't know who *they* are, Eric."

When he squeezed her hand again, a jolt of electricity ran up her arm to lodge in her chest. What was happening to her? She didn't have time for entanglements or romance while running for her life alongside Kadie's and Houston's. Maybe that was why she reacted to the tall, dark and handsome stranger. He offered her a small light in the darkness, and she was grateful to him. Sure. That was it. Once he dropped her hand and never touched her again, she'd be able to convince herself of that.

"That's what we do here at Secure One." When she raised her brow, he chuckled for a moment. "Okay, so that's not our purpose, but we've been involved in some high-profile cases that we solved because of the targets on our backs."

"But you don't have a target on your back. I do. I'm no one special."

"Never say that," he insisted, squeezing her hand tightly. "The moment I met you at Dirk's, I knew you were someone special. The moment you walked through the doors of Secure One, you became family. That's how Cal runs this place, so you may as well know that right now. You aren't leaving here until we clear your name and find Kadie."

"Those are a lot of promises when you don't know if you can keep them," she whispered, her gaze on his lips as he focused on hers. That was when she remembered not to whisper. She lifted her gaze until he held hers, and she was drawn to place a finger against his lips. "Remind me to speak louder if that's what you need. I don't want to make life harder for you."

When she dropped her finger, he cleared his throat as though he were as surprised by the contact—and her words—as she was. "Will do. You're observant, which is good. That will help us with this mess. As for making promises I can't keep, that statement proves that you don't know what we're capable of at Secure One, but you'll learn. For now, you must put your leg up with some ice and rest until morning."

Her head shake was frantic. "No. There's no time to rest. We have to start searching for Kadie."

"There is time for you to rest while I fill the team in on what's happening. While I do that, Mina will look at the note. Our boss, Cal, flies back tomorrow afternoon or evening with the rest of the team. Once they're here, we'll have enough people to help us search for answers. We'll find Kadie and clear your name, but we can't do that if we're exhausted. You included." He stood and held out his hand to her. "Houston needs you to be strong enough to care for him while you're here too."

Tentatively, she placed her palm into his. His hand was so warm that it instantly calmed her and made her feel like everything might be okay. "Don't you have to turn me over to the police?"

"Should I? Yes. Do I *have* to? No. We don't have to do anything."

"But there will be repercussions for you if you don't, right?" she asked, following him to the door. He took her elbow so she could lean heavily on him as her leg started to ache now that the local anesthesia was wearing off.

"Only if we can't prove that you're innocent. Once we do, we'll hand over the evidence and you to the police, and you'll be cleared. That won't happen until your sister is safe and the threat has been mitigated. The events of this evening are enough to tell me that whoever has decided to set you up plays to win. Do you understand what I'm saying?"

Sadie's throat was too dry to speak, so she just nodded. She understood that she could have died tonight, and if she wasn't careful and didn't listen to everything this man told her to do, she could still find herself dead and unable to protect Houston. As they walked down the hallway to the med bay, she had to ask herself if all of this had to do with something she'd seen, heard or done at Dirk's house. Nothing else made sense. Had she seen or heard something odd or unusual at work that she hadn't registered?

She begged her tired, concussed mind to think, but all it did was pound. The answers to the thousand questions running through her head would have to wait until she'd had some sleep and the headache dissipated. With any luck, her head would be clear by morning, and she could help the team sort out all the moving parts of this mystery. A glance at Eric told her that a guardian angel had been watching over her tonight when that car had tried to take them out. Both by keeping them alive and having them land on the property of a team that fought for the underdog, no matter the evidence stacked against them.

"WHAT DO WE KNOW?" Mina asked as soon as everyone was gathered in the conference room.

"Cal called and they're flying back in the morning," Eric said to open the meeting. "They should be here no later than nine. He knows we need help."

"Good. We need the entire team back here if we're going to have enough staff to go around," Mina said.

He pointed at her. "Exactly what I told Sadie before I forced her to rest with Houston. I got as much out of her as I could tonight. She was exhausted and in pain."

"How did she react when you told her there was a warrant for her arrest?" Efren asked.

Eric lifted a brow at him. "She became so overwrought that she passed out in my arms."

"Hard to fake that," Mina said. "Not impossible, but hard."

"She wasn't faking," Eric said between clenched teeth. He wanted to jump down Mina's throat but held himself back. He had to play it cool, or they would start to think this was about more than just helping the underdog. "Once she came to, it was easy to see that she had no idea what was happening." He walked to the whiteboard where he'd written a list of information and tapped it with his finger. "This is the timeline of events since a few weeks before I met her at Dirk's."

"Wait, her sister is missing?" Mina asked, pulling a notepad in front of her. "I didn't see a missing person report on our basic background check of Sadie."

"The police blew her off. Kadie left a note, but Sadie says there's no way her sister wrote it." He turned to Efren. "Sadie said the note and a sample of her sister's handwriting were in her car."

"I put everything in the guest room since I didn't know where they'd be staying," Efren confirmed.

"I'll get to work on running those samples through my programs in the morning," Mina said, and Eric turned to her. "If we can prove without a doubt that two different people wrote those notes, that's another point on Sadie's side of the column that she's being set up."

"I don't need columns to tell me that," he said, leaning on the table. "The woman has no idea what's going on. She's just trying to care for her nephew and keep them alive. We need to do a deep dive on both Sadie and Kadie to see if they're tied to the Loraines in a way even they aren't aware of on the surface."

"Where is the baby's father?" Roman asked from where he sat at the table. "He might be our best place to start."

"She doesn't know. All Kadie would say was that she wasn't sure who the father was. She had a one-night stand and never got the guy's name."

"Do you think Sadie would agree to a DNA swab of Houston?" Mina asked, and everyone turned to her expectantly. "If we run the baby's DNA through CODIS, it's possible the father could be in the database."

"Or a family member," Roman said, standing and leaning on the table like Eric. "Good thinking, babe."

Mina smiled, but Eric could tell she still wasn't feeling well. Her face was drawn, and her skin had a pallor. It was time to wrap up the meeting so everyone could sleep.

"That's a great idea, Mina," Eric agreed. "I'll talk to Sadie about it in the morning. It might take some convincing, but I'll do my best."

"In the meantime, I'll do the handwriting analysis and start a background search on Kadie," she said, writing on a pad.

"In the morning," Roman said firmly, glancing at her, and she nodded. "We all need to call it a night and start fresh tomorrow."

"Agreed," Eric said, his frustration mounting at the lack of information and the late hour. "Efren and I will do shifts with the rest of the guys to cover all the accounts. I'll turn everything over to Lucas at 5:00 a.m. when he comes on shift. We'll reconvene when Cal is back and Sadie is rested."

Everyone agreed and they gathered their things before they left. Eric insisted on taking the first shift so Efren could take his leg off and rest his limb. There was no sense in trying to sleep right now. If he did, his mind would conjure up the horrors he'd already lived through once. Better to keep his mind busy trying to help Sadie.

When Eric strolled into the control room, he stopped short. Lucas Porter was at the monitors with his trusty companion, Haven, under his feet. "Lucas? What are you doing here? Your shift doesn't start for a few more hours."

The man turned to him with an easy smile. "I know,

but after all the commotion, I couldn't get back to sleep, so I thought I'd help out with the accounts so you guys could rest."

"That's appreciated, Lucas." He pulled out a chair and fell into it. "I'm exhausted, but my mind is swirling. I'll sit here and stare at a computer monitor until I fall asleep or the sun rises."

Lucas chuckled as he hit a toggle switch to flip his screen to a different camera. "I've been there. I'm so lucky to have Haven to keep me on the straight and narrow now. Ever think about getting a service dog?"

Eric glanced at him for a moment and shrugged. "I have, but my lifestyle doesn't lend itself to caring for a dog. I'm often off on jobs that wouldn't work with a dog in tow."

"They're trained animals, Eric," Lucas said with an eye roll. "They can be away from their person. They don't like it, but they can. They can also be invaluable in the field because, again, they're trained animals."

Eric ran his hands over his face a few times and slowly leaned back in his chair. "I don't need a dog as much as better hearing aids."

"I wasn't talking about your hearing loss."

Lucas fell silent, and Eric held his tongue. He knew Lucas was talking about his PTSD. After all, that was why Lucas had Haven, but Eric preferred to pretend he hadn't seen the horrors of that day every time he closed his eyes. Pretending was more manageable than admitting he had no control over anything that happened in this world. His chuckle was sardonic when it left his lips. It wasn't but a few months ago that he'd been telling Mack he needed to find help for his PTSD from that day when their worlds had exploded. Talk about the pot and the kettle.

"If the team needs extra hands, Haven and I are in," Lucas said. "Whether in the control room or the mobile command station. I joined Secure One because I believe in what you guys do."

Eric nodded once. "Noted, but now that you're here, it's because you believe in what *we* do. We're a team, and you're part of that team now. Once Cal arrives, we'll meet with all the big names. You want in?"

"Absolutely," the man said, sitting up straighter. "Anything I can do to help."

Eric thumped his back and nodded. "We're lucky to have you, Lucas."

They were lucky. They all knew it. Lucas had been working as the head of security for Senator Ron Dorian's estate when they'd crossed paths. After Secure One had saved the senator's daughter and taken down a serial killer terrifying the nation, Lucas had emailed to ask if they ever hired other disabled veterans to join the team. The email had come at an opportune time for both of them. With all the press they'd gotten starting with taking down The Madame and The Miss and solving the Red River Slayer case, they'd had more clients than manpower. Cal had pulled Lucas in for an interview immediately.

The fact that Lucas had severe PTSD from his time in the war wasn't a sticking point for any of them. Everyone on the team had it to some degree. When a human experienced war, it changed them on a molecular level. No one left their time in the military without some form of PTSD, whether they'd served in peacetime or wartime.

Lucas controlled his with medication and by keeping Haven by his side. He was also meticulous, insightful and eager to prove himself as a team player. Cal had hired him immediately after his background check had cleared, so he'd been working for them for almost six months. Eric had been the underdog enough times to know what Lucas was feeling now that he had his feet under him.

"It's time for you to spread your wings around here," Eric said, pushing himself to stand. "In fact, since you took the initiative to cover for me, I'm going to bed. The main team will be back in play at 9:00 a.m. I'll get you in on the meeting. Good enough?"

"Better than good enough. See you then."

He held his fist out for a bump, which Eric delivered before he turned and left the room. Suddenly, his burdens didn't seem so heavy. It was time to lay his head down before the start of what was sure to be another busy, confusing day.

Chapter Six

Houston banged on the table and squealed with the glee of an eight-month-old with scrambled eggs. Through the large serving window, Sadie watched one of the men re-fill his plate from the chafing dishes and sit beside Houston to eat. She liked that the kitchen was set up so the cook never had their back to the dining room.

"What is going on in here?" Eric's voice boomed through the kitchen, and Sadie spun away from the stove, spatula still in hand, as her heart pounded against her ribcage. She couldn't be sure if it pounded from the scare or from having his voice surround her again.

"Uh, breakfast," she said, remembering to speak clearly since there was so much noise in the other room. "Are you hungry?"

"You're supposed to be resting."

She returned to the pan and stirred the eggs momentarily before facing him again. "Where did you get the idea that a woman with a hungry infant gets to rest?"

Eric smiled, and she did an internal fist pump to get that much out of him. He was always so stoic. Maybe he came by it naturally or maybe it was the job, but seeing his smile at the start of the day was lovely.

"That's a fair point, but why are you feeding everyone?"

Rather than answer, she turned to the stove, flicked the heat off and made him a plate. She answered as she handed it to him. "Because everyone was hungry?" His brow lowered to his nose, and she bit back an eye roll. "I made Houston breakfast, and one of the guys wandered down when they smelled food. Before long I had an entire pack of hungry men lining up for breakfast. It's like no one ever cooks for them."

Eric was already shoveling food into his face, but when he swallowed, he grinned at her again. "It's been a long time since we've had a cook here. Cal has been buying premade meals for the freezer and someone cooks something every few days, but it's not like when Charlotte was cooking."

"Who's Charlotte?" she asked, checking on Houston over her shoulder. He was strapped securely into a chair with his baby sling, but with so many people telling him he was cute and making sure he finished his breakfast, she had no worries he'd get hurt.

"Mack's fiancée. Charlotte is the reason they're in DC. She received an award at the White House for the Red River Slayer case."

Sadie snapped her fingers when she remembered. "That's right. She started working here as the cook?"

"She started as a sex-trafficked woman who found refuge here during a case. When she stayed on at Secure One, she replaced Marlise in the kitchen when Marlise was promoted."

"Who's Marlise?" She felt like she was playing *Who's on First?* with this guy.

Her confusion made him laugh, and he shook his head as he set his plate down. "In fairness, you haven't met the whole team yet. Marlise is Cal's wife. They should be back any minute."

"Thanks for the information. I would hate to put my foot in my mouth. That said, if they're on their way, I'd better clean up this mess so we can get to work."

"We?" he asked, raising a brow.

"You don't think I'm going to sit here meekly while you rescue me, do you?"

"The thought had crossed my mind—not rescue you so much as help you out of this jam."

Sadie worried her lip between her teeth as she watched Houston blow raspberries at Mina. "I do need help out of this jam. I have no idea how to keep Houston safe and clear my name at the same time."

"That's why we're going to fight for—"

"Secure one, Charlie," came a voice from the doorway.

Eric snapped to attention and turned to the giant of a man blocking the door. "Secure two, Echo."

"Secure three, Romeo," Roman said from the dining room.

And so it went around the room as it appeared to be how they welcomed their team back into the fold. When everyone started talking at once, Sadie grimaced as the decibel level climbed. She couldn't help but wonder how Eric even functioned in that environment. Then she noticed him flick his finger near his ear before he did some fancy handshake with the man in the door. It was impressive, considering the steampunk-looking prosthesis Cal wore on his hand.

"Glad you're back, boss. How was the flight?"

"As gentle as dove's wings," the man said, his eyes crinkling as he smiled.

Something told Sadie this man could be as sweet and loving as your nana, or as hard and mean as an assassin. She hoped she never saw the latter.

"Good to hear. I'm glad you're back. We need the manpower."

"As always," Cal said with a chuckle and a shake of his head. "You must be Sadie?"

He stepped around Eric and stuck his hand out for her to shake. It was a unique experience when his three prosthetic fingers wrapped around her flesh. "I am. It's nice to meet you, Cal. Eric was schooling me on the who's who of the Secure One team."

"Good to hear since you'll see these faces for the next few days. I need to get settled, and then we'll meet in the conference room in thirty?"

"I'll be there. Do you want breakfast? There's plenty here," Sadie said, motioning at the warming dishes on the counter.

"You made breakfast?"

"The baby was hungry," Eric answered, and she pretended not to notice his eye roll.

Cal's laughter cut above the din of voices, making Sadie smile. "One thing led to another" was her only explanation.

Cal grabbed a plate and dug into the eggs. "I'm not one to turn down good home cooking. We've missed it around here. Thank you for feeding everyone."

"It was no problem," Sadie said, knowing she wore a ridiculous smile. Seeing someone appreciate her work was gratifying, and she tossed a withering look of *I told you so* at Eric. "I work as house staff for Dirk, but I often help out in the kitchen when there's a big party. I love it when I get a chance to stretch my cooking wings. Anyway, I'll clean up the baby and meet you in the conference room in a few minutes."

She tried to walk past Eric, but he grabbed the crook of her arm. "I'll be down to your room to escort you in ten."

"I don't need an escort," she said, shaking her arm free of his grasp. Every time he touched her, electric heat slid through her belly. That needed to stop if she was going to get out of Secure One with her life and her heart intact. He lowered his brow and waited until she sighed. "Fine. See you in ten."

Sadie plastered a smile on her face and walked into the dining room to collect Houston. She didn't like being ordered around by a man, even if he was trying to help her, but she forced herself to remember she had bigger problems. Eric was trying to keep her out of jail so nothing happened to Houston. She would lose him to CPS if they took her into custody, which was out of the question. Her only objectives were to find Kadie and keep Houston safe. She'd do whatever she could to make that happen, even if it meant being bossed around by a tall, dark, brooding stranger. She would go as far as making the ultimate sacrifice so Kadie and Houston could live. Sadie had already come to terms with the idea that she might not walk away from this situation alive, and she was okay with that as long as Houston was safe.

After wiping Houston's face and freeing him from the sling, she swung him into her arms and waved as she left the room. It was time to start the day and stop thinking about the man who had an unseen power over her after such a short time. When they were together, his warm hands and the look in his eyes didn't help matters. She had to focus on her goals, to clear her name and bring Kadie home. Anything else was a distraction she couldn't afford.

AFTER A SHARP rap on the door, Eric dropped his hand to his side and shook out his shoulders. He was steeling himself for the fight to come, but there was no choice. If Sadie didn't agree to the DNA swab for Houston, it would cut them off at the knees when it came to finding Kadie. He'd convinced Sadie to trust them when she was skeptical and untrusting of everyone and everything, so he hoped for that reason she'd listen to the reasons why they needed Houston's DNA to find his mother and keep her nephew safe.

The door cracked open, and Sadie stuck her head out. "Hi, I'm almost ready to go. We'll be out in a few minutes."

She went to close the door, but he held it with his palm. "I need to talk to you privately first." Fear skittered through her eyes. "Don't worry," he whispered, stepping closer to the door. "It's not Kadie."

The door swung open for him to enter, but not before he noticed her shoulders relax a hair. Once he was inside, she pushed the door shut and walked over to the floor, where Houston was playing on a blanket. She picked him up and tucked him into her arms as though she alone could protect him. She couldn't, and he hated to be the one to prove that to her, but he'd have to if she wanted to get out of this alive.

"You're not taking Houston from me."

He took a step closer and cocked his head. "I have no

plans to do that. Why would you think I would? You're both safe here until we sort out how you're involved in this mess. Just take a deep breath and hear me out."

She nodded once, but he noticed she didn't let go of the baby. "Usually when someone says *hear me out*, they have something bad to say."

"Not so much bad," he said, lowering himself to the bed to sit. "Maybe uncomfortable for you, but I want you to understand why we need to do it." She motioned for him to explain, so he did. "We need to take a DNA sample from Houston. It's just a swab of his cheek. Once we have his DNA, Mina can run it through CODIS to see if there's a match."

"What is CODIS, and why does it matter?"

"CODIS is a DNA database that the FBI developed. It's filled with DNA profiles from all over the country. If you have a sample from a crime scene or victim, you run it through the database to see if it matches anyone's profile already on file."

Eric watched her eyes and waited. Since losing his hearing, he'd mastered the art of hearing what a person said with their eyes. He saw the moment the ball dropped. "You're trying to find his father." Eric tipped his head in agreement. "No. It doesn't matter who his father is. He's not going to help us find Kadie."

"You can't say that with certainty since you don't know who Houston's father is yet. If we can find his father, that gives us a new path to try to trace your sister's whereabouts. It will also help us see if there's a connection between your family and the Loraines."

"I'm telling you, Eric, we don't know the Loraines!"

He held his hand out to calm her so she didn't upset

the baby. "I know what you're telling me, but my job isn't to take your word at face value and stop looking. That doesn't do anyone any favors. For all you know, you ran into one of the Loraines at Dirk's, had an interaction with him and never even knew who he was. If we can tie you to a Loraine, then we have better insight into why the cops think you wanted one of them dead. Does that make sense?"

"I understand why you want me to do it," Sadie said, walking up to him. This time her eyes yelled the fierce determination of a mama bear. "But I am not this baby's mother, and I cannot give you permission to find the man my sister has decided won't be part of his life. If she wants to find out who the father is, she can run the DNA test once we find her."

"That doesn't help us now, Sadie. You're not hearing me," he said, frustration filling the room so much so that Houston started to whimper. "Taking Houston's DNA may be the only way to find his mother. We have nothing to go on, the police refuse to look for Kadie and with the arrest warrant active, we can't even take you outside the compound. If you don't agree to this, our hands are essentially tied. Every minute that we don't do something is another minute that Kadie is in danger." He'd tried to deliver that harsh reality with kindness, but he saw the grimace of pain on her face before she turned away.

Sadie kissed the top of Houston's head to calm him as she paced around the room. Every time she looked at the baby, Eric noticed her eyes overflowed with the love of a mother despite not having given birth to him. He had to respect that she was Houston's protector, but at the same time, he had a job to do. There was a woman missing and in danger and another woman being accused of a crime she hadn't committed. Secure One was the only protection Sadie had, and he prayed she saw that before it was too late.

When Sadie turned back to him, she had a mask of neutrality firmly in place. "If I agree to this DNA swab and you find Houston's dad, can you promise me we can go down that path without contacting him? There's no way I'm going to introduce Houston to his father without my sister's permission. Do you understand me?"

Eric held up his hands in defense. "I read you loud and clear. There's no reason we have to contact Houston's father in a public fashion. Mina needs a name, and then she can find everything we need to know."

Sadie brushed another kiss across the top of Houston's tiny head, and he reached up and patted her face as though he was giving her permission to do the test. She laughed, though Eric could tell she wanted to cry, and kissed the baby's palm.

"You have my permission, then. The only thing that I want is to get Houston's mama back. Whatever happens to me is inconsequential as long as he's with Kadie."

"Never say that again," Eric said, standing and stalking across the room. He stood in front of her as white-hot anger tore through him at the thought that she would sacrifice herself for her sister. Did she think so little of herself that she believed no one would miss her? He'd only known her a few days, but when she left Secure One, he knew she would leave a gaping hole in the part of him that he hid from the world. "What happens to you is consequential, both to this little boy and your sister. Never, ever let yourself believe that you're inconsequential, sweet Sadie. That's a good way to give up when the going gets tough. I don't know you that well, but I do know that's not your constitution, so get that straight in your head this instant."

Her eyes widened at his tirade, but he noticed her spine stiffen when she raised her head and gave him a jaunty salute. "Sir, yes, sir," she said with a small smile on her lips.

"Good," Eric said with a nod. "We'll make sure nothing happens to either one of you while you're under Secure One's roof. With any luck, we'll reunite your sister with both of you in seventy-two hours. First, we need to give Mina a path to follow."

"Then let's hit the woods," she said, taking a step back as though being that close to him was unnerving. Maybe it was. In fact, he hoped it was. Because as long as she was unnerved by him, she would keep her distance. If she came too close, he couldn't promise that the mutual heat flaring between them wouldn't consume them.

Chapter Seven

Sadie walked through the door of the conference room with Eric and came face-to-face with the full force of the Secure One team. She stopped short at the end of the long table, and Eric put his hand to the small of her back.

"Thanks for joining us, Sadie," Cal said from where he stood at the whiteboard.

Sadie glanced around the table with a nod. "Thank you for trying to help me with the nightmare my life has become. I'll make breakfast, lunch and dinner for two weeks if you can find the reason someone wants me dead."

"Don't say that too loud," Lucas said with a chuckle. "It's been months since we've had anyone to cook for us. Everyone sure did love a hot breakfast this morning."

"I'm glad it made them happy, and I'll gladly make dinner tonight too. We all have to eat, and it makes me feel like I'm contributing to the team while I'm here."

"I can't argue with that," Cal said. "Unnecessary, but if you want to, no one else will argue either." He winked, and she blushed, glancing down at the table for a moment until Mina spoke up.

"Where's Houston?"

"I left him with Selina," Sadie explained. "Eric suggested it would be easier without him here."

"She needs to focus on the plan without worrying about the baby," he explained before turning to Efren, who sat on the left side of the table. "I told Selina you'd be down later to fill her in on the plan."

"Great," Efren muttered. "It's like you enjoy throwing me to the wolves or something."

Sadie was confused why everyone was snickering, but she figured that was a story for another day. "Selina did the DNA test for Houston before we left. We have to find my sister, and if that's the only way to do it, then it was a chance I had to take."

Mina motioned Sadie over to an empty seat next to her. "It may be the only way to find her, which sounds dramatic, but when someone disappears into thin air—not even leaving a digital trail—it's nearly impossible to find them. Houston's father is the only unknown in her life, correct?" she asked.

"At least to us," Sadie agreed. "She swears she doesn't know who he is, but I wonder if that's true. Either way, that doesn't help us now."

"Exactly," Mina agreed. "If we can find Houston's father, there may be a connection there that we don't have right now. Every second we waste is another second Kadie is in jeopardy."

Sadie took a quick glance around the room. "You mean, you all believe me? You believe that Kadie didn't run away?"

"I looked at Kadie's note this morning," Mina said, slipping it out from the folder on the table. "I believe Kadie wrote this because she left you a secret message within the note. She purposely wrote it so you would question the authenticity of it. At least the authenticity regarding her intentions."

"I don't understand what you mean," Sadie said, her gaze sliding to the note. "I read that one hundred times and never saw a secret message."

Mina held up her finger and pulled out a copy of the note with most of the words blanked out. "It almost escaped me, but when I scanned it into the computer, I noticed that some of the words were darker than the others. It was hard to see with the naked eye, but the computer magnified it. I concentrated on just those letters and got the message she wanted you to know."

"I didn't run. Taken. Protect Houston. Find me," Sadie read, her eyes filling with tears as she gasped for breath. Her world started to spin, and Eric grasped her shoulders and squeezed, bringing her back to center. "I knew it." Her voice gave out, and she closed her eyes, resting her forehead on her palm. "I knew she'd never leave Houston that way."

Eric rubbed her shoulders as the room fell silent and she worked to keep it together for both Houston and Kadie. "Do you need a break?" he asked, resting his warm hand at the base of her neck.

Sadie lifted her head and wiped a wayward tear from her cheek. "No, I'm okay. This makes it clear that she's in danger and we can't waste a minute."

"Give us a timeline on how long she's been missing," Cal said from the board, making a new column to write in.

"It's been ten days now. Kadie went to work like any other day. I know my sister, and there wasn't a hint that anything was different that morning when she kissed

Houston goodbye. An hour later, her work called to see if she was coming in. They told me she hadn't arrived and wasn't answering her phone."

Cal wrote *October thirteenth* on the board. "Okay, so you went looking for her on the thirteenth?"

"Immediately. I put Houston in my car, and I followed her route to work. She wasn't anywhere along any of the routes she would normally take."

"You didn't find her car abandoned either?"

"No," Sadie said, sucking in a breath. "That part worried me the most and was another reason the cops wouldn't look for her. They said she had to have run if she had her car."

"Not necessarily," Lucas said from across the table. "If enough people were in the car that stopped her on the road, it would be easy to take her and her car."

Cal pointed at him and wrote *Multiple attackers* on the board. "What did you do after you went looking for her?"

"I went back to my apartment hoping she was there. She wasn't, and that's when I found the note on my bed. It hadn't been there when I left to look for Kadie."

"Is the building open to anyone?" Cal asked.

"No, you need a key to get in the front of the building and another key for the apartment. The apartment was locked when I got home."

"Which means they had Kadie's keys at that point to get in and out without being noticed."

"I didn't even think about that, to be honest. It's possible the apartment complex still has the security footage!" Sadie said with excitement.

"Lucas," Cal said from the board. "After the meeting

is done, take Sadie to the control room and work with her to contact the apartment management about security footage?"

"You got it, boss," Lucas answered, shooting a smile at Sadie.

She felt better knowing that all of these people had her and Kadie's backs. "Should we ask for as much footage as we can get?" she asked, turning to look at Eric. "Just in case they came back?"

"That's not a bad idea," he agreed, glancing at Cal for confirmation. "You haven't been back since you found the note from Kadie?"

Sadie shook her head and turned back to face Cal. "After I found the note, I was super freaked out. I gathered all of our things and took Houston to my friend Julia's. We've been staying there ever since. She watches him while I work."

"I agree with getting as much footage as possible, then. If you haven't been back, you don't know if they came looking for something in the apartment or left a ransom demand," Cal pointed out.

"I never thought of that!" She gasped the words more than she spoke them. "I should have stayed at the apartment, but I was so scared for Houston that I didn't even think!" Tears filled her eyes again and she choked on a sob. "I'm a terrible sister!"

Eric's fingers squeezed her shoulders. "You're not a terrible sister. You did the right thing. Staying in the apartment was dangerous when you knew they could get to you there. You had no other choice."

"Eric's correct," Cal said as Mina handed her a tissue. "We just have to consider all possibilities when it comes to why these people took Kadie."

"But if they left a ransom demand and I never got it, they may have hurt Kadie!"

"No," Eric said, squeezing her shoulders again. "It's not a secret where you work, correct?" Sadie shook her head no. "Considering the note you got yesterday telling you to run, we all know someone else is aware that you work for Dirk. I would venture a guess it's not hard to ask around in Bemidji for directions to Dirk's place. If they wanted ransom, they'd know where to find you."

Cal motioned for Eric to stand next to him at the whiteboard. Sadie didn't know if that was because he wanted his help or if it was because that way Eric would be able to hear him better. If there was one thing she noticed about this team, they all worked together to support each other and work around their disabilities.

"I didn't think of that, to be honest. Mostly because I wasn't part of the events at Fettering's place, but I think we're all on the same page now," Cal explained. "Sadie, did Kadie act normal during the weeks leading up to her disappearance?"

Sadie appreciated that he'd said *disappearance* and not that she'd run. She paused to think about his question, recalling the last month before Kadie had been taken. "For the most part."

"But?" Eric asked, drawing out the word.

"It's probably nothing."

"Give it to us," Cal encouraged her. "You never know what might be important."

"Well, she started taking Houston out every night for a walk. Even if I offered to keep him for her on my nights off, she insisted on taking him. She claimed she was trying to lose the baby fat, but she had no baby fat. She barely gained any weight with Houston."

"How long were the walks?" Eric asked, while Cal had the marker posed on the board.

"Hours? She was gone so long a few times that I got worried and called her. She didn't answer the calls but texted me she was fine and would be home soon. How long she was gone on the nights I worked, I can't say."

Cal wrote it down on the board. "Which means she could have been trying to get in shape or she could have been secretly seeing someone?"

"Again, yesterday I would have said no, but today I can't say that and believe it."

"Anything else?" Mina asked, taking her hand in hers. "A change in eating habits, sleeping habits or attitude? Anything she may have said that made you wonder at the time but then you forgot about?"

Sadie racked her brain to come up with anything that might help them find Kadie. "There were a few times she was late getting home from work last month. I mean like hours late, not just a few minutes."

"That had never happened before?" Mina asked, and Sadie shook her head.

"No, and she used to always text me to let me know if she was going to be late. She didn't do that those times. I called her work, and they told me she'd left at her normal time."

"Did you confront her when she came home?" Cal asked.

"No. Kadie always apologized and said she lost track

of time at the grocery store or running errands. I took it at face value since she'd come in with bags."

"And she had no excuse for not letting you know?" Eric's question was curious but also moody—as though it made him angry that her sister would disrespect her.

"Her phone was dead both times."

"Or that's what she told you," Mina said, and Sadie answered with a shrug.

"Is it fair to say that Kadie's personality had changed over the last month?" Cal asked, and this time Sadie nodded.

"I never really thought about it, to be honest, but it had changed. I would say for the better, actually. Kadie was a new mom, working and trying to juggle everything on little sleep, so I was happy when she started walking with Houston. It got them out of the house, and Houston slept better, so she got better sleep as well. I wasn't home at night, so I couldn't get up with him to give her a break."

"I just have one question," Mina said, her brow lowered. "How did you work all night and then take care of Houston during the day? When did you sleep?"

"In bits and pieces," Sadie answered with a chuckle. "I napped when he napped, and when she got home at three, I slept until nine and then went to work. Working the night shift for Dirk meant tasks that took longer but were less physical. If I had an evening shift for a party, Julia would watch Houston until Kadie got done with work." She paused and then sucked in a breath. "Julia could be in danger if anyone figures out that she knows me."

"I have surveillance on her," Cal said. "She hasn't been approached by anyone as of yet."

"I need to let her know I'm okay," Sadie said, but Eric shook his head.

"Can't happen. Too risky."

"She could call using a Secure One line. They can't be traced," Mina gently said.

"No," Eric said again, taking the same stance he had earlier in her room. It screamed dominance. "Any contact with Julia could put the woman at risk if they think she knows something she doesn't."

"If that's the case, it's already too late," Cal said. "By way of association, if anyone discovers they're friends, she's going to get a shakedown for information. Sadie needs to call Julia and let her know she's safe but give her no information about where she's staying. It's all over the news that Sadie is wanted for murder, so I'm sure Julie has to be shocked and worried, right?"

"Absolutely, but she won't believe it," Sadie said with conviction. "She's probably terrified though."

"Does she work somewhere during the day?"

"Yes, she's a receptionist at a staffing agency."

"You'll call her there. There could be a listening device at her home, so it's smarter to call her where she can't be overly loud about who is on the phone. The call will put her mind at ease and also get us information. We'll give you a list of questions to ask her, but we need to know if anyone has contacted her about you in a way we can't surveil."

Sadie could tell that Eric didn't like it, but he finally gave his boss one stiff nod.

"Do we have everything up on the board that we know so far?"

Eric held up his finger and grabbed a marker. He

wrote the words *Winged Templar* on the board and circled them. "This name is still an unknown entity. Mina,
have you had any luck tracking down that moniker?"

Mina shook her head. "No. I couldn't find anything
connected to the mob, but we both know that means
nothing. I'm still working on it. Don't give it to the cops
yet."

"I have no intention of doing that," Eric said with an
eye roll. "They'll assume it's Sadie's mob name or something equally ridiculous."

Sadie couldn't help it. She snorted with laughter, slap-
ping a hand over her mouth. "Sorry, but this whole thing
is outrageous."

Cal was grinning when he spoke. "The update I got
from the Bemidji police earlier this morning was that
Howie Loraine was killed in typical mob-style point-
blank range before his head was removed to sit upon his
chest. They are currently doing a deep dive into Sadie's
life to see how she's connected to the mob."

"For heaven's sake!" Sadie growled, anger and righ-
teous indignation filling her. "I'm not connected to the
mob in any way, shape or form. I'm an underemployed
maid trying to help my sister raise her son. I didn't put
a hit out on anyone! Like, how does one even go about
that? Is there a number in the phonebook? Do I google
1-800-HitsRUs?"

Mina slipped her arm around her shoulder. "We know,
Sadie. Cal is just telling us what the police are doing
in their investigation. It's important to know if they're
keeping you as a suspect or tossing out the warrant."

"Mina is correct. We know you have no connection
to the mob," Cal said. "We've already done backgrounds

on you, but we'll let the police busy themselves looking for a connection that isn't there while we do the hard work of solving the case." Everyone around the table chuckled at that comment. "You see, the Bemidji police are missing the most important person that Secure One has, and that person is Mina. She will find the important connection if there's a connection to be found."

Eric must have noticed she was confused because he returned to the whiteboard and pointed at a picture on the board. Below the picture were arrows, one going to the name *Sadie* and one to the name *Kadie*. "If Mina can find a connection between Howie Loraine and you or Howie Loraine and your sister, then we can trace where the interaction occurred. Once we know the point of contact, we can dive into Howie's life at that junction to see why someone set you up to take the fall for his murder."

"Wait," Sadie said, standing from her seat. "Is that a picture of the Loraines?"

"Of the three boys, yes," Cal said. "This one here," he said, pointing to the middle man in the picture, "is the victim, Howie, this is Randall Junior." He pointed to the man on Howie's left. "And this is—"

"Vic." Sadie walked up to the whiteboard to peer at the image. How could this be possible? Her heart pounded in her chest as she stared at the image. She had to be mistaken. There was no way the answer was this simple. She put a shaky finger on the man to the right of Howie. "I think this is Vic."

"Victor Loraine?" Cal asked with surprise.

She spun toward him with her breath quick in her chest. "Is that his name? We only knew him as Vic."

Eric came up behind her and grasped her shoulders

almost as if he knew she needed the warmth of his hands to ward off the chill of the truth. "You knew him as Vic? How do you know him?" he asked as Cal picked up the marker again.

When Sadie spun around to face him, she was immediately pulled in by the intensity of his gaze. "Um…" She forced herself to look away for a moment. If she didn't, she'd never finish a thought. "I… We…met him at a Halloween party."

"How long ago was that?" Cal asked.

"I want to say it was, like, two years ago? I know it was before Kadie got pregnant. She had an instant crush on him, and they danced together at the party. He asked her out before the night was over."

"You're saying Kadie went out with Victor Loraine?" Eric asked.

"She went out with this guy," Sadie said, pointing at the man in the picture again, "but he told us his name was Vic Larson."

"We just found our connection, people," Eric said. "Mina—"

"Already on it," she answered as she started typing into her laptop.

"Why would he lie about his name?" Sadie asked.

Eric met her gaze again and held it. "I can't say for sure, but he's the only Loraine son who has stayed above the law. He may not like to associate with the name."

"He's the family's black sheep, so to speak," Cal explained. "I imagine using his real last name in this state is difficult. *Larson* gives him anonymity."

"Okay," Sadie said, "even if that's true, what good

will it do him to lie when he eventually has to come clean about it?"

"I can't say, but we found our connection regardless." He turned to Mina. "Can you work with this?"

"Are you kidding me?" she asked with a chuckle. "You're making this too easy on me. I'll update you soon." She stood and walked over to the board. "Sadie, do you remember how long Kadie dated Vic?"

"As far as I know, they only went out once."

"Do you think this could be the one-night stand Kadie was referring to?" Eric asked as Cal wrote on the whiteboard.

"No," Sadie insisted. "It was long before she got pregnant with Houston."

Mina dropped her hand from the board. "As far as you know, Kadie only went out with Vic once? You can't say for certain that they didn't go out more than that and your sister didn't tell you?"

"Honestly, three weeks ago, I would have told you no. But today, I can't say that and believe it. I'm starting to think Kadie kept more secrets than I realized. We always vowed to tell each other everything, but clearly I'm the only one who stuck to that vow."

"Listen," Eric said, catching her eye again. "It's possible that the secrets she kept were to protect you and Houston. Don't assume the worst until you know why she did what she did, okay?"

Sadie nodded, trying to break their connection but was unsuccessful. She was connected to him if he was in the room, like it or not. When Eric stared at her lips like he wanted to kiss them senseless, she didn't want to break the connection.

He's reading your lips, Sadie. Nothing more. She kept telling her brain that, but it wasn't listening. She wanted him to kiss her senseless, which was a bad idea when she was up to her neck in deception. At this moment, she didn't know up from down, and allowing Eric to get close would only complicate the situation. Sadie swallowed hard and reminded herself she had to be strong for Houston. She had to concentrate on finding Kadie before it was too late.

A phone went off and everyone checked theirs, but it was Efren who was being paged. He stood and grabbed his notepad. "I'm needed on the west side of the property. There's a section of the fence that's offline. Are you guys okay here?"

"Go," Cal said with a nod. "When you're done, we'll hopefully have footage to watch from the apartment building. Find me in the control room."

"Ten-four. Tango out."

"Let's adjourn for now," Cal said, putting the marker back on the whiteboard. "Once Mina has time to run some of this information down and we get some of the footage from the apartment building, we'll come back together. In the meantime, you know how to reach each other if situations arise."

Everyone nodded and stood, leaving the conference room for their stations. Sadie still hadn't broken her connection with Eric.

"Are you ready to call the apartment management?" Lucas asked when he stood.

Without taking her gaze off Eric, she nodded once. "I have to check on Houston first though."

Eric grasped her shoulder and squeezed it. "I'll check

on him when I go down to fill in Selina since Efren got called away. If he's sleeping, we'll leave him alone. If he's happy, he can stay with Selina until you're done on the phone. Here," he said, turning and grabbing a black box off the table. "Take this walkie. I'll keep you updated on his status."

Sadie slid it from his hand, his warm skin brushing across hers with just the hint of warmth and tenderness. She wondered what it would feel like to have him caress her face, her body or to have him hold her through the night.

Stop. Focus.

She held up the walkie. "I'll be waiting."

Chapter Eight

Eric stuck his head inside the door of the med bay and noticed Houston asleep on the gurney. Selina stood from the computer and walked over to the door, motioning him outside to talk.

"You must have eyes in the back of your head," Eric said as a greeting.

"I saw you on the computer screen. Is there a problem?"

"No, why would there be?"

"Because you're here instead of Brenna."

"He got a call to fix a fence. I told Cal I'd fill you in."

"Any day is a lucky day when I don't have to deal with that guy," she said on an eye roll.

Eric bit his tongue to keep from popping off on her. Whatever was going on with her had nothing to do with Efren Brenna. He was just the unfortunate person she'd picked to wear her target and take her bullets.

"How's the baby?" He held up the walkie. "I promised Sadie I'd let her know as soon as I saw him."

"Sleeping like one." Selina glanced back to the gurney for a moment, and a smile filled her face. "He's such a good boy. As long as he's fed and dry, he never makes a peep."

"That's helpful considering what we're dealing with

right now. I'm glad he can be away from Sadie for a bit while she helps us with the case. She's calling the apartment management now to see if there's any security footage from the day Kadie disappeared."

"Someone did deliver the note to her room," Selina agreed.

"And that someone had a key, which means it's possible they were caught in the lobby somewhere. Will you keep Houston until she's finished working with Lucas?"

"Houston is not a problem. What can I do to help while he's asleep?"

"Keep working on the DNA, and let us know the moment it's available so Mina can get it into CODIS. We found a connection to Sadie and the victim from the storage unit."

"Do we have a name for the victim? I've been down here since they showed up, and no one has filled me in."

"Howie Loraine. Mob-style execution before his head was removed and put on his chest to fit in the trunk. They're claiming Sadie paid for the hit."

Selina said nothing, but her eyes were wide as saucers. Eric wasn't sure she was breathing so he grasped her arm. "Selina?"

She jumped and took in a quick breath. "Did you say Howie Loraine?"

"Yeah, the youngest of the Loraine brothers...do you know them?"

"N-no," she stuttered. Her lips said one thing, but her eyes said another, and Eric was instantly on edge. "I just remember when their dad was arrested. That was messy."

"Yeah, and the fact that one of Randall Loraine's

sons was killed mob style tells me they're still somehow wrapped up with them."

"So how are Sadie and this Howie kid connected?" Selina asked, her shoulders straightening as she dropped a mask down again. Her reaction to that name was visceral and something Eric couldn't ignore, but for now, she had slipped back into operative mode.

"They don't, but Houston's mom, Kadie," he explained, pointing at the baby, "dated Howie's middle brother, Victor. Mina is running that down for us right now to see how long they dated and if Kadie ever met any of the other brothers."

"Do you think Vic—Victor is Houston's father?"

He saw a bit of fear on her lips when she said the name before she locked it down again.

What was going on with her? This wasn't the same woman he'd worked with for years. Something had changed during the Red River Slayer case, and she hadn't been the same since.

"Sadie doesn't think so, but I'm planted solidly in the other camp. I think there's a good possibility that Houston is a Loraine. If Mina finds a timeline of how long they dated and when they were last seen together, it could line up."

"If that's the case, we have to protect this little boy, Eric. No one can know he's here. No one." Her hands were shaking, and he held her shoulder to calm her.

"What am I missing here, Selina? What do you know that I don't?"

She glanced around the hallway, her eyes filled with fear and worry. There was something else there that Eric couldn't put his finger on, but he was deeply concerned for the woman in front of him.

"Just take my word for it. If that boy is a Loraine, they'll do anything to get their hands on him. No one can know he's here!" she hissed, her voice low enough he couldn't make out her words clearly and had to read her lips.

Before he could say another word, her face changed again and she was back to the calm, organized Selina he recognized. "I'll get the DNA to Mina for upload. If Houston is related to the Loraines, we'll know soon enough since Randall will be in the system as a convicted felon. I'll keep you posted."

With that, she turned, slid the med-bay door shut and walked over to Houston. Eric noticed the shudder that went through her as she stroked the baby's downy head. That left him to wonder just what Selina was hiding from the rest of the team.

LUCAS SHOULDER BUMPED Sadie when she hung up the phone. "That was tough, but you pulled it off."

She let out a breath while she nodded. "For a minute there, I didn't think they bought the story. I'm glad they finally agreed to send the footage over."

"I'm going to let Cal know we were successful, and then I'll set us up in command central to watch the footage. You'll have to be there in case we find something."

"I need to check on Houston," Sadie said, eyeing the black box Eric had given her. He'd messaged that the baby was sleeping, but she wanted to check on him herself. Everything about this was scary, but Houston grounded her. He motivated her to fight to find her sister and bring her home.

"That's fine. It will be at least thirty minutes before the footage arrives by email. Go check on the babe and bring him to the control room if you have to. We'll make it work."

"Okay, thanks, Lucas," she said, standing and stretching. "I'm going to grab a bite to eat too since I missed breakfast."

"You cooked breakfast," he said with a chuckle.

"Doesn't mean I remembered to eat it." She winked as she turned and walked toward the door.

The truth was she hadn't forgotten to eat. She just hadn't been hungry. The moment her sister had disappeared, so had her appetite. Add in the responsibility of Houston and now an arrest warrant for murder hovering over her head, and she was a hot mess. Sadie would force herself to eat and sleep so she could be there for Houston, but the idea that Kadie was in danger while she went about life as usual made her sick to her stomach.

Sadie stepped into the hallway and walked straight into a wall. She glanced up when she heard his exhale of breath. Their gazes met, and for a moment neither of them spoke, both too consumed by the electricity zapping through the air.

"Where are you going in such a hurry, Sades?"

Sades? When did he start calling her Sades?

"To—to check on Houston." She hated how tongue-tied she got around Eric. He unnerved her in the best and worst way possible. She forced her mind to take a step back from his intensity so she could think straight.

"We're waiting for the apartment manager to send over the footage. It should be here within the hour."

"Excellent news. I'm glad you could convince them to turn it over."

"It wasn't easy, but I could tell they didn't know about my 'legal troubles'—" which she put in air quotes "—so they bought my story about an intruder."

"I hope it helps us move this along. Every second we search for Kadie is a second Houston doesn't have his mother." His words hit her like bullets. She closed her eyes and sucked up a breath. "I'm sorry. That was insensitive."

"But true," she whispered, knowing he wouldn't hear the words, but he'd read them on her lips. Her tiny pink lips would melt under his if he ever kissed her. Before she could open her eyes, he'd pulled her into a hug. She stiffened at first, unsure how to feel about being in his arms, until his heat relaxed her and she sank into him. She'd longed for a hug of reassurance but had no one to ask—until now. She was sure that was all it was until he started to rub her back with his warm, gentle hand.

"We're going to find her," he promised, and she slid her arms around his waist and held on for dear life.

"We have to," she said, remembering to speak clearly since he couldn't read her lips. "She didn't do anything wrong. I don't understand the game being played, so I'm taking my toys and leaving the sandbox."

The rumble of laughter from his chest ran the length of her, the sound warming her head to toe while the sensation made her feel like she had a home and a family. She hadn't felt that way in far too long. Sure, Houston and Kadie were her family, but having someone of her own to lean on, depend on and laugh with was what she yearned for more than anything.

But it couldn't be Eric Newman. He was off-limits physically, logistically and emotionally. Physically he was standoffish. It was understandable. He lived a different life than she did and always would. Emotionally he was unavailable. There was no question he'd brought demons back from war—and that was expected, but he still let them control him. She saw it every time he held Houston. A shadow would cross his face that said his time at war had been ugly. Sadie wanted to ask him about it but was afraid he'd never speak to her again if she did.

This hug doesn't feel standoffish, that voice inside said.

She sighed internally. The hug was nothing more than a moment of comfort. Her sanity depended on believing that, but when Eric leaned out of the hug and captured her gaze, he made that impossible.

He zeroed in on her lips and then licked his, narrowed the gap and brushed his against hers. It was soft, tender and too quick, but it told Sadie he experienced the same heat and magnetic pull between them. She wondered if he'd felt the same electric spark she had when their lips had touched.

She didn't have time to ponder the question before he spoke. "Speaking of Houston," he said, clearing his throat though his gaze was still on her lips. "I just checked on him. He's fine."

Sadie blinked several times before she could respond. Her body was on fire with need and desire, and her brain had stopped functioning the moment his lips had touched hers. Why had she been cursed with poor timing? She hadn't found anyone who was interesting or engaging for years, and the one time she did, her life was a hot mess.

He's off-limits. Kiss or no kiss, that voice reminded her.

"I'm happy to hear that, but I can't leave Selina to take care of him. She has a job to do too. I'll go get him, and he can sit on my lap while we watch the footage."

"Right now, Selina's most important job is to take care of the baby."

"Houston is not her responsibility," Sadie said with a shake of her head. "I know I haven't been here long, but I get the vibe that she has more to offer the team than what anyone allows."

The corners of his eyes crinkled from a grimace. "Is it that obvious?"

"It is to someone who lives the same kind of life. Being underemployed puts you on the defense and the offense at the same time. You want to defend your skills and prove them. You have to keep your boring, unchallenging job while looking for opportunities that would put your real skills to the test. I won't let Houston get in the way of Selina being able to flex her skills."

Eric slung his arm around her shoulders, leaving a burning trail of desire across her still-heated nerves. "You don't have to worry about Selina or the team. Your only focus is on yourself, your sister and your nephew. You let us worry about Secure One as a whole. That said, I have it on good authority that Selina is waiting for Houston's DNA from the lab. Once she has it, she'll get the report right to Mina who will run it through CODIS. If he's related to the Loraines, we'll know soon enough since Randall's DNA is in the database."

"He's not a Loraine," she said, immediately on the defense.

"Maybe not, but it makes the most sense to start at the beginning of the path, and right now, that's with the Loraines. If there's no connection to them then we'll pivot."

Sadie noticed Eric was working too hard at keeping his expression neutral when he spoke. He believed Houston was a Loraine too. It wasn't like she hadn't considered it, and while there was always a chance that Kadie had slept with Victor Loraine, she didn't believe he was the father.

"I was going to ask you how Mina does all of this hacking without getting caught. She's hacking government websites."

"You really want to hear that story?" Eric asked, walking them into the kitchen and flipping on the light.

"I do. I'm fascinated by what Mina can do with a computer. If she can trace Kadie down using a mouse and a keyboard, I'll forever be grateful to her."

He pointed at the coffeepot across the counter. "Better fire that up, then. We're going to be here awhile."

Sadie took the opportunity to break their connection and prepare the coffeepot. Once it was gurgling, she couldn't help but touch her lips. Eric had kissed her and then pretended as though it hadn't happened. Maybe he'd realized it had been a mistake the moment his lips had touched hers and wanted to move past it? That was probably what she should do too, but that was easier said than done when living in close proximity.

"Don't overthink it." He came up behind her and plastered his body the length of her back as he leaned into her ear.

"It's kind of hard not to," she answered, her eyes closed since he couldn't see her face. She swallowed around the dryness in her throat and took a breath. "I can't explain the draw between us."

He turned her and grasped her shoulders. "Neither can I, and we don't have time to unpack what's happening between us. We have to concentrate on finding Kadie."

"I agree," she said with a single nod.

"Once Kadie is safe and reunited with Houston, then we can concentrate on this draw between us."

He dropped his hands and slid a stool out to sit. While Sadie prepared mugs for the coffee, he gazed at her with an intensity that left her nerve endings singed. In the next breath, he launched into how Mina had found her way to Secure One via the FBI, as though anything mattered but the promise he'd just made.

Chapter Nine

Eric stood behind Sadie and Lucas, arms folded across his chest with his eyes focused on the screen in front of them. They had the footage from the morning of Kadie's abduction, which he was now convinced was the case, and had found the moment Sadie had left with Houston to go look for her sister. If they were going to catch the guy on camera, the time was coming soon.

"I find it hard to believe they wouldn't know there were cameras in the building," Sadie was saying as Lucas ran the recording. "Everyone has cameras these days."

"There," Lucas said, pausing the video on a guy who had walked into the lobby. He wore black jeans, combat boots and an army-green jacket. "Is he wearing a mask?"

They all leaned in together to get a closer look. "Looks like it," Sadie agreed, and Eric could hear the disappointment in her voice. "A mask of Richard Nixon."

"Original." Lucas huffed the word more than he said it. Disappointment was evident in the room.

"He's wearing gloves," Eric noted while they watched the suspect approach the apartment door. "And he's got a key."

"Those are Kadie's keys," Sadie whispered. "She keeps

a little teething ring on them for Houston in case they get stuck in line somewhere."

They waited, and in less than thirty seconds the masked man had walked into the apartment, returned, relocked the apartment door and slipped out the side door.

"I wish they had cameras on the outside of the building," Eric growled. "If they did, we could trace the car he gets into."

"We asked, but they said they don't have them outside other than at the doors. I'm making some calls to see if there are any cameras on other buildings that might capture the parking lot," Lucas explained.

"Good—stay on that. We know this guy is young, just by the way he moves, average height and white by the color of his neck where it meets the mask."

"That's not much to go on." Eric heard the weight in Sadie's words. He couldn't help but wish he could do something more than stand there.

"No, but at least we know that she was absolutely abducted and forced to write that note. Let's keep watching and see if they come back."

Lucas hit the Double Speed button, and they watched people come and go, but no one other than Sadie approached the apartment door. Eric's phone rang, and he motioned for them to keep going with the video, then stepped out the door to answer the phone. He could see who it was on caller ID, and he needed to take the call.

"Dirk," Eric greeted the man on the other end of the line. "How are things over there?"

"Things would be better if the cops could find my former employee and arrest her."

Eric was going to pretend that he hadn't heard the

word *former* in that sentence. He didn't want to break the news to Sadie that her boss had abandoned her. "I don't know how I can help with that, sir. Secure One is not the police."

"You seem to solve more cases than they do," he snapped, and Eric had to bite back laughter. He wasn't exactly wrong, but wouldn't he be surprised to know Sadie was in the other room.

"Is there something you need in regard to your security at the property, Dirk?" Eric asked, using the placating tone he had perfected for working with demanding clients.

"Yes! You can find Sadie! Are you listening? The cops won't let anyone near the storage units, and I'm losing business!"

"Again, I remind you that we aren't the police and we have no say over what they do or don't do. I can call the chief at the Bemidji PD and find out when they'll release the storage units, but that's as far as I can go in my role as your security expert. It hasn't been forty-eight hours yet, so I'm not surprised they haven't cleared the units. It should be within seventy-two hours."

"I can't wait another day! Find out how much longer," Dirk snapped, his usual snippy tone firmly in place. "People need things from their units, and this is making me look bad!"

Eric opened his mouth to speak, but the phone went dark. "Nice. He hung up on me." With an eye roll, he opened his phone app and clicked another number. Since his hearing aids were already connected to Bluetooth, he might as well follow through on his promise, even if his client was annoying.

"Chief Bradley here."

"Chief, it's Eric Newman from Secure One." He went on to explain what he needed and listened to the heavy sigh of the chief before he spoke.

"Fettering has made it very clear how he feels about this investigation, but I can't have other cars in that storage unit until I'm sure that the evidence response team has everything they need. I predict we'll be able to clear the area by the end of the day, but I won't rush it."

"I don't expect you to, Chief. I am simply touching base on the request of my client."

"More likely he yelled at you and then hung up."

Eric couldn't help but smile. "Seems you're familiar with Mr. Fettering. I'll let him know to cool his boots for a few more hours. Any luck on finding Miss Cook?"

"None. She's fallen off the face of the earth with that baby. Almost as if someone was offering her protection…"

"That is odd," Eric said, stopping himself from saying *just like her sister* since he wasn't supposed to know that Kadie was missing. "Would you do me a favor?"

"Depends on what it is. I'm rather busy trying to solve a murder over here."

"This has to do with the murder. It might even help you find the actual killer because I sure as hell know it's not Sadie Cook."

"So you say. If I could get a warrant, I'd be running my people through Secure One to look for her, but I have no proof to show a judge."

Eric's grin grew wider. "No, you sure don't, and she's not here anyway, so you'd be wasting your time. That said, I was thinking about the way Howie Loraine was killed."

"What about it?"

"I'm sure you're familiar with what happened eight years ago with the Loraines?"

"I've read the reports. I was chief of police in Iowa at the time, so I was rather removed from it."

"Then may I suggest you look into Medardo Vaccaro's organization."

"The Snake? What does he have to do with this?" Eric heard the skepticism in the chief's voice loud and clear.

"Let's not split hairs here, Chief. What happened to Howie was a mob hit, and we all know that Vaccaro and the Loraines used to be tight. It's not outside the box to think they still are and Howie crossed a line Vaccaro didn't like."

"You're suggesting the mob is framing Sadie Cook to take the fall for a hit?"

"It's possible," Eric agreed, his chest tight as he worked to convince the chief there were other avenues to explore when it came to who'd killed Howie Loraine.

"Aliens are also possible."

Eric bit back the sigh and flexed his shoulders. "Chief, something reeks, and it's not Howie Loraine's dead body. You can't tell me you don't feel the same way."

"I do," he agreed slowly. "None of it makes any sense, which is why I'd really like to speak to Miss Cook and try to clear her as a suspect. I don't suppose you happen to know her whereabouts at this point in time?"

Eric's gaze drifted to the control room where Sadie sat holding a toy for Houston while she watched the footage. "I do not, but with or without Miss Cook, concentrating on the right avenues—the ones that make sense—should clear her name and reveal the real killer. That's all I'm saying."

"You're saying a lot for a guy who just works for a security company."

"Sir," Eric said, biting back the disrespect that sat on his tongue. "I may work for a security company now, but the core group of us were MPs in the army. We know when something stinks of a setup."

"I'm busting your chops, Newman. I know you have a unique history with the law. I will try to clear Fettering's units today. I'll keep following my other leads in hopes something pops up to clear Miss Cook. Until that time, or until I can speak to Miss Cook, the warrant will remain active."

"Ten-four," Eric agreed before hanging up.

The phone fell to his side with a sigh of frustration. They needed that warrant canceled. At some point, they'd have to move Sadie and Houston out of Secure One, and they couldn't afford to get hit with a charge for harboring a fugitive. His mind's eye drifted back to the moment his lips had touched hers. He realized that he wanted her name cleared for other reasons too. Reasons that he shouldn't even have been considering but couldn't banish from his mind.

A rush of air swooshed past him, and he glanced up to see Sadie as she ran into the bathroom and slammed the door. Lucas, now holding Houston, ran to the door calling her name but stopped short when he saw Eric.

"What happened?" Eric asked, torn between talking to Lucas and going after Sadie. He settled for taking Houston from Lucas and cuddling him into his chest.

Lucas motioned him into the control room after giving Haven a command to rest. "We found something on the footage."

"Show me." He sat and waited for Lucas to load the video. When he hit Play, Eric leaned into the screen, trying to get a better look at the guy approaching Sadie's door. "Wait. Is that…"

"Victor Loraine," Lucas confirmed.

Eric's whistle was long and low. "What is he doing?" Lucas held up his finger for him to wait, and sure enough, Victor knelt and slid something under the door. "Dropping a note. I think it's fair to say he knows Kadie better than her sister thought."

Lucas pointed at him in agreement. "She called the apartment manager on-site and asked them to go into the apartment, get the note, take a picture and send it to us. When she hung up, she took off."

"I would imagine she's stressed and near her breaking point," Eric said, glancing at the door to see if she had returned. "Sadie is coping with a lot right now, including taking care of her nephew without knowing when or if her sister is coming back." He stood and pushed the chair in. "I'm going to check on her. Let me know when the letter comes in, and we'll reconvene." Eric picked up a walkie-talkie and clipped it to his belt.

"Ten-four," Lucas agreed as Eric left the room.

First, he'd leave Houston with Selina for a few minutes so he could find Sadie. He reminded himself she was a woman in need of a friend and nothing more.

Maybe one day, he'd believe it.

Chapter Ten

Sadie sat on the toilet in the small bathroom and tried not to hyperventilate. This was too much. She could only imagine what Eric would think when he found out Vic had come to their apartment. She was ridiculously naive for not knowing that her sister was involved with this guy. She'd honestly had no idea. Kadie had done a fantastic job keeping her in the dark about Vic, but now Sadie wished she hadn't. A little part of her worried that Victor Loraine was Houston's father, and if that was true, life just got dangerous. It would be disastrous if they couldn't find Kadie before Vic learned he was Houston's father.

"Oh, no," she groaned aloud. "What if he already knows?"

There was a knock on the door, and she snapped her head up, holding her breath so they would go away and leave her to freak out in peace.

"Sadie? It's Eric. Come out so we can talk."

"I don't want to talk," she said and waited to hear his footsteps moving down the hallway.

"I can't hear you through the door, Sades," he said, and she suspected his lips were pressed to the door. "We need to talk."

With a heavy sigh, she pushed herself up off the toilet and threw the door open. "Can't a girl have an existential crisis without an audience?"

"Not here," he said with a grin. "Here we approach the problem head on and find a way to fix it."

"I don't know that there's any fixing this," she said with a shake of her head. "What's that saying? You can't unscrew what's already been screwed?"

Eric's snort made her smile. "Yeah, something like that. Let's go talk."

"I want to see Houston."

"Okay, we'll talk on the way to the med bay," he agreed. They started walking, and he waited for her to speak, but she wasn't going to. The less she said, the better right now. It didn't take them long to get to the med bay, and Eric pressed his thumb on the fingerprint reader. When the door slid open, he announced himself. "Secure one, Echo."

"Secure two, Sierra," Selina said, spinning around in her chair with a happy Houston on her lap.

As soon as Sadie saw her nephew, she ran to him, scooped him into her arms and hugged him. "I'm sorry I ditched you, baby." She kissed his cheek noisily, and he giggled, his belly jiggling with the motion. Sadie noticed Eric smile at Houston, and soon he was tickling his belly as she held him.

"He's a good boy," Selina said, and Sadie couldn't help but notice it was the first time since she'd been here that the woman looked happy. "We were watching *Sesame Street* and playing pat-a-cake. He's probably getting hungry and then will need a nap."

"I'll feed him," Sadie said before Eric suggested anything else. "We're waiting for some information to come in anyway."

"Sure, that would be great. I'll do some work while you're gone. When Houston's ready for a nap, bring him down and he can stay with me so you can work."

"Thanks, Selina," Eric said with a pat to her shoulder. "I'll bring you some lunch too. How's everything coming along?"

"I've sent the information to Mina. If the father's DNA has been stored in a database, we'll know soon enough."

Sadie swallowed over the nervous bubble of fear that lodged in her throat. "I'm embarrassed to say that I think Kadie does know who Houston's father is and purposely kept me in the dark."

"There's nothing to be embarrassed about, Sadie," Eric said, resting his hand on her back. It was warm, and she focused on that rather than the fear spiraling through her. "You had no reason not to take Kadie at her word. You're a wonderfully supportive sister, and that's what you should focus on."

"He's right," Selina said, standing and handing her Houston's blanket. "Kadie may have been trying to protect you from the truth."

"That Victor Loraine is Houston's father?" she asked, and both Selina and Eric tipped their heads in acknowledgment. "That's my worry right now. Especially if he knows he's the father. A part of me wants that note to tell us he is the father, and part of me wants it to be something dumb about how much he adores Kadie and wants to be her boyfriend." She waved her hand in the air. "Or something meaningless to the investigation, I guess."

"Note?" Selina asked, glancing between them with confusion. Sadie couldn't be sure, but she swore she noticed a look of panic on Selina's face when she'd mentioned Victor's name.

"Lucas and Sadie were watching the footage from the apartment building. About three days ago, Victor Loraine showed up and shoved a note under the door," Eric said to fill her in. "We're waiting for the apartment manager to get the note and take a picture for us."

"Which means a Loraine is still in your lives. And no one knows you're here, right?" Selina asked. Sadie noticed a tremble at the end of the sentence and she glanced at Eric in confusion, but he was dialed into Selina and not paying her any attention.

"No one," Sadie repeated immediately. "I don't even have a phone or any way to contact the outside world. Well, I guess the apartment manager knows I'm still around, but he's sending the information to my regular email, not the Secure One email, and I called from the untraceable phone."

"Good," Selina said with a jerky nod. Sadie could see the relief flow through her. "You'd better get the baby fed before the note arrives."

There was no question that Selina was dismissing them, so she nodded and left the med bay with Eric's hand resting at the small of her back. She grabbed on to the sensation of warmth that it offered and focused on it. She didn't want to need this man, but the longer she remained at Secure One, the more she wanted him.

The kitchen was empty when they walked in, and she flipped Houston to her hip and opened the fridge. "We're out of baby food," she said over her shoulder. "It might be eggs again."

"Give him to me," Eric said, pulling Houston from

her arms and holding him against his chest so he could see what she was doing. "Now you don't have to work one-handed."

"Thanks." She smiled at his thoughtfulness—and at the way he looked holding a baby. He was a big, bad security operative until you put a baby in his arms. The baby softened him and made him approachable as a person rather than a guard.

"You're welcome, and we're not out of baby food." He pointed at the counter where jars were stacked. "Mina had more baby food and formula delivered this morning. They also dropped off a high chair. We want him safe while he's here."

"Bless her," Sadie said, her hand to her heart as she shut the door and grabbed some jars. "I was wondering what I was going to do when I ran out."

"Now you don't have to worry. Houston won't suffer for something that isn't his fault. It's not your fault either."

She shrugged as she made his bottle. "Maybe not, but I still feel as though we're putting everyone out here. Maybe I shouldn't feel that way, but I do."

She shook the bottle until it was mixed and then handed it to him. "He will drink some of that while I make his food."

She watched as Eric handed Houston the bottle and he sucked at it hungrily, his hand patting the bottle as he lay cradled in Eric's arms.

"Do you see your family often?" she asked, smiling at her nephew as he hummed with happiness.

"No. They didn't support my choice to join the military."

"No offense, but that's kind of a crappy thing to do to someone you love."

"Offense taken," he said with a smirk, and she grimaced. "People always say that as a precursor to something that's true but pointed. You're correct though. I still talk to one of my brothers and one of my sisters. My parents are already gone, so at least they don't have to watch the destruction of the family unit at my expense."

"Not really," she argued, spooning baby food into a bowl to warm it. "They're using you as an example in a twisted, misaligned way. You aren't the enemy and didn't start the war."

"True, but my participation in it made me the enemy in their eyes. Especially after…"

She spun and waited for him to answer, but when he didn't, she raised a brow. "Especially after what, Eric?"

She waited, but the only thing she heard was silence.

Chapter Eleven

Sadie remained quiet, hoping that he'd finish his thought, but he didn't. The longer he gazed at Houston, the paler he became. She couldn't decide if she was seeing a ghost or if he was channeling one.

He stroked Houston's leg absently, his breath heavy in his chest. She was about to speak when he did. "I'm sure you noticed that we all have battle scars?" She nodded but didn't speak. "There was a mission. We were moving a diplomat's family to a safe house. Mack was with the family, Cal and Roman in the lead car, and myself and a gunner in the rear. I'm sorry—I don't talk about this. Ever."

She stopped his hand from caressing Houston's leg. "I didn't ask you to talk about it, Eric. You don't have to show me your demons for me to trust you."

He glanced up and captured her gaze, then flipped his hand until he was holding hers. "Mack keeps telling me to talk about it more to help it fade. Lucas says I should get a dog like Haven so I have something else to concentrate on."

"What do you believe?" she asked quietly. "That's what matters more than anything."

"I believe that people died that day for no reason," he

answered, his eyes flashing angrily. "People were injured for no reason. Cal almost lost his hand. Mack can't walk without braces, and I can't hear a thing without these pieces of plastic." His words were growled and angry. Houston looked up, and his tiny hand patted Eric's chest twice as though he alone could comfort him.

"I'm sorry that you had to go through that, and still have to deal with it, when it wasn't your war to fight."

"We were supposed to save that family, but we didn't. We didn't," he said with a shrug, dropping her hand to stroke Houston's leg again. "We didn't save them, and it ended our careers in the military. In hindsight, I'm glad I got out, but I would have preferred it had been on my own terms."

"I'm sure every disabled veteran feels the same way." She leaned her hip on the counter and held his gaze. "But you know you were never going to save them, right? If the terrorists wanted them dead, there was no stopping them. Unfortunately you were in the way of them completing their mission."

He pointed his finger at her and then let it drop back to Houston's leg. "Cal, Roman and I know that without question. It took Mack much longer to understand that he wasn't to blame. I get it. He drove the car and felt responsible for them but still couldn't change or stop it. Charlotte helped him see that in the end he saved a lot of lives by what he did do."

"I'm not going to say *no offense* because you will take offense at this without a doubt. You still harbor a lot of anger about it, right?"

"We all do. We always will. What happened might fade into the background of our lives, but it will always be there. We will always carry the ghosts of the people we lost. That comes with the territory of being special ops for the military. Will I always be angry about it? Yes. I accepted that I could end up on the battlefield when I joined the special ops team. I accepted that I could end up dead. I can't accept that a little boy died a horrible death and I couldn't stop it. Do you know what I see every night when I close my eyes?"

She shook her head, but didn't speak, hoping he'd pour out some of his anger for her to carry.

"I see his tiny leg," Eric whispered, his fingers gripping Houston's leg again. "It came out of the door." His voice was choked when he lowered his arm to imitate what he'd seen. "This tiny, innocent leg sticking out of the door, and then just a ball of flames. That little leg is burned in my memory forever as the symbol of an unwinnable war with tragic consequences that were too high. I lie in bed at night in silence, but in my head, I hear it all again."

"I'm sorry," she said, remembering not to whisper or he wouldn't hear her. "I'm sorry I can live in total oblivion because you can't."

He tipped his head in confusion as he straightened Houston in his arms. "I don't understand."

"I was here when you were there. You saw things over there that I'm oblivious to because you waded into that battle. I'm free to walk around and live my life." She paused and shook her head. "Well, you know what I mean. You carry the horrific memories of freedom so I don't have to."

His breath escaped in a whoosh, and he held Houston closer as though he was taking comfort from the tiny being in his arms. "I honestly never thought of it that way."

"You should," she said, resting her hand on Houston's belly. "He's safe and happy with food in his tummy because you held the line for him without ever knowing him. To me, that's a hero. That's selflessness I don't have within me. You carry burdens you shouldn't have to, but you do it so Houston and I don't know the horror of war firsthand."

"And I would never want you to," he said, holding her gaze. "Ever. Not you, my nieces or nephews, or even my siblings who think I'm the enemy."

"It's gotten worse, hasn't it?" she asked, and the look in his eye told her she was correct. "Since Houston got here, I mean. The memories have been harder to suppress."

"The boy who died, he was older than Houston but just as innocent. That leg..." he said, only a puff of air coming out as he stroked Houston's tiny foot. "I just... I need to stop seeing that leg."

"I wish I could carry that memory for you, Eric. I can't, but I can make sure that Houston doesn't make it worse. Give him to me."

"No," he said, tightening his arm in the cradle where he held her nephew. "While he's made the memories more frequent, I think in a way he's also offering me a chance to heal from it. I don't know if that even makes sense." He gazed up at her from under his brows, and she nodded slowly.

"He's giving you a second chance to keep a child safe from harm."

"I need that second chance," he agreed, a small smile

on his face as he tickled Houston's belly. "I need to prove to myself that my ears don't override my instincts."

"Your ears?" Sadie put the food in the microwave and waited for him to answer.

"When you go from sound to silence in the blink of an eye, you struggle to compensate for it with your other senses."

"I can't pretend to understand," she said, stirring the baby's food. "If it matters, I think you do an excellent job of communicating. I'm sure that's little comfort when you're the one who deals with the frustration of communication every day." She took Houston from his arms and fit him into the high chair, where she spilled some cereal onto the tray for him to eat. "Maybe instead of compensating for the loss of your hearing, you should use it to your advantage."

"Maybe you don't know anything about it," he growled.

She heard the offense in his words, and she held up her hand. "I'm not saying I do, Eric. It was only a suggestion and not meant to upset you. I care about you, and knowing that you live in a state of frustration makes me sad."

"You care about me?" he asked, watching her spoon sweet potatoes into Houston's mouth. "We've only known each other a few days."

"The length of time we've known each other doesn't preclude me from caring about you, Eric. You're a good man with a kind heart. You're dedicated to helping people, which is something few people can say these days. I'm forever grateful to you for taking the risk of protecting me and Houston when you didn't have to."

"You're innocent, and we'll prove it," he said, his

words gentler now. "For the record, I care about you and Houston." He fell silent as she fed the baby, his happy squeals and babble filling the empty kitchen. "Just out of curiosity," he finally said, "how would I use being deaf to my advantage?"

"In a way, you already do it. You just need to decide it's an advantage instead of a disadvantage."

"Which is?"

"Lipreading," she answered, wiping Houston's face and kissing his cheek. "You see it as a necessary evil right now rather than a skill the other men don't have." She motioned at the door behind him. "Efren didn't know that the guy in the car said the words *Winged Templar*. You were the only one there with the skill to see that. Do you see what I'm saying?"

He was silent for a long time but finally nodded. "I never thought of it that way. I do have that advantage when my position allows it."

"You're good at multitasking with it too. I've watched you the last couple days and noticed your gaze is always tracking other people in the room. You're always taking in other conversations by reading their lips."

"True," he agreed, lifting Houston from the chair while she washed off the tray. "That's an interesting take on it. I'll think about how to incorporate it. You're observant, Sadie."

Her shrug was nonchalant, but on the inside, she was cheering that they'd had a breakthrough. "I try—"

"Secure one, Whiskey." The black box on Eric's belt crackled with Mina's voice.

He grabbed it and held the button down. "Secure two, Echo."

"Conference room in five," Mina said. "We have the letter, and you'll want to see it."

"Ten-four. Echo out." He stuck the box back on his belt and shifted Houston to his hip as he raised a brow. "Ready to take one step closer to finding your sister?"

She set the towel down and took a deep breath before she followed him out of the kitchen. Like it or not, she was going to learn what her sister was hiding. If it helped them find her, then she'd swallow her embarrassment in front of the team and do anything to bring her back to Houston. As she followed Eric back to the med bay, she couldn't help but think how good he looked with a baby in his arms. She watched the muscles of his back ripple as he shifted his load, and she wondered what they would feel like under her hands as he lifted her and carried her to his bed.

Her eyes closed, and she shook her head—*Focus, Sadie, and not on the man before you. Your sister is in danger, and you are being accused of an atrocity you didn't commit.*

She heard the internal chastising and made note of it, but the man she followed was too enigmatic to ignore. She wanted to know what made him tick, and that drew her to him like a moth to a flame. Sadie was sure she'd get burned, but in the end, the pain would be worth it.

Chapter Twelve

The conference room lacked most of the big players when Eric walked in. It was just Lucas and Mina waiting for them, which told Eric things were about to get real. Sadie had been quiet since they'd left the med bay, but he supposed he had been too. Every time they talked, this tiny woman gave him too many big things to grapple with in his mind. It almost felt to him like she could see inside him and read the list of people and events that haunted him. It freaked him out if he was honest, but he didn't have time to fixate. There were steps to follow in this investigation, and none of them included kissing Sadie Cook. He had to keep his mind on the steps. Learn what Vic Loraine knew, apply it to find the missing mother, bring her home and move Sadie out of Secure One and his head for good. His inner demons laughed. Fat chance of that ever happening. He'd have to try though.

"Mina, Lucas," Eric said as they walked in. "Where is everyone? I thought we were having a meeting."

"Cal and Efren will be down shortly. Everyone else is tied up with other clients."

"Should we call Elliott and see if he's available for extra work?" Eric asked.

Mina tossed her head back and forth a few times. "That's not a bad idea. Maybe we could have him take over a couple of our clients closer to him. Let me talk to Cal."

"Who's Elliott?" Lucas asked, glancing between them.

"He's one of our guys who installs and maintains security systems closer to the border," Eric answered.

"Of Wisconsin?"

"Canada," Mina said to clarify. "He's near International Falls. He hadn't worked here long when an old friend needed help in his hometown of Winterspeak. He went up to help her develop a security plan for her tree farm, but—"

"They fell in love," Lucas said with a groan. "Why does that always happen here?"

Mina's laughter filled the room. "Well, in fairness, they had been best friends through high school, so it wasn't completely unexpected. Anyway, he helps Jolene on the tree farm and with their new baby but has stayed on the payroll. I'll talk to Cal about reaching out to him. If he's interested, it might be a good way to take some of the everyday strain off our shoulders for clients he's closer to."

"I'm sorry this is taking up resources and adding strain to the already thin staff," Sadie said, lowering herself into the chair. "Maybe you should just turn me over to the chief in Bemidji. All I request is that you keep Houston until I'm released again."

"No." The word left his lips without conscious thought. "That's not going to happen. Don't worry about our team. We've proved time and again we're strong enough to handle the most ruthless criminals. Protecting a baby and his aunt is like a cakewalk for us."

"He's right," Lucas said, pointing at Eric. "We got you and Houston. We'll keep you safe until your name is cleared. You can trust Secure One. Just ask Mina."

Mina nodded at that statement—she'd been the one to steer Secure One into the personal-protection arena they'd gotten so good at in the last few years. Lucas patted Haven to settle the dog on the floor. "If we turn you over to the police, you could end up in jail, where you're vulnerable to the person who set you up in the first place. Eating a bullet for something you didn't do isn't fair, so it's not going to happen."

Eric motioned at Lucas before he sat. "What he said. Besides, we're up to our neck in this case as Fettering's security team." He turned to Mina. "Have you found anything on the Winged Templar yet?"

"No, but," she said, holding up her finger, "I am layers deep into the organization now. I have a good feeling that I'm getting to the bottom of it. From what I can see, the mob bosses of their different divisions, which is what they call their regions, use code names. Makes sense, right?"

"Generally speaking," Eric agreed. "If they have a code name, it's so no one knows their real one."

Mina pointed at him. "Which means we'll always be one piece short of a full puzzle, but if I can build the rest of the picture around that missing piece, we might be able to find the Winged Templar's image and then run that through facial recognition."

"You're saying it's nearly impossible," Sadie said with a shake of her head.

"Nearly, yes, but not completely. There are ways—I just need a bit more time."

"Take all the time you need," Cal said, walking into the room with Lucas. "We're not sharing the name with the cops anyway. Do we have an update?"

"Yes," Mina said, grabbing a remote and aiming it at the projector. "We have the note that Vic left for Kadie. I'm going to warn you, Sadie, the revelations in the note are jarring."

Sadie set her jaw. "I'm prepared for anything."

With a nod, Mina flipped the note up on the screen and started to read aloud. "'Kadie, are you avoiding me? Did I do something wrong? I love having you and Houston with me at night, but I haven't been able to reach you for days. I'm scared that you've taken Houston away from me but also scared you weren't given a choice. I love you, Kadie. I love our son. I want nothing more than to be a family with our baby boy. I know you're still scared about my family, and I hope they aren't the reason that you left, both figuratively and literally. Please, if you get this note, at least let me know you're okay. I love you. Vic.'"

The room was silent as Sadie stared at the note. Eric could tell she was trying to process all of the information and stay detached from it at the same time.

"Essentially, he knows his family is capable of making someone disappear," Eric said, his tone angry.

"No," Sadie said. "He knows his older brother is capable of making someone disappear because he's all that's left of his family now."

"Unless their father is pulling the strings from prison," Cal pointed out. "He was one of Vaccaro's top guys before he got pinched."

"Also a possibility," Mina said. "I'll put my ear to the ground on that one."

"Maybe Vic warned Kadie about his family and what they were capable of and it spooked her," Lucas suggested. "Maybe she did take off in the hopes of protecting Houston, you and Vic?"

Sadie shook her head immediately. "No, she wouldn't do that. I know I've said that before and been wrong, but I'm not about this. She was taken. We already have evidence to prove she didn't leave by choice. Now we need to figure out where she is."

"We need to talk to Victor," Cal said, motioning at the note. "He doesn't come right out and say it, but it gives me the impression that he knows there are reasons why someone would go after Kadie."

Sadie spun on him and stuck her finger in his chest. "You promised! You promised we wouldn't contact the father."

Her growl was cute, but he didn't laugh or smile. He just wrapped his hand around her finger and held her gaze, closing out everyone else around them. "That was when we thought the father didn't know Houston existed. Clearly that's not the case." He motioned at the note still up on the screen. "The man knows Houston is his son, and he's worried about them. Yes, we need to talk to him to find out what he knows, but we also need to let him know his son is safe. That's the very least we can do."

Eric noticed Mina grab her tablet and start punching buttons. "What's up, Mina?"

She popped her head up. "Before I came down, I started running Houston's DNA against the samples we have from the Loraines." She turned the tablet around for them to see. "I just got a hit. Randall Loraine Senior is not excluded as the grandfather of Houston and has a 99.998% likelihood of being the paternal grand-father. Likely, a son of Randall Loraine Senior is the father of the sample submitted and the results support the biological relationship. That combined with the note is enough for me to call him the biological father of Houston Cook."

"Me too," Eric said with a nod as he rested a hand on Sadie's shoulder. "I know that's not what you wanted, Sadie, but we have to play the hand we're dealt."

She rested her forehead in her palm and sighed. "It's not that I don't want Kadie to be happy or Houston to have a father if they've found a life with Victor. If Victor Loraine is his father, then Kadie is in real danger and Houston could become a pawn in a dangerous game."

"Agreed. That's why we need to pull this guy in and talk to him," Cal said, leaning on the table. "He could have information about where they may have taken Kadie."

Sadie motioned at the note still up on the board. "Clearly not. If he knew where she was, he wouldn't have left that note."

"Cal means he may not know he has the information," Eric patiently explained. "When asked the right questions, he may provide an answer that even he didn't know he had."

She worked her jaw around and finally nodded. "Okay. I follow that train of thought. He knows his family better than anyone, so he's a valuable resource. Let's pull him in and have a chat."

"Not here," Cal said. "I don't want a Loraine to know where my property sits—right side of the law or not."

"That's smart," Eric agreed. "We need a neutral location, and we're not bringing the baby."

"Then he may not come," Sadie jumped in. "He's going to want to see Houston."

"When he pats our back, we'll pat his." Cal set his tablet down on the table and leaned over it. "I'd rather keep the baby tucked away with Selina here. If we take him out, there's a chance that whoever took Kadie tries to grab him. We could be under surveillance since they know we're Fettering's security."

"I didn't think of that." Sadie chewed on her lip. "How are we going to convince Victor to meet with us if we can't bring Houston?"

Eric straightened his shoulders before he spoke. "His brother just died, right?" Cal and Efren nodded, then waited for him to finish. "We contact him as the security team for Dirk Fettering. We tell him his brother had a storage unit at Dirk's place and we need his help to open it and clear it out."

"I'm listening," Cal said, sitting on the edge of the table and crossing his arms.

"We lure him to a unit that will serve as a meeting space. We bring a video of Houston playing happily but with no identifying features of his location."

"I like it." Cal pointed at Sadie. "Take her, or leave her here?"

"Pros and cons?" Eric asked, glancing at Efren and Mina.

"Excuse me, but *her* is right here," Sadie said with enough force to own the room. "There are no pros and cons. I'm going. He knows I'll always protect my sister and nephew. If I'm there, he'll talk."

"She's not wrong," Eric said, lifting a brow at Cal.

"She's not, but it's about moving her safely. It's ninety

minutes to Bemidji. That's a lot of exposed time, even if she's hidden in the back of a van. It's risky since we don't know if someone is watching us."

"We take mobile command." Eric waited for Cal's reaction and noticed his lips pull into a tight line.

"Still risky."

"Roman and I will leave at the same time in a distraction car," Mina said. "We can even put a baby seat in the back as added incentive." She glanced over at Sadie for a moment. "With a wig and a hat, I could be Sadie from a car length away."

Efren nodded. "Absolutely. I'll drive a follow car just in case they're approached. Once you're at Fettering's, we'll circle the wagons back here and decide what kind of manpower you need there."

Cal raised his hands in the air and let them drop. "All right, let's do it. Who's going to call Vic?"

"I'll do it," Eric said. "Since I'm running point on the team at Dirk's."

"Good. Line him up. We'll get you a fake contract for a storage unit in Howie's name while you get ready to roll."

Eric held up his finger. "I'm rethinking this. How quickly can Marlise get me that contract?"

"Minutes. Why?"

"We should have mobile command in place before I reach out to him. We need to be on-site so if he shows up immediately, we're there. If he asks anyone else about the unit, he's going to learn there isn't one."

"I see your point," Cal said. "Be ready to roll in thirty?"

"I need to check on Houston," Sadie said as she jumped up from her seat.

"A fast check, and then get a bag packed. We won't be back until tomorrow at the earliest. Be prepared to stay longer," Eric instructed.

"But Houston…"

"Will be fine with me and Selina," Mina assured her, squeezing her hand. "We'll be his stand-in aunts and take good care of him. Remember, you're leaving him here for his safety but you're going so you can bring his mother home to him, right?"

Sadie nodded, and after a smile and a thank-you, she headed to the med bay.

"Do you think she's ready for this?" Mina asked.

Eric stared out the door for a moment before he turned back to his team. "I don't know Sadie that well, but I do know one thing—she would do anything for her sister and that baby. She'll roll with the punches like a pro because she's motivated to bring her family back together."

Cal tapped the table. "Let's try to keep the punches to a minimum this time around." He grabbed his tablet and walked to the door. "I'll get everyone else updated. See you in the garage in thirty. Charlie out."

Eric glanced at Efren and shook his head. "Keeping the punches to a minimum will be easier said than done."

Chapter Thirteen

Sadie paced around the small office in the back of mobile command. Any minute now, Vic would knock on the door to the RV. When that happened, she could no longer deny the truth. Houston was a Loraine, and that meant one thing for her little family—danger. With her sister still missing, Sadie knew that to be the absolute truth. They had to find Kadie, and if they had to use Victor Loraine to do it, so be it. Her mind immediately flew to the worst-case scenario—finding Kadie dead. The thought sent a shiver down her spine, and she lowered herself to the couch to rest her stressed-out body.

"You can't think that way. Kadie is alive and waiting—no, depending on you to find her." She said it aloud as though that might manifest it into being.

They had to find her because there was no way she'd be able to turn Houston over to his father and walk away. Anger bubbled up inside her. Anger at Kadie for not telling her the truth about Houston's father when they'd had a chance to work through it together. What did she think Sadie was going to do? Disown her?

Sadie's shoulders slumped forward, and she forced herself to face the truth. Kadie had been protecting her.

She was the older sister, and she always tried to keep Sadie safe. If she knew Victor's family was dangerous, she would keep whatever secrets she had to in order to protect her sister.

The knock sounded loud on the RV door, and Sadie stood instantly, fear rocketing through her. She had to face Vic and tell him the truth about where his son was. Eric would be beside her, but getting a lead on where Kadie might be would be up to her. Vic had to trust her before he'd trust Secure One. If he didn't trust Secure One enough to tell them his family's secrets, they had no hope of finding Kadie. Sadie focused on the goal and forced everything else from her mind. She had to play this exactly right if they were going to find her sister. That meant sharing Houston with his father, and she hoped Vic would sacrifice just as much to keep him safe.

She could hear murmuring in the central part of mobile command. The two bedrooms had been soundproofed to allow better sleep for the operatives who weren't on shift. She glanced around the office she stood in, which was about the size of a closet but had been optimized for Cal's disability. The computer equipment and setup made everything accessible when he wasn't wearing his prosthesis. The sofa against the other wall opened into a bed, though she couldn't picture a guy the size of Cal sleeping on it.

The core team dynamic of Secure One was unique. Cal, Roman, Eric and Mack had all served on the same special ops Army Military Police team for years before being injured together on a mission. They anticipated each other's weak points and made sure they were filled so everything went along like clockwork. The men were all different, but they all had one thing in common: integrity. Her own experience told her that. Before the accident, Eric had only met her for a brief snapshot in time, but he refused to let her face any of this alone. That said something to her.

There was a knock on the door, and then Eric said the phrase she'd been waiting for. "Time for a chat," his deep voice said, and she inhaled a breath, steeling herself for what was to come.

Sadie grabbed the door handle, blew out her breath and pushed it open to come face-to-face with the man she had come to rely on in just a few short days. It wasn't a hero-worship thing either. They had a profound connection that she couldn't explain. She was drawn to him, and when they were together, Eric made her feel like everything would be okay. And not just about Kadie and Houston, but for her. There was an emotional connection she had never experienced before—and wasn't sure she ever would again.

She'd been with several men, some longer than others, but none of them had made her feel the way Eric did with a simple look or brush of his hand against her back. He made her feel like she was the most crucial person in the room and he would do anything to keep her safe. When he looked at her, his expression said he'd do anything for her, but Sadie knew the truth—the one thing Eric wouldn't do was consider a relationship with her.

She flashed back to the story of what had happened the day he'd lost his hearing. He still hadn't come to terms with it, and until he did—and accept how it had changed his life—he never would. Until he learned how to move his life forward while carrying that burden, there would never be room in his heart for anyone else. In fairness, he carried the atrocities of too much war and the faces of too many who he couldn't save, so learning to live again with those souls now part of him might be too much to ask.

"Ready?" he asked, grasping her shoulder in a sign of solidarity and strength.

"As I'll ever be."

Eric led her down the hallway to the front of mobile command that housed their complicated visual command center. Vic sat in a chair, his elbows braced on his thighs and his hands folded together as though he were praying. She took a split second to take in his side profile. He was different from the other Loraine brothers. He wasn't all muscle and hard lines. He was young, wore a baby face like none she'd ever seen before and had a dad bod before he even knew he was a dad. There was something about him that was genuine and honest though. Sadie could understand why her sister had been drawn to him.

"Sadie!" Vic said, jumping from the chair and running to her. He had wrapped his arms around her before Eric could even move. "I'm so glad you're okay! What are you doing here? Have you seen Kadie? Where is Houston? Why are they saying you killed my brother? You didn't, right?" he asked as he took a step back.

"Of course not!" Sadie exclaimed. "I don't even know your brother. I didn't even know your name until they figured out your real identity."

He held up his hands in defense. "I wasn't saying that you did kill my brother. I'm just so confused right now. Hold on a minute—Howie doesn't have a storage unit here, does he?"

"No," Eric answered. "But we needed to talk to you without tipping off anyone else in your family."

"Which means you know about my family."

"It would be hard not to," Sadie said. "But we're not here about your family. We're here about my family."

"Your family is now my family, Sadie. I love Kadie. Before she disappeared, we were putting together a plan to be a family somewhere away from the tentacles of the Loraine dynasty. She was going to talk to you about it as soon as we had everything in place, I swear. Do you know where she is?"

"We were hoping you could tell us that," Eric said.

"If I knew where she was, don't you think I would have gone to her by now? I've been worried sick! Does she have my son with her?"

"No," Sadie answered quickly. "I have Houston."

"Is he here? I want to see him!" Vic demanded.

Eric stepped between them. "Houston is tucked away safely and well cared for. Right now, we need to focus on where his mother is and how to get her back to him. Once we do that, you can see your son."

Vic glanced between them in defiance for a moment but finally relented. "I've had a bad feeling in the pit of my stomach since she missed our usual nightly visit. What happened, Sadie?"

She ran him through what had happened the day Kadie had disappeared and the events that had transpired since. "We have no idea where she is, Vic. Once we discovered that you're Houston's father, you were our only hope of finding a lead to follow."

Vic slowly lowered himself back to the chair and rubbed his forehead. "The first night she didn't show up at our apartment, I thought she just needed time to think." He turned to face them, and Sadie noticed the look on his face was part rapture and part pain. "I asked her to marry me the night before she disappeared."

"And what did she say?" Sadie asked.

"Yes, but that was followed by an immediate question about how my family would be involved."

"Why was she worried about how your family would be involved?" Eric asked.

"She was worried they were going to come after Houston once they found out he was a Loraine. Let's not split hairs here—we all know who my father is and who he worked for. Let it be said that Loraines raise Loraines no matter what."

"Even so," Sadie cautiously said, "you're a Loraine. If you and Kadie are together, then a Loraine is raising Houston. Why would that be a problem?"

Victor rubbed his palms on his pants for a moment, and Sadie noticed his Adam's apple bob before he spoke. "The problem is I'm not just the black sheep of the family—I've been disowned. And as far as my family is concerned, I don't exist as a Loraine anymore."

"Our intel indicates you aren't involved in the family business. Either the legal or illegal one," Eric said. "Is that accurate?"

"Accurate to a *T*," Vic promised. "I've had nothing to do with my family since my father was arrested and put in prison. I didn't have much to do with them before that either. When my mom died, I lost the only person who defended me in that family. I didn't know exactly what my dad was doing, but I knew he was working for The Snake. It wasn't hard to figure out that it wasn't on the right side of the law. Once I left for college, I never looked back. I'll work sixty hours a week if I have to just to make sure every penny that I earn is honest."

"Yet despite all that, my sister is still in danger because she chose to be with you. It's easy to understand why she was worried being with you would be dangerous for Houston."

"But nobody else should know that Houston is my son!" he exclaimed, standing from the chair.

Eric made the *calm down* motion with his hands. "We understand your frustration, Vic. We're all stressed, but we have to approach this in a logical manner. Is it possible your family is responsible for Kadie's disappearance?"

Sadie noticed he had asked the question deliberately, as though his precision would net them the answer they desperately needed.

"Absolutely. There isn't a doubt in my mind."

"Okay, second question. Assuming they're the ones who have her, would they set up Sadie to take the fall for your brother's death just to get their hands on Houston?"

"Why do you think I sent that note to your work? I didn't know if you were with Kadie, but I was worried you were in danger. I remembered Kadie saying you worked for Fettering, so I sent the note just in case you were still in town." Vic put his hands on his hips. "My family would literally do anything you could conjure up in your mind, and worse, to remain in favor with Vaccaro. Do I think that they would try to steal Houston away from me? Absolutely. That's why I rented an apartment under an assumed name just so I could see Kadie and my son."

"Despite all of that, my sister is still missing."

"Sadie got the note," Eric said, his jaw ticking, "and she ran with Houston. Someone followed her and ran her off the road."

"Luckily I ended up on Secure One property. I don't know where I'd be if I hadn't."

"You'd be dead," Vic said, his words defeated. "You and Kadie would both be dead, and my son would be in the hands of evil. Thankfully they failed to bring you and the baby to Randall Junior that night. That means Kadie's still alive. We have to find her. I don't want Houston to grow up without a mother. We have to find her, and then we have to take Kadie and Houston somewhere safe. Somewhere my family and Vaccaro can never find them or hurt them again."

"How do you know that Kadie is still alive?" Eric asked, taking a step forward to put himself between Vic and Sadie.

"She's still alive because you have Houston. Until they have the baby, they won't kill her. They might need her for leverage. I should have known this would happen. I wanted Kadie and Houston in my life, and I didn't take enough precautions. We should have left town immediately. That's on me. Truthfully I don't know why it matters so much that I have a son. I never had anything to do with Vaccaro. He doesn't even know who I am."

"Oh, don't fool yourself," Sadie said, her hands in fists at her sides. "Vaccaro knows everything about you, right down to your underwear size. He knows what you do, where you go and who you see. Why? Randall Senior was running one of Vaccaro's biggest operations. Just because your father is in prison doesn't mean you're not being watched. In fact, they probably saw you come here tonight!"

"I—I should have considered that," Vic said. "Did I just put everyone in more danger?"

"No," Eric said stepping in and placing a hand on Sadie's shoulder. She tried to concentrate on the warmth it offered while she took some deep breaths. "Your brother was found on this property, and if anyone looks, they'll find a contract between him and Dirk for a storage unit. They'll also see that I called you to come look at the unit."

"So, what happens now? How do we find Kadie while we keep Houston safe?"

"When you leave here tonight, you're going to call Randall Junior. You'll request an audience with him," Eric instructed. "You'll insist you need to see him tomorrow, and when you're in the house, you're going to look for any possible evidence that your brother has Kadie."

Vic took several steps back until he bumped into the command console. "I haven't been in that house in over twelve years. I have no intention of breaking that streak. Think of a new plan."

"Not even if you could save my sister's life?" Sadie demanded.

He shrunk back, his eyes filling with tears. "I'm sorry—you're right. It's just that I wasn't made the same way my brothers were. I'm not good at deception and games. I'll do anything for Kadie though, and that includes taking on my own family."

"Good," Eric said with a head nod. "As long as you're in, Secure One will keep you safe. Are you ready for a fast lesson in how to be an operative?"

Vic stiffened his shoulders and pushed his chest forward. "Where do we start?"

Eric turned to Sadie and grasped her shoulders gently. "Are you okay with this?"

He asked the question as though there was no one in the room but them. As though nothing mattered more than her answer.

"Just like Vic, I'll do anything I have to do to save my family," she said.

"Even when it scares you?"

"Especially when it scares me."

Her answer brought a smile to his lips, and he gently chucked her under the chin, his thumb caressing her jaw as his hand fell away. "That's because you're a warrior."

Eric turned away to address Vic, but Sadie didn't notice. She was too busy replaying the way his touch had left trails of heat along her jaw and the way his kindness with her and Vic touched her heart. Eric Newman was becoming less of a mystery she needed to solve and more the man she wanted in her life with every passing second.

Chapter Fourteen

"I can't believe I left a defenseless baby alone." Sadie paced the small hallway as though every step would bring her closer to Houston.

"You didn't leave him defenseless. He's with trained operatives, one who also happens to be a nurse."

"I know, I know," she muttered, rubbing her forehead. "I'm still trying to wrap my head around Kadie having a second life that I knew nothing about, Eric. It's not something I ever thought she'd keep from me. What did she think was going to happen if she told me she was in love with Vic? None of it makes sense."

"It does make sense," Eric said gently. "Kadie was protecting you."

"I'm sorry," she said, as she turned to face him. "Kadie had months to get used to the fact that Vic was a Loraine, now I'm left to play catch-up while trying to keep it together for Houston's sake. He's coming here tomorrow?"

"That's the plan," Eric agreed. "Cal will bring him and the rest of the team. Selina will monitor mobile command and help you with Houston. When Vic is done at the homestead, he will come here and let us know if he saw any sign of Kadie. We'll be monitoring him the entire time he's inside the Loraine mansion too. If he hits on anything, we'll know immediately."

"I wish we didn't have to wait until morning."

"Me too, but we have to protect Houston. I want to make sure we're safe here before they bring him."

"The mansion," she said, as she started pacing again. "Only Randall Junior lives there now, correct?"

"Now that Howie is dead, yes, besides the hired help. Vic hasn't lived there since he left for college. When his father was arrested, he never went back. That decision probably saved his life. If he had returned home, he could have been dragged into Vacarro's shenanigans without even knowing it."

"Don't get me wrong," Sadie said, turning to make eye contact with him. "I'm glad that Kadie found Vic and not one of the other Loraine boys. Vic loves my sister and his son—I can see that when he talks about them. I may not like that she kept secrets from me, but I also understand why she did it."

"She's the big sister. It's her job to protect you," he said with a nod.

"True, at least in her mind, but I don't have to like it." She started pacing again, and he snorted, the sound loud in the quiet space.

"I can't make you like it, but I can help you see it's time to accept it."

"That's going to be about as easy as me convincing you that the car bomb wasn't your fault."

He couldn't hide his sharp intake of breath. "That's not a fair comparison," he said through clenched teeth He hated that he couldn't hide the hurt that laced his words.

"I didn't intentionally mean to hurt you when I said

that, Eric. I did though, and I apologize. I shouldn't have compared the two." She reached out to touch him, but he spun away from her.

He walked to the front of mobile command, where a panel of bulletproof sheeting closed off the cab and protected the team from unexpected attacks. The cameras on all four corners of the vehicle also gave them a bird's eye view of the area. They'd parked mobile command inside the gated storage-unit area, so they should be safe tonight. Dirk was reopening the units tomorrow for clients, but the security measures would be considerably tighter than in the past.

"During the day, I don't think about what happened. I'm busy enough that I can keep those memories at bay. It's only when I take my hearing aids off and lie down to sleep that the torment begins," Eric said. "Since you and Houston arrived, I haven't been able to keep those memories at bay during the day. It's overwhelming to get hit both day and night. I used to allow the memories to wash over me while in bed, as a way to make it through the next day. Now it's wave after wave all day and night. I'm always on edge and find it hard to relax."

She walked toward him, and he could feel her heat and energy as though he were a magnet and she was the metal. In a beat, her soft, warm hands caressed his back and then up over his shoulders in a pattern that relaxed him and put him on edge simultaneously.

"I'm sorry, Eric. We inserted ourselves into your life in a way that's uncomfortable and makes your life harder. That's not fair. I'll go back to Secure One and keep Houston there while you're here."

He turned, ready to agree. If he banished Sadie to Secure One, he wouldn't have to face the trust he saw in her eyes—trust that he would bring her sister home. If she wasn't here, he could force himself to work relentlessly, shoving the memories back where they belonged for another decade. Before he could speak, his lazy gaze ate her up head to toe. Dammit, how did she have so much power over him in such a short time? He didn't know the answer, but he knew she wasn't going anywhere. "I don't want you to go. It's not your fault that I can no longer control the memories. That's my fault. I refused to deal with what happened because I thought it would be easier to pretend it didn't happen. All that's gotten me is fourteen years of suffering. You brought it to a head in an irrefutable way, and that tells me my life needs to change. If I don't do something, it will eat me alive."

"Do you know how to do that?" Her question was soft and gentle, but it was also heavy and loaded. He struggled to answer it since he didn't know how.

"Maybe I'll take Lucas's advice and look for a service dog."

"For your PTSD, or to be your hearing guide dog?"

"Both?"

Sadie's smile brought one to his lips too. "If you take the question mark off that answer, it's a solid plan. Not that what I think matters. I think what you think is the only thing that matters."

"That was quite a sentence," he said with a chuckle. "I understood what you meant though. This is what I know—I've spent too many years trying to bury a ghost rather than exorcize its demon. I watched Cal and Mack go through it all while trying to pretend the same didn't apply to me. My learning curve is high, but the events of the last few days have leveled out the curve for me."

Sadie's laughter was soft when she nodded. "We all have to take our own path with things, Eric. If we aren't ready to make a change in our lives, it will never truly stick. It happens for each one of us at a different time and place in our lives. It's about having the wisdom to know when the time has come and grab onto whatever rope is dangling there for us to hold."

"Houston gave me the wisdom to see the time has come, but oddly enough, he was also the dangling rope," he said. "When I picked him up for the first time and stared into those little eyes, I realized he had his entire life ahead of him, and I didn't want anything to mar it. That's what I've been doing by pretending those people didn't mar a part of my life. They existed. They were real. Their trust was mine for just a hairsbreadth in time, but they weren't mine in being. It was because they belonged to someone else that we all suffered that day. No amount of wishing or denial will change that, right?"

"You're exactly right, Eric, but also, trying to face a situation like this head on without any help could make things worse. I'm worried about you," Sadie said, resting her hand on his chest.

"I wish I could benefit from talk therapy," he said, cupping her cheek to caress her chin with his thumb. "Unfortunately it never worked for me in the beginning."

"Maybe because you weren't ready to face it yet? Would trying again be worth the risk?"

"That's possible," he agreed. "Here's the thing—talking about it won't make it go away. PTSD doesn't go away. We all know that. Sometimes talking about it, keeping it all mixed up and frothy week after week, just makes it worse. I need to find better ways to cope so the memories slowly fade and become less tangible over time. From what Lucas tells me, Haven has helped him do that. He has something else to focus on when the memories overtake him. Haven is there to pull his focus back to the present immediately. That's why I was thinking about getting a dog that could help me with both my hearing disability and the PTSD."

The admittance forced a heavy breath from his chest, and he closed his eyes for a moment. "I wasn't expecting to have this conversation tonight, but the truth is it's the most important conversation I've had in years. You've only been part of my life for a short time, but you're the only person I could trust with the truth, Sadie. You're the only one I trust not to judge me."

"I would never judge you, Eric. It feels like I've known you—"

"Forever," they said in unison.

His gaze held hers, and what he saw in her blue eyes said they shared a connection neither had been expecting. He lowered his head until their lips were only a breath away. Rather than pull away, she closed the distance and brushed her sweet lips against his. His chest rumbled with pleasure, so she lifted herself onto her tiptoes and turned her head—permission to take the kiss further.

He cupped the back of her warm neck and pulled her against him until their bodies connected. Her heart pounded against his chest when she dropped her jaw and let his tongue take a tour over the roof of her mouth before it tangled with hers. He was sure his lungs would explode from lack of oxygen, but he didn't want to stop. He didn't want to break the spell. He didn't want to think about anything else when his lips were on hers. When his lips were on hers, he thought about what life might be like with her if he could take that leap of faith. Desperate for air, he ended the kiss but rested his forehead on hers.

"What is this connection between us?" The question was asked in desperation, as though she wouldn't live to the next minute without knowing the answer.

"I wish it made sense to me. If you're in the room, I can't help but react to you. I want to tell you things I've never told anyone else before. Being in a combat zone didn't scare me as much as my reaction to you has the last few days. I was prepared for a war zone. I wasn't prepared for you, Sadie Cook."

"I'm not staying. Maybe that's why?"

"No." One word that held fervent denial. "Because I want you to stay. For the first time in fourteen years, I want someone to stay. That in and of itself is…" He put his hands to his head and made the *mind blown* motion.

"I've never met anyone like you, Eric Newman. Maybe I can't explain the connection yet, but I do know that it has nothing to do with my situation and everything to do with who we are as individuals. The way you hold Houston, the way you take care of me and the way you sacrifice for your teammates tells me that you care. It tells me that you're protective but in a positive way. Growing up, we never had a father figure in our life," she said. "As an adult, I've realized that not having a male presence in my life has made it not only difficult to date but to know when I'm being taken advantage of. I've never been able to discern when someone likes me for me or when someone wants something from me. I never have to worry about that with you. You are you, and you are real all the time, no matter what is going on around you. I can trust you to keep me safe, but you're also teaching me how to love and be loved."

"Love?" he asked, a brow in the air.

"Figure of speech, but you know what I mean, right?" she asked, nervously flipping her hand around in the air.

He caught her hand and held it to his chest. "I do know what you mean, Sadie. I don't want you to think I'm making light of what you're saying because I'm not. I'm struggling to wrap my head around this too. What I see in your eyes when you look at me...it makes me want to be a better man. It makes me want to change the things that I can change and cope better with the things that I can't—"

Before he could finish the thought, her lips were on his. She owned the kiss in a demanding yet gentle way. She took his face in her hands and stroked his five-o'clock shadow tenderly, all while she kissed the lips right off him. When they broke for air again, she took his hand, turned and walked toward the bedroom. Enchanted by her beauty and confidence, all he could do was follow.

Chapter Fifteen

Sadie's heart was hammering in her chest as she walked through the bedroom door and he followed. What was she doing? This was so not her MO. She didn't have casual sex with men who she'd only known for three days.

But is this just casual sex? that voice asked. *Or is this going to be something more?*

She couldn't speak for Eric, but she knew in her heart it was something more. It was also something that likely would not end in her favor. Once they cleared her name and brought Kadie home, she would have to leave Secure One. It wasn't hard to see that none of the guys at Secure One had time to date. How could they when they were always working? Cal, Roman and Mack made it work because their significant other also worked at Secure One. Sadie didn't work there. She had to remember there was an end date on this thing between them. She could move forward and take everything from him until that day arrived, or she could play it safe and walk away from this now.

Eric slid his warm hands up her back to knead her neck. "Everything okay?" He leaned in to ask the question, his breath hot against her ear, running goose bumps down her back. The sensation told her that while none of this would last, she could enjoy a moment of pleasure during a time of uncertainty and fear.

"Everything's fine," she said. "I paused when I remembered we didn't have any protection."

His strong hands gently spun her around to face him. "You're serious about this?"

"I mean, only if you want to." She hated that he could hear the waver in her voice.

Without breaking eye contact, he pressed her hand to his groin. He didn't say a word, just lifted his brow.

"Well, hello, big fella," she purred, taking a tour of him until his breath hitched and he grasped her hand. "We still don't have protection."

"Oh, sweetheart, I'm always prepared." He held up a finger and darted to the med bay, returning with a handful of condoms.

"Looks like someone has plans. Did you buy a case?"

"Yes," he answered, walking toward her until the backs of her knees hit the bed.

"You get that much action in mobile command?"

"No." This time his answer was low and growly. "We use condoms for other things besides raincoats."

"Oh, really?" The question was more a breath than words. "Water balloons?"

He slid his hands up under her shirt from her waist to her ribs, gripping them gently. "Makeshift water canteens," he said, blowing lightly on her neck as his hands worked their way to the edges of her breasts. "Waterproof phone bags." His thumbs stroked her nipples until she lost track of the conversation. She wanted to touch him, so she ran her hands across his chiseled, warm chest and back down to his hips where she rested her hands. "Fire-starter protectors."

"They sound versatile."

"They are," he agreed, taking a nip of the skin across her collarbone before he kissed the same spot to wash away the pain. In one fluid motion, he pulled her shirt over her head and took a step back. "Gorgeous." His voice was low and filled with desire as he ate her up in her lacy bra. "Pretty bra, but it has to come off."

It was a flurry of hands as they tore their clothes off, throwing them into a pile on the floor. Barely naked, Eric was already kissing, sucking and tasting Sadie's skin in a slow but deliberate trail down her chest.

"If you're trying to turn me on, it's working," she moaned as he dipped his tongue into her navel.

When he raised his head, he fiddled with both hearing aids before he lifted her by the waist and set her on the bed.

Sadie grasped his face and trailed her thumbs over the tiny wires and down to the earpieces. "You can take your ears out if that's more comfortable."

"Take my ears out? Oh, no, darling, I was turning them up. I want to hear every moan and squeak you make as I make love to you."

With a smile she lowered herself to the mattress and crooked a finger at him until he followed her down. He kissed his way across her left breast and up her chest to her chin.

"I'm not very good at this," she said, her hands buried in his hair. "You could say my experience is advanced-beginner level."

Eric lifted his head to meet her gaze. "But you've been with a man before, right?"

"Yes. I just meant *experienced seductress* isn't one of my titles."

His laughter was loud in the room as he kissed his way back to her navel and dipped his tongue in to take a taste. The sensation covered her in goose bumps, and her hips bucked for what was to come. "I don't want an experienced seductress, Sadie." She spread her legs, and he moaned as he kissed his way down to her center. "You're already better at this than you think."

She hummed when he kissed his way up her thighs. "I'm still willing to learn."

"Then let me teach you how I make love to a woman," he murmured, setting his tongue on her swollen bud.

Sensations overtook her, and her hips bucked at the sweet, sweet torture he doled out until she couldn't stand it a minute longer. "Eric, I want you," she cried, pulling him to her mouth by his hair. "Please." The word was a begged prayer against his lips. She grasped him in her hand, and he pulsed hard against her grip. Captivated by the feel of him in her hand, she slowly rolled on the condom he'd handed her.

Once protected, he poised himself at her opening and grasped her face to make eye contact. "We're at the *no going back* moment. If we do this, there's no going back to the people we were yesterday."

"I don't want to go back, Eric. I want to go forward with you."

Permission granted, he entered her on a gentle thrust, and she cried out from the pure joy and pleasure of being complete. Something had been missing in her life all these years, and now she knew what it was—Eric. He was her destiny and always would be, regardless of how long they were together.

"God, Sadie." He sighed into her neck as he carried them both up to sit on a cloud of pleasure. "It's never been like this before."

"Eric," she moaned, her mind overflowing with so many emotions and sensations. "I want to take this leap with you."

With a guttural yes, he shifted and together they jumped into an oblivion where they could have a life together, if only for a moment in time.

ERIC WONDERED IF this was what it felt like to be a caged animal. He hated having to wait for someone else to do a job he could do faster and better. Except this time he couldn't, and the wait was killing him. It didn't help that Selina had arrived at mobile command before sunup with Houston—and with an attitude that grated on his last nerve.

To add to his living hell, he couldn't stop thinking about the woman he'd made love to for half the night. She was incredible, and he did not deserve her in any way, shape or form. He turned and noticed her bracketed in the doorway with the sun streaming in to highlight her golden hair. She rocked Houston side to side as he slept, occasionally kissing the top of his head. The scene was so sweet that it broke his heart. He knew he could never give her that life. She deserved a husband, two-point-five kids and a white picket fence. He couldn't offer her that. All he could offer was too much time away, too many memories that wouldn't go away and no chance of having babies with the job and lifestyle he lived.

Could he live a different lifestyle for her? The answer to that was complicated. He probably could, but what he would do he didn't know. He'd graduated high school and within two weeks had been at basic training. He'd been trained as a special ops police officer, but after losing his hearing, being a civilian cop was out. That was why he'd worked at Secure One since leaving the army. Secure One was safe. It was a place where everyone understood him and the things that he went through, but they also knew there was nothing he could do to change the things he'd brought back from the war.

To put it another way, they all carried the same ghosts. Those ghosts were stacked by the years, not months, that they'd done bad things to protect good people. It was hard for any civilians to grasp the magnitude of their service, both good and bad, but somehow Sadie did. She understood that he fought a battle every day even all these years later. Most people would jump ship and run, but Sadie had simply picked up a bucket and helped bail.

Sadie glanced up and met his gaze. She offered him a shy smile, and he turned away. He couldn't do this right now. He had to focus on her sister and bring her home safe. Then he had to free Sadie of this murder charge so she could go on with her life. The sooner she left Secure One, the sooner she could find someone who deserved her love, devotion and desire. His body tightened at the thought of it. She was all sweet curves and soft edges in a way he had never experienced before. Sure, he'd been with plenty of women, but none of them had made him feel the way Sadie did. None of those women had made him want to leave his current life behind and go anywhere with her. That was the truth of it, even if it could never be reality.

Eric turned his attention to Selina and the computer screens in front of her. She had agreed to help him in mobile command while the rest of the team dealt with Dirk and the issues surrounding the security at the storage units. He should have been running point on that, but he couldn't be in two places at once. Since he had been the one to talk Vic into visiting his brother at the Loraine mansion today, Cal had insisted he remain in mobile command with Selina, Sadie and the baby.

Vic was inside the Loraine mansion. He sat on a couch in the living room across from Randall Junior. Vic's button camera on his jacket showed them everything he saw in real-time. He had refused to wear a microphone, afraid Randall would see it and know he wasn't there just to grieve their brother.

"How long are they going to sit there and talk?" Selina asked. It was more like a grumpy growl, and it drew Eric's attention from the screens.

"They haven't seen each other in a long time, so I explained to Vic that he needs to make it look like he's there for a reconciliation. Anything else will raise Randall's suspicion, and Vic will be the next dead body on our hands."

Selina didn't respond. She kept her gaze on the screens with her jaw clenched tightly. Eric could not figure out for the life of him what was going on with her. From the moment she'd arrived at mobile command this morning, she'd been skittish, standoffish and downright rude to Sadie when she'd asked how Houston had done during the night. He walked over and knelt next to the bank of computers so she didn't have a choice but to make eye contact with him.

"Selina, what is going on?"

"Nothing is going on." She said the four words with such disdain that it made him snort.

"Nice try. There isn't one of us here who can't see that something has changed with you. Efren has been your punching bag, but I'm starting to think this has nothing to do with him and everything to do with you. Or something you don't want to tell us that is happening in your life."

"You can think whatever you'd like, Eric. I'm here to do my job, which lately has been undefinable."

Eric had already suspected that was part of the situation, but it certainly wasn't all of it. "Then I say it's time you talk to Cal about your job and your hopes for your future at Secure One, and see what he says."

"What if I don't like what he says?" she asked, side-eyeing him.

"Then you counteroffer or you give him your notice. But one way or the other, at least you know. The animosity you're carrying about the situation has to be exhausting."

"That's rich coming from you."

"Meaning what?" He didn't like the barb at the end of that sentence, but he couldn't take it back, nor would he. He wanted an answer.

"It means that you carry plenty of animosity. You wear it like a cloak of armor, reminding everyone that we're so lucky because we can hear. You never take into consideration the fact that we know that and we all have your back. It's easy for you to sit there and call the kettle black, but you forget that you're the pot." She snapped her lips closed, focused her attention on the screens and refused to say anything more.

Rather than respond to her catty observations, he stood and watched the screens for a few more seconds. Vic was still sitting there talking to Randall, and every so often they caught a glimpse of his beer bottle going to his lips. He'd been there for over an hour now, and Eric hoped he was still nursing the first beer. They couldn't risk he would get tipsy and give up his reason for being there. An hour was long enough to chew the fat anyway. It was time to start looking for Kadie.

He walked over to Sadie in the hallway and leaned against the wall to talk to her in low tones. The baby was sleeping on the floor of Cal's office on a giant bed of blankets. Sadie was watching over him, but she turned, knowing instinctively, as she always did, that he would need to read her lips.

"What's going on with Vic and Randall?" Her gaze flicked to the front, but she was too far away to see the screens.

"Right now, Vic is still talking to Randall in the living room. I wish he'd taken a microphone with him so we could hear what they're saying."

She rested her hand on his chest, and her warmth spread through his body, automatically relaxing him. He loved it and hated it at the same time. No woman had ever done that to him before, and it was likely no other woman ever would.

"It would have been nice," she said, "but I understood where Vic was coming from. If for any reason they found a microphone on him, not only would Vic be in terrible danger, but so would we and Kadie. We have enough bad vibes to carry right now—we don't need to add more."

"I know you're right, but it's still frustrating for someone like me to sit around and wait while someone else gets the answers I need to do my job."

"It's equally as frustrating for me when I know my sister could be in that house somewhere, scared, hurt and wondering if we're ever going to find her. All I can do is trust in the process and trust that you know the best way to find her and bring her home to her son. If I could, I would take her place and let them do whatever they wanted to me if it meant Houston had his mother."

"No." The word came out in a way he hadn't been expecting. It was forceful and, if he was honest with himself, possessive. "Don't even think that way, much less say it aloud. We will find Kadie, bring her home to Houston and keep you all safe in the process. It's what we do. You have to trust me."

"I do trust you, but I don't trust the Loraines. Any of them."

He didn't need to hear her words to read the meaning behind them. "Listen, I know where you're coming from, but I think Vic is on the up and up."

"I'm reserving my opinion on Victor Loraine until we get Kadie's side of the story. Right now, we're taking the word of someone I don't know with ties to a family that doesn't know how to do anything but lie. Forgive me if I can't trust him at first sight," she said.

"No apology necessary, Sadie. I know where you're coming from, and I understand how you feel. We did a deep dive on Victor Loraine, and there is nothing—at least nothing anywhere on the light or the dark web—

about him. I've had a lot of experience on making snap first impressions about people. Sometimes it was a matter of life and death, and I can tell you if Victor Loraine had walked into our camp unannounced, I would have pegged him as an ally and not a foe. That said, I respect how you feel and I ask that you reserve judgment until we know if Kadie is in that mansion."

"This is a terrible thing to say, but I actually hope she is at the mansion," Sadie said. "If she's not, I don't know who took her or why."

He grimaced before he could stop it.

"What? You promised to always be honest with me, Eric."

At that moment, he wished she had never uttered those words, but he had and he was a man of his word. "It's entirely possible if Randall Loraine doesn't have Kadie that The Snake does."

"Vaccaro? You think a mob boss has my sister?"

Her voice was loud enough now to wake the baby, and he put a finger to her lips. "All I'm saying is with Howie Loraine involved, there's more than a fifty percent chance that The Snake has something to do with it. We have our ears to the ground, but so far we've heard no chatter about The Snake picking up a woman in Bemidji."

"Your ears to the ground? You mean Mina?"

He winked and smiled, enjoying the moment of levity in a tense situation.

"We have movement," Selina called out, snapping them both to attention.

Sadie glanced at Houston, who was still sound asleep, and then motioned for him to go. They stood behind Selina, watching the bank of computers in front of her.

"What's going on?" Eric asked.

"Randall got a cell phone call, so Vic made a motion that he was going to the bathroom, I have to assume, and Randall nodded. Now Vic is wandering the hallways."

"He's looking for something," Eric said.

"He's looking for some*one*," Sadie said. "Kadie."

"I hope so. That's what he's there for. Otherwise this has been a waste of precious time."

The camera went screwy and out of focus momentarily before Vic's face filled the screen. He had twisted the camera toward himself like a selfie and started to speak. Eric immediately said, "Office. He's going to the office." The camera shifted again, and then Vic was moving down a hallway.

"You have to give them credit—the place is pretty swanky," Sadie said as Vic passed expensive artwork on the walls. "I'm surprised that lure of the place didn't suck Vic back in after college."

"Once you escape a place like that, you never go back," Selina said. "Ever. This is a big ask. I hope you appreciate what he's doing for you."

"You mean what he's doing for his family, right?" Sadie said, her tone of voice an obvious challenge to Selina. She glanced at Eric, who shook his head no and darted his gaze to Selina for a moment. Thankfully Sadie backed down just as Vic walked into a home office fit for the Godfather.

"Hey, honey, I'm home," Selina sang. "Show us the goods, Vic," she cooed to the screens, widening and tightening different views and angles in front of them.

They all leaned in while holding their breath. None of them knew what he was looking for, but it was evident that Vic did. He had a plan that he was hoping would lead him to his future wife.

"How long has he been gone from the living room?" Eric asked Selina, who punched up a timer on the screen.

"Only two minutes. Vic should have at least three more before Randall gets suspicious." She pointed at the camera still monitoring the living room that Vic had so kindly tucked under the couch cushions. Randall was talking on the phone, his head nodding.

Eric slid his gaze back to the computer screen where Vic was searching the office. He had lowered himself to the executive chair and was going through the desk. There was a monitor on the desk that was off, but no computer could be seen anywhere. He couldn't hear Vic, but he could sense his desperation as his motions grew frantic. Eric prayed he was still being quiet.

Selina had her eye on Randall, who still sat on the couch seemingly laughing along with whatever the caller was saying on the other end.

"He needs to hurry up in there," Sadie said. "I doubt his brother is going to leave something out that will point him directly to where his girlfriend is being held hostage."

"Nothing ventured, nothing gained," Eric said. "You're probably correct, but he's still got to try. That's why we sent him in. He knows his brother better than any of us, and he can think like a Loraine. We can't."

The camera got a shot of Vic running his fingers along the edge of the desk. Suddenly the computer monitor came to life and the camera jerked. That was the moment Vic laid eyes on the woman he loved. He held the camera up, scanned the screen and then turned it to show his face.

"'Help! I don't know where this is,'" Eric read as he watched his lips move.

A sharp intake of breath had Eric's head swiveling. Sadie had turned white as a ghost as her knees collapsed. He scooped his arm around her waist so she didn't fall and held her to his side.

Vic was still talking to the screen. "'We have to find her! We have to get to her! She needs help!'"

"There's nothing we can do," Selina said without turning. "He needs to follow the plan and rendezvous with the team before we try to save Kadie. We don't even know if that feed is from inside Randall's house."

"Of course it is!" Sadie exclaimed. "She's right there on the screen!"

"Selina's right, babe," he gently said, trying to soothe her. "It could be a remote feed from somewhere else."

"We also can't go in alone," Selina pointed out. "We're not the cops."

Vic still had the camera up to his face. "'Remote feed?'" Eric read. "He's asking that as a question," he told them. "Which means he doesn't know if she's on-site either."

"Oh, we've got trouble," Selina said, pointing to the monitor and the empty chair where Randall had been sitting.

"Get out, get out," Eric chanted, hoping Vic would sense the danger coming at him.

Vic must have heard his brother coming or calling for him because he reached out, searching for a button to turn off the monitor. It was too late. His brother stood in the doorway wearing a satisfied yet smug grin. Eric leaned in as Randall walked toward his brother. Vic's coat camera was pointed directly at Randall now, and Eric didn't want to miss a word Randall had to say. He tightened his grip on Sadie and waited while the two men faced off.

"'What are you doing, little brother?'" Eric read on Randall's lips.

He couldn't see Vic's response, so he waited for Randall to speak again.

"'You didn't think I'd believe you were here to mourn our lost brother, did you?'" Eric read slowly. "'You... years.'" Eric paused. "He probably said he hasn't seen him in years."

Vic slid out from behind the desk and inched toward the door. Whatever he said made Randall laugh.

"'I don't know what you're talking about, Vic,'" Eric read. "Something about the computer." He was frustrated but watched as Randall approached Vic, who tried to skirt past him to make for the door. Then a gun appeared, aimed directly at the camera.

"Dammit!" Selina exclaimed.

"Vic better do some fast talking," Eric muttered. "We can't save him at this point. He's got to save himself."

He leaned closer to the monitor, hoping Randall would give them enough information to find Kadie. Eric also hoped he didn't shoot his brother. Randall stood still while wearing that smug smile on his face. They could only assume Vic was speaking to him.

"'This will be touching,'" Eric read, breaking the silence when Randall spoke. "'I can see the headlines—Loraine brother dies wrapped in his lover's embrace.'"

The gun waved toward the door, motioning Vic to start walking. Terrified to the point of shaking, if the camera was any indication, he had the wherewithal to walk backward so they could still see Randall in the camera.

"'It's a secret,'" Eric read. "'I'd kill you now, but The Snake wants no dead bodies to deal with unless he orders it.'"

Vic visibly started and must have said something to his brother because Randall sneered. "'Enough talk,'" Eric read. "'Time to see your lover girl.'"

Vic turned slowly to walk down the hallway, allowing them to see the direction he was going. Hopefully he'd be able to show them where to start looking.

"For not being an operative, this guy is intuitive," Selina said as she typed a message to Cal.

The two men paused near a door while Vic turned the handle. He took a step forward, and immediately the camera went dark. Before Eric could say anything, the door to mobile command nearly flew off its hinges, announcing the arrival of the cavalry.

Chapter Sixteen

Eric hung up the phone and disconnected his hearing aids from the Bluetooth. "Cal and the guys are digging into Howie's financials." He offered the information to anyone in the room who was listening, but Lucas and Mina had their heads buried in their computers.

As soon as it had become evident they wouldn't see more from Vic, they'd circled the wagons as a team to make an extraction plan. To do that, they needed more space, so Dirk had given them a heated storage unit to use so they could spread out the team between there and mobile command. Eric wasn't letting Sadie out of his sight, so he moved her and Houston into the storage unit with him until they had a better plan to keep them safe.

His gaze traveled to the woman he had too many feelings for in such a short time. He couldn't stop thinking about how she'd made him feel last night when she'd offered him her body and her heart. Maybe she hadn't come right out and said *I love you* with words, but she didn't need words when she trusted him with her body. Eric swore internally. He never should have allowed himself the pleasure of being with her. It would be impossible to let her go once they had Kadie back safely. He knew and accepted that he would have to let her go, despite wanting to keep her close to him.

The thought gave him a jolt. He'd never thought that about a woman before. All the women he'd been with had been well aware they were there for a bit of fun and nothing more. They'd all been okay with that. Sadie said she was okay with it, but Eric knew she wasn't so much okay with it as accepting of it.

"We have a hit," Mina said, jumping up from the desk and giving him a start. "Roscoe Landry, age fifty, is a mob boss for Vaccaro. It's said his underlings call him the Winged Templar."

Eric did a fist pump. "We have another connection. The guy who dropped the trunk said they had to follow the Winged Templar's orders."

"Which to me sounds like the person responsible for the hit."

"Yes," he agreed, "but we can't prove it. How do we prove it?"

"I wish I knew who these guys were. I'd trace them back until I found the original hit order. We don't know if the guys who dumped him also killed him. They could have just been on disposal duty."

"We tried running facial recognition on the video we took, but it was too dark and far away. Wait." Eric clapped his hands together. "We need to use the victim."

"Use the victim?" Mina asked for clarification. "You mean trace Howie back until we find a connection to Roscoe?"

Eric pointed to her, and she ran back to the computer to start typing.

"What does any of that mean?" Sadie asked, pacing

the small area around the playpen where Houston sat happily, babbling at his toys.

"If we can find hard evidence that Howie and Roscoe are linked, you're off the hook."

"Just because they knew each other?"

"No," Eric said with a head shake, "because Howie was killed in a mob-style execution, and Roscoe is one of The Snake's top bosses. Once we know if Howie and Roscoe are connected, we look for a double cross by Howie. I assure you there is one. If Howie crossed him, Roscoe would order the hit and deflect the blame."

Sadie's head tipped to the side in confusion. "If that's the case, maybe he shouldn't have had him killed execution style." Her eyes rolled, and she mumbled what he thought was the word *men*.

"I never said he was smart." Eric winked and turned to Lucas. "Anything from Vic?"

Lucas shook his head. "Nothing usable. I know he's got the camera because it keeps shaking, but there's nothing other than blackness."

"Have you found the blueprints for the Loraine home? We need to know where that door leads to. If we have to go in, I want everyone to have the floor plan memorized."

The team knew Vic, and likely Kadie, were still inside the Loraine mansion. The GPS tracker in his shoe told them that much. What it didn't tell them was where inside, which was the reason they needed the blueprints.

"I'm working on it," Lucas answered, but Eric could hear the frustration in his tone. "Mina might have to make a go of it. Trying to get them through legal channels isn't working."

There was a knock on the door. "Secure one, Sierra."

Eric walked to the door and answered. "Secure two, Echo." Then he opened the door to allow her in. They were working out of a corner storage unit with a small side door, so they didn't have to open the main door as people entered. Selina had been their go-between for information, but when she burst through the door this time, her arms were loaded with long cardboard tubes. She dumped them onto the table in the center of the room and stepped back.

"What's all this?" Eric asked, homing in on her stiff shoulders and fisted hands.

"The blueprints for the Loraine mansion."

"What? How?" Lucas asked, standing immediately. "I've been working on getting those for hours."

"Don't ask questions I can't answer," she said through clenched teeth. "Just help me get these up on the wall."

Lucas glanced at Eric, who gave him a slight head tilt to go ahead and help her. He waited while Selina tacked the blueprints to the wall in an order that only she understood. She gave Lucas one- or two-word directions until all the prints were up. They stepped back, and Selina grabbed a marker. She started writing and marking things on the blueprints while everyone stared in stunned silence. Eric sensed the entire room was wondering the same thing—how had Selina gotten the blueprints, and how did she know the things she was writing on them?

"No way," Mina said to break the silence. "That was way too easy."

"What was too easy?" Sadie asked, handing Houston his bottle before walking over to Mina's station.

"I found the connection between Howie and Roscoe. Howie Loraine was engaged to Roscoe's daughter."

Eric stepped forward, certain he had misheard. "Say that again?"

"Howie was engaged to Roscoe's daughter, Lydia."

"Is there any evidence that Howie was working for Vaccaro?" he asked, an idea beginning to take root in his mind.

"Not that I can prove yet, but if he was engaged to Roscoe's daughter, the likelihood is high that he was working for Vaccaro."

Sadie put her hand on her hip. "If Howie was engaged to Roscoe's daughter and possibly working within the organization, the next question we have to answer is why did Roscoe have him killed?"

Eric couldn't stop the grin that lifted his lips. "She's good. It's like she's always been part of this team. That was my exact thought. Do you have any theories, Sadie?"

"I don't know much about the mob," she answered, "but I have watched a lot of mob movies. And it seems like the only thing that gets you killed in the mob is a double cross or personal affront."

Mina pointed at her. "What she said. Being engaged to the mob is a dicey place to be. It's highly possible there was a personal affront, especially with a guy like Howie. There could also be a double cross, which might be harder to track down. I'll keep looking." She went back to her keyboard, and Eric turned to Sadie.

"Things will move quickly once we figure out the connection between Howie and Roscoe. You'll return to mobile command and stay locked up tight with Houston."

"I won't stand around while someone else saves my sister! I'm going with you."

"No, you're not." This time it was Selina who answered. "You know absolutely nothing about an operation like this, which makes you more hindrance than help. If you go out there with no idea what you're doing, you will end up dead."

"She's not wrong," Eric said with his brow in the air, "and I can't allow that. You need to be here with Houston to keep him safe until we bring Kadie back."

He had to bite the inside of his cheek when Sadie planted her fists on her hips, puffed out her chest and jutted her chin in a sign of fierce determination. She clearly wanted to help save her family, no matter what they said.

"No," Selina said again. "The Loraine mansion is complicated, has too many entrances and exits, and is no place for someone without formal security training. We bring you along and the next thing we know, Randall will have three hostages. That simply cannot happen. Besides, I'm going with the team, which means someone must be here to care for Houston."

Eric turned on his heel to face her. "Are you going to be able to work with Efren?"

She took a step forward and stuck her finger in his chest. "For your information, I can work with anyone on this team. I don't appreciate the insinuation that I'm not a team player. I have always been a team player and will continue to be one. Now, let's step over to the blueprints and devise an attack plan."

"Well, well. Someone has decided to stop waiting to be told she's part of the team and just be part of the team. I like it. Keep it up."

Before he could say more, Cal announced himself. "Secure one, Charlie."

"Secure two, Echo," he responded, then opened the door for Cal, Mack, Efren and Roman. "You're just in time to get the lowdown on the mansion's layout," Eric said, motioning at the wall where the blueprints hung. "Mina is following up a lead on the connection between the Winged Templar and Howie."

"You found one?" Cal asked with his brows up in surprise.

"It was too easy," she said without breaking stride on the keyboard. "Howie was engaged to Roscoe's daughter."

Efren's whistle was long as he set his hands on his hips. "Hell hath no fury like a woman scorned."

"My thought exactly," Mina said, her gaze never leaving the screen. "If it's here, I'll find it."

"While she's doing that," Cal said, motioning to Mina, "let's break down the mission. Regardless of the connection, we must get Kadie and Vic out of that mansion."

Selina motioned them toward the blueprints spread across the wall. "This is Randall's office," she said, pointing to a room she circled in blue. "This," she said, pointing at a small opening she had circled in red, "is the door they walked through."

"Where does it go?" Roman asked from where he stood by Mina, a hand on her shoulder.

"According to the blueprints, it's a closet. Unless you have this set of prints." She pointed at the bottom row. "They show the tunnels. If I were a betting woman, I would say they're in this area somewhere."

"Tunnels?" Cal asked, stepping forward and letting his gaze wander the blueprints.

"We already know Kadie's at the mansion since Randall Junior told Vic he was taking him to see her. That said, he won't keep a hostage anywhere the hired help can happen upon her."

"He needs a secret room?" Sadie asked, and Selina gave her the so-so hand motion.

"Something like that."

"Do the tunnels go to a secret room?" Cal asked, pointing at a long, narrow hallway on the blueprint.

Her finger went up one blueprint and pointed at the room to the left of the door Randall had taken Vic through. "This is Daddy's private library. Here—" she moved her finger to the end of the room "—is a trapdoor with a ladder."

"And you know this how?" Efren asked, his head cocked as he stared at the blueprints.

"Because I do my job," Selina answered, her teeth clenched together.

"No, there's more to this than just doing your job, Selina," Cal said. "How did you get these blueprints?"

She spun on the group and walked up to Cal, sticking her finger in his chest. Eric grimaced. No one was insubordinate to their leader without suffering the consequences. "I will not answer any questions about what I know and how. I will share my knowledge with the team on how to stay safe and accomplish the mission. Is that clear?"

Eric stood frozen, as did the rest of the team. Even he could have heard a pin drop until Cal spoke. "Clear. For now," he added. "But we will address all of this," he said, motioning at his chest with his prosthetic finger, "when this case is resolved."

Eric stepped forward, the peacemaker in him wanting to settle things down for everyone. "Listen, Selina, we're grateful for any information you can give us about the mansion." Her shoulders were stiff and unyielding as she faced them. It was never more apparent she was hiding something, which didn't come as a surprise. Everyone knew that Selina's past was a dark hole she never discussed. But none of that mattered right now. "We have to move if we want to find Kadie and Vic before they're moved or killed."

"And we can't count on the cops," Efren said, stepping forward. "They still believe Sadie ordered the hit on Howie. They're going to be no help."

"Agreed," Selina said turning back to the plans on the wall. "Since we can't involve the cops, this will be considered breaking and entering."

"Considering we're rescuing hostages, I'm sure such a minor charge will be overlooked. Were anyone to learn of the mission, that is," Lucas said, his arms crossed over his chest.

She stiffened her spine and raised her chin. "If we're all in agreement, then what I'm about to tell you will make this job twice as easy but twice as dangerous. Are we all in?"

"Secure one, Charlie," Cal said.

"Secure two, Romeo."

"Secure three, Mike."

"Secure four, Echo," Eric said with a wink at Sadie.

"Secure five, Whiskey."

"Secure six, Tango."

"Secure seven, Bravo," Marlise, Cal's wife, said.

"Secure eight, Lucas."

"Secure nine, Sadie."

Eric reached out and took Sadie's hand, squeezing it.

"Secure ten, Sierra," Selina said, and then with a respectful nod, she turned back to the blueprints. "I can't confirm but I do suspect that this doorway is a set of stairs that goes to the same place the trapdoor does in the library," she said, pointing at that long empty space again. "Otherwise, it's another entrance to the library. Either way, it will take them to the tunnel."

"What do they use the tunnel for?" Cal asked.

"Escape," she answered immediately. "That said, there are also storage rooms on each side of the tunnel."

"Storage rooms?" Eric asked, releasing Sadie's hand and walking to the front so he could hear and see Selina better. "Can you explain?"

"More like cubbies, I suppose," she answered. "Places to store off-season sports equipment, clothing and household stuff."

"Or perfect for stashing a woman away for a few days," Eric said.

"Yep," Selina answered, pointing at the tunnel again. "There's plenty of space for Randall to hold Vic and Kadie while he waits for orders from The Snake. We now have confirmation that's who he's working for since he came right out and told his brother. Thanks to Eric's lipreading skill, we know that Vaccaro is pulling the strings. I assure you, where the mob is involved, danger quickly follows, so we need to get into that tunnel and get them out of there before The Snake gives an order we can't stop."

"How do we do that?" Cal asked. "Better question is once we get into it, how do we get out?"

Selina returned to the table and unrolled a smaller blueprint still waiting to be opened. "Tunnels always have an entrance and an exit, right?" she asked, getting head nods from the crew. "So does this one. The exit, or what we'll make our entrance and exit, is next to the garage in the back of the house. It's hidden in plain sight as an egress window. This is all the information I have on security around the yard," she said, passing out a paper packet to everyone.

"Hello, connection, my name is Winner," Mina gleefully said as she spun in her chair to face everyone. "Howie Loraine was engaged to Roscoe's daughter but was playing Hide the Salami with a model in Chicago."

"Hide the Salami?" Cal asked with his brow up.

She just laughed and clapped her hands. "Once a playboy, always a playboy where Howie Loraine was concerned. In their eyes, the only answer was to fix the problem."

"That made a bigger problem for us," Selina said with a shake of her head. "Knowing that, we have to move. You get five minutes to read that, ask questions and start your mission prep. I want to be rolling as soon as it's dark. That gives us—" she checked her watch "—an hour and twenty-two minutes to have our ducks in a row."

"Who's running this mission anyway?" Cal asked, taking a step toward the table.

"I am," Selina answered, leaning forward on the table. "Trust me when I say if you all want to walk out of there alive with our two hostages, not a soul around this table will argue with me."

Eric waited while Cal debated his next move. The Selina of the last thirty minutes was someone he didn't know, and he suspected he wasn't alone in that feeling. That was confirmed when Cal took a step back and nodded once. "Mission leader is Sierra. Mission foreman is Echo. Mission communication manager is…" He turned to Lucas and gave him a finger gun with his prosthesis. "Lima."

The unexpected declaration of a call name brought a smile to Lucas's face as he nodded at their leader. Lucas had officially been accepted onto the elite team at Secure One, and Eric knew he'd work twice as hard to prove that he deserved that distinction.

Cal turned to the rest of them. "Everyone else, get your assignments from Sierra. Let's get this couple back to their baby." Selina might've been running this mission, but he still ran the show.

Chapter Seventeen

Sadie paced the room, anxiety and the need to do something filling her to the breaking point. Houston slept in the playpen, blessedly unaware of how dangerously close he was to becoming an orphan. He'd become Sadie's responsibility forever if his parents didn't make it out alive. It also meant she'd have to run far and fast to keep him out of Randall Loraine's hands. Could she handle being a single mother of an infant? Absolutely. Did she want to? No. She wanted her sister home, alive and raising her son. Sadie couldn't fathom life without her sister in it.

"Secure one, Echo."

Sadie walked to the door, unlocked it and let Eric into the tiny room at the back of mobile command. "Hi," she greeted him after she closed the door.

"Cal got a call from the chief of police in Bemidji. You've been cleared of Howie Loraine's murder."

"What? How?" She took a step closer to him, desperate for the news to be true.

"We tipped them off to the Winged Templar. Once Mina had his real name, the Chicago police raided his home and found the contract paperwork on the hit."

"Did the paperwork show that I didn't order the hit?"

Eric nodded, and she let out a sigh, her shoulders slumping. "I'm so glad to be out from under that suspicion."

"You're one step closer to getting your life back."

She fisted the front of his shirt in her hand. "What's happening tonight, Eric? I need to know the plan."

"Nightfall is here, so we're gathering our final supplies to approach the mansion and enter the tunnel. If our luck holds, that's where we'll find Kadie and Vic and get them back here safely."

"I'm going," she said, her tone no-nonsense and forceful.

"Absolutely not," Eric said in a tone of voice that to anyone else would leave no room for argument.

"Listen to me, Eric! Kadie is my sister," Sadie hissed, stabbing herself in the chest with her finger. "I need to be there when she comes out of that mansion! She doesn't know any of you!"

"Vic is with her. I'm sure he's filled her in on who we are and that we're working to rescue them. He'll also tell her that you are keeping Houston safe. Once we get them out, the team will bring her right to you and Houston."

"You don't know that Vic is with her! You don't know that she's even in that mansion! What if she's injured and needs a hospital? I have to be there, Eric!"

"Listen to me, baby. It's too dangerous. We've talked about this. If you're there, then I'm worried about you and I can't afford to have my attention split that way. It's hard enough to make sure that I'm communicating and getting all of the information correctly from the rest of my team. If my mind is partially focused on your safety too, the mission will fail."

"You don't have to worry about me. I will stay wherever you tell me to stay."

"I'm telling you to stay here," he said. "I'll be brutally honest with you, Sadie. The idea of having you there where I can't protect you terrifies me. I've never felt this way about anyone before. That also terrifies me, but in ways that I can't put into words."

"Maybe you can," she said, taking a step closer and putting her lips on his for a brief moment. "Maybe you can put it into three words."

"That's the problem," he said, his forehead balanced on hers. "Putting it into those three words is dangerous."

"That makes it real?" Sadie asked, her heart pounding at the idea that he loved her too. "Is it possible to fall in love in less than a week?"

"If I've learned one thing working at Secure One, it's that it's possible to fall in love in one breath. I've seen it happen multiple times. But I never expected—"

"It to happen to you?" she asked, her voice soft and tender. The brush of his forehead against hers when he shook his head told her more than any other answer he could have given her. "You're afraid to be vulnerable again, right?"

This time he nodded and took a step back. She reached up and flicked the button on his hearing aids until they were off. His eyes widened, and she held her finger up. Then she said those three words. She waited while his eyes did the hearing for him. "I love you, Eric Newman. That may complicate life, but it also completes it. I'm not letting you go out there without telling you how important you are to me."

She flipped the switches back on his aids and waited

for him to speak. "Why did you turn my hearing aids off?"

"I wanted there to be no question about what I said. You trust the things you see more than the things you hear. I wanted you to see that I love you and that I'll always find a way to show you as much as tell you."

Before she could say another word, he pulled her into a tight hug, both arms wrapped around her and his lips against her ear. "I love you too, Sadie Cook. Oh, boy, does that complicate things, but I've never felt like I needed someone else to breathe. Then you came along, and suddenly I needed to see you morning, noon and night. That's why it terrifies me even to consider putting you at risk. Anything can happen out there, and you could get hurt."

"I could say the same about you," she said, leaning back so he could read her lips. "I'll do whatever you think is the best, but Kadie has to know that I've been looking for her and that I've kept Houston safe."

He grasped her shirt and pulled her to him, kissing her in a frantic tangle of tongues that neither of them would forget anytime soon. "Those will be the first words out of my mouth," he whispered against her lips. "I want you here, locked safely behind these doors where there's not a chance you can get hurt."

His lips attacked hers again, and she leaned into the kiss, dropping her jaw so he could drink from her the courage he would need to go out and face the risk for both of them.

When the kiss slowed, she said those words again so he could feel them. "I love you, Eric. Do not get yourself killed out there, do you understand me?"

"Loud and clear." He leaned back and tucked the hair back behind her ears. *I love you too*. He mouthed the words this time so seeing was believing. "We should keep how we feel about each other under our hats for now. I don't want any distractions within the team tonight."

"Agreed," she said with a head nod.

As though the idea of keeping it between them was too powerful for him, he walked to her, grasped her chin and laid a kiss on her that would carry her through until he was back in her arms.

ERIC TIGHTENED THE straps on his bulletproof vest, checked his gun and tucked it into his holster at his side, and flipped his night-vision goggles down over his eyes. He forced himself to put Sadie from his mind and concentrate on nothing but the mission—find Kadie and Vic and bring them out safely.

"You're sure about this?" he asked Selina, who stood next to him. "You're positive there's a way in from the back?"

"There's no question in my mind that we can get into the mansion this way. I know it's hard for you to trust me, but I promise you if we're going to find them and bring them out, this is the only way."

"Are the cops in position?"

Selina pushed the button on her earpiece. "Secure one, Sierra. Do we have a go?"

"Secure two, Charlie. Detectives are approaching the door as we speak. Hold your position."

"Ten-four."

He pulled his gun and waited. "I don't want the cops to screw this up," he growled.

"There's a fifty-fifty chance," Selina agreed. "But we didn't have a choice. If we didn't bring the cops in on this, we'd get hit with more charges than we could wiggle out of without damage to the business. Once I showed the chief the video of Randall holding his brother at gunpoint, they decided maybe they should take a second look at the brother. We've only got one chance at this while he's distracted by the cops. We need to make this happen."

"If they can keep Randall Junior busy for a few minutes, we can do the rest."

"I hope they have more than just detectives approaching that door. I hope they have the SWAT team. There are way too many exits to cover here. Not to mention Randall's personal bodyguards won't favor the cops arresting him."

"That confuses me," Eric admitted. "Why does Randall Junior need bodyguards if he's not doing anything illegal?"

Selina snorted to hold back her laughter. "Randall Junior obviously took over the business when Randall Senior went to prison. That's why he needs bodyguards. Of that, I have no doubt."

"How do you know so much about the Loraine case?"

She flipped her night-vision goggles down over her eyes and pulled her gun from her holster, pointing it at the ground. "I told you before that I won't answer questions. That still stands."

"I hope you realize at some point that excuse won't hold water and Cal will demand answers. Keep your secrets—I've got other things on my mind tonight."

"Like the woman back at mobile command who's waiting for you to be her hero."

"I'm not her hero, Selina." Eric's gaze darted around the yard, searching out danger.

"It's okay to love her," she said.

"Who said anything about love?"

"One doth protest too much, if you ask me. I'm happy for you, Eric. Sadie is your perfect match. You don't have to confirm that for me to know I'm right. All I'm saying is don't be afraid to take that chance. Real, all-encompassing love like that is hard to come by in life. Don't pass it by just because you don't think you deserve it."

"Why would I think that?"

"Oh, I don't know, because of what happened in the sandbox? We all know that you haven't dealt with your ghosts from that time. Maybe it's time to let somebody help you carry the burden."

"This still feels a lot like the pot and the kettle," Eric said.

"Except it's not," Selina pointed out. "You have someone within your reach who wants to be part of your life. Don't blow it, Eric. You might not get a second chance."

"Noted," he said through clenched teeth. "Be ready—we've got to be close to go time."

She nodded, pulling her gun close to her vest and crouching in the shooter's position. He'd go first, covering the open ground while she covered him. The empty stretch of grass ahead of them felt one hundred miles long. He reminded himself it was his job to get across the space, find Kadie and bring her back to her sister, and then walk away. While he absolutely loved Sadie and she made him feel things he had never felt before, they could never be together. There was no way he would drag somebody as sweet and innocent as Sadie into his life just to poison her too.

"Secure one, Charlie." His hearing aid crackled to life with Cal's voice. "The detectives have made contact with Randall Junior. It's go time."

"Ten-four. Echo and Sierra out."

Eric fiddled with his hearing aid for a moment. The earpieces kept them connected, but the app that ran it to his hearing aid couldn't have full control. Once he had surround sound again, he glanced at Selina, who gave him a nod. He took off in a runner's crouch, his gun pointed at the ground as he ran. He could bring it up and get off a shot in a split second, but he hoped he'd get across the yard to the safety of the brick garage without notice. Selina had assured them the backyard didn't have motion-sensor lights or alarms. How she knew that they weren't allowed to ask, which meant they were putting trust in her word against their better judgment.

He had no doubt Selina was already following him, even though she should've been waiting for him to cover her. She knew this property too well for her to have learned it all by studying the blueprints. There was a reason she had this much knowledge about the Loraine mansion and the people inside. At this moment, he didn't care what Selina's secret was. They all had secrets, and no one had the right to judge someone else for theirs. That said, if they were going to get out of this alive with their hostages, he was going to have to offer blind trust in a way he never had before.

Once his back was plastered along the cold brick of the garage, he spotted Selina moving toward him. The night was silent, which meant thus far, Randall was cooperating with the detectives. They just had to avoid any motion sensors they didn't know about, Selina's assurance or not, and they had to be sure if they ran into any SWAT members they made it clear they were friend and not foe.

His mind slid to mobile command, where the woman he loved was waiting for him to be the hero. That was a heavy load to carry. Even heavier than when he'd been in the army and carrying the load of a country on his shoulders. Back then, the people he was protecting had been nothing more than an idea of the larger picture. Tonight, the idea was concrete, and he remembered every curve of her body and the feel of her soft skin under his.

Selina slipped through the night and up alongside him, snapping him from his thoughts of Sadie and bringing him back to the present situation. Selina crouched as she assessed the backyard with her night-vision goggles. She whispered, but he didn't hear a thing.

He tapped her on the shoulder. "You can't whisper. Look at me when you speak."

She turned and nodded. "Sorry—forgot. From what I can see, everything looks clear. Do you see anything?"

"Negative," he replied.

"Are you ready to go in?"

"Let's do it. Eyes forward, guns ready, be prepared for anything."

Her laughter took him by surprise. "Oh, you don't have to tell me that. I know how things can turn on a dime when it comes to the Loraine mansion."

Before he could reply, she was motioning him forward along the back of the garage until she came to a halt and knelt.

I had to find the opening, she mouthed, pointing at the ground.

Eric aimed his gun at the ground and waited while Selina pulled back the 'grass' to reveal an egress window cover.

"You can't even tell it's there," Eric whispered. The glass had been covered with artificial turf to make it blend in.

"Once we're down there, we have to make quick work of that window. It will be locked from the inside."

"Ten-four," Eric whispered, then waited as she lifted the glass and it rose on hinges. He pointed his gun into the hole, and his night-vision goggles revealed a short metal ladder that led to the window below. "You go first. I've got you covered," he said, motioning at the ladder with his gun.

Selina hesitated for only a moment before she slung her gun into the front of her pants, backed up to the opening and descended the ladder within a matter of seconds.

Silence was of the utmost importance now, so she made the hand motion for him to follow. Before he ducked under the cover, Eric did a full sweep of the yard in front of them. He saw no one moving nor any lights in the distance. He quickly descended the ladder far enough to grab the cover and pull it closed. He didn't want a surprise attack. At least Selina would hear someone opening the cover above them.

The window keeping them from the tunnel looked like a simple double pane side slide open, but he suspected it was something far more secure than one of those. Selina confirmed that when she lined the window with duct tape and used a center punch to break the pane. She quickly did the same thing with the second pane, making a hole just big enough to reach the levers to unlock the window.

"I have to admit this is too easy," Selina said, making eye contact. "As soon as I open this, be ready to fire. There could be a silent alarm on it or they could be waiting."

"Ten-four," he said, standing to the side of the window. He expected her to slide it open, but instead, the window swung open into the well. He swept the area below them, surprised when there was another ladder that they'd have to descend to reach the floor of the tunnel. How deep did these people need to bury their secrets?

With a nod, he motioned Selina down the ladder. When she hit the bottom, she immediately pulled her gun and swept the area ahead of her. In a moment, she motioned him down, so he followed her, being sure to pull the window nearly closed to prevent sound traveling down the tunnel.

Once he was standing next to Selina, she pulled out a folded paper from her chest pocket. It was a map of the tunnels, and she held it out for him to see with his goggles. She pointed to where they were and where Vic and Kadie might be tucked away. The tunnel was easily the length of a football field and originated in the main house library. The several closet-sized storage rooms along the way held their interest. If you were going to squirrel someone away for an extended period, this creepy dungeon would fit the bill.

They moved forward, but Eric didn't like that they

were heading toward the house rather than away from it. The air was thick with intense fear. Eric had felt this kind of fear before. He tried to focus on this mission rather than the ones that had failed. There were twice as many humans in the world doing evil as those doing good. That made it impossible to win every time.

Immediately, his mind's eye went to the woman waiting for him to return. She was everything to him, even if they couldn't be together. He would do anything to bring her family back to her. At the end of the day, her family would be the only thing she would have, so he owed her that. Eric understood that he could love someone, but he lacked the ability to love someone unconditionally. No, that wasn't true. He loved Sadie unconditionally. He lacked the ability to love her freely because he knew he could lose her in the blink of an eye.

He'd seen that happen so many times during the war. One minute he'd been talking to his buddy, and the next minute his buddy had been gone. Vaporized. Shot down. Bleeding out. Asking him with a waning, gurgling voice to pass those last words to their wife or girlfriend. Those words had been burned into his soul and always would be. Sadie shouldn't have to suffer the scars too. She said she understood what he'd been through, and maybe she did to a degree, but at the same time, she didn't. She'd never been there at 2:00 a.m. when he was drenched in sweat and covered in scratches from his fingernails or curled into a ball in the corner of the bed sobbing into a pillow. She'd never seen that, and he didn't want her to. Sadie deserved the kind of man who could offer her stability in life. That would never be him.

Selina held up a fist, telling him to halt. She motioned

to the left with two fingers, reminding him that was the first room they had to clear. The door was solid wood and locked from the outside with a padlock like one used to lock up athletic equipment or bicycles. He waited while Selina cut the padlock, and then they both took a deep breath before she swung the door open. His night-vision goggles showed him winter skis. His heart sank.

Selina closed the door, pulled her gun back to her shoulder and motioned forward. He followed with his gun aimed at the ground as they approached the next door. This one was also padlocked, but it only took Selina a moment to cut it loose. With a nod, he crouched and aimed his gun at the door. When she pulled the door back, it revealed a woman with her hands tied to her feet and a gag in her mouth.

Kadie Cook was alive.

Selina put her gun behind her back and walked into the room while Eric covered her. Selina whispered into Kadie's ear, and the woman began nodding frantically. She was trying to hold her hands up, so Selina quickly cut through the ropes and let them fall to the floor before she removed the gag. She held her finger to her lips and motioned out the door. Kadie nodded her understanding.

Selina approached Eric and knelt, pulling her Secure One phone from her vest. She typed something in and held the screen out for him to read.

We're near the end of the tunnel. Randall could be right above our heads. Time to go silent mode. She doesn't know if Vic is here, but she did hear a commotion a few hours ago. We have one room left to check. If he's not there, we take her out and regroup?

Eric gave one nod, confirming the plan. His left hearing aid gave a warning beep in his ear that the battery was almost dead. Frustrated, he reached up and shut down the aid, leaving the right one on. Selina motioned Kadie behind her, and they sandwiched her as they moved toward the final padlocked room. Eric knew they were dangerously close to the stairs and the library. He held his breath when the bolt cutters loudly snapped on the last padlock. Selina motioned for Kadie to take a step back, and then with one motion, she opened the door and brought her gun up to her shoulder.

Vic was draped across a chair, his hands and feet tied and a gag in his mouth. His head listed to the side while he blinked his eyes repeatedly. Randall had clearly knocked him around before putting him in the room. His limp posture worried Eric, and he prayed the man could walk. The one thing he did notice was the relief in Vic's eyes when he saw them. Selina quickly cut the ties from his hands and feet and then removed the gag. Surprise and fear bloomed across Vic's face when he got a good look at her. He stood on quivering legs and stumbled backward away from Selina, mouthing something Eric struggled to read.

He swore he'd said *Ava Shannon*. Before Eric could step in, Selina leaned forward and blocked his view of Vic's lips. Whatever she said to Vic made him nod with excitement. She put an arm around him and helped him out of the room where Kadie, to her credit, was silent when she ran to him and slid under his other arm to help hold him up. Selina motioned to Vic's head, and Eric immediately noticed the bloodied mat of hair. She gave him the good-to-go sign, so they turned back toward the trapdoor.

If everything had gone to plan, Cal and Efren would be waiting to help them bring out the hostages while Roman and Mack worked the perimeter to ensure they all got out safely. He grabbed his Secure One phone and punched in the agreed-upon Morse code he would use if they found the hostages. He waited and was rewarded with the reply telling them everyone was in position. With a nod at Selina, he picked a steady but slower pace than he liked as he headed for the trapdoor. Vic needed both women to support him, which meant they could only go as fast as their slowest member. He tossed around helping Vic but decided they were all better off with both hands on his gun if confronted. After a tense few minutes, they reached the ladder, and Eric punched a code into the phone again. The window swung open to let in a bit of the night sky, and he tipped his head up.

Cal's hand lowered into the hole, and he made a fist and then held out a finger—*Secure One*. They were good to go. He whispered into Kadie's ear that it was safe and urged her up the ladder. Eric waited as Efren helped her, but he held the stop fist up to Selina as she tried to get Vic to climb the ladder. Eric could see he would never make it up on his own. They needed another team member to come down and help him up. Within seconds of helping Kadie out, Efren was climbing down the ladder. As an above-knee amputee, Eric didn't want him trying to help a half-conscious man up a vertical ladder. He wanted him to cover their butts with his gun. He'd been a sharpshooter in the army and could take out a threat in the dark with one hand tied behind his back.

"Cover me," he whispered to Efren as he helped Vic toward the ladder.

"No, she's dead. I know she's dead. She's dead." Vic was rambling as though the knock on the head had done more damage than they'd thought.

Eric didn't have time to worry about it, except that he was too loud. He leaned into Vic's ear and whispered, "It's Eric from Secure One. If you want to see Kadie and Houston again, you must quiet down and climb this ladder. They're waiting for you."

"Kadie? Is Kadie safe? Houston? Houston is my son. Why is she here? She's dead."

They were out of time, so he took one of Vic's hands and placed it on the metal, hoping the unexpected chill would clear his head a bit. It seemed to work as he immediately put the other one up and slowly climbed the ladder even while murmuring. It wasn't ideal considering the situation, but if they could get him out into the fresh air, that might help clear his head and quiet him down.

"You should stop right there," a voice said from their left. Eric spun slowly and came face-to-face with Randall Loraine Junior. "Since you're holding the next Loraine heir hostage, I was planning to exchange his mother for my nephew. There is a low likelihood of you getting out of here alive until you tell me where he is."

"You're outgunned, Loraine," Eric said in the voice he reserved for dire circumstances. "It's three against one down here. My team will shoot first and ask questions later." Their semiautomatic rifles were pointed at Randall, who carried only a 9 mm.

"We'll see about that," he said and pushed a button on his watch. The tunnel lit up, blinding Eric and Selina for a moment until they ripped their night goggles off. Thankfully, Efren still had the man in his sights.

"You can't win here, Loraine!" Efren yelled as Eric got his bearings back.

Selina lifted her head and pointed her gun at Randall's center mass. "You heard him. Back away."

"No!" He jumped backward, tripped and fell, then crab-walked to get away from the woman in front of him. "You're dead! They said you were dead!"

Before anyone could react, Randall brought his gun up and got off a shot. Selina's pained grunt filled his ears as she fell to the side just as Efren's shot rang out. The sound blasted through his aid, and Eric struggled to clear his head as the tunnel went dark. On instinct, he flipped his goggles back down and located Randall as he limped down the tunnel. He aimed but didn't pull the trigger. He couldn't shoot the man in the back as he ran. They'd have to leave him to the cops. "Randall is headed to the library! Selina is down! Need medic!"

He turned to Efren, who was tending to Selina on the ground. "What's her status?"

"Looks like a belly wound. Loraine got her under the vest—we need to get her to a hospital ASAP!"

"I can walk," Selina grumped, but Eric wasn't sure if he'd heard correctly. "I said I can walk!" She pushed at Efren until he stepped back.

That brought a smile to Eric's lips. A man couldn't count Selina down and out yet.

Efren helped her to her feet, her arm across her belly as she walked to the ladder. "It's just a flesh wound," she insisted as she put her foot on the first rung of the ladder.

Eric glanced at Efren. "Help her up. I'll cover your back."

With only a few moans from Selina, Efren was able to get her up the ladder where Roman and Mack helped her through the opening. Eric wasted no time on the ladder and joined them at the back of the property.

Flashing lights filled the backyard as a medic team ran toward Selina, who was now lying on the ground. Her bulletproof vest was open, her black T-shirt now silky with her blood.

Eric knelt next to her and leaned into her ear. "Who is Ava Shannon? Why do they think you're dead? How do you know Randall Loraine?"

Selina met his gaze, and a whimper left her lips. "I told you there are questions I can't answer. Those are three of them." Then her eyes drifted closed.

Chapter Eighteen

Sadie ran down the hallway carrying Houston, the nurse having pointed her in the right direction to find her sister. "Kadie!"

A curtain was thrown back, and a face so much like her own stared out. "Sadie!" her sister cried as soon as she saw her. "Houston!" The baby let out a squeal, and then they were together, hugging, laughing and crying as Kadie kissed her son's head, checking him over for injuries. "I knew you'd take care of him."

Sadie ended the hug and helped her sister sit with Houston on her lap before she dropped his diaper bag. "He's fine," she promised, hugging her sister again. "I'm so happy to see you," she said through her tears. "When they told me they had to take you to the hospital, I imagined all the worst scenarios."

"I'm okay," she promised as Sadie lowered herself to another chair. "That was a precaution, but the doctors said I'm fine and don't need to be admitted. I'm waiting on Vic to come back from the CT scanner."

"Kadie, what happened? How did you end up at Randall's?"

Kadie rubbed her cheek against Houston's as he snuggled in against her neck. "I was driving to work, and two

SUVs boxed me in and forced me off the road. I didn't even have time to grab my phone before I was tossed in the back of one of the SUVs and they all drove off. One of the guys even took my car. I have no idea where that is."

Sadie didn't have the heart to tell her it was probably in a chop shop somewhere and she would never see it again. "Did they take you right to the mansion?"

"I don't know. They blindfolded me, and eventually we stopped somewhere dark. Maybe a garage? That's where they made me write that letter. Did they send it to you?"

"I found it on my bed when I came back from searching for you," Sadie explained. "I knew it wasn't your handwriting. Mina, from Secure One, said you wrote it but you did it in a way I'd know you didn't want to."

"Yes!" Kadie exclaimed quietly so not to scare Houston. "I knew you wouldn't believe I wrote it, and I hoped you'd run."

"I did, after Vic sent a note to my work. That's how I ended up with Secure One. They've been protecting me and Houston since someone ran us off the road near their property. Randall treated you good?" Sadie asked, afraid of the answer but also needing to know.

"He didn't have a choice. I refused to tell him where Houston was. To be honest, that dude isn't the smartest guy I've ever come across. He was so mad when they brought me to him and Houston wasn't along. He also doesn't have the stomach for violence. He wouldn't let his bodyguards slap me around and insisted putting me in a dark room alone would break me."

"I'm so sorry, Kadie," she whispered, squeezing her hand.

"There were so many times I wanted to break down

and cry, tell him everything if he'd let me out of that room, but then I pictured this sweet boy. I would live through anything, or die trying, to keep him safe."

"How did they know who you were or that you even had Houston?"

"I'm afraid that's all my fault," Vic said as they rolled him back into the room still on a gurney. "Houston, my sweet boy."

The baby leaned back at the sound of his voice and let out another happy squeal. Kadie stood so they could hug as a family. Sadie's heart broke from the sweetness of the reunion. If she had doubted Vic's love for her sister and his son a few days ago, she no longer did. Tears ran silently down his cheeks as Kadie stroked his forehead, being careful of the stitches in his head from the beating he'd taken. Houston clung to him like a spider monkey, so Kadie left them locked together while she kept her hand on the baby's back.

"Randall told me while he was walking me to the dungeon that Dad has kept someone on me since I left for college. He suspected I would try to have a family outside the family." Vic's eyes rolled, and he shook his head. "We were careful, but a few days before Kadie disappeared, his guy saw me open the door for her and Houston. It wasn't hard to do some research and find out who Kadie was, and even without solid proof, they suspected the baby was mine."

"Then why put me in the crosshairs with the note?" Sadie asked. "Why didn't they leave the note for you?"

"Randall said he knew Kadie lived with you and not me. He thought if they left the note for you, you'd run straight to me with the baby and they could grab him.

They didn't realize that you didn't know who I was. When you disappeared completely, they had to do the legwork to find you."

"Which they did when they ran me off the road?"

"No," Vic said, shaking his head. "They still didn't know where you were. That's why I got a beating from his bodyguards. They wanted me to tell them. I passed out and woke up in that room."

"Do you think it was just a coincidence with an impatient driver?" Sadie's world spun to the side, and she was glad she was sitting down. If it had been an accident that put her on the course to fall for Eric while they'd worked to rescue her sister, that told her how truly special it was to have him in her life.

"In the rain, it could have been," Vic said, rubbing his forehead. "So many things had to come together to save this little boy. It was all my fault to begin with by thinking my family didn't care what I did. I put everyone I care about in danger."

"Will it continue to?" Sadie asked, her brow in the air. "I doubt The Snake is going to go away just because your brother and father are in prison."

"My brother and father were the ones who didn't want me to raise a Loraine, not The Snake. The problem is my brother won't stay in prison. The Snake will get him out, but I have a plan to make sure they all leave me, and my new family, alone."

"How?" Sadie and Kadie asked in unison.

"Through lawyers and mediators, I plan to approach Vacarro about a protection order, so to speak. I don't know him well, but I do know that he doesn't put time or energy into anything that doesn't serve him. Our little family doesn't serve him, which means he'll be happy to have this black sheep out of his hair."

Kadie wiped the rest of his tears from his cheek and then kissed his forehead. "We can worry about that once you're feeling better. Your brother is in jail for shooting a security officer, so we're safe for the next few days. Try to rest."

Sadie stood and squeezed her sister's shoulder. "I want to go check on Selina. Are you guys okay if I leave Houston with you?"

"Of course," Kadie said, turning to hug her. "We'll be fine."

"Okay, let me know when you need a ride home and I'll get it arranged." Sadie kissed the top of Houston's head and waved as she left the little family to spend some time together alone. Her first stop would be to check on Selina, and then she was going to find the man she loved.

THE HOSPITAL NOISE was a buzz saw to Eric's head. There was so much happening at once that he had to shut his only working aid down or lose his ability to focus on anything. Selina had been rushed into emergency surgery the moment she'd arrived at Sanford Hospital. Randall's bullet had lodged somewhere in her abdomen, and it was going to require exploratory surgery to remove it and ascertain what damage had been done.

Cal grabbed his shirt and pulled him into a room off the waiting area. "What the hell happened out there?"

Eric held up his finger and turned his aid back on. "I missed something." The words were spit out hard and fast as his fingers raked his hair. "He shouldn't have been able to get the drop on us, but I didn't hear his approach!"

"From what the team tells me, no one heard his approach. It was like he materialized out of thin air."

"But he didn't," Eric growled. "He was there. I missed him." He jabbed himself in the chest and forced the truth from his lips. "The battery died on one of my hearing aids. It hasn't been holding a charge and it was my fault for not checking them before we left!"

Cal grabbed his shoulder and squeezed it. "It had nothing to do with your aid being down, Eric. We all missed him moving out of the main house. I was running point on the scout team, and I watched him escort the detectives to the door. He was in the basement with you in a quarter of the amount of time he should have been when we calculated it. That means there's another door to that tunnel somewhere. A door Selina didn't know existed."

Eric was still shaking his head. "I'm resigning effective immediately," he said, lowering himself to a padded chair. The weight of the last few hours sat heavy on his shoulders, and he couldn't bear knowing that his friend had been injured because of his failure.

"You're absolutely not doing that." Eric turned to see Sadie blocking the doorway, her eyes firing daggers at him. "Nothing that happened out there tonight was your fault."

"You can't tell me what to do," he said, his voice harsh in the quiet room. "And you don't know anything about what happened out there tonight. You weren't there!"

"I wasn't there, that's true," she agreed, stepping inside the room. "But you brought my sister home to me, and that's what I'll remember about tonight. Am I upset, sad and feeling guilty that Selina got shot? Yes, but it wasn't your fault. If anything, it was my fault for pushing you guys into trying to save my sister! I will owe Secure One and Selina for the rest of my life for what the team did to help my family when the cops wouldn't lift a finger. What I won't do is allow you to blame yourself for what happened as a way to push me away."

"It was no one's fault," Cal said with exasperation. "Eric, you know we all accept the same risk when we run these operations. Did I think we'd be rescuing hostages when I started Secure One? No. I had no idea we'd be rescuing women and taking out serial killers, but here we are, aren't we? You have skills beyond being a security guard—don't think they haven't been noticed. I've seen what you've done to integrate technology into the team to accommodate us better as we do this job." Cal held up his prosthesis. "My hand, Mack's legs, your ears, Mina and Efren...we all benefit from the perceptive changes you've made on the team. I'm guilty of not saying it enough, but what we did tonight would not have been possible without the technology we have because of you. So, no, you're not resigning. You can be mad about it, but you've worked too hard to use your disability as an excuse to avoid living. Does living real hurt sometimes? It sure does, but that doesn't mean it's not worth the pain."

"Living real?" Eric asked in confusion. "I don't think I heard you correctly."

"You did. I said living real. What that means to you is up to you. To me, it means giving myself grace again. It means enjoying life and accepting love from a woman who understands that some days will be harder than others. It means letting the rough days be rough so that rough day doesn't turn into a rough week or month. Marlise taught me that accepting love doesn't make me weak. It means I'm strong enough to ignore the doubts and let someone else see all my ugly."

"And there's always plenty of ugly to see in my soul," Eric hissed, his gaze drifting to Sadie, who still stood in the doorway. "You're too pretty for that kind of ugly, Sadie Cook."

"I don't remember any ugly, Eric Newman," she said, her finger pointing at him as she walked toward him. "All I remember is the sweet way you held my nephew when he was crying, swaying him back and forth to offer him a safe place to be frustrated about life. I remember the way you shielded me from danger and the way your lips feel on mine when we kiss—"

"That was a mistake," he ground out, interrupting her. There was no way he could sit there and listen to her tell him all the ways they were perfect together. Not when he knew he had to let her go. "We were a mistake. I never should have gotten involved with you and Houston. I should have turned you over to the police. If I had, our friend wouldn't be in surgery right now!"

"And my sister would be dead." Her voice was so quiet if he hadn't been watching her lips, he wouldn't have heard her.

"You don't know that. What I do know is, this—" Eric motioned between them with his hand "—is over. I can't protect you, and as you learned, the world is dangerous, even in small-town Minnesota!"

"I don't need you to protect me, Eric Newman. I need you to stop pretending that this—" she motioned between them with her hand the same way he did "—isn't right. You're a big, bad security guy, whoopie! I'm not scared of your world, and I don't need protecting. I need someone to love me. Someone like you—"

"I've got an update on Selina," Mina said, racing into the room and interrupting Sadie.

Eric braced himself for the news while pretending he didn't want to pull Sadie into his arms forever. "How is she?"

"Out of surgery. She's going to be okay," Mina said, her folded hands near her lips. "The doctor couldn't tell me much since I'm not her medical power of attorney, but he did say she's going to be fine in a few weeks."

"Thank God," Cal and Eric said in unison.

"Cal, the doctor wants to speak with you," she advised. "He's at the nurses' station."

"On my way," he said, skirting past Mina and Sadie and jogging out the door.

"I'm so glad she's going to be okay," Eric said, his hand in his hair as he turned to pace away from the two women. When he turned back, only Mina stood before him. Good. It was time Sadie hit the road. She had a life that no longer included him. He had nothing to offer her. He never made that a secret—she just wasn't listening. Ironic, considering.

"In the FBI, we had a word for guys like you, Eric."

"Excuse me?"

"Is there one?" she asked, hand on her hip and her nose in the air. "I heard what you said to Sadie. Real jackhat move, Newman."

"Jackhat?" He was throwing every defense he had her way to shut her down. The last thing he needed was a lecture from Mina Jacobs about his love life or lack thereof.

"Would you like me to write down what I have to say so it's extremely clear and you can refer to it when you're alone in your cold, empty bed?"

"That's low, Mina," he said, crossing his arms over his chest. "I can hear you."

"I never said you couldn't. I was implying that you won't, and there's a difference. *Couldn't* means you have no ability to. *Won't* means you refuse to. Sadie is the best thing to ever happen to you, but you act like she's putting you out by existing."

"I'm no good for her, Mina!" he exclaimed, throwing his arms up. "I have nothing to offer her in the emotional department or for her future. She's better off without me."

"So that's it? You get to make that decision for her? You get to be the judge and jury of her life? How would you feel if someone said you couldn't be with Sadie because you deserve better."

"There is no one better than Sadie Cook!"

"You made my point. You'd be angry, upset and sad if someone said that and then took away your chance to change it. That's what you just did to Sadie."

"I don't know how to have someone else in my life, Mina. Sadie is young and innocent and deserves a life outside the walls of a compound that exists to protect the protectors."

"Yes, protection from harm. Not from love. Look around you, Eric. Love comes in all different ways. It's up to you to recognize it when it comes your way."

The chair was there for him when he fell into it, his limbs heavy with sadness and dread. "I don't know how to love, Mina. Not anymore. It's been too long."

"Nice try, but love is like riding a bike. You never forget how even if you're a little rusty initially. You have to oil up the chain, straighten the brakes and set the seat to the right position. Once you've done that, it's smooth sailing, even over the bumpiest road." She motioned at her left below-knee prosthesis as though to prove a point. She had been through a lot, and Roman had been by her side for all of it.

"I'll think about it."

"While you're thinking about it, think about how to apologize to that girl. Think about groveling and begging for her forgiveness. If she does forgive you, then she's a better woman than I because I'd kick you to the curb."

He frowned and ran his palms over his legs. "I'm scared, Mina."

"I know you are, Eric," she said, dropping her arms and walking over to him. She squeezed his shoulder to remind him that she was still his friend. "But that's not a reason to treat someone cruelly. You tell them the truth and let them make their own choices."

"That's what I'm scared of," he admitted, staring at the empty doorway.

"That she won't choose you?"

"Yep," he answered with a sad chuckle. "I know if I were Sadie, I'd run."

"But you're not her, so you owe her an apology."

Her words were valid, and guilt filled him. The same guilt that filled him every night when he lay alone while wishing he wasn't. The guilt that a little boy had died before he'd ever had a chance to live and that he wanted to live even though the little boy couldn't.

"The doctor said she's going to need some time to recover," Cal said, walking into the room and breaking the silence. "But physically, she'll be fine. It's time to regroup with the team."

Cal and Mina turned to go, and Eric knew this was his only chance to bring up what had happened in the tunnel earlier. Selina was going to be okay, but if they didn't figure out her secrets, she wouldn't stay that way for long. It was time to follow his instincts again and be the leader the team needed.

Chapter Nineteen

"Wait." Eric stood and rubbed his hands on his pants when his friends turned back to face him. "What I say here needs to stay between us." They both nodded, so Eric turned to Mina. "I need you to do a deep dive on a name for me."

"What name?"

"Ava Shannon."

"Where did you hear that name?" Mina asked, shifting so she could look between him and Cal.

"I saw the name on Vic's lips during the raid. I wondered if it was pertinent." He didn't say that the name had been directed at their friend.

"It's weird that he would say the name in that setting," Mina said. "Ava Shannon is dead. I ran across her when I was researching Howie Loraine. She was Randall Senior's second wife. Some say an arranged mob marriage to offer him up as the family man again as they started their counterfeiting business. She was killed eight years ago during the raid on the mansion."

Eric lifted a brow in part confusion and part surprise. Interesting that both Vic and Randall Junior had thought Selina was Ava. It had to be a bad case of the doppelgänger among us. Eric wondered if it was a mistaken identity, but instinct told him Selina was in danger even if she wouldn't tell them why.

"How does this apply to the team?" Cal asked, stepping forward to stand behind Mina.

"I don't know that it does."

"Listen, I'm tired of people trying to hide stuff from me. I've got Selina in a hospital bed with a huge chip on her shoulder and closed lips. I don't need the same from you."

Eric's gaze flicked to the door, and then he took a few steps closer to the only people he trusted in his world. "Vic was looking at Selina when he said the name. She's lying in that hospital bed because Randall called her that right before he shot her."

Mina glanced up at Cal, and Eric could read the surprise on their faces. "That's more than a little weird," she said.

"And considering Selina's behavior since Howie Loraine landed on our radar, I think it's pertinent," Cal added.

"I don't know why," he said, uncomfortable with what he was about to admit, "but my instincts tell me Selina is in danger. Serious danger." Cal did a fist pump that made Eric pause. "What was that?"

"Me rejoicing. That's the first time you've listened to your instincts since we left that sandbox over a dozen years ago."

"That's not true." His words were defensive, but on the inside, he wondered if they were true. Had he shut out his instincts along with everything else?

"Believe what you want, but I know what I know,"

Cal said. "As for Selina, I agree that she's in danger. What's our plan?"

Cal and Mina looked to him for the answer, so he straightened his spine and inhaled. "We do a deep dive on Ava Shannon. I'm talking right down to the kind of underwear she wore," he said, glancing at Mina, who was smirking while she nodded. "And while we're doing that, we keep someone on Selina. She's never alone."

"She's going to hate that," Mina said with a chuckle.

"She's not going to have a choice." Cal's words left no room for argument. "There's no way she can fight any-one off in her condition. She's defenseless right now."

"Can we spare Efren?" he asked.

Cal lifted a brow in amusement. "You want to put Brenna on her?"

Eric held up his hands in defense. "He's trained in guarding bodies, that's all. I'd trust him with my life, which means, in my opinion, he's the best choice to keep Selina alive until we figure this out."

"Or she talks," Mina said.

"She's not going to talk," Cal argued. "She's had plenty of chances to talk. She'll keep her secrets until she's scared good and straight."

"Or she's tired of having a babysitter. Especially one she can't stand," Eric finished.

"She will be out of it for a few days, so you run point with Efren. Let him know what's going on and facilitate whatever he needs," Cal said to him. "Mina and I will do the deep dive and see what we can come up with on Ava Shannon."

"Hopefully it's not what kind of underwear she buys," Mina said with laughter as she turned to go. "Now that we know Selina will be okay, Roman and I will head back to Secure One. I'll sleep on the way so I can start searching when we get there. I'll keep you posted. Whiskey out."

They watched her go, and then Cal turned back to him. "I'm following behind them. You got this?"

"Absolutely, boss."

Cal grasped his shoulder for a moment and squeezed it. "For the record, you did exactly what I would have done out there tonight. We can't predict everything that might happen when we're out in the field. All we can do is be prepared and react to them, which is what you did. Tonight you listened to your instincts and you saved lives. That's what you should focus your thoughts on. Nothing else."

"Easier said than done, but I'll work on it."

Cal slapped him on the back gently. "That's enough for me. Charlie, out."

Alone in the room, Eric took a deep breath and stretched out his neck. It was time to talk to Efren and do what he could to protect a friend. He forced the image of Sadie's sadness from his mind as he walked to the waiting room and found Efren. With a crooked finger, he motioned him into the hallway.

"I need a favor, but you aren't going to like it."

"Hello to you too," Efren said with a chuckle. "Not the best way to start a story, bruh."

"I wish I had a story, but I don't. Right now, I've just got a gut feeling, and my gut tells me Selina is in danger."

Efren tipped his head to the side as though he agreed with him. "My gut may be saying the same thing. That or I shouldn't have had coffee from the cafeteria."

The comment lifted Eric's lips briefly before they fell again into a tight line. "I want you to stay here with her until she's released. Don't take your eyes off her until I get back to you with more information."

"Done. I'm not sure how Selina will take the news though."

Eric imagined her reaction to Efren being her body-guard and it dragged a chuckle from his lips. "She'll be on pain meds, and her IV tube will only reach so far. You should be safe."

"Fair point. I'll need some things if this will be an extended stay." He motioned at his leg. He was wearing his running blade rather than his day-to-day leg.

"Of course. Text me a list. I'll head back to the mo-bile command center and gather it. We'll also get you a vehicle."

"In case I need to make a quick getaway from Selina?"

Eric's gut twisted. "No, in case you need to make a quick getaway with Selina. I'm not certain, but I will tell you that Vic and Randall recognized Selina tonight. They thought she was their long-dead stepmother. Con-sidering his head injury, I could ignore Vic's mumblings, but Randall was of sound mind when he thought he saw a ghost and shot her. Understand?"

"Understand," Efren said, biting his lip. "I'll work on getting answers from her, but I doubt they'll be more than a hand gesture or two."

Eric couldn't help it. He smiled. "You might be new here, but you do have her pegged. Give me an hour to gather what you need, and then I'll be back to check on our mystery patient. In the meantime, if you need any-thing, you know our numbers."

"You got it, brother," Efren said, giving him a fist bump before he walked to the nurses' station to inquire about Selina's room.

Eric jogged to the elevator and stepped in. As the doors slid closed, he couldn't help but wonder if they were also closing on his time with Sadie.

HOURS LATER, Eric sat in his vehicle at the exit of the gas station. He'd just left the hospital again after checking on Selina. It had been a long night, but in the light of the morning, she would be fine. She'd have a few new scars, and not all of them physical, but she was just grateful to be alive. She'd stopped talking to him the first time he'd mentioned the name Ava in their conversation. She'd feigned weakness and closed her eyes as though she had passed out. He knew better, but he couldn't make her talk. Instead, he'd left her in the capable hands of Efren in hopes that she'd eventually get sick of having a babysitter and fill them in on her past.

Cal had been right about one thing—he'd always had good instincts. It was time for him to start trusting them again. What had happened that day on their mission had been out of his control. He knew that even if it wasn't easy to remember or believe. Those people had died, but not because his instincts had been wrong. In fact, that day his instincts had told him nothing was as it seemed, but he hadn't been in charge of that mission and had had no say over when it happened. Even though his instincts had been correct, he'd stopped trusting them. Last night, when he'd watched Vic and Selina interact, those instincts had kicked back in and hadn't given him a choice but to listen.

Nothing was as it seemed with Selina Colvert. He had plans to find out what the truth was and make sure she was protected until it was resolved. That was what they did at Secure One. They worked together as a team, but they were also family. Family took care of family. Mack had dropped off a vehicle for Efren to use and collected the mobile command to drive back to Secure One.

Eric had texted Cal that he was on his way back, but Cal had other plans. He told Eric he had to stop pretending he didn't care about Sadie and follow through on the apology he owed her. Then he texted him Sadie's address.

Taking another swig of the gas-station coffee, he didn't even recoil at the battery acid as it slid down his throat. His taste buds had quit after the third cup of bad coffee at the hospital, but he needed the jolt of caffeine to help him think. He focused on the pros and cons of turning right versus left.

Right would take him back into Bemidji, where he could find Sadie's apartment and talk to her. Maybe. If she was there. He didn't know because he hadn't seen or heard from her since he'd told her to go away last night. Everyone on the team had found a way to call him on his bad behavior toward Sadie, leading him to believe they hadn't done a stellar job hiding their feelings for each other.

Left would take him back to Secure One, where he could keep living life fake, as Cal would say. Eric preferred to call it living safe. He was good at doing his job while holding people at arm's length. At least he had been good at it—until he'd met Sadie. Now he wasn't sure about anything in his life.

That was a lie. Eric was sure of one thing—he'd fallen in love with Sadie the moment he'd laid eyes on her. He was also sure she deserved better than he could offer her, but Mina had pointed out he didn't get to make that decision. Sadie had to do that for herself.

He watched a Lexus pass him going north and let his mind wander to Sadie. All he could see was the look in her eyes when he'd told her they were over. There had been hurt and sadness but also determination to be the strong one in the situation. She wouldn't cry or scream or curse him out. His instincts said she was going to fight. She would regroup and give him time to face what had happened to his friend.

He gasped, leaning back in the seat as though the weight of the entire world was on his chest. Sadie had shown him with blinding clarity that he hadn't just lost his hearing—he'd lost his ability to listen. He shut everyone out, including his own instincts, and pretended he'd lost those in that war zone too. The truth was just the opposite. Losing his hearing had let him hear his instincts. Now it was his job to *listen*.

Eric punched a button on the car's display. 1786 W. Moreland Road was programmed into his GPS thanks to Mina. Cal had said Sadie lived in apartment 124. A quick glance at the clock told him it was only 6:00 a.m. and she was probably sleeping. He should take the left, drive the ninety minutes home and do the same thing. Sleep would help him put things right in his head before he saw her again.

He let off the brake and flicked his signal light on, waiting for a bakery van to pass before he turned...right. "She deserves more than you, man, but Mina's right.

You can't make that decision for her. Regardless, she deserves an apology from your lug head."

The drive to Moreland Road wasn't long or complicated. Too quickly, Eric was parked in the lot of Sadie's apartment building. He knew she was home since Cal had dropped her off when he'd left the hospital to head back to Secure One and she hadn't had time to replace the Saturn.

He climbed out of the car and walked to the door, taking a deep breath before he pushed the button for apartment 124 and waited for someone to answer. Silently, the door clicked open, so he pulled the handle and stepped into the vestibule of the building. He followed the signs and walked down two hallways to find her apartment. When he stopped at her door, he took a deep breath and raised his fist to knock.

The door swung open, and Sadie stood before him wearing buffalo-plaid sleep pants, a white T-shirt and fuzzy slippers. She was the most gorgeous woman he'd ever laid eyes on. At that moment he knew he'd do anything to have her, even if that meant he had to live real. Fear rocketed through him, but he tamped it down. He had been in a war zone and survived. With Sadie's help, he could survive the first few months of living real. That is, if she was still willing to give him the time of day.

"Hi," she said, leaning against the door. "How's Selina?"

"She's out of recovery and in her room. She's grateful to be alive and happy Kadie and Vic are okay. Efren is with her. Can I come in?"

Sadie stepped aside and held the door open, motioning for him to enter. Once he was inside, she closed the door and leaned against it as he took in the space.

"You're packing?"

"Usually what you do when you have to move."

"What about Kadie and Houston?"

"Kadie and Houston are with Vic at his apartment. The doctors would only release Vic from the hospital if he had someone to stay with him. After her ordeal, there was no place else Kadie wanted to be. She planned to sleep for hours with her baby and the man she loves. Mack drove them home before he headed back to Secure One."

"She's decided to make a go of it with Vic?"

"She has," Sadie agreed, sitting on the couch, so he had to sit as well if he didn't want to be leering over her. "She understands now that Vic has nothing to do with his family, but she will try to convince him to move somewhere far away from Bemidji."

"Probably a good idea for their future," Eric agreed. "If he lives here, he'll always be known as the other Loraine brother."

"Which shouldn't be derogatory considering he has moral character, but somehow it would be," Sadie said with an eye roll. "He's decided to contact Vaccaro through a lawyer and strike a truce deal with him. He wants to live a normal life and raise his son without The Snake or his brother watching over him."

"I hope he can achieve that type of life. Randall was arrested, but you know he'll be cleared of the charges as soon as The Snake sends in a lawyer. Hopefully if Vic strikes a deal with Vacarro, Randall also falls in line and leaves his brother's family alone. It will be difficult to get free of them, and I feel bad that you and Kadie got wrapped up in that mess."

Sadie shook her head at his words. "I don't. If Kadie hadn't fallen for Vic, we wouldn't have Houston. He's worth every bit of trouble we must endure to raise him to be a good, caring, loving man who does the right thing, just like his father. I never realized how much Vic went through at the hands of his family, but his life hasn't been easy. He deserves happiness now."

"I agree, and I hope you'll get to see them often," Eric said with full sincerity.

"We'll work it out," she answered, but he heard how unsure she felt about the situation. "I'll always be part of Houston's life."

"What about mine?"

"I got the general impression you weren't interested in me sticking around." Her words this time were haughty, and he heard the anger underlining them even if she was trying to keep it light.

"That's why I'm here."

"To make it clear that you aren't interested in me sticking around?"

"No," he said, standing and walking to her before he fell to his knees to take her hands. "To make it clear that I'm interested in you sticking around. I want you to stick to me like glue."

"You have a weird way of showing it, Eric Newman."

"I know." He gazed at her sweet face and brushed her hair behind her ear. "Mina made that very clear."

"Why does that not surprise me?"

"She was right though. You do deserve an apology and the independence to make your own decision. I don't have the right to tell you what you want or don't want. All I can say is I'm sorry for being a jerk the last few days. You came into my life and flipped it on its ear. I couldn't keep up with the emotions swirling inside me, and I got scared. Those emotions made the ghosts I live with pop up when I least expected it—"

"I understand, Eric," she said, running her finger down his cheek. "I understand that you can't control those ghosts and it's terrifying when they pop up unexpectedly."

"Yeah," he said with a breath. "But you've shown me that I must find a way to keep them buried, even if that means seeking outside help."

"You're tired of living with them unchecked. That's understandable. It must be torture to relive it over and over."

"Living fake," he said with a nod, and she tipped her head in confusion. "Cal told me it was time to live real. That all these years, I've been living fake, meaning that I shut my emotions down. I finally figured out that doing that also silenced my instincts until the day you walked into my life. Meeting you was the first time those instincts wouldn't be quiet."

"You knew I was in danger."

"Yes, that, but also my instincts told me you'd change my life."

"Clearly not for the better," she muttered, but he read the words on her lips.

His fingers grasped her warm chin, and he forced eye contact with her. "You're wrong. My life is so much better because I met you. I sat in a gas-station parking lot for far too long when I left the hospital this morning. It gave me time to think where it was quiet." He chuckled and pointed at his ear. "I guess I could have shut these off and gotten silence, but that wasn't what I needed."

"You needed clarity."

Eric pointed at her. "Yes, it made me realize that my soul fell in love with you when our eyes met. It was that simple. The rest is what's complicated."

"If you believe in love, and trusting in each other, then the complicated parts become a little less complicated each day."

"That's what I want to believe, but it's going to take me some time to learn how."

"I know," she agreed with a soft smile.

"Please don't move. Please stay and teach me how to uncomplicate the complicated parts of life."

"They didn't tell you, did they?" she asked, a smirk on her lips.

"Tell me what?"

"I quit my job at Dirk's and took a new one. I'll be working as a chef, where I can stretch my wings and finally do what I love."

His shoulders deflated, and he hung his head momentarily before glancing up at her. "Congratulations. You deserve it, Sadie. You're an excellent chef, and the guys will never let me forget it."

"Thank you," she said, her face beaming from his compliment. "Unfortunately I have to move for the job. Cooking for all those hungry operatives will have a learning curve, but from what I'm told, they're tired of the MREs. Even if they're better than the ones they got in the army. Something tells me they'll be pretty easy to please."

Eric's heart pounded hard as he lifted himself onto his knees. "MREs? Army?"

"Secure one, Cook."

A smile lifted his lips, and his heart slowed to a normal rhythm as he gazed at the woman he loved. "Cook isn't part of the phonetic alphabet."

"I know, but it is my last name, and from what I hear you have to be part of the team for a bit before you get a code name. I'll be starting tomorrow morning as the chef in residence, but a little stork told me that in about seven months, I may also be pulling in some hours as the nanny."

"Stork? Nanny?" He paused, and his eyes widened. "Mina?"

A smile lifted Sadie's lips when she shrugged. "We'll wait for the official announcement, but I have it on good authority that Secure One will need that high chair Mina ordered."

"You're going to work with us at Secure One?" His words were more of a plea than a question.

"You didn't think I would let you off the hook that easily, did you? I'm prepared to dig in and prove to you that not only do you deserve love but you deserve happiness and a better way forward."

"You've already proved that, Sadie. I need help learning to accept it."

"Learning to accept love or happiness?"

"From my viewpoint, they go hand in hand." He took hers and twined their fingers together. "Once I accept your love, happiness will follow."

I accept you, Eric, she mouthed, stroking his cheek. The warmth of her love warmed more than his skin. It reached his heart and wrapped around that too. To be loved by someone who wanted nothing from him was magical. "I accept your pain, sorrow, challenges and strengths." He opened his mouth, but she put her finger against his lips. "And I know that your challenges may get worse over time. I also know that you'll adapt to whatever comes along because that's who you are, Eric. You adapt in ways that even you don't notice. I don't have my head in the sand about the challenges we'll face in the future, but my heart still beams at the idea of spending my life with you. That feeling," she said, shaking her fist near her chest, "is what tells me I have to fight for you."

"No, you don't," he promised, leaning forward and placing his lips on hers for a moment. "I'm done arguing. I want this. I want you. I want a life that's real, even when it's messy. You understand a messy life, but you keep returning to help clean it up. I love you, Sadie Cook."

"And I love you, Eric Newman. I have since the moment my heart told me I could trust you to keep us safe. You didn't let me or anyone else down. I know you think you did, but there was nothing you could have done differently."

Was that true? His analytical mind ran everything backward in a heartbeat, offering only one conclusion. "There were things I could have done differently, but that doesn't mean the outcome wouldn't have been the same."

"Or worse," she said, her words defiant. "The outcome could have been much, much worse."

"I need to help Selina with what she's facing, even if that takes me away from Secure One."

"We do," she said, emphasizing *we*. "And we will—together. You didn't think I would walk away because you scowled at me, did you?"

A smile lifted his lips. "It would have been easier if you had, for both of us."

She plastered her lips to his and kissed him like a woman who knew what she wanted. She kissed him like a woman who wanted him and no one else. "Would it be easy to walk away from that?"

"No," he whispered, grasping her face and returning the kiss. He climbed onto the couch to straddle her lap and pressed her head into the back of the couch with his kiss. She whimpered—from pleasure or pain he didn't know, so he eased off. "You were going to be impossible to walk away from. I knew that from the start. I don't know how things will go at work, but I know I want to give us a chance."

She popped open the first button on his shirt but held his gaze. "To start," she said, pausing to open another button. "You'll drive me to Secure One, and I'll put my suitcase in your cabin. Then we'll crawl into your bed and sleep for twelve hours. When we wake up, I'll work my magic."

"In my bed or the kitchen?" he asked, one brow raised as she pushed his shirt off his shoulders and onto the floor.

"Can it be both?"

"Nothing would make me happier."

"Then I say, secure one, Cook," she whispered, trailing kisses down his chest.

"Secure two, Echo," he whispered as her love filtered into his heart to heal it a little more.

* * * * *

Don't miss the stories in this mini series!

SECURE ONE

The Silent Setup
KATIE METTNER
October 2024

The Masquerading Twin
KATIE METTNER
November 2024

Holiday Under Wraps
KATIE METTNER
December 2024

MILLS & BOON

INTRIGUE

Seek thrills. Solve crimes. Justice served.

Available Next Month

Protecting The Newborn Delores Fossen
The Perfect Murder K.D. Richards

....

A Colby Christmas Rescue Debra Webb
Wyoming Undercover Escape Juno Rushdan

....

Killer In The Kennel Caridad Piñeiro
The Masquerading Twin Katie Mettner

Available from Big W and selected bookstores.
OR call 1300 659 500 (AU), 0800 265 546 (NZ) to order.
Visit **millsandboon.com.au**

6 brand new stories each month

INTRIGUE

Seek thrills. Solve crimes. Justice served.

MILLS & BOON

This Christmas, could the cowboy from her past unlock the key to her future?

Don't miss this brand-new Four Corners Ranch novel from *New York Times* bestselling author

MAISEY YATES

In-store and online November 2024.

MILLS & BOON

millsandboon.com.au